THE CONFESSION

EDEN FALLS ACADEMY

the confession

JUDY CORRY

Copyright © 2023 by Judy Corry

ISBN: 978-1-957862-19-4

ASIN : B0BKFLSMZC

All rights reserved.

This is a work of fiction. Names, characters, organizations, places, events, and incidents are either products of the author's imagination or are used fictitiously. Any resemblance to actual persons, living or dead, or actual events is purely coincidental. No part of this book may be reproduced in any form or by any electronic or mechanical means, including information storage and retrieval systems, without written permission from the author, except for the use of brief quotations in a book review.

Cover Design by Judy Corry

Couple Illustration by Wastoki

Edited by Precy Larkins

Proofread by Jordan Truex

www.judycorry.com

Also By Judy Corry

Eden Falls Academy Series:

The Charade (Ava and Carter)

The Facade (Cambrielle and Mack)

The Ruse (Elyse and Asher)

The Confidant (Scarlett and Hunter)

The Confession (Kiara and Nash)

Kings of Eden Falls:

Hide Away With You (Addie and Evan)

Rich and Famous Series:

Assisting My Brother's Best Friend (Kate and Drew)

Hollywood and Ivy (Ivy and Justin)

Her Football Star Ex (Emerson and Vincent)

Friend Zone to End Zone (Arianna and Cole)

Stolen Kisses from a Rock Star (Maya and Landon)

Ridgewater High Series:

When We Began (Cassie and Liam)

Meet Me There (Ashlyn and Luke)

Don't Forget Me (Eliana and Jess)

It Was Always You (Lexi and Noah)

My Second Chance (Juliette and Easton)

My Mistletoe Mix-Up (Raven and Logan)

Forever Yours (Alyssa and Jace)

Standalones:

Protect My Heart (Emma and Arie)

Kissing The Boy Next Door (Lauren and Wes)

For my daughter Jade

*Also...for all the #TeamNash fans.
It's about time our favorite billionaire heir gets his own happily ever after, right?*

PLAYLIST

"Made Up Story" by Andi
"Sometimes" by K E M A L & NEIMY
"The Search" by NF
"Not Like I'm In Love With You" by Lauren Weintraub
"Devil's Work" by Andi
"Lovely" by Fly By Midnight
"see you later (ten years)" by Jenna Raine [feat. JVKE]
"would you love me now" by Joshua Bassett
"Why Try" by Ariana Grande
"end from the beginning" by Savanna Leigh
"Coke and Mentos" by salem ilese
"Girl Next Door" by Robyn Ottolini
"Tell Your Mom" by Georgia Webster
"Fumbled the Bag" by Jenna Raine
"Enchanted" by Taylor Swift
"Fictional" by Khloe Rose
"Your Daughter" by Chase McDaniel
"A Thousand Years" by The Piano Guys
"One Life" by Ed Sheeran

1

KIARA

"READY FOR THE first day at your new summer job?" my mom asked when I walked into the kitchen of our small cottage on Friday morning.

"I guess so." I stepped up to the counter where she was pouring her cup of coffee. "I just hope my boss is nice."

"Nice?" Mom asked, her brown eyes sparkling. "I don't think you have anything to worry about there. In fact, I have a feeling that she'll be the best boss you've ever had."

"Pretty sure that's debatable." I shrugged as I grabbed a blueberry bagel to put in the air fryer to toast. "I mean, she *is* making me work the morning after my high school graduation. What kind of boss would ask something like that of an eighteen-year-old?"

"The kind of boss that has a huge graduation party to set up for the teenage sons of her billionaire bosses and needs all the help she can get."

Did I mention that my mom was the head of staff for the Hastings family—the seventh richest family in the United States—and had just hired me as one of the household maids?

Because yeah...her job was exactly why we currently lived in the two-bedroom cottage on the Hastings' thousand-acre property.

Had I always dreamed of cleaning the bedrooms and bathrooms of the family I'd lived next door to when I graduated from high school? Not exactly. But culinary school was expensive, and since the Hastings family actually paid a decent wage, I couldn't turn the position down when my mom had a maid go on maternity leave for the summer and needed someone to fill the temporary opening.

"I guess pleasing your billionaire bosses is a good reason," I said. "Even if I had to leave my own grad night early in order to get enough sleep for today. We can't have a tiki torch or inflatable slide out of place for tonight's party, can we?"

"Not on my watch." Mom added a splash of half-and-half to her coffee. Then looking at me, she said, "But I thought you said you didn't mind leaving your party early."

"I was kidding." I smirked at my mom as I shut the air fryer door and hit the bagel button. "Two hours was more than enough time at that party."

If it hadn't been for my best friend, Alessi, dragging me there, I probably wouldn't have even gone in the first place.

My senior year at the local high school hadn't exactly been "the best year ever."

But I guess that was to be expected when you date a college boy for six weeks only to discover six weeks too late that he already had a *girlfriend* and you were unknowingly the "other woman" in their relationship.

Yeah...that happened. Hazard of being new in town, I guess.

And since Tristan's *real* girlfriend also happened to be the most popular girl at Sherman High with lots of friends happy to avenge her honor...it had been a rough senior year, to say the least.

Stupid Tristan for being hot, older, and way too charming for anyone's good.

And stupid me for falling for the smooth-talking players who always broke my heart.

I kept telling myself that someday I might actually find a way to date a guy who was sweet and considerate—someone who actually treated girls right.

But since guys like that never paid attention to me—for more than a few hours, at least—I wasn't holding my breath.

A memory of a brief encounter from last summer flashed through my mind, but I quickly chased it away. Thinking about that night would only make me crazy.

Because while the guy from that night—the one with ocean-blue eyes and a heart-stopping smile—had seemed to be the sweet and caring sort when we'd spent a magical evening together, in the end, he was just like all the other guys with short attention spans.

Like a baby who hadn't developed object permanence yet.

They'd give you all of their attention when you were right in front of them and make you feel like the princess in a fairy-tale. But once the clock struck twelve and you were out of their sight, it was like they forgot you even existed.

Even if you lived right across the backyard from them.

"Can you grab the extra folding table from the main laundry room?" Mom asked me after directing the other staff members on where to place the tables already outside on the terrace. "We had to bring an extra table in there yesterday when we were ironing the linens."

"Sure," I said. Then glancing at the big round tables already outside and thinking they looked rather heavy, I asked, "Do you think I'll be able to carry it myself?"

"It's one of the buffet tables," Mom said. "It's pretty light, so I think you'll be able to manage."

"Okay." I sighed, slightly anxious about just walking into the Hastings' house like I belonged there. Usually when I came over here, my mom or another staff member let me in the door.

What if someone from the family was in that part of the house?

Would they think I'd broken in?

For security measures, the family members were always introduced to each person who joined the staff—that way they'd know whether to call their security team if a random stranger showed up in a staff uniform.

A family worth as much money as them dealt with opportunists every once in a while and could never be too careful.

But since today was a busy day for everyone, I hadn't been given the usual staff orientation that my mom always gives the Hastings' employees.

Mom noticed me stalling. Seeming to understand my hesitation, she said, "Just go through the staff entrance over there." She pointed to a large white door that led into the section of the house where the chef's kitchen and laundry room were located. "I told Mrs. Hastings that you'd be filling in for Cynthia. It's okay for you to do your job, Kiara."

"Okay." After drawing in a deep breath, I headed inside the house.

The air conditioning hit me when I walked through the staff entryway. I'd been in here with my mom several times before and knew that if I continued down the long hallway with marble floors and high ceilings, I'd find the chef's kitchen behind the first door on the right. And just a few feet down the hall from that was the door that led into the laundry room where I would supposedly find the buffet table.

I turned the brass doorknob. After peeking inside to make sure none of the Hastings' family members were randomly in there, I opened the door the rest of the way. The main laundry room was huge, about five times the size of ours at the cottage. It had a long marble island where the folding took place, three washer-and-dryer sets, several ironing stations, and walls lined with cupboards where the family's extra tablecloths, towels, bedding, and other linens were stored.

I glanced around the room with the morning sunlight shining through the wall of windows, and a second later, my eyes landed on the long table my mom had sent me in here to grab.

It was still set up, so I would need to tip it on its side to push in the legs before I could carry it out the door. But just then, a male voice sounded through a crack in the door opposite the one I'd come in.

I turned to look at the door that led into the main house and saw that it was partway open. One of the other maids must have forgotten to shut it earlier.

"Is your freshman fan club coming to our party tonight?" a deep voice that I recognized as belonging to Carter Hastings came from the kitchen.

Carter was the second oldest Hastings boy, one of their two eighteen-year-old sons who would be honored at the graduation party tonight. And from the question that he just asked, I assumed he was talking to his slightly younger half-brother Nash.

My guess was confirmed a second later when Nash's tenor voice said, "I'm sure most of them will be coming. I invited everyone from the drama program, anyway."

Nash was one of the stars of the drama program at the

fancy prep school that the Hastings teens attended. He'd played the Phantom in the academy's musical presentation of *The Phantom of the Opera* this past winter and had done such a great job that he'd been offered scholarships to Yale, Berkeley, and Boston College because of it.

Yeah...he was *talented*.

"You ever going to tell them that their chances of dating you are about zero out of one hundred?" Carter asked, most likely referencing the pack of fifteen-year-old girls I'd seen following Nash around their backyard a few weeks ago. "Or are you planning to allow them to continue thinking that you're actually going to choose one of them to be your summer fling before you head off to university?"

"I don't know," Nash said. "I was thinking I'd just let each girl think I would've picked her if the school year hadn't ended so fast and I wasn't going to Yale in the fall."

Carter chuckled. "I guess that's one way to do it. String them along for four months, and then ghost them when summer comes."

"I wasn't trying to string them along," Nash said, and I imagined him running his fingers through his golden locks, giving it the tousled look I loved on him. "I mean, they all knew I wasn't looking for a girlfriend." After a short pause, he added, "It's not my fault I'm so charming."

There was a sarcastic note to his voice, so I knew he wasn't saying it out of arrogance and was merely joking.

But as I was one of those girls who had noticed how charming Nash was, I couldn't really fault anyone else for falling for it, too.

And because I hadn't seen him since Sunday morning and was apparently experiencing withdrawals, I set the corner of the table that I'd mindlessly held in the air for the past minute back on its legs and tiptoed over to the door to see if I could get a peek at Nash through the crack.

A moment later, my gaze found the two Hastings boys standing on either side of the kitchen island.

Carter sat on a stool, wearing a navy-blue suit and tie—most likely the outfit he planned to wear to their graduation ceremony this morning. Nash stood on the other side of the island with his back to me, wearing a teal T-shirt and shorts.

From behind, Nash and Carter were nearly identical with the same blond hair, broad shoulders, and athletic builds. The only real difference between them being that Carter was slightly taller—though Nash seemed to be narrowing that gap this year since he was an inch or two above six feet now.

The boys looked pretty similar from the front angle as well, definitely brothers with their dad's genetics seemingly stronger than the genes they got from their different moms.

But even though they were both cute, Nash's aqua-blue eyes had always been just a little kinder.

He had a light to him that I didn't know if I'd ever seen someone have.

"Just don't come complaining to me when they all start crying as they're saying their goodbyes at the end of the night." Carter leaned against the back of his stool and picked up a blueberry from his yogurt parfait. "I told you back in February that you needed to stop encouraging your little harem."

"My harem?" Nash chuckled and shook his head. "Now that's a way to make it sound way more exciting than it actually is."

"You can thank Ava for that nickname." Carter smirked at his brother.

"Yeah, well..." Nash leaned forward and set his bowl onto the marble counter. "Not all of us can be so lucky to have a beautiful Cohen twin as our girlfriend. Sometimes we just need a bunch of freshman girls to cheer us up."

"And did they cheer you up?" Carter arched an eyebrow.

"I guess." Nash shrugged his broad shoulders. "I mean, if you're asking if I'm over Elyse, then yes. I finally got over her."

He had a crush on Elyse?

Elyse was the identical twin sister to Carter's girlfriend, Ava, and one of the girls who had moved into the house next door this winter.

When I'd seen her play Christine in the musical, opposite Nash, I'd already been jealous of her since I'd sell my soul to have Nash look at me the way he'd looked at her during their performance.

I'd eventually made myself feel better about that by convincing myself that he had only looked at her that way because he was an amazing actor.

But apparently, it hadn't all been an act.

He'd had a crush on her at one time, at least. Possibly while they were in the musical together.

And if Elyse Cohen—a statuesque brunette who looked like she could walk the runway at one of her famous fashion designer mother's shows—was his type, then there was little chance that he would *ever* be attracted to someone like me since I was basically the opposite of that.

I mean, I wasn't an ogre or anything. I liked how I looked well enough when I caught my dirty-blonde-haired, brown-eyed reflection in the mirror.

But my affinity for baking, paired with the genetics I'd gotten from my Latina mother, had given my hips enough width that my booty would definitely stick out like a sore thumb among the rail-thin models if I ever accidentally found myself on a runway.

Nash picked up his bowl again and rinsed it out in the sink.

After putting it in the dishwasher, he said to his brother, "I guess I better change into my suit, so I don't miss our graduation."

"You better hurry," Carter said. "Because we're supposed to be there an hour early, and I know how long it takes you to fix your hair."

Nash chuckled before glancing back at Carter. "We both know who spends an hour in front of the mirror every morning making sure every hair is in the exact right place."

I didn't get to hear Carter's response because it was then that I realized where Nash was going. Instead of heading up the grand staircase just outside the kitchen like I expected, he was walking toward the laundry room instead.

And if I didn't move right now, he would hit me in the face with the door and discover that I'd just been eavesdropping on them.

So with my heart jumping into my throat, I quickly dashed back to the table I was supposed to be retrieving. I was setting the table on its side and trying to figure out how to get its legs to fold under when the door swung open and Nash stepped into the room.

"Oh, h-hey." He stepped back, startled. "I didn't realize anyone was in here."

"Yeah, hi." I glanced over my shoulder, my face growing hot as I worried he would somehow know I had just been spying on him and his brother. "My mom wanted me to take this table outside."

I pushed on the table legs again so it would look like I was actually trying to do my job, but I must not have been strong enough, or was doing something wrong, because they refused to budge.

Thanks for letting me look like an idiot in front of Nash today.

"I asked one of the housekeepers to iron my shirt this morning," Nash's voice said from closer behind me. "I'll just grab it and get out of your way."

When I turned to look at him again, he was walking toward a rack in the corner with a couple of dress shirts and a navy-blue suit.

He pulled the first shirt off the rack and checked the size as if to make sure it was his and not his dad's or one of his brothers'. When he looked up again, I realized I was staring at him, so I cast my gaze at the table with my hands on my hips.

"Did you need help with those legs?" Nash asked, seeming to realize I had no idea how to do the job my mom asked me to do.

"Yeah. They seem to be stuck," I said.

I assumed that the son of a billionaire had moved a table like this probably about as many times as I had, since he was the one with the huge staff that ran his household. But after putting his shirt back on the rack, he stepped up beside me and said, "I think we just move this part first." He pointed to a little metal rectangle that I hadn't noticed on the folding mechanism. "And then..." He slid the metal piece out and stomped on the folding mechanism. "You just do this."

The table leg folded in immediately, and before I could try to take over the other side, he had the second leg folded in.

"How did you know how to do that?" I asked, slightly in awe, and yeah, also thinking the way he'd just done that was hot in a "man who knows how to fix things" sort of way.

He shrugged. "We had a table like this on set for the last play I was in, so I got lots of practice moving it on and off the stage and storing it away."

"Cast members have to help with the stage-crew stuff, too?" I asked.

"We do try to make ourselves useful sometimes." He gave

me one of his dazzling smiles. I knew it was stupid to feel faint and dazed when all he'd done was to be friendly, but...wow. He really was gorgeous when he smiled like that.

Okay, he was gorgeous even without the smile. Nash Hastings was movie-star and sun-kissed, male-model hot. But since this smile was just for me and not one of the girls in his harem, it did funny things to my stomach and made me want to find a way to get him to smile at me like that all day.

It was probably ridiculous for me to have a crush on a guy I didn't actually know all that well.

Aside from a party last summer, the extent of our interactions over the past year that I'd lived here could all fit in a ten-minute time span. Hellos and head nods didn't take more than a few seconds each.

But sometimes it was better to pine for someone from a distance. To see him from your bedroom window at night or hear him laughing with his friends when you were sitting on your front porch, just imagining what it would be like to be the person he was laughing with.

It was when you got to know someone better that the rose-colored glasses started to fade away and you discovered little flaws or quirks that made them more human and less fantasy.

And I wanted to keep this fantasy going for as long as I could. Because even if all of our interactions were surface level and had the distance expected of the billionaire heir and the head of staff's daughter, it at least made it possible to keep the magic I'd imagined last summer alive.

Our unfamiliarity helped me believe that if he actually got to know me, he'd act the same as he had when we'd met in the woods behind his house.

If I confronted him about why he didn't seem to remember that night or recognize me the next day, but then possibly got a response that I didn't like, it would only make it harder to pretend that that night meant as much to him as it had to me.

"Does this just go on the terrace with all the other tables?" Nash asked, bringing me back to the present.

"Just outside the dining room doors, I think."

"Perfect."

And before I knew it, he was carrying the table out of the laundry room.

"Oh, you don't need to do that," I said, chasing after him once I realized what was going on. "That was supposed to be my job."

"It's okay," he said, glancing over his shoulder briefly. "It's my party. I should help out at least a little."

"It's my first day on the job, though," I said, catching up and trying to take the table from him. "I don't want everyone to think I'm lazy and got the job because my mom hired me."

"Oh you're working here?" He stopped momentarily when we were back in the hall that led outside.

"Just for the summer." I tucked some hair behind my ear. "I'm filling in for Cynthia while she has her baby."

"Oh cool."

"Yeah..." Did he know who Cynthia was?

Probably not.

He didn't seem to be making the connection that I'd be cleaning his room this summer, anyway.

Seeing where he slept.

And showered.

Picking up on more of the pieces of his personality and what was important to him in a way that I hadn't been able to discover from a distance.

Noticing that his bedroom light always turned off before Carter's was about all the insight I had, because though my room was across the backyard from his, I couldn't actually see that far into his bedroom.

Not that I'd tried.

That hard...

I promise I'm not a creepy stalker!

"Is your graduation today, too, then?" Nash started carrying the table down the hall toward the terrace again.

"It was yesterday." I stepped quickly after him to keep up.

"Nice."

"Did you go to a party or anything afterward?" he asked. "Because this has to be an early morning for you, if you did."

"I went for a couple of hours," I said, slipping in front of him so I could open the door to the terrace. "But since I have work today, I was okay leaving early."

I thought about telling him how being around my graduating class wasn't exactly the best of times. But then we made it to where the other staff members were putting the tablecloths on the big round tables.

Nash looked around like he wasn't sure what to do, so I held my hand out for the table instead and said, "Here, I can take that from you now. Thanks for carrying it out for me."

"No problem."

We each took a step toward each other, and as he transferred the table to me, I caught a slight whiff of his cologne.

Does he smell this good all the time? I wondered as I sucked in another breath.

Because, um...no wonder he always had his harem following him around. If I didn't already have a crush on him, I would have been hooked from his scent alone.

It was a woody and spicy scent that made me think of cuddling next to someone you loved by the fireplace or afternoon walks in the woods.

It probably reminded me of those things because my dad's

cologne had been similar, and those were things he and my mom had always done together before we had to leave him and our life back in Florida.

"Is something wrong?" Nash asked, breaking me from the memories of my past life. When I looked at the concerned expression on his face, I realized I must have zoned out for a moment too long.

I cleared my throat. "Yeah, sorry." I nodded, forcing a smile. "I—um—" I shook my head. "Y-your cologne just reminded me of someone."

"Who?" He arched an eyebrow. "Your boyfriend?"

"No..."

"Ex-boyfriend then?"

"No." Tristan's cologne had not smelled nearly this good. "Just someone I haven't seen in a long time."

Is he trying to see if I'm single?

I chased that thought away. He was just making polite conversation.

But since I didn't know how much my mom had told Mr. and Mrs. Hastings about why we had to leave Florida, or why we never really brought up my dad to anyone, I just left it at that.

"Well," Nash said, running his fingers through his golden blond hair as he looked around the busy terrace, "I should probably change into my suit before I'm late for my own graduation."

"Of course, yeah," I said, not knowing why my cheeks were suddenly flushing. "Have fun graduating today."

Have fun graduating today? Why had I said that? Graduations were always boring.

"Thanks," he said. And since he was polite, he didn't look at me like I was an idiot.

He turned and headed toward the door that led into his

family's dining room. As I carried the table over to the place my mom had instructed, I just hoped that Nash would somehow forget any of the embarrassing things I'd done or said so I could hopefully keep from being remembered as the idiot who didn't know how to disassemble a folding table.

2

NASH

"CONGRATS ON GRADUATING!" My sister Cambrielle pulled me in for a hug when I went to greet my family after the commencement ceremony on the academy's large back lawn. "I can't believe everyone is leaving me behind next year."

"I know," I said, hugging my petite sister tight and speaking into her hair. "How dare we all be a year older than you."

"It's really not fair." She stepped away from the embrace, and that was when I noticed the tears in her eyes. She wiped at them and laughed like she was embarrassed for getting emotional. "I mean, I'm so much more mature than you. I should have been born first."

"You being more mature than me is definitely debatable." I chuckled, despite feeling emotional myself about spending these final moments with the students I'd become friends with over the past four years. "I mean, it's a credit to how mature I actually am to allow my baby sister to hang out with my cool, older friends. And even more mentionable is how I didn't fly off the handle when you started dating one of my best friends."

"Yeah, you didn't freak out *at all* when you found out Mack and I were secretly dating." She pushed my shoulder and rolled her eyes. "Which, if we're basing maturity off of that, you kind of just proved my point that you aren't the one who should be wearing that cap and gown today."

So maybe I'd gone *slightly* berserk when I'd caught one of my best friends making the moves on my sister last fall. But with the reputation Mack had regarding his previous flings, it wasn't exactly unfounded.

In fact, my protective-older-brother vibe should have been celebrated.

Thankfully though, Mack had been on much better behavior with Cambrielle for the past several months and they now had a relationship that I was *slightly* jealous of.

"We'll just have to agree to disagree on who should have graduated today then," I said, even though Cambrielle actually could have graduated along with the rest of us today and been just fine going to college next fall.

My parents finished congratulating Carter on being number two in our graduating class, barely missing the title of valedictorian that had gone to one of our other friends. Then my mom turned to me, holding her arms open, and said, "You looked so good up there, honey." She pulled me in for what I liked to call her "mama bear hugs." "I'm *so* proud of you."

"Thanks, Mom," I said, hugging her back just as tight. "I couldn't have done it without you."

Which was literally true. If she hadn't picked up on some of the demons I was dealing with last summer, I might not have even made it to graduation. I might have ended up in a ditch somewhere with the trajectory I was on.

I hugged my dad and oldest brother, Ian, next and was planning to go ask my favorite teacher for one last photo together when my freshman friends stopped me in the middle of the field.

"We're going to miss you so much next year," my friend, Marlene, who had taken me to the Valentine's dance said. "Drama club just won't be the same without you."

"You ladies are going to be amazing without me," I said as I looked into the faces of the girls who had been there to boost my ego when I'd been dumped by a girl I'd fallen for too fast. "And I heard Rick Peters is planning to audition for Tony when you do *West Side Story* next fall, so I think the drama program will do just fine."

All of my freshman friends would be fine without me, too.

I went around the circle, giving each of the girls a hug and telling them how much they meant to me.

I'd been wondering this past month, as my high school career came to an end, if I had wasted my time chasing all of the wrong girls while the rest of my friends had managed to find a serious relationship this year. Because even if I tried to look like I was having fun and enjoying the attention of my freshman friends, deep down, I just wanted someone I cared about to love me back the way I loved them.

My mom always told me that I fell hard and fast—which was true. But was it too much to hope there was someone out there who could feel that way about me? Because not only was it lonely sometimes, but being the only single guy among my siblings and best friends was getting more and more weird when we all hung out together.

They were cool and didn't do couple things all the time. But ever since Scarlett and Hunter started dating again, it felt like I was the ninth or eleventh wheel when we all got together.

I checked the time on my watch. I still had an hour before my parents expected me at my graduation dinner, so I decided to see if I could get that last photo with my drama teacher, Miss Crawley, and thank her for everything she'd taught me over the past four years.

Of all my teachers, she seemed to care the most and always knew just what I needed to push me to be better...even if it meant watching my rival, Asher, play Jean Valjean instead of me our junior year.

Was that lesson excruciating at the time? Yeah, my ego took a major hit and I'd spiraled into a depression for months after. But even if it had been a hard lesson at the time, I probably wouldn't have worked so hard for the Phantom's role if I hadn't experienced that failure the year before.

It took a few seconds to spot the petite woman with wavy blonde hair among the crowd full of maroon caps and gowns, but after standing on my tiptoes to tower over everyone, I saw her chatting with a girl who looked my age.

"Think I can get one last hug from my favorite teacher?" I asked Miss Crawley when I stepped up behind her.

The twenty-nine-year-old woman turned to look at me over her shoulder. Then with a smile that lit up her whole face, she said, "Of course." We hugged. Before I could thank her for everything she'd taught me, she gestured at the girl beside her and said, "Oh, and before you disappear, I need to introduce you to my niece."

"Your niece?" I looked at the girl with shoulder-length brown hair, noticing then that she had the same green eyes as my teacher.

"Yes, this is my niece Alessi. My sister's daughter." Miss Crawley put her hand on her niece's back. "My car got a flat tire this morning. She was sweet enough to pick me up so I can get it out of the shop after this."

"Nice to meet you, Alessi," I said, noticing how pretty she was. "Are you here visiting your aunt?"

"No." She shook her head, her pink lips turning up in a smile. "I'm from here. I just went to the other high school."

And I briefly wondered if my dating failures had happened

because I was looking at the wrong school. Because, wow, Miss Crawley's niece was gorgeous.

And the universe must have wanted me to talk to this beautiful girl a little longer because Miss Crawley excused herself to go take a photo with my friends from drama club, Asher and Elyse, leaving Alessi and me to make small talk.

"You're lucky you have such a cool aunt," I said, deciding our mutual acquaintance was as good of a conversation topic as any. "She's actually my favorite teacher from the academy."

"My aunt Sloan is the best," Alessi said. "Hence why she's my favorite."

"Tell me how that's possible?" I asked, wondering how Miss Crawley, who was in her late twenties, could have a niece my age. "She's too young to have an adult niece, isn't she?"

Alessi's smile broadened. "Oh, she's, like, eleven years older than me."

"Really?"

She nodded. "My mom was the oldest of my grandparents' kids and Aunt Sloan was the youngest. So they're, like, twelve years apart."

"That makes sense, I guess."

Just because my family with four kids only spanned six years didn't mean everyone had so many kids that close in age.

Not that my dad had planned it. Dad hadn't even known that Carter, who was seven months older than me, even existed until he was eight years old. Before Carter, he thought he only had two biological children since Ian was from my mom's first marriage.

Alessi glanced over her shoulder to where her aunt was taking a photo with another student now. To me, she said, "My aunt said some of her students are planning to help out with the entertainment for the Midsummer's Renaissance Fair. Are you one of those students?"

"Actually, I am." I smiled. "I'm helping out with the Greenshow."

My friends and I would be wearing renaissance costumes and performing a few different skits inspired by that era several times over the three days that the fair would be going. The months without a new project to focus on were always the hardest for me, so it was nice to have something already on the calendar to look forward to this summer.

"Has she roped you into doing anything?" I asked, knowing that if Alessi was close to her aunt at all, there was no way she hadn't been asked to help somehow.

"I'm planning to sing a few of my songs." She blushed like she was embarrassed. "And play my guitar."

"You're a singer-songwriter then?" I raised an eyebrow, impressed.

"I'm trying to be," she said, glancing down modestly. "I have a few songs on the music platforms and a small following on social media, so nothing huge yet. But I'm trying to get my name out a bit more this summer before school starts in the fall."

"Did you just graduate, too?" She looked my age but could have also been a year younger than me.

"Yeah, from Sherman High yesterday," she said. "I'll be going to Eden Falls University in the fall."

"Nice. I'll be at Yale."

"So, not too far from home," she said. Yale's campus was only a twenty-five-minute drive from Eden Falls.

"Can't beat the East Coast," I said.

I'd considered going to Berkley for a short time after they offered me a pretty good scholarship. But I wasn't quite ready to live that far from home, so I'd stuck with Yale. I'd be working at my dad's company full-time this summer and part-time during the school year to help pay for it.

Most people assumed that because my parents were extremely wealthy, it meant they just gave us everything.

Which, yeah, was a pretty accurate assumption since they gave us a lot.

But once we graduated, we were expected to at least pay for our books and half of our housing so we could slowly ease into the responsibilities that came with adulthood.

I still didn't know what I'd do without a housekeeper while I was at the Yale dorms, but at least I'd have a meal plan to keep me fed while I was away from my family's chef, Marie.

Yeah...I know, I'm spoiled.

My phone buzzed with a text. I checked my watch to see who'd sent it and saw a message from my brother.

Carter: **I'm heading to the parking lot now. Meet me there in five if you want a ride back to our party.**

"Looks like my ride is about to leave," I told Alessi. "My graduation dinner starts in a few minutes."

"Well, it was nice to meet you..." Her face looked contemplative, like she was trying to think of something. Then, seeming to realize something, she said, "Actually, I don't think I ever got your name."

"Oh, it's Nash," I said. "Nash Hastings." I offered her my hand to shake, surprised Miss Crawley or I hadn't said it when we were first introduced.

"Nash *Hastings?*" Her eyes lit up, like she'd heard of my last name before.

Which shouldn't surprise me, really. Anyone who knew anything about Eden Falls would know that my family had been one of the first to settle in the area.

But instead of mentioning that, she surprised me by saying, "I totally know who you are now. My friend actually lives in the house behind yours."

"Really?"

She nodded. "I'm good friends with Kiara Matheson. So I've totally been to your house before."

"You have?" I furrowed my brow, sure that I would have remembered her.

Had I met her on one of the nights I'd blacked out?

But then she added, "I mean, I haven't been to *your* house. Like, I've never stepped foot in that mansion you live in. But I definitely went to your property several times this year while hanging out with Kiara."

Okay, so maybe I hadn't forgotten meeting her. Which was a relief. It was always uncomfortable when someone had to tell me about a night I was fully present at—physically, at least—but had zero recollection of, thanks to the substances I'd been abusing at the time.

"Well, that's cool," I said, hoping she hadn't noticed the mini panic attack I'd just had. "It's surprising I've never bumped into you before, though."

She shrugged. "Your family's property is huge, so it's not that surprising."

Miss Crawley came back to us then. "I'm so sorry, that took longer than I wanted. But if you have time, I'd still love to get that photo with my favorite Phantom."

"Of course."

Miss Crawley asked Alessi to take the photo for us, and after handing Alessi my phone so I'd have a copy too, we posed for the camera.

I gave Miss Crawley another hug, feeling more emotional than I should even though I'd see her again in a couple of weeks. I said one last goodbye and thanked her for being the amazing teacher and mentor that she was.

"It was nice to meet you too, Alessi," I said before leaving. "I'm sure I'll see you at the renaissance fair."

"If you're lucky, you'll see me the next time I visit Kiara." She winked.

"Well, I'll be spending a few hours in my backyard this evening, so if you happen to be visiting tonight, you should drop by the party."

"Maybe you'll get lucky tonight then."

I smiled, liking that she was flirting with me.

At least I was pretty sure that was a flirtatious comment.

I pushed the thought away. I'd never been very good at figuring out if someone was actually flirting with me. I had a lot of experience in liking girls and thinking they liked me back, only to have them choose a different guy.

So I wasn't going to even start to get ahead of myself.

Even if Alessi was beautiful.

I shook my head. *She probably has a boyfriend.*

And I'm not even interested.

Crushing on girls I'd just met was in my past and not my future. And after going strong for six months without crushing on anyone, it would be in my best interest to at least wait until I was at Yale to put myself out there again.

3

KIARA

"THANK YOU." A woman with silver hair whom I knew to be one of Nash's grandmothers said to me as I cleared her dishes during dinner. "The food was delicious."

"I'm glad you enjoyed it." I smiled, setting her dishes in the crook of my left arm. "You must be very proud of your grandsons."

"I am," she said, her blue eyes sparkling in the early evening light. "I always tell my friends that if I had to do it again, I'd go straight to being a grandma and skip the motherhood part. Grandkids are where the real fun is."

"I'll have to remember that." I chuckled, enjoying the aging woman's candidness. I grabbed a couple more plates from the table before carrying them back to the prep kitchen.

My first day of work for the Hastings family was almost done. In just about thirty minutes, I would be finished with my duties and able to curl up on my couch with my pug, Duke, to watch *The Great British Baking Show*.

And take a shower. Yes, I'd probably take a shower first

since working in the sun all day had left me sweatier than I normally liked.

But even if it had been a long day, it had been a good one. And though most of my work next week would be solitary, I did enjoy being with the other staff members. There were some fun personalities in the group, and this summer was setting up to be a good one.

The dinner portion of the graduation party had been a success as well. The food was getting rave reviews from the guests, Carter and Nash seemed to be enjoying themselves, and their parents looked very proud of them both.

Earlier, as Mr. Hastings went on about Carter's many academic and extracurricular accomplishments, I thought I saw Nash's smile falter for a moment. But he'd been all smiles again when his dad moved the spotlight onto him immediately after and went on to talk about everything he had accomplished during his high school career. Which were many.

And yeah, hearing about how talented and amazing Nash was had only made him hotter.

There was just something attractive about a guy who was driven, talented, and successful.

I set the dishes I'd been carrying on the counter with the other dirty plates and utensils. On my way back to the terrace to clear more dishes, my phone buzzed.

I slipped it out of my pocket to see who it was and found a message from my friend Alessi.

Alessi: **How have you never told me how hot your neighbor is?**

I furrowed my brow and sent her a response. **Which neighbor are you talking about?**

The Hastings did have three very attractive sons. And the guy next door, Mack, wasn't too bad to look at either.

My phone buzzed again. **I just met Nash after his graduation and wow, that boy is fiiiine.**

She'd gone to his graduation?

Me: **Why were you at his graduation?**

A twinge of jealousy pulled at me as I thought about what might have happened there.

Alessi: **My aunt Sloan needed a ride to the tire shop so she introduced me to him when I went to pick her up.**

I was about to text back "oh cool" when another message came through.

Alessi: **No wonder you love living in that cottage. The view you have is amazing.**

It's pretty great, I texted, trying not to give away my feelings for the youngest Hastings boy.

Did she like him then? Because if she was interested, that couldn't be good. Alessi was basically every guy's type: gorgeous, outgoing, and a huge flirt who always got what she wanted.

And while it felt like I'd made a tiny bit of progress by having an actual conversation with Nash this morning, it was probably just an unmemorable conversation to Nash—easily forgettable if my bombshell of a best friend tried to step in.

I hadn't told Alessi about my crush because she wasn't exactly known for being great at keeping secrets. But should I say something to her about it now? Just so she'd at least know that I liked him, too?

Another text came through before I could figure it out.

Alessi: **Nash invited me to come to the party tonight. Will you be working the whole time?**

Me: **I just have to help through the rest of dinner and then I'm off for the night.**

Alessi: **You should come hang out at their party with me.**

Wouldn't that be weird, though? To crash a party I wasn't invited to?

Sure, I'd been welcome at the dinner...since I was a *server*. But the party tonight was for Nash and Carter's friends and classmates. Not the girl who lived behind them.

Alessi seemed to sense my hesitation through the phone because she texted, **It should be fun. I bet there will be tons of cute guys there too. Maybe some who will be sticking around here for the summer that you could have a summer fling with to make Tristan jealous.**

Was she already planning to have a summer fling with Nash then?

Probably.

Alessi never wasted time when it came to guys.

Especially not hot, talented guys who also happened to be from a family worth billions.

Me: **What about Dante? I thought you had a good time with him at the party last night.**

Alessi: **He was fine. But I don't know. Nash is just, like, so much hotter.**

I couldn't argue with that since I was partial to him myself.

Alessi: **So will you come with me?**

Me: **Sure.**

I mean, if she was going to try to hang out with the guy I liked, I might need to be there so he would have the option of getting to know me better, too.

Then if nothing else, I could say that I at least tried to get to know him before Alessi swept him away with her bubbly personality.

Alessi: **I think I'm going to just have to walk from the front gate. There are so many cars here.**

I finished putting on a summer dress after the quick shower I'd taken. Then I picked up my phone off my bed to respond to my friend.

Me: **Just park at the cottage. There should be space in our driveway. Then we can just walk into the party together.**

That way I wouldn't have to look like I was crashing the party by myself.

"You look nice." Alessi greeted me with a smile when I opened my front door a few minutes later. "I love that color on you."

"Thank you," I said, appreciating her compliment on the light-blue dress that I'd just bought. "You look amazing, too."

Which was no surprise. Even though Alessi and I came from a similar social class—her parents were both schoolteachers—she was such a thrifty shopper that she always found the best deals on high-end clothes.

"Are you ready to go?" Alessi asked, looking me over.

"I just need to put on my sandals."

I went back to my room and grabbed the sandals I'd gotten right before we moved here from Miami last June. After slipping them on, I made sure all the lights were off and Duke had one of his favorite chew toys before locking the front door.

"Where do you think Nash is?" Alessi asked as we walked down the stone path that led from the cottage to the back lawn. "Did you happen to see what he's wearing tonight?"

"I haven't seen him since cleaning up their dinner," I said, glancing around at the clusters of teens standing on the lawn.

"He was wearing a suit then." Which he'd looked amazing in, by the way. "But I'm sure he's changed into something more comfortable for tonight."

They had their volleyball net set up and a few inflatable slides and games that my mom had rented from the local fun center, so I imagined he would have changed out of his fitted suit for all of that.

Nash, from what I had observed, was very much the life of the party, so I could see him getting right in the middle of all of the fun.

In fact, I was pretty sure my mom said it was Nash who had made the special request for the wipeout game I'd seen being set up in the corner.

"Let's check the inflatables first," I said.

"You think he's over there?" Alessi looked sideways at me, like she didn't expect the son of a billionaire to be into the kind of activity that kids gravitated toward.

"Maybe," I said. "I'm pretty sure he'll be there at some point anyway."

We walked across the lawn, and I noticed several heads turn our way. It was like the Hastings boys' friends and classmates were confused at why two unfamiliar girls would be at their graduation party. But I tried to ignore the wave of imposter syndrome washing over me and appear like I was confident enough to be there—and not currently wondering if tagging along with my friend to the party of my billionaire neighbors was a bad idea.

Like, would Nash, Carter, or Cambrielle give me one look and tell me to go back to washing dishes in their extra kitchen?

I didn't think so. They were all super nice and not the stereotypical spoiled spawn of what could be considered American royalty...

But I hadn't exactly been invited to hang out with them

since moving in, so there was a possibility that this could end in humiliation—with me needing to quit my job and move out so I never had to face them again.

I drew in a deep breath to calm my nerves. When that didn't work, I bent closer to Alessi and said, "Are you sure Nash invited you here?"

"We were flirting, so I guess his invitation could have been a joke." She shrugged. "But he did say I should drop by the party, so I'm pretty sure we're welcome."

"Okay," I sighed, trying not to think too much about her mention of Nash flirting with her. "But if they look at me weird, I'm going straight back home to watch my baking show with Duke and leave you here to explain."

Alessi laughed and linked her arm through mine. "It's going to be fun."

We made it to the corner where the inflatables were. My Nash radar was apparently even better fine-tuned than I thought because it only took me a second to spot Nash jumping over and under the two giant padded beams swinging around the game.

"Is that him?" Alessi squinted her eyes in his direction. "In the navy-blue T-shirt?"

"Yeah, that's him," I said, watching him successfully jump over the swinging arm that had just knocked two other girls to the padded ground.

"Awesome. Let's go join him."

And even though I was nervous to just jump in and join the game, I started walking toward the game's entrance with Alessi.

But when that round stopped and the swinging arms slowed, only one person jumped off.

"Looks like we only have room for one more right now," the guy running the game said. "Which of you wants to go on?"

"Do you mind if I do?" Alessi looked at me.

"Go ahead," I said. Then looking down at what I was wearing, I added, "I'm wearing a dress anyway, so it's probably best for me to stay off."

I had shorts on underneath, so I wouldn't be giving anyone too much of a show if I happened to get knocked over. But since possibly falling on my face in front of Nash wasn't exactly a look I was going for either, I was fine sitting this one out.

Alessi kicked off her shoes on the grass beside me, and when she climbed on, Nash noticed her immediately. A huge smile took shape on his handsome face as she walked closer.

"You made it after all," I thought I heard him say. "Does that mean it's my lucky day?"

To which she called back, "It must be."

I didn't know what they meant by that exchange, but I hoped his talk of her showing up meaning he was lucky didn't mean he was hoping to *get lucky* with her in the way a lot of people meant that phrase.

Was Nash the type of guy who frequently *got lucky* with girls he just met? I didn't think he was.

But I guess it would help explain what happened between us last summer...

The guy running the game started it up again. As Alessi and Nash were ducking under and jumping over the large beams, Hunter Blackwell, one of Nash's friends who had been a regular at the coffee shop during my Sunday morning shifts this past year, stepped up beside me.

"Hey," he said in his deep voice. "How are things going?"

"Pretty good," I said. "My friend and I decided to crash your graduation party."

"I can see that." His green eyes smiled at me with amusement. "I noticed you two when you made your grand entrance."

"Yeah." I chuckled. "I'm sure it was super grand."

He shrugged his broad shoulders. "I call it like I see it."

"Well, thanks for pretending for me," I said. "I might be feeling like a bit of a party crasher."

"Did your invitation get lost in the mail again?" he asked, knowing exactly where I lived and that I was basically invisible to Nash and his family—thanks to an email I'd desperately sent Hunter's advice columnist alter ego earlier this week.

"I think so. But my friend," I pointed to Alessi, "who just met Nash today, I might add, got an invitation."

"Really?" Hunter raised his eyebrows. Then after watching Nash and Alessi interact and probably noticing how flirtatious the exchange looked, he said, "Does your friend not know how you feel about Nash?"

"No." My cheeks warmed as I remembered exactly what I'd written in that email to Hunter. How I'd asked for advice on how to get a guy who barely knew I existed to notice me.

And how Hunter had emailed me back saying that he was happy to play matchmaker if I wanted.

I sighed. "Alessi isn't exactly the best at keeping secrets, so I haven't told her. The last time we talked about guys, she was trying to convince me to find a summer fling to make my ex jealous."

"While she goes after a summer fling with Nash..." Hunter nodded his head knowingly, like he had just taken the thoughts out of my brain.

"She's definitely the summer fling kind of girl," I said, looking back to Alessi and Nash and not liking how she was tugging on his arm to hold him in place when the beam came back to them.

She was all over him.

Ugh.

"Want me to play matchmaker tonight?" Hunter asked. "I'm headed back to Manhattan in the morning, but I could try to get us all on the same volleyball team or something after this."

"That's sweet of you to offer," I said, genuinely thankful that Hunter was thoughtful enough to help me out when we were barely more than acquaintances. "But sadly, I don't think me playing volleyball would be helpful. I'm sure it might even make it worse since I'm not coordinated that way and bound to humiliate myself."

I was much more comfortable getting my exercise in the form of bicycling or surfing. Ball sports were not my thing.

"Well, we'll have to think of something else then," he said. "I'm determined to pay you back for keeping my secret identity a secret."

"I think how generously you tipped me for your chai lattes was more than enough."

He pushed his fingers into his pockets, seeming somewhat bashful about my mention of his generosity.

Which was another reason why I liked Hunter. He was such a laid-back guy that he never sought to be the center of attention. But even if he liked to keep so many of his good deeds a secret, I had noticed them. And I was that much closer to paying tuition for next year because of him.

"Any fun plans for the summer?" Hunter asked.

"Just working for the Hastings," I said. "Living the glamorous life of a housekeeper."

"Nice," Hunter said. "I'm sure they'll appreciate your hard work."

"I hope so," I said. "What about you? You said you're headed home to Manhattan tomorrow. Does that mean this is the last night you'll get to hang out with your friends?"

"It definitely won't be the last time," he said. "Mack and Scarlett will be at Columbia with me and everyone else is going to schools within an hour of New York, so I'm sure we'll find ways to get together here and there. Plus, we're all planning to meet up at the Hastings' house in the Hamptons for the Fourth of July weekend. So we'll see each other again." He hooked his thumbs in his pockets. "What about you? Are all of your friends headed in different directions?"

"Alessi and I are both going to Eden Falls University this fall." I nodded toward Alessi again. "So we'll be sticking together."

"Nice."

I was about to ask Hunter if he planned to keep his high school advice column going now that he'd graduated when his girlfriend Scarlett, a tall girl with auburn hair, walked up to us.

"I was wondering where you'd disappeared to," she said, slipping her hand into Hunter's. "I found a few people to play volleyball, so we're about ready."

"Awesome," Hunter said. He nodded at me. "I've been trying to convince Kiara to play with us. But so far, she's not biting."

"I'm not saying Hunter and I are the best at volleyball or anything," Scarlett said, amusement dancing in her brown eyes. "But if you like winning, you should totally play with us. We'll make sure you're on our team."

"I'll think about it," I said, enjoying her competitiveness.

"We can make sure Nash is on our team, too," Hunter said. And when my eyes went wide at him basically revealing to Scarlett that playing with Nash was a big incentive to me, he quickly added, "Because he's also really good at the sport. Definitely not for any other reasons."

"Just because he's a good volleyball player?" I said in a chiding tone, tilting my head to the side.

"Of course. I mean, unless you want me to do it for other—"

"I like winning things," I said, cutting him off before he

could tease me any more about my secret crush. "So sure, I guess I'll be on your team."

"Perfect," Scarlett said, thankfully not seeming to catch on to what had just happened. Then putting her hands on either side of her mouth, she called out to Nash. "Hey, Nash, we're starting the volleyball game in five minutes and you're on our team, okay?"

Nash looked over and gave her the thumbs up before yelling, "I'll be there."

Volleyball with Nash's friends ended up being more fun than I had expected. And while I was clearly the weakest link on our team, Scarlett, Hunter, and Nash had obviously played together enough through the years that all I had to do was step off to the side when the ball came my way, and they would take care of everything.

Was it the best look to be so bad at a sport in front of a guy I was trying to get to notice me? Probably not. But I was glad that I'd joined the game because I had managed to get a few serves over the net and had received a high five from Nash each time.

Which, let's be honest, was kind of a big deal.

I mean, our hands had touched for, like, a full two seconds during the game.

I chuckled to myself as I thought about the ridiculousness of my crush. Since when did I get so giddy about a high five?

Since it came from the guy I'd had a crush on for close to a year, that's when.

"Are you ladies thirsty?" Nash asked, coming up behind Alessi and me after the game. "We have a drink bar on the terrace."

"A drink bar?" Alessi asked. "Your parents are cool with that?"

"It's not *that* kind of a drink bar." Nash chuckled. "My parents definitely aren't serving alcohol to minors tonight." A weird look crossed his face. "But we do have some soda machines up there with different mix-ins."

"That sounds fun," I said.

Nash nodded. "My sister Cambrielle is obsessed with the soda shop in town and suggested the idea."

We walked across the lawn toward the steps that led up to the terrace. When Alessi looped her arm through Nash's as we headed up the stairs, I noticed a few girls scowling at the new development.

And all I could think of was, *Oh yeah, I totally feel you, girls.*

But I wasn't about to just step off to the sidelines quite yet, so when we made it to the soda bar, I cleared my throat and asked Nash, "Do you have any recommendations for a good drink mixture?"

"I know a few," he said, grabbing a couple of large plastic cups and handing one to me and another to Alessi. "Is there a certain soda you like better than others?"

I looked at the different options. "I think out of all of these, my favorite would have to be Dr Pepper."

"Yeah?" Nash said, a smile lifting his lips. "Then I'd suggest a Dr Pepper with the raspberry puree and coconut creamer."

"Really?" I asked, never having heard of those flavors all mixed together. "Those taste good together?"

He nodded. "Cambrielle converted me to that drink," he said as he filled his cup with the ingredients he'd just mentioned. "I used to be a sparkling water or lime rickey guy, but every once in a while a good DP really hits the spot."

"I'll have to try that then," I said before filling my cup with the same ingredients he'd just used.

I stirred my drink with the straw. After taking a long sip, enjoying the way the raspberry puree gave it a little something special, I said, "That's actually really good. You and your sister have great taste."

"We do," he said, taking a sip of his own drink.

"What would you suggest I mix with my Mountain Dew?" Alessi asked, gesturing to her cup that was already full of the yellow soda.

"I think the watermelon syrup and piña colada puree taste really good with that," Nash said.

"Wanna make it for me?" Alessi asked, a flirtatious smile on her lips.

"Sure." Nash set down his drink and took her cup from her hands. And as Alessi chatted with him while he mixed her drink for her, I hated that his cheeks were slightly flushed.

Did he already like her then?

Should I start looking at bridesmaid-dress options to wear to their wedding?

Nash helped Alessi put a lid on her soda, and then we all went to sit on the patio furniture that had a good view of the lawn below.

I was sipping on my soda and trying to think of something to talk to Nash about when Alessi pointed to a tall guy with curly black hair. "Hey, Kiara. That guy's pretty cute," she said. "Think we should have Nash introduce you to him?"

"What?" I asked, my cheeks flushing with heat as I tried to figure out why she would suggest that. Then I remembered what she'd said earlier about finding my summer fling tonight. "Oh yeah, maybe."

"You want me to introduce you to Ben Barnett?" Nash asked, a confused expression on his face.

"Are you friends?" Alessi asked. "Because I may have bribed Kiara into coming here with me tonight by promising that I'd help her find a summer fling."

"You had to be bribed to come to my party?" Nash looked at me with amusement in his eyes. "Spending an enchanting evening in the company of someone as amazing as myself wasn't compelling enough?"

"No, it's not that—" I tried to say.

But then Alessi touched Nash's arm and said, "She already had plans to Netflix and chill with her pug. But since she's always been such a good wingwoman for me, I told her it was time I finally returned the favor. Plus, she has an ex that we need to make jealous when we go to the college parties this summer."

Netflix and chill with my pug?

What a way to make me sound super cool, Alessi.

"So do you know that guy?" Alessi asked, clearly not realizing how lame she'd just made me sound. "Is he single?"

"Who, Ben?" Nash asked.

"If that tall, dark, and handsome guy is named Ben, then yes," Alessi said. "He looks like the kind of guy Kiara's ex would be jealous of."

She thought Tristan had a type of guy he'd be jealous of? Was that a thing with guys?

I doubted it.

Especially not guys who had happily gone back to dating their original girlfriend as soon as she'd slapped him on the wrist and told him to never cheat on her again before they kissed and made up.

Yeah, Tristan couldn't care less about me moving on with anyone.

Nash's gaze zeroed in on the guy again, but a second later,

he was shaking his head and saying, "I wouldn't go after Ben if I were you."

"Is he taken?" Alessi frowned. "Or just not from here?"

"Oh, he's single," Nash said. "But I'm pretty sure he's headed back to North Carolina soon."

"Oh dang." Alessi frowned, making a show of acting sad on my behalf. "Long-distance relationships do suck."

Nash seemed to find Alessi's level of investment in this humorous. "Not to mention the fact that Ben is also a jerk."

"He is?" Alessi asked.

Nash nodded. "He tried to do some dating prank on my sister and a bunch of other girls from our school this past fall. Like, he was stringing several along at the same time. So, I'd probably find someone else."

"What about that guy?" Alessi pointed to a tall guy with black hair and a jaw that could cut glass who had just walked onto the terrace.

"That's Asher," Nash said. "And he's already spoken for, I'm afraid. Elyse from next door is dating him."

"Hmmm." Alessi looked around as if trying to find another target for my summer fling.

But before she could point to any other guys, I cleared my throat and said, "Hey, so, you can probably just stop this wing-woman business. I'm not actually interested in a summer fling. I already have my eye on someone else."

"You like someone?" Alessi's eyes lit up, and I realized too late that I shouldn't have said that last part. "Who is he? Do I know him?"

I scrambled for something to say, but since I was terrible at lying, I decided to go with some version of the truth.

"Yeah." I tucked some hair behind my ear. "It's a guy that I met at The Brew a couple days ago."

I just wouldn't mention that the guy was Nash and I'd "met

him at The Brew a couple days ago" when he'd dropped by the coffee shop with his siblings for a mango smoothie and sandwich.

"Did you get his number?" Alessi asked.

What should I say?

I didn't want Nash thinking I was actually interested in another guy, did I?

Or would it be better to make it look like I at least had options?

Nash and Alessi were both looking at me like I should have answered the question by now, so I quickly said, "I, um, had to help a customer and didn't have a chance."

"What about you?" Alessi swiveled in her seat to face Nash better. "Do you have a girlfriend I should be worried about?"

"No," he said, looking like he was fighting a smile. "I'm single." Then bumping his knee against hers, he asked, "What about you?"

"I'm single..." Alessi said. With a flirtatious upturn of her lip, she added. "For now."

When they both got a spark in their eyes, I felt like the invisible third wheel.

Of course, when I finally hang out with my crush, he ends up liking my best friend.

4

NASH

"NOW DON'T you look like a young business professional," Regina, our head of staff, said to me when I came down the main stairs wearing a suit and tie on Monday morning. "I'm guessing your dad has roped you into a summer job."

"Yeah," I said, looking just past where Regina stood. Kiara was following her mother out of the laundry room, holding a stack of sheets and wearing a black and white housekeeping uniform that all of the cleaning staff wore. "My dad said I should at least give the family business a fair try before fully committing to a life on the stage."

"It is a pretty good family business to be part of," Regina said matter-of-factly.

"I know," I said, running my hand across my tie to smooth it down.

Which was why all of my siblings and I would be working there this summer.

I'd never been super interested in working in my dad's office before because I'd always wanted to be an actor and star in movies. But since I could make more money working for my dad than I ever could even as an A-list star, I figured it would be stupid to not at least try.

Then later, if I saw my siblings living the life of a billionaire while I was demoted to millionaire status when we were older, I would at least know that I'd given it a shot.

I made it to the bottom of the stairs, and while Regina said something to Kiara, I walked past them and into the kitchen to see what Marie had whipped up for today's breakfast.

"I'm just going to give some instructions to Belinda real quick," Regina told her daughter as I scooped some bacon and eggs onto my plate. "Then we can go upstairs and run through the rooms you'll be working on today."

Regina disappeared down the hall a moment later to where I assumed Belinda was working this morning.

"It looks like we both have something in common," I said to Kiara once we were alone.

"We do?" she asked.

"Yeah." I grabbed a piece of toast and added some strawberry jam to it. "We're both working for our parents this summer."

"Oh yeah..."

"Nepotism at its best, right?" I set the knife back down and grabbed a cluster of grapes to put on my plate.

"Umm..." She furrowed her brow, not seeming to like my comment.

Realizing I must have offended her, I hurried to say, "Not that you wouldn't have been the best person for the job, anyway." I swallowed. "I'm sure your mom hired you because you're really good at cleaning. I mean, she's your mom, so she would have seen how clean you keep your room or not."

She nodded. "Yeah... I mean, it's only a temporary position and I don't think there were a lot of people who applied, anyway."

"Oh, so you had to apply?" I asked, honestly having no idea what the process looked like for the people who came to work in my home. "Did you get an interview and all that?"

"No..." She seemed to think for a moment and then said, "So I guess it really was nepotism." And when she ended by chuckling lightly, I was relieved that my earlier comment hadn't offended her too much.

"Well, it looks like we do have something in common after all." I shot her a smile before taking my plate to the other side of the island to eat.

As I started eating my first piece of bacon, I watched Kiara out of the corner of my eye. When she pulled out her phone like she was uncomfortable just standing there in the room with me while waiting for her mom to return, I was reminded of something.

"Hey, do you mind if I ask you a slightly weird question?" I asked after washing my bacon down with a gulp of orange juice.

"Uh, sure..." she said hesitantly.

"Well, I was wondering if I could possibly get your friend's number from you." When she gave me a weird look, I added, "I thought I hit the save button when she gave it to me on Friday, but when I went to text her yesterday, it wasn't there."

"You tried to text Alessi?"

"I was hoping to ask her on a date." We had such a great time at my graduation party that it would be fun to see if we got along that well on a one-on-one basis.

Because let's face it. Being the only single guy among my group of friends this summer would be lame. And even though I'd be headed to Yale this fall, the idea Alessi and Kiara had planted in my head about having a summer fling actually didn't sound so bad.

I'd given myself the last six months to get over Elyse. And

summer was for fun. I'd had such a crappy summer last year, I wanted this one to be different.

In the very least, it would be nice to have someone to hang out with when we all went to the Hamptons in July.

Okay, I was getting way ahead of myself. I was only asking Alessi on *one* date right now. I didn't need to start planning everything else out yet. That was what the "old Nash" did.

But when Kiara gave me a weird look after I mentioned wanting to ask her friend on a date, I wondered if maybe I was being too eager. "Alessi said she wasn't dating anyone, right?"

"She's single," Kiara said.

"Okay, cool." I sighed, relieved. It would just be my luck to ask another girl out who liked someone else. I pulled my phone out of my pocket. "So can I get her number?"

That seemed to snap Kiara out of whatever she'd been thinking about because she tapped on her phone screen a few times and said, "Do you want me to just text you her contact info?"

"Sure."

I gave her my number, and a few seconds later, my phone buzzed with a message.

"I'm guessing you're the 4695 number that just came through," I said.

"Yep."

I opened the text and saved Alessi's number into my contacts. Then I smiled at Kiara and said, "Perfect. Thanks."

"No problem," she said, her voice sounding like she might need to clear her throat. "I'm sure Alessi will be excited to get your text."

"I hope so." A small thrill of nerves flashed through me.

A moment later, Regina's footsteps sounded on the marble floor in the hall. At the sight of her mother coming our way, Kiara slipped her phone back into the front pocket of her uniform and picked up the stack of sheets that she'd momentarily set on the side table.

"Good luck in my room today," I said.

"Thanks?" She frowned, like she wasn't sure why I'd just said that.

"You're the one taking care of our rooms while Cynthia is on maternity leave, right?" Or had I just heard her wrong on Friday when she'd told me whose job she was taking?

But understanding washed over her face a second later. "Oh yeah, of course." She paused for a moment before saying, "I hope you'll have a good first day at your job." Then with a slight smile, she added, "A job that you most definitely didn't get just because your dad owns the company."

"I will." I grinned, liking that she was being playful with me now that we'd gotten some of our earlier awkwardness out of the way. I hadn't spent much time around Kiara since she and her mom had moved in here last summer, so I wasn't quite sure how seriously she took herself.

I was grateful to see that maybe she could handle some joking around after all.

I was hoping to get to know her best friend a little better, so getting on Kiara's good side would probably be a good idea.

Regina joined her daughter at the bottom of the staircase. After waiting for Carter and Cambrielle to pass them on their way to the kitchen, they both went up.

"Is Kiara working here now?" Carter asked after doing a double take at the two women walking up the stairs.

I picked up my fork again. "She's filling in while Cynthia has her baby."

"Oh, nice," Carter said. "Cynthia told me she was hoping she'd go into labor this weekend."

"Do you know if she did?" I asked, curious how much our housekeeper kept in contact with Carter. Did he know her well then? Because I'd only just barely noticed that she was pregnant a few weeks ago.

"I really don't know." Carter shrugged as he grabbed a plate off the counter and started loading it with the breakfast spread. "But I'm sure Regina will have us sign a card when she does."

"True," I said. Regina was awesome like that. She kept everything running around here so we barely had to think about things like that getting done. We just knew that they would.

Which was why my mom told Regina that she was never allowed to quit.

Our last head of staff had been with our family for ten years, but already, only a year into her job, Regina had proven herself irreplaceable.

And her daughter had already proven to be quite helpful, too.

Which reminded me about her friend's number I now had sitting in my phone.

So while Carter and Cambrielle chatted about what they expected work would look like today, I pulled up a new message box and typed out a text to the beautiful girl I'd been thinking about since Friday.

Hey, I was wondering if you'd be up for a date this week. (This is Nash Hastings btw.)

I let my thumb hover over the send button for a few seconds, making sure I was really ready to ask a girl out after six months of only flirting with my freshman friends.

It felt good enough to me in the moment though, so I tapped the send button and listened to the swoosh sound as it went through the air and to Alessi's phone.

Hopefully, by the end of the day I'd have a date scheduled.

5

KIARA

DOES *this room even need cleaning?* I wondered as my mom took me around Carter's bedroom on Monday morning.

I was getting my tour of the wing where all of the Hastings kids' bedrooms were located. I didn't know what I'd expected the bedrooms to look like when my mom showed them to me, probably something super fancy and big—and they were all definitely huge and breathtakingly beautiful. But for some reason, I'd expected them to at least look like they needed *some* tidying. I mean, Carter's room looked way cleaner than my room had ever looked. And he'd even made his bed this morning.

But I guess billionaires didn't like dust, so maybe that was why I'd be cleaning the already spotless rooms twice a week?

My mom showed me Cambrielle's room next, which was beautiful and feminine and basically my dream room. But aside from a few throw pillows that she'd left on the floor by her bed in her rush to get to her new summer job, there really wasn't much left for me to clean up before I vacuumed.

Ian's room was the next one down the hall from Cambrielle's and would probably be the easiest room of all to clean since no one was currently living in it. All I'd have to do was wipe down the bare dresser and end tables and vacuum. No tidying would probably ever be needed unless there came a point when he decided he was sick of the pool house and wanted to sleep in his old bedroom for a night or two.

But since he seemed to be living it up as a bachelor, from what I'd observed of the college-aged girls he snuck home a few nights a week, I had a feeling the pool house would fit his needs perfectly for the summer.

"And as you probably guessed already, this last bedroom belongs to Nash," Mom said, turning the handle to his door and opening it.

My heart raced at the thought of finally seeing the room where Nash slept. A second later, I was following my mom into my crush's bedroom and taking in his belongings.

His room had a nautical-type feel to it, decorated in white, navy blue, and yellow. A king-sized bed sat in the center of the far wall, right between two huge windows. There was a couch along one wall and a keyboard along the other where I assumed Nash must sit when he was practicing the songs for the musicals he was in.

I'd noticed that none of the other siblings had televisions in their rooms, and it seemed to be the case for Nash as well. Which was kind of interesting to me because I'd thought I was one of the only teens in America who wasn't allowed to have a TV in her bedroom.

There were a few trophies on the built-in shelves off to the side of his couch, and right above it was a whole collage of Polaroids with snapshots of Nash and his friends at school and what looked like backstage at different performances.

"Like the other bedrooms," my mom said, bringing me back to the tour she'd been giving me, "Nash has an ensuite bathroom, which will need deep cleaning on Mondays and a quick wipe down on Thursdays. And his closet is just inside the bathroom."

"Got it," I said, glancing through the bathroom door that was partially open. I couldn't see the whole bathroom, but there was a huge soaker tub in one corner that made me curious if Nash was the type of guy who enjoyed taking baths.

"Belinda does all of their laundry on Mondays, so you may see her come in and out of their closets today as she puts their fresh clothes away."

I nodded.

"Anyway, I think that the four bedrooms and their accompanying bathrooms will keep you busy for most of the day," Mom said, guiding me out of Nash's room and into the family room just beyond the bedrooms. "But if you have extra time, you can vacuum this room and the theater room that's just through those doors." Mom pointed to the double doors on the opposite end of the room. "Any questions?"

I pressed my lips together and looked around. "I don't think so. I just use the cleaning stuff from the hall closet you showed me, right?"

"Yes." Mom nodded. "Everything you need should be on the cart in there. But if you find you're out of something, just text me and I'll send someone up with whatever you need."

I nodded, looking back toward the hall with all the bedrooms. "Does someone else clean Mr. and Mrs. Hastings' room?" Their room was on this same floor, just down the opposite hall.

"Jordan handles all the rooms in their hall, so you won't need to worry about that."

"Okay, cool."

"We don't have a set lunchtime, but when you're hungry and at a good stopping place, feel free to take your hour lunch then."

"Sounds good," I said.

My mom left me then, so I went to the closet to get the cleaning cart I'd be taking around all the rooms with me this morning.

Was this the cologne Nash had been wearing on Friday? I wondered, picking up the cologne bottle with the words Creed Aventus on it.

It was late in the afternoon on Monday, and I'd already cleaned most of the rooms on my list for the day. Cleaning the bedrooms of a wealthy family wasn't something I could ever see myself doing long term, but I'd been able to listen to my favorite podcasts all day and I only had Nash's closet left to vacuum, so the day hadn't dragged on too long.

I took the lid off the cologne, briefly wondering if Nash would be able to tell if I sprayed it in here when he got home.

Deciding that he probably would and that it would breach some sort of housekeeper/boss code of conduct, I opted for just bringing the nozzle close to my nose and breathing it in.

And yep, after just a tiny whiff of the scent that I imagined heaven smelled like, I was pretty sure this was the same cologne.

I set the bottle back down on the bathroom counter that I'd just wiped down and resisted the urge to smell the lotion he had next to it.

I'd been doing that all day: resisting. Resisting all the urges

I'd felt as I moved through Nash's room to open his drawers and cupboards or dig around his bookshelves to see exactly what he had in here and what kinds of things he deemed worthy of living with him in his room.

I was like a thirsty person who'd spent the last year in the desert, and now that I was currently surrounded by water, I wanted to drown in it. Learn all there was to learn about what made Nash Hastings tick.

But since I never knew when another staff member might be walking in to put laundry in Nash's drawers or drop off a graduation gift or card that someone had sent him in the mail—man, this boy had a lot of people who loved him—I'd kept my snooping to a minimum.

Even though I had been practicing a Herculean amount of self-control, I had managed to learn a few new things about my crush next door. From his book collection, I learned that Nash was a fan of superhero graphic novels. The trophies I'd meticulously dusted told me he had won many of the drama competitions he'd been to over the past four years.

The swim shorts that he'd set to dry over the edge of his soaker tub told me he had gone for a swim early this morning. The meditation beads and journal sitting on the end table by his couch told me that even though he was outgoing and high energy so much of the time, he also saw the importance of being introspective and still.

And the huge container of peanut M&Ms, which was hiding under the crocheted blanket on his couch when I'd gone to fold it, told me he had a secret sweet tooth that his family may or may not know about.

I smiled as I grabbed the vacuum from my cart to take it into his closet where I'd be finishing my workday. I kind of loved that the guy I'd crushed on from afar this past year, and whom I had put on a slight pedestal, had his own little candy stash in his room. It humanized him. And as someone who also had a pretty big sweet tooth herself, it was nice to have that commonality.

Was he into baked sweets, too? Because if so, I would be more than happy to hook him up with some of those. My mom and I could only eat so many of the brownies or pastries I made each week in my quest to own a bakery one day.

I got to work vacuuming the closet that was almost as big as my bedroom. After a while I checked the time on my watch and saw it was already after five o'clock.

Crap! I needed to hurry up and finish before Nash got off work and found me still cleaning in here.

But it was like the universe knew I was in a hurry or something, because just before I could finish, the vacuum decided it was time for me to empty the dirt from the canister.

I sighed and blew out a quick breath to puff my hair out of my face. It took me a minute to figure out how to remove the canister, and then I had to figure out where the best place would be to empty the dirt. I ended up grabbing one of the trash bags from my cart. Deciding it could be a messy affair, I took the bag and the canister out onto Nash's balcony and worked to empty the dirt out there.

I checked the time again. It was already five-fifteen. If Nash left his work at five on the dot, he might be here in as little as ten minutes given the twenty-five-minute commute to his dad's business headquarters.

I wiped my brow and hurried back into his closet. I tied off the garbage bag and dropped it on my cart before rushing to figure out how to put the canister back on.

I was just pushing the power button when Nash's closet door suddenly opened. Nash stepped through with his tie already loose around his neck and his white button-up half undone.

I jumped when I saw him, and he must have been surprised to see me, too, because he gasped and instantly took a step back.

"H-hi," he said, his shock showing on his face. "Sorry, I didn't realize you were still cleaning in here."

"Yeah, sorry," I said, standing up straighter. "It took me a while to figure out the vacuum earlier. And um, I think I'm slower than Cynthia."

"It's okay," he interrupted before I could continue rambling. "I'm sorry you've been cleaning so long."

"Yeah, it's been a long day." I pushed some stray hairs out of my face. But then realizing that it probably sounded like I was complaining about my job to the person who helped keep me employed, I hurried to add, "I mean, not that I'm complaining. I'm definitely not. I'm grateful for the job. And—"

"No, I get it." He chuckled, amusement lighting his eyes. "Cleaning all day seems like hard work."

"Seems like?" I furrowed my brow, curious why he'd said it like that.

"I mean..." He rubbed the back of his neck and shrugged. "I grew up here so...I haven't exactly needed to do much of that for myself."

"I guess that makes sense," I said, my gaze following his hand as he dropped it back down. My eyes were suddenly transfixed on the little bit of his tanned chest that I could see in the gap of his shirt. I blinked my eyes shut and cleared my throat before saying, "I should have realized you probably didn't do a lot of cleaning."

Okay, I was sounding like an idiot now. I'd blame it on all the chemicals I'd used today...if the Hastings actually had me using cleaning products like that. But instead of using the cheap, toxic cleaning supplies that I'd used growing up, they had all non-toxic and natural cleaning products.

So any brain fog I might be experiencing could only be blamed on the long day and my nerves over being five feet away from Nash when he had clearly come into his closet to undress.

Should I feel cheated that I hadn't been hidden more discreetly in here? Would I have gotten to see him with his shirt all the way off if he hadn't noticed me sooner?

I pushed those thoughts away. I could fantasize about a shirtless Nash on my own time.

I was worried for a moment that he might have noticed me acting a little off, but instead of saying anything about my strange behavior, he said, "I was kind of surprised that my parents decided to go ahead and fill Cynthia's spot this summer. They've been talking about how Carter and I need to learn how to take care of our own spaces before we head off to college. But with you working here now, I guess they're going to just let us learn once we're in our dorms."

"You won't have a housekeeper at Yale?" I asked.

"No." He dropped his tie on the island in the middle of his closet. "Sadly, I don't think my parents will let me take you in my suitcase."

"Huh?" I furrowed my brow, caught off guard by that last sentence.

He chuckled. "I mean, unless you want to skip your plans for next fall..."

It was probably a bad sign for my level of interest in Nash that an offer like that could actually tempt me.

If it was serious, that is.

Which it wasn't. He barely knew me.

And he's interested in my best friend.

Ugh. I couldn't let myself forget about that.

"Do you have any fun plans for this summer besides working?" he asked as he removed his blazer from his shoulders and hung it over a velvet hanger.

"Not really," I said, allowing my gaze to linger on his broad shoulders. "I'm just trying to make as much money as I can, hence the summer job." I gestured at the vacuum whose handle I was still holding. "My goal is to go to college and not get into any debt."

"That's smart." He seemed to consider the idea, but I could tell that he didn't really have a concept of how hard that would be for a regular girl from a middle-class family whose mom was still paying off a lot of the debt her dad had gotten their family into.

I had no idea if Nash had any scholarships to his Ivy league school, but I figured his parents would be filling in any of the gaps financially for his higher education.

"So you'll just be working here all summer?" He turned back to me when he'd finished hanging his jacket.

"For the most part," I said. "I'm also planning to have a booth at the renaissance fair this summer."

"Really?" he asked, seeming intrigued as he opened one of the drawers that Belinda had filled with his clothes an hour ago. "What kind of booth?"

And that was when I realized I should probably hurry up.

"Sorry," I said apologetically when he pulled out a shirt. "You came in here to change and I'm stopping you."

"No, it's fine. You can finish vacuuming. I'll just change in my bedroom in a minute." He grabbed a pair of shorts from another drawer. I expected him to leave so I could finish up, but he leaned against the doorframe instead and asked, "So what kind of booth will you have at the fair?"

"Oh, um, it's a dessert booth," I said, surprised he was actually interested enough in our conversation to ask.

"A dessert booth?" His eyes lit up. "That sounds delicious."

I smiled, liking his enthusiastic response. "I'm hoping people will think so."

"What kind of desserts are you making?"

Was he actually really interested? I'd assumed he only started talking to me because he was just nice and extroverted, but he could have left by now without seeming rude.

But was he actually interested in the little details of my life? Someone he barely knew?

I tucked some hair behind my ear. "I'm making brownies, tarts, and croissants. Things like that. Oh, and probably some scotcharoos, too."

"Scotcharoos?" he asked like he wasn't familiar with the name of the treat my dad requested for his birthday each year.

"They're like peanut butter rice krispies with a layer of melted chocolate and butterscotch chips on top."

"Oh, I think Marie made those before." He nodded.

"I think most people call them Oh Henry Bars," I said. "But scotcharoos is the name my grandma had on the recipe she gave me."

Not to be confused with scroteroodles, like my best friend from Florida had accidentally kept calling them the first time we made them together.

Oh how I missed that girl. Sadly, we lost contact when my mom and I moved.

"Well, I'll have to make sure to visit your booth while I'm there." His gaze went down to the vacuum. "Anyway, I'm sure you'd love to finish your work for the day, so I'll stop bugging you."

"Okay, thanks," I said, resisting the urge to tell him that he wasn't bugging me at all and that he could probably read the constitution to me right now and I'd still be hanging onto his every word.

Yeah...he doesn't need to know about that.

He took a step through the doorway. Then taking the door handle in his hand, he said, "Um, I'll just open the bathroom door again when it's safe for you to come out."

"Sounds good." I swallowed, trying not to focus too much on the fact that Nash Hastings would be changing just on the other side of the door.

What even was my life right now?

6

NASH

I OPENED my bathroom door like I said I would when I was dressed, waved to Kiara when she looked up from her vacuuming, and then went back to my room to figure out what I was going to do with the rest of my night.

Cambrielle and Carter said they already had plans to go on a triple date with their significant others and our friends Asher and Elyse, so I was left on my own for the night.

I briefly wondered if I should try and text my "freshman fan club," as Carter had lovingly named them, but I was pretty sure most of them had left town by now. Plus, now that I was moving on to a different stage of life than them, it was probably best for me to spend more time with people in the college phase of their lives.

I pulled my phone from the pocket of my shorts and considered texting Alessi to see if she wanted to hang out. But when I opened our text thread from earlier and read the messages where we'd planned our date for Wednesday, I decided asking to hang out today would probably mess up the timeline for all of that.

Not that I actually knew the perfect strategy for dating. I'd messed it up enough times in the past to know that whatever method I'd tried didn't work.

I was never sure where the line was for playing it cool and pursuing a girl. I'd played it too fast with Bree Peterson in September when I tried to kiss her on our first date and got her cheek. And then I played it too cool with Elyse and waited too long to ask her out.

If I'd asked her out when I first realized I liked her at the soirée my family had put on for Carter's birthday back in October, I probably would have had a better chance at winning her over because Asher wouldn't have been around to steal her attention.

I was like Goldilocks and the three bears, and after playing a lot of too hot and too cold, I was trying to find the spot that was *just right*.

So I'd waited two and a half days to ask Alessi out and scheduled our date for two days later instead of for tonight or tomorrow.

That way, I hopefully didn't appear too eager but also didn't leave too much room for another guy to swoop in before I had a chance to find out if we even jived well.

Don't get ahead of yourself, Nash. It's just a date.

I didn't need to start thinking of Alessi as a prospective girlfriend three days after meeting her.

But that was how I always was. I fell fast and hard.

Though thankfully, when it didn't work out, I was usually able to move on pretty quickly.

You know...except for the fact that I hadn't actually been interested in a girl since Elyse dumped me.

Six months ago.

I pushed those thoughts away. I was happy for Elyse and

Asher. They seemed happy. And we weren't even going to college in the same city, so it couldn't have lasted anyway.

The sound of the vacuum stopped, bringing my attention back to the present. When Kiara walked into my room with her cart all ready to go, I asked her, "Now that you're off from work, do you have any fun plans for your evening?"

She looked up, seeming surprised that I was asking her about her plans. Then she shrugged and said, "I'll probably grab some dinner at home and then go bug Alessi at work."

"You're hanging out with Alessi tonight?" I sat up a little straighter. But then telling myself I didn't want to look too interested in that, I made myself slouch back down again.

I needed to play it cool like Carter always did with girls.

Cool and aloof.

So in what I hoped seemed like a minorly interested voice, I asked, "Where does she work?"

"At Charlie's Food Hut."

"Is she a waitress?" I asked, trying to remember if I might have ever seen Alessi working there when I'd visited in the past. Charlie's always did have the really cute girls from town working there.

"She's a server there."

Hmm...I wondered, trying to figure out a plan. Would it be weird for me to just show up at Charlie's and order food randomly?

Probably.

But would it be weird enough for her to think I was stalking her?

Hopefully not.

Or I could just ask the girl currently in front of me if she wanted to hang out tonight and get the bonus of seeing her best friend...

"Hey, so I actually don't have anything to do tonight and

know I'm just going to be bored..." I said, devising a plan in my head as I spoke. "Would it be weird if I tagged along with you?"

A surprised and then confused expression crossed her face, and for a moment I worried she'd think I was weird for basically inviting myself into her plans for the night. But after a few seconds, she shrugged and said, "Sure, that sounds fun."

"Yeah?" I asked, the tightness in my chest loosening with relief.

"Yeah..."

"Cool." I smiled. "And since I haven't had dinner yet either, we could just grab some food there too, if you want. It will be my treat. Then we can both bug your friend together."

"Okay, sure..." She seemed to need to think about that for a second. Finally, she nodded. "Yeah...that sounds fun."

"Should we go now?" I stood from my bed, ready to get on with our plans.

"Can I change first?" She looked down at her black and white housekeeper uniform then back to me.

"Of course."

I opened my bedroom door for her to push the cart through, but when I followed her out into the hall, she gave me a confused look.

"I promise I'm not stalking you." I chuckled and held up my hands. "I was just done here and figured I might as well go out with you," I said to explain why I was walking down the hall with her. "Then we can drive in my car together."

"Oh, okay, sure." She seemed relieved that I wasn't doing anything weird.

I promise I'm not trying to stalk you, Kiara. I'm just anxious to see your friend.

Did that make me seem creepy?

I needed to not be creepy.

Creepy guy was never a good look for anyone.

I pushed the thoughts away. I was just being social. Just making new friends.

"Here, let me put this away for you," I told Kiara when we got to the closet that her cart went in.

"Thanks," she said, seeming simply thankful for my offer and not like I was coming on too strong.

Which was good. *Cool and aloof*, I told myself as I pushed the cart into its spot and shut the closet door. "Cool and aloof" was the way to make a good impression.

And while I was at it, making a good impression on Kiara might be a really good idea, too. Best friends always influenced their friends on whom they should or shouldn't date. And if I showed Kiara a great time, maybe she'd put in a good word for me.

So actually, my date with Alessi on Wednesday kind of started with the lead up of tonight.

And if I could show Kiara how fun and what a good guy I could be, hopefully I'd be one step closer to a great date with Alessi.

7

KIARA

NASH and I made it to the front door of my cottage, and before I opened it, I briefly wondered what it would look like in there.

My mom and I weren't messy people or anything, but we did sometimes leave random things on the counter or kitchen table in our rush to get to our next activity.

I hadn't made my bed either this morning in my rush to get to work on time...but Nash probably wouldn't try following me into my room though, right? So it should be fine.

I drew in a deep breath and pushed open the door like I wasn't nervous at all about the guy I liked seeing where I lived.

"Hey, Kiara," Mom said when I walked inside. When she noticed the tall guy behind me, she sat up a little straighter on the couch and said in a more upbeat voice, "Oh hello, Nash. I didn't realize you were behind her."

"Yeah," I said, glancing over my shoulder to Nash who seemed to be taking in the living room. "Nash and I were just going to Charlie's to grab dinner and say hi to Alessi."

"That sounds nice." My mom smiled at Nash.

I worried she might say something more about how it's nice

we were finally spending time together after living so close, but thankfully, she didn't. Instead, she asked me, "How was work? Did you get everything done?"

"I got the bedrooms all cleaned," I said. "But I'll have to finish those other two rooms tomorrow."

"Sounds good."

I glanced back at Nash who was currently getting his legs sniffed by Duke. He didn't look like he seemed to mind the interrogation though, because he bent over to pat Duke on the head.

"I'll just go change real quick," I told Nash. "Then I'll be back."

"Sounds great," he said, looking up from my pug briefly. "I'll just hang out with your mom and this guy."

I hurried to my room to change into some shorts and a T-shirt, going for a casual vibe that didn't look like I was trying too hard while still hopefully looking cute. When I walked back out a few minutes later and saw my mom and Nash chatting like you always imagined a guy would talk with a girl's parents before their first date, a sudden flush of nerves washed over me.

Because I was going to dinner with Nash Hastings.

It wasn't an official date or anything. I knew that. He'd already told me this morning that he wanted to ask Alessi out.

But he'd asked me to go to dinner with him and he was paying and even driving us there…so when you put all those facts out there, most people would think it was a date, right?

If only we weren't going to dinner at Alessi's work because he wanted to see her.

So, yeah. Not a date.

So close, and yet so far away.

"Ready to go?" Nash asked, getting up from the couch.

"Yep." I nodded. Then to my mom, I said, "I'll be back later."

"Have fun but don't stay out too late," Mom said. "You've got work early in the morning."

"I'll bring her home early," Nash said to my mom, giving her a smile. "I've got a job now, too."

We walked out the door. As we headed down the path that led to the garage where Nash's convertible was parked, I realized I still didn't know what he did for work.

So I asked, "I never heard what you're doing for work this summer. Did you have a good first day?"

"My dad has Cambrielle and me mostly filing paperwork and organizing the files, so kind of boring but it went okay."

"Will you be doing that most days?" I asked, imagining that someone with as much energy as Nash might get bored at that kind of a job.

"Just until the files are all sorted to match the current clients. Then I think his assistant will find another odd job for us to do."

"And it's just you and Cambrielle doing the filing and sorting?" I asked when we came to a spot on the path that turned into a little bridge that went over a small stream of water.

He nodded. "Carter started working part-time for my dad when basketball season ended, so he's already on the fast track to running the place one day."

"So Carter plans to stick with the family business?"

"It's basically understood that Carter will be the CFO and Ian will be the CEO when my dad retires." Nash shrugged. "Cambrielle might decide to go after the COO spot too, if she ever gets tired of ballet."

"And you've never been interested in working there long term?" I asked.

"It just sounds like too many cooks in the family kitchen." Nash rubbed the back of his neck. "Plus, sitting behind a desk for the next thirty years might make me go crazy. I have too much energy to stay in one place for very long."

"I'd have a hard time sitting behind a desk, too," I admitted. "Which is why I'm hoping to work in an actual kitchen." When he furrowed his brow like he didn't understand what I meant, I added, "I'm going into the culinary arts program at Eden Falls University."

"Really? That's so cool." Nash seemed to perk up. "Does that mean that the dessert booth you'll be running isn't just a one-time side hustle?"

"I'm hoping it turns into more than that." My cheeks warmed, giving away my self-consciousness as I talked about my plans for the future. I knew my dreams probably seemed small compared to what Nash and his siblings had going for them. But since it was my actual dream, I said, "I've always thought it would be fun to open a bakery."

"That's so cool," Nash said, his eyes smiling like he was genuinely enthusiastic about my future plans. "And now that I know how much you like baking, I bet your desserts are amazing."

"My mom and I like them, anyway," I said with a shrug, hoping to come off as confident but not too prideful.

We made it to the north side of the Hastings' huge house where the garages were located. After leading me to the fourth garage, Nash punched in a code and the door opened to reveal his lime-green BMW with the top already down.

"Want me to put the top up so it doesn't mess up your hair?" Nash asked as he walked over to the passenger side and held the door open for me to climb in.

I froze momentarily as I tried to decide. I'd always wanted to drive in a convertible like this. And who knew when or if I'd ever have a chance to ride in Nash's car again.

So deciding it was okay if my hair got a little windblown as we drove into town, I said, "I think keeping it down sounds fun."

"You sure?" He arched an eyebrow like he knew from experience with other girls that getting your hair blown at forty-five miles an hour on the winding road into town wasn't always a welcome event.

But I showed him the hair elastic that I always kept on my wrist and said, "I can pull my hair back in this so we should be good."

"Okay, great." He smiled. After I climbed into the seat, he shut my door and walked around to the driver's side.

The drive to Charlie's took about ten minutes since the Hastings' estate was on the outskirts of town. When we pulled into a parking spot, I pulled down the visor to check how my hair had fared. After pulling the ponytail down and running my fingers through my hair, I turned to Nash and asked, "Does it look like I just rode in a convertible?"

He turned toward me, letting his gaze run over my hair. "You look great. There's just…" Then before I knew it, he was reaching over and smoothing down the hair at the back of my head.

Chills immediately raced down my spine at his gentle touch. And when he looked at me with those amazing blue eyes of his and said, "There, that's better," I about melted into a puddle in his passenger seat.

Nash just touched my hair!

I recovered a moment later, and when Nash unbuckled and climbed out, I followed suit.

Charlie's was a locally owned burger shop that had been around since the fifties. It was decorated mostly in red and white with a black-and-white tile floor to contrast the red booths. It was famous for its chocolate shakes and cheese fries and served as one of the most popular hangouts for the popular kids at Sherman High.

It was always busy no matter what time of day, so when we got inside and there were only two booths left, I was tempted to tell Nash that I'd save the table while he ordered the food just so we'd have a good place to sit.

Although, having to wait for a table would just mean I'd have a little more time with Nash, so maybe not getting a spot right away would actually be a better option.

Deciding that I'd much prefer standing in line with him instead of stealing glances at him from a booth, I stepped up beside Nash and looked up at the menu on the wall behind the counter.

"Does Alessi usually work at the counter?" Nash asked. "Or is she in the kitchen?"

"She usually works behind the counter," I said, not liking the reminder that he was only here because he wanted to see my friend. "She's probably just delivering someone's food."

Just as I expected, when I turned my head to look at the dining area, I saw Alessi walking through the tables with an empty tray in her hands.

When she was about ten feet away, she seemed to notice Nash because the corners of her plump lips turned up into a smile. But then her gaze landed on me, and her smile faltered. For a second, I thought she was disappointed to see me until I realized how this situation might look.

So I called out, "Hey, Alessi," and waved her over. Then leaning in close, I whispered, "Don't worry. This isn't a date. Nash heard I was coming here to hang out with you tonight and asked if he could tag along because he wanted to see you."

Her expression brightened immediately before she looked up at Nash again, gave him a quick hug, and said, "What a great surprise to see you here."

"We figured we'd come bug you at work," Nash said, squeezing her back before stepping away. And I kind of hated that he seemed to perk up a little more now that Alessi was with us.

"Well, I'm kind of busy right now." Alessi gestured at the room that was almost at max capacity. "But if you guys stick around long enough, I should be able to hang out with you on my break."

"I think we have a couple of hours to chill." Nash glanced sideways at me. "Right?"

And even though the jealous part of me wanted to say that actually, we probably needed to hurry so I could get to bed early for work tomorrow, I said, "As long as your boss doesn't mind us hogging a table all night, I don't have other plans."

"Great." Alessi's smile broadened. Then holding up the tray in her hand, she said, "I better get back to work."

Nash and I got in line to order food. As we waited for the two women ahead of us to order, Nash asked, "So, do you have a usual order that you get every time you come here?"

"Not really," I said. "I usually get different things depending on what I'm in the mood for."

"Really?"

"Is that weird?" I asked, suddenly self-conscious that he might be judging my fast-food habits.

"No, definitely not. That's actually what I always do, too," he said. "But everyone else in my family thinks I'm weird since they always get the same thing."

"If that's true, then why did you always order the same thing at The Brew?" I asked, skeptical that he might just be trying to make me feel less weird. "Didn't you always get the mango smoothie and green eggs and ham sandwich?"

The sentence was out before I realized that this might make me sound like I had some sort of obsession with him. Which was definitely not a look I should be going for when I could literally see his balcony and window from my bedroom.

I didn't want him thinking I was a stalker or anything.

But he just shrugged and said, "I just get the smoothie every time because I'm a baby and hate the taste of coffee."

"I guess that makes sense." A slow smile spread across my lips because of the way he said that. "I hated it before I worked there. But then I found that if I added the right amount of milk and creamer to it, I could force it down."

He arched an eyebrow. "But you still don't like the taste?"

"Not really." I smiled sheepishly. "I keep trying it with the hopes that I'll acquire it someday."

He chuckled. "Saying something is an *acquired* taste is basically saying it's disgusting but has some health benefits."

"True," I said. "So maybe I should just go with the mango smoothie instead."

"I highly recommend it," he said. "Plus, I'm pretty sure that this cool girl named Kiara might even have the secret recipe." He winked.

"I think you might be right," I said, trying not to blush over the fact that Nash had just said I was cool before winking at me.

Was he flirting with me? Because the giddy teenager still inside of me wanted to think that this whole conversation was a lot like flirting.

The couple ahead of us finished their order, so we stepped up to the counter. Nash said, "I'll take the Charlie Burger, a cherry limeade, and a small cheese fry." Then he looked at me to signal that he was done, so I ordered a BLT, a sparkling water with strawberries, and some jalapeño poppers.

Once Nash had paid, Alessi made our drinks up for us. Then after getting them across the tall counter, Nash led me to a booth in the back corner that had just been wiped clean. As I followed him to the table, I allowed myself to check him out from behind. I'd been trying not to stare too much this afternoon, so now that his back was to me, I had a chance to really take him in.

And the look from this angle was definitely a good one. He wore a navy-blue T-shirt with an athletic fit that hugged his every muscle just right. His shorts were just the right length that I liked on a guy and showed that he had already spent a good amount of time in the sun this spring, and possibly did a lot of calf raises while he was getting his tan.

It was probably weird to be attracted to a guy's leg hair, but yeah, Nash had just the right amount and it did not hurt the overall appeal he had at all.

Nash slid into his seat, and I took the bench opposite him. After taking a sip from his drink, he asked, "So did you quit your job at The Brew to work at my house this summer, or will I be seeing you there on Sunday when I grab breakfast with my siblings this weekend?"

"I ended up quitting." I took the wrapper off my straw and folded it into a knot out of habit. "It was a good job, but they could only fit me in part-time and I needed something more full-time for the summer. I might try working there again next school year though, if it works with my class schedule."

"Oh yeah, because you'll be sticking around here for college."

Did he think I was lame for staying close to home for college? There were definitely some people at my old school who seemed to think that going to the local university was less of an accomplishment than going to one of the bigger schools.

Which was probably why my insecurities had me saying, "I thought about going somewhere else for a minute when things got bad last fall but..." I trailed off when I realized I was bringing up a topic I didn't actually want to go into. So I ended with, "It just made more sense to stay here and save money."

But of course Nash picked up on what I'd been about to say because he asked, "Things got bad?"

"Yeah..." I started, trying to figure out how much detail to go into about all the drama that had happened after finding out I'd been the other woman in Tristan's relationship.

But then Alessi showed up at our table with our food and chatted with Nash for long enough that when she left, he just turned back to me with a smile and said, "Well, this burger is bigger than I expected."

"I hope you're hungry," I said, my eyes going wide as I took in the Charlie burger that had three huge beef patties with a bun and toppings between each layer.

"I'm sure I can pound it," he said, picking it up in his nimble fingers.

I was just admiring how neat he kept his fingernails when Alessi came back to the table. "I almost forgot this for your poppers." She held out a small container of ranch to me. "I know how much you like our ranch."

"I do love it," I said, taking the ranch from her hand. To Nash, I said, "Charlie's ranch is the best."

"Oh I know," Nash said, a twinkle in his eye. "My family loves it so much that we insist Marie keeps it in stock for us."

"Lucky," I said, thinking how nice it would be to have people that basically waited on you hand and foot and did whatever you asked of them.

"Anyway," Alessi said, bringing my attention back to her. "You two enjoy your meal." Then raising an eyebrow at me, she added, "Just don't have too much fun together, okay?"

Had she caught on to the flirty vibe we had earlier and was feeling threatened by it?

Because I had seen him first...

But when she walked back to the front counter, I reminded myself that I did not need another guy making a mess of my social life.

So I'd just be tiptoeing around my feelings for Nash for the next little while and hoping things worked out for the best.

8

NASH

"I'LL SEE YOU ON WEDNESDAY," I told Alessi when Kiara and I finally got ready to leave Charlie's after spending the last two hours there.

"I can't wait," she said. And when she smiled at me, butterflies fluttered in my stomach because she looked like she meant it.

Kiara and I drove back to my house. Since it was dark and the garage was on the end farthest from the cottage she and her mom lived in, I offered to walk her home.

"So I gather from that interaction at Charlie's that you and Alessi have a date planned later this week," Kiara said as we walked past the pool house.

"I asked her this morning." I ran a hand through my hair. "Thanks for giving me her number, by the way."

"Of course." Then after taking a few steps, she asked, "Do you have any fun plans in mind for your date?"

"I was thinking about taking her on a hike to go explore this cave on my family's property."

"Wow," she said, her eyes going wide. "That's really adventurous."

"What do you mean by that?" I frowned, wondering why she'd just made that face.

"It's just..." she started before clearing her throat. "That sounds like a fun date and all. And a lot of girls would probably have fun doing something like that. But..." She scrunched up her nose as she looked up at me. "Alessi is, like, the last person I could see going on a hike and enjoying it. I mean, she might pretend if she likes you enough, but she's the girl who would get doctor's notes to get out of doing laps in PE and always says that if someone was to catch her out exercising in nature, they need to look behind her to see who's chasing after her with a knife."

"So you don't think she'll like that?" I asked, feeling disappointment creep over me.

"I'm about ninety-nine percent sure that she wouldn't enjoy that."

"Dang..."

She must have sensed my disappointment and lack of better ideas because she quickly said, "But, like, if you want to do that, don't let me persuade you away from it. Who knows, maybe she'll like you enough to get her shoes muddy."

"I don't want our date to seem like torture." I already had a history of dates going off the rails, I needed the odds stacked in my favor and not against me from the start. "What do you think Alessi would like doing instead?"

"You want me to help you plan your date?" she asked, her tone not as enthusiastic as I'd hoped.

"You know her way better than me," I said, hoping to persuade her. "And you're a good friend, so you probably want her to have a good time, right?"

"Right..." She sighed. "Well..." She bit her lip as she

thought. "If you really want to impress Alessi, she'd probably like to go to dinner at a nice restaurant. She always talks about wanting to eat at Jacob's Steakhouse."

"Okay, that's doable." Jacob's Steakhouse was one of Eden Falls most upscale restaurants, but I was pretty sure I could get a reservation. "Anything else?"

Just dinner wouldn't be enough of a date, would it?

"I don't know... movies are always a safe bet, aren't they?"

"Yeah..." *But they're so cliché, too.*

"I don't know." She shrugged. "You could also give her flowers or chocolates. She's always talked about wanting a guy to really spoil her on a date."

"What kind of flowers does she like? Do you know?"

"I don't know," she said. "But her favorite color is purple, so maybe a bouquet with purple and white flowers?"

"Perfect." I pulled out my phone to jot down these ideas in my notes app. Looking back at Kiara, I said, "Thank you so much for saving me. I'm so glad you asked what my plans were. I could have easily blown it."

"Yeah, of course." She smiled, though it seemed forced for some reason. "No problem."

Was she looking at me like that because she actually didn't want me to go on a date with her friend?

Had I done something over the last couple of hours to make her think I wasn't good enough?

I pushed the thoughts away. My mind was just trying to take me back down old thought patterns. Kiara wouldn't have warned me about the no-hiking thing if she wanted me to fail. My insecurities were just making me see things that weren't there.

We made it to the bottom of the steps that led up to Kiara's front porch. When she stopped and looked up at me like she was ready to say goodnight, I said, "I had fun hanging out with you tonight."

"Me too," she said, glancing up at me through her lashes. And for a moment, I got a weird sense of déjà vu—like I'd been here before.

But that was impossible since we'd never really hung out like this until tonight.

Which was kind of strange, wasn't it? We'd lived just across my backyard from each other and were the same age, and yet we'd never spent time together until the past few days.

"It's kind of weird that we haven't hung out before, isn't it?" I found myself asking, wondering if she had thought the same thing. "Why do you think that is?"

"I don't know." She tucked some hair behind her ear. "Going to different schools probably helped with that."

"I guess so," I said. "But now that we don't go to rival schools, we'll have to hang out again soon."

"I'd like that," she said, and the way she smiled as she said it told me that it was true.

Which meant that any disapproval I'd sensed earlier really must have been in my head.

"Cool, well…" I stuck my hands in my pockets, unsure what to do next since this hadn't actually been a date. "I guess I'll see you around."

"I'm sure you will."

She pulled her keys out of her pocket to unlock the door, but they slipped out of her hands and onto the stone landing.

I bent over to pick them up for her, but she moved at the same time, and we accidentally bonked heads.

"Sorry!" I said at the same time she did.

We both laughed awkwardly. Then after looking to make sure she wasn't reaching for her keys that were still on the ground at the same time as me again, I quickly bent over, retrieved them, and handed them to her.

"Thanks," she said, rubbing her forehead where we'd collided.

"Of course." Then taking a step back, I added, "And now I'm going to go put some ice on my head."

She let out a light chuckle and said, "Yeah, me too."

9

KIARA

ARE THEY BACK YET? I opened my Instagram app for the fifteenth time, hoping to see if Alessi had given an update to her stories since the last time I checked...five minutes ago. It was Wednesday night—Nash and Alessi's big first date—and I was in my room getting ready for bed.

Alessi was always documenting her days for her social media followers, but even though her date with Nash had started four hours ago, so far, there had been nothing.

Were they making out right now?

Had they had a super romantic night and ended up parking somewhere? Because I hadn't seen Nash's bedroom light switch on yet, which meant he hadn't come home and gone to bed.

I'd caught a glimpse of Nash earlier since I had to chase Duke all the way to the front of the Hastings' house when he escaped from my backyard. Nash had just been walking out the front door, wearing a black polo shirt and dressy pants that were tailored to his long legs just right. He also wore a different pair of sunglasses than he had yesterday when we'd driven. I didn't think he could be more attractive, but he somehow became even hotter.

He'd seen me chasing Duke across their front drive and chuckled like he found my naughty dog hilarious. And when Duke ran up to jump on his legs, Nash had thankfully picked him up and handed him to me so I could stop running around their property like an idiot.

Yeah, instead of looking all put-together and cute like Alessi probably had when he picked her up right after that, I'd been a red-faced, sweaty mess.

Why had I told him not to take Alessi on the hike to that cave? That way she would at least have had to break a sweat in front of him, too.

Though, since it was basically impossible for Alessi to look bad, any sweat would probably just have made her appear to be *glistening* in the sunset.

Why did they have to meet at Nash's graduation? Right when I finally had a reason to interact with him most days?

The universe really had stupid timing sometimes.

Oh well. I sighed and stood to close my curtains since it was time for me to stop thinking about this and go to sleep. I was only going to make myself crazy if I kept stewing over what Nash and Alessi might be doing together right now.

I would just have to text Alessi tomorrow morning to ask how the date went.

I was reaching for my curtains to pull them shut when Nash's bedroom light switched on across the way.

Did that mean he was home?

Maybe I could text him to find out how their date had gone? Use the excuse that I was curious if my tips for their date had ended up working out...

I opened my messaging app to the thread from when I'd

sent him Alessi's contact info. *Should I do this?* I wondered as my fingers hovered over the keyboard on my phone.

Or would that be weird?

Yeah, it would probably be weird to text him seconds after his light had turned on. He'd know for sure that I was waiting up for him.

I pressed the lock button on my phone. I would just wait to ask Alessi about it tomorrow, then I wouldn't look like I had an obsessive interest in what may or may not have happened between them.

Please just don't tell me that you made out.

I could handle them spending time together. But if they went to the falls, or any other hot make-out spot, I didn't want to know. I'd rather live in the delusional dark.

So I closed my curtains then went to put my phone on my charger.

I was about to climb in bed and turn off my lamp when the screen of my phone lit up with a text.

My heart skipped a beat. Was it Nash?

But then I saw Alessi's name in my notifications along with a text that said, **Nash Hastings is the most perfect guy I've ever been on a date with.**

No. My heart plummeted.

Nash wasn't supposed to be the "most perfect guy for her." Not when I wanted him to be that for me.

My stomach twisted just thinking about what this might mean. Were they already boyfriend and girlfriend then?

Since I needed more details now, I swiped up on my phone to respond.

Me: **So I'm guessing your date went well?**

I drew in a deep breath as I waited for her response. *Just because she thinks he's perfect doesn't mean he feels the same...*

Though Alessi was basically every guy's type, so their feel-

ings were probably mutual.

A few seconds later, her response came through.

Only, instead of having Alessi's name attached to it, the text was from Nash?

Nash: **How did you know I went on a date tonight? Who is this?**

Crap! I looked at the top of my phone's screen.

I hadn't opened Alessi's text when I responded to her. I'd accidentally texted Nash since our previous conversation was the last thing up on my screen.

And now Nash knew that I had saved his number in my phone while he obviously didn't save mine.

Should I just tell him it's a wrong number?

My phone vibrated again.

Nash: **Your number looks familiar so maybe we know each other??**

Yeah...it looks familiar because I used it to send you my friend's number a couple of days ago.

But since I didn't want to be the lame girl who saved a guy's number when he couldn't care less about saving mine, I decided to start typing out the words, **Sorry, I think I got the wrong number.**

But before I could send it, I had the last-minute thought that this might actually be the perfect time to see if he remembered something else...

A way to find out anonymously...

So I deleted what I'd written and instead said, **We do know each other. We met at a party last summer.**

His response came a few seconds later.

Nash: **We did?**

Yeah...I figured he didn't remember anything from that night based on what had happened the next day.

Nash: **Can you give me some details?**

It was at your house. Your parents were having a garden party. Everyone was dressed up.

But to leave it more vague, I said, **It was a party at this really big house last summer. Near the end of July. People were dressed up in costumes.**

I was dressed as a peasant girl.

Nash: **I think I remember that party. The beginning of it anyway. And you were there?**

Me: **I was there.**

I had helped Marie bake the pastries for the party and then I'd carried them around on trays for the guests after dinner. The Hastings had the staff members dress up that night in renaissance-period clothing—wanting to make the evening extra special.

I'd worn a long, pink wig to fit in with the fairytale-like environment. False lashes. Dramatic makeup, the whole shebang. I'd looked amazing.

And based on the way Nash had flirted with me all through dinner, I'd thought he agreed.

Until the next day when I'd tried to meet him again and he didn't show.

And then again when I'd run into him the next week and he had zero reaction.

Maybe the makeup and wig had made me look too different from my normal look?

But if he'd been attracted to the real me beneath the pink hair and dramatic makeup, he would have at least given me a second look after that night, wouldn't he?

I re-read his question from above and decided to give him a few more details to see if it sparked anything.

Me: **We kept making eye contact during dinner.**

Then when dinner ended, you found me again and we talked and danced.
   That was the condensed version, anyway.
   What actually happened had been much more of a roller coaster ride.
   I'd had fun the first two hours since the environment had been so magical. But the merriment of the night had disappeared when I received a text from Alessi saying I'd been tagged in a photo on the Sherman High Gossip page. Someone had taken a photo of me while I was working at The Brew and used photoshop to paint a red A on my chest.
   I'd immediately gone to the link and found the photo, along with a caption that basically called me a homewrecker. They'd written an "introduction" post about me that said I was new to Eden Falls but would be attending school with everyone in a few weeks. Then they'd warned my future classmates to keep a close watch on their boyfriends because I was out to seduce all the guys in town.
   My mom had seen me a few minutes later in the chef's kitchen in the Hastings' house, trying not to cry as I wondered how I'd make it through the rest of the night when I felt like throwing up.

"Just head home," Mom said as she pulled me close for a hug. "The busiest part of the night is over. We'll be fine without you."
   "Thank you," I said, squeezing her back. "I'll see you later."
   I slipped my phone into the pocket of my dress and then walked back outside around the edge of the party. I took the stone path through the woods and had almost made it home without anyone seeing me having my meltdown. But when I was about thirty yards away from the cottage, a wave of nausea

passed over me and I had to stop for a moment to vomit in a bush.

I was just using the fabric at the bottom of my dress to wipe round my mouth when Nash came walking up the path in his short-sleeved button-up and dark-blue trousers. He'd heard me being sick and offered me some mouthwash, which he was coincidentally carrying in his pocket.

I guess when you're a Hastings, you always needed to be ready with kissably fresh breath—a hazard of being both hot and wealthy.

After I cleaned up and used the mouthwash, Nash walked me over to a nearby bench and asked if he could arrange for his driver to take me home.

It was dark, and even though we were closer than we'd been earlier, he didn't seem to recognize me. And while I had fun making flirty eye contact with him during dinner, I was grateful he didn't realize I was the girl who had just moved into the cottage two months ago.

I would be running into him enough here and there that I didn't need him picturing me barfing every time we bumped into one another.

"I don't live too far," I said. "So I can just walk home from here. But thank you."

"But if you're sick, you probably shouldn't be walking," he said. "It's really no problem."

And since I didn't want him to find out I was the girl who lived behind him, I told him I wasn't sick. Then I briefly explained that someone had posted something mean about me online and it had simply upset me.

"Someone made a mean post about you?" he asked, seeming surprised.

"Just gossip." I nodded. "But I'd prefer not to go into it, if that's okay. I think talking about it more will just make me feel sick again."

Nash seemed to understand, and instead of prying, he gave me a gentle smile. "Okay, let's not talk about that then." He was quiet for a moment and then said, "I know this is probably really bad timing, but I was actually hoping I'd get a chance to talk to you tonight."

"I was hoping to talk to you, too," I admitted. "Though I wish it was under better circumstances." I chuckled and wiped at the corner of my eye that still had moisture clinging to it.

"I'm sorry you had a rough night." He reached over and tucked a lock of pink hair behind my ear, the gesture sending a rush of warmth across my neck and scalp. Then he asked, "Do you want to get out of here?"

And even though I knew I'd probably kick myself later for not going somewhere with him, I said, "I should probably be getting back home."

I moved to stand, but at that same moment, the quartet my mom had arranged to play for the party began playing a beautiful arrangement of "A Thousand Years."

Nash turned his gaze to the party through the trees. After listening to a few measures of music, he glanced back at me and said, "Can I at least get one dance with you before you leave?"

And when he looked at me with those mesmerizing blue eyes of his, I couldn't say no.

So I let him help me stand, and then he pulled me into his arms for a slow dance right there in the middle of the stone path.

He smelled amazing, like mouthwash and expensive cologne. And for those few minutes, it felt like I was living in a fairytale. I was Cinderella and had snuck into a ball I hadn't been invited to in order to dance with the prince.

The music ended way too soon, and even though I'd told

Nash I needed to get home, I suddenly didn't want to pull away from him to disappear inside.

Because even though I'd felt sick to my stomach moments before, being in his arms had calmed me. He felt safe.

Comforting in a way I hadn't felt before with a guy.

My temple rested against Nash's strong jaw as we stood there together, and in that moment, I felt at peace.

After a few minutes, the next song began. And in a voice just above a whisper, Nash said, "Thank you for dancing with me."

"Thank you for asking me," I replied just as softly.

But neither of us made a move to step away and end the moment that could only be described as magical.

When Nash tilted his head down and seemed to swallow, I wondered if he might kiss me. And even though I'd felt calm moments earlier, that single thought made my heart race since guys like Nash had never given me a second look before.

He angled his face toward me, his hot breath warm on my neck.

And I just waited.

Waited for this boy I barely knew to make the move I wanted him to make.

He breathed in a deep breath, and the anticipation in my veins pulsed even more.

But he didn't do anything.

I was about to give up on interpreting any signs he might be giving me when he whispered, "I'm trying to get up the nerve to kiss you. But I'm worried you'll run away if I do."

I didn't think my chest could get so tight, but I suddenly couldn't breathe. How was this guy so sweet?

I'd literally never met a guy who would say something like that—allow himself to be that vulnerable.

So I'd found my own courage and said, "I won't run away."

A moment later, he was tilting my chin up with his fingers and his lips were pressing gently, tentatively, against mine—as if still unsure I would allow it.

So I kissed him back, more thankful than ever that he'd let me use his mouthwash. And even though the kiss was short—just a few seconds—it was one of the best kisses I'd had in my life.

We pulled away. He kissed me one more time on the cheek and said, "Can we meet again? Tomorrow at Eden Falls at sunset?"

"Yes," *I said breathlessly, both surprised and excited that he wanted to see me again so soon.* "I'll meet you there."

10

KIARA

I SIGHED as I stared blankly ahead, remembering how long I'd waited by that beautiful waterfall, thinking Nash would come around the bend at any moment. But instead of having a second magical night, I'd gone home two hours later with no sight of Nash.

As the days went by and he didn't seem to recognize me as the girl he'd danced with and kissed, I started to wonder if I'd only dreamed it. I had a really vivid imagination, so it was possible.

But when I'd walked down that path one evening and stopped by the bench Nash and I had sat on, I'd found the small mouthwash bottle in a rose bush and knew it had been real.

He'd just forgotten, or blocked it out somehow.

Or he was using his impeccable acting skills to pretend like the moment had never existed.

He *was* extremely talented.

My phone lit up with a new text from Nash.

Nash: **At the risk of sounding like a complete jerk, I really don't remember that night very well.**

My chest fell.

Me: **You don't?**

I sighed and looked at the empty mouthwash bottle that I still had sitting on my dresser.

Nash: **I was in a weird place last year. There are kind of a lot of nights that I don't really remember...**

I frowned as I re-read his text. *There were a lot of nights he didn't remember?*

Did he have a really bad memory then?

No, he couldn't be such a great actor if he had a terrible memory.

But since I'd rather keep that memory to myself and not give Nash another chance to disappoint me, I decided to make up some details from that night instead of using anything real.

Me: **I had blue hair at the time. I was the tallest girl on the dance floor. With a humpback.**

Nash: **Really?**

Okay, now this was just kind of wrong and weird. So before I caused him any more confusion, I texted, **No, sorry, I think I took the joke out too long. I was bored and I think I have the wrong number.**

It took another minute before he replied again.

Nash: **So you weren't at one of my parents' parties and you're not a girl my age?**

I decided to ignore that first question since I didn't want to tell any more lies and focus on the second part instead. But to keep him from knowing that I knew exactly how old he was, I texted.

Me: **Depends on how old you are.**

Nash: **18**

Me: **I'm 18 too.**

Me: **And a female.**

Nash: **Ok cool. Nice to clear that up. I'm a male.**

I laughed at how formal we were being now. But then I said, **Good to know.**

11

NASH

"THANK you for the advice you gave me for my date with Alessi," I told Kiara when I came home from work and found her packing up her cleaning cart in my room on Thursday evening. "I think Alessi really enjoyed it."

"Glad I could help," she said as she moved to the wall to unplug the vacuum cord from the outlet.

As she started wrapping the cord around the vacuum, I debated on whether to press her for any information Alessi might have shared with her about our date. Kiara was still a lot closer friends with Alessi than she was with me, but I'd like to think that we were close enough that she would be okay sharing a few details on what Alessi might have said about our date.

So even though it probably made me seem needy, I pushed my hands into my pockets and asked, "Um, have you heard anything from her?" I cleared my throat. "Like, did she say anything to you about our date?"

Kiara looked up from the vacuum. With a shrug, she said, "She texted me last night and said she had a good time."

"She did?" I asked, my chest feeling lighter.

"Yep." Kiara finished wrapping the vacuum cord up and stood. She hesitated for a moment then asked, "H-how was it for you? Did you have a good time with Alessi?"

Knowing that she was most likely just asking so she could relay the information back to Alessi, like any good friend would do, I said, "The date was great. Alessi is a lot of fun to hang out with."

She'd been fun to talk to and she'd laughed at my jokes, which was always good. Things had gotten slightly awkward when the waiter messed up her order and she wanted me to ask him to take her steak back. But everything had gone smoothly after that.

"That's good you had fun," Kiara said. She looked around my room as if checking to see if anything else needed to go on her cart before she left. And as she walked back into my bathroom and closet, I thought over my date from the night before.

Besides the slight hiccup at dinner, the meal had gone really well. And the movie went even better. I'd been looking for the sign that Alessi might want to hold my hand as we sat in the luxury recliners, but she turned out to be bolder than the girls I usually asked out. She ended up taking all the guesswork out of that by taking my hand in hers about twenty minutes into the movie. Which had been really nice.

When I dropped her off at her house, I hadn't been sure how she'd feel about a goodnight kiss—I'd had trouble reading the signs for that in the past—so I ended up playing it safe and just went in for a hug.

Hopefully, that was the right move for a first date with someone you just met.

Kiara came back into my room after doing her last inspection. After lifting the vacuum onto the cart, she asked, "So do you think you'll ask Alessi out again?"

"I think so," I said. I was definitely interested. "But we're actually going to this birthday party for her stepbrother tomorrow night. So it should be fun."

"You're going to Miles's party?" She furrowed her brow.

"Yeah..." Was she surprised Alessi had invited me? Had she just been exaggerating what Alessi had said about our date, so I wouldn't feel bad?

But then she said, "That's just... I didn't realize Alessi wanted to go to that. Last time we talked about it, she was annoyed with him and didn't want to celebrate his birthday twice since her family will be celebrating again on Sunday."

"She seemed excited about it when she mentioned it last night," I said, rubbing the back of my neck. "In fact, you should come too."

"You think so?" she asked, seeming torn.

"Of course. It should be fun."

"It does sound fun..." She bit her lip. "But also, possibly awkward. Miles is best friends with my ex..."

"And you're not sure you want to run into your ex at the party?" I guessed.

She nodded. When her eyes met mine, I could see she was having some sort of internal battle.

"But you and Alessi are going together?" she asked, like my answer might sway her one way or another.

"I'm picking her up at eight-thirty tomorrow night," I said. "If you want to come, I can totally give you a ride, too." Then just because she looked like she might need a little more swaying, I added, "If your ex does show up and causes drama and you want to leave early, I can totally take you home."

"You don't mind leaving parties early?" She raised an eyebrow, like she somehow knew I had a reputation for being the life at the party last year.

But since that wasn't really me anymore and I'd made some changes to keep me from getting too out of control, I said, "I'm really okay with it. And if Alessi wants to stay longer, I can just come back to get her."

"Okay," she said. She seemed to think it over for just a second longer before she nodded. "I'd love to go with you guys."

Me: **I hope your work is less awkward than this movie I'm watching tonight.**

I looked at the text I'd sent Alessi a few minutes earlier, noticing that it still only showed it was delivered but not read.

It made sense, I guess. She was working tonight and wouldn't be able to respond to my texts until she had her break at eight o' clock.

Which left me with no one else to text since most of my other friends were currently in my family's theater room with me, watching the weird movie.

I didn't know where Mack had heard about it, but based on the acting alone, I doubted there were more than ten people in the whole world who would recommend this as good entertainment.

It was supposed to be an adventure movie where this group of friends get together for one last hurrah five years after college, but then their flight goes down in the ocean and they end up stranded on a deserted island and have to fight to survive.

The storyline was okay, but something had definitely gone wrong with the actors, or maybe the director was one of those odd ducks who thought excessive eye movements and quirky lines would give the movie a special artistic flair that was just lost on me.

I pulled up the contacts on my phone, deciding to scroll

through them to see if there was anyone else I could text to pass the time with.

I'd gotten rid of my social media accounts last summer after realizing it was bringing way more drama into my life than was healthy, but it was bored moments like this that made me think a funny video or meme would be great for passing the time right about now.

I scrolled past a few of my freshman friends' names and considered texting them. But after hovering my thumb over Ginny's name for a few seconds, I continued scrolling through. I hit the K's a few seconds later, and as I looked for Kiara's name, I realized I never saved it when she'd texted me Alessi's info.

Which was kind of weird. I scrolled back up again, wondering if I might have spelled her name differently, but nope, there was no Kiara, or Keara, or anything else that would resemble her name in there.

Maybe I still had the text from her?

But after scrolling through my messages, there was nothing. I must have accidentally deleted her message when I was cleaning out the storage on my phone earlier this week because it was too full.

Which was too bad. She probably would have been fun to text. Or even have come hang out with us tonight. At least I wouldn't have been the weird ninth wheel with all of my friends.

I looked at the couch in front of me where Addison was sitting with Evan. I guess they weren't dating like everyone else in here was, but they did have an interesting dynamic that made me wonder what exactly was going on with them. They said they were stepsiblings, and Hunter had told me that Evan had been friends with Addison's older brother for a few years before Addison's mom married Evan's dad...but they were literally always together. I didn't think I'd ever seen Addison without Evan standing right beside her.

Maybe they just got along really well? Kind of like how Carter, Cambrielle, and I hung out all the time?

But I'd seen things here and there—touches and looks that were just nothing like what I'd ever do to my sister that made me wonder if there was a more taboo relationship going on behind the scenes.

They'd just moved into an apartment together. They were both planning to attend Eden Falls University in the fall, and the apartment was close to campus but...it was still kind of weird.

But I guess it was so they wouldn't have to worry about ending up with a bad, unknown roommate?

Someone screamed in the movie, and I looked up to see that a girl had fallen through a hole and into a cave. As a guy lowered himself down so he could explore it, since of course you'd decide to explore the cave instead of finding a way to help the girl climb right out, I decided to take a photo of the screen and send it to the random stranger who had accidentally texted me last night. I captioned it with the words: **Saw this and it reminded me of that night we went spelunking.**

Then I waited to see if she would be as much fun to text today as she was last night.

555-203-4695: **Oh yeah. How could I forget? We had so much fun that night. Did your head end up being okay?**

I chuckled. Glad she was playing along with my weird mood.

Me: **Just a few stitches and I was good as new.**

555-203-4695: **Good. Wouldn't want to mess up that beautiful head of hair you have.**

Me: **Definitely not.**

555-203-4695: **I mean, you do have hair right?**

555-203-4695: **Not that it would be bad if you didn't. Bald guys are cool too.**

Me: **I have hair.**

555-203-4695: **Nice. Me too. Wow, we have so much in common.**

Me: **It's blue, right? I'm considering having mine dyed, so we'll match the next time we see each other at a party.**

555-203-4695: **I bet you'd pull that off amazingly. But sadly, I'm back to my natural hair color of dirty blonde.**

Me: **Looks like we actually do have our hair color in common then.**

Me: **What's your name, anyway? I have you as "555-203-4695" in my phone right now, but somehow it doesn't quite match the image I have in my head of you from our cave exploring adventures.**

The message went from *sent* to *read* and the three dots hovered on the screen for a moment before disappearing, like she was hesitating to give me her real name.

Realizing texting a random stranger personal details about yourself was different than bantering back and forth, I decided to take my question back and quickly texted: **Never mind. You don't have to tell me. We're strangers.**

Her response came in right after that.

555-203-4695: **Okay, yeah. I'd probably like to just stay anonymous for now.**

Me: **Ok cool. I'll just put you in my phone as "Wrong Number Girl" instead.**

And so I wouldn't lose this girl's number the way I'd lost Kiara's, I hurried to save her contact info.

Wrong Number Girl: **Such an accurate nickname. Makes me wonder if the name I'm saving your number under fits reality.**

Me: **What name are you giving me?**

Wrong Number Girl: **I'm saving you as "hot sounding, flirty guy." It definitely fits the image I have in my head for you, at least.**

Me: **I don't want to sound like I'm bragging but...I'm pretty sure that name fits perfectly.**

Wrong Number Girl: **I thought so.**

I thought about asking her what a "hot sounding, flirty guy" would look like in her head, but the movie ended and everyone started standing up to leave. I slipped my phone back into my pocket so I could walk my friends out.

But as I walked behind Asher and Elyse down the hall past my bedroom, I couldn't help but wonder if Wrong Number Girl actually lived in Eden Falls or if I'd seen her before.

The area code and prefix of her phone number were definitely local. The same as mine. Just the last four digits were different.

Was it possible I'd run into this girl around town and just didn't know it?

12

KIARA

I WALKED down the path from my house toward Nash's garage on Friday night. I'd run into Nash again when he got home from work with his siblings, and we'd arranged to meet by his garage at eight-fifteen to go pick up Alessi before the party.

Had I purposely timed my workday out so that we would bump into each other when he was off work? Perhaps.

But since we hadn't exactly arranged where to meet when we talked about the party yesterday, and he didn't know that he already had my phone number, I had to get creative.

When we chatted, he'd initially suggested that I give him my number so he could just text me when he was ready to leave, but I'd managed to sidestep that by suggesting we just meet at his car at eight-fifteen—thankfully, he did not bring up the number exchange again.

Man, I really should have thought that through.

Probably should have just given him my real name when he'd asked me about it last night and gotten the deceit out of the way before I got too far in. It would have passed for just a strange coincidence that I'd texted him again, right?

Okay, so he definitely would have known that I'd saved his number on Monday and had been stupid enough to ask him about his date on Wednesday. But would that have been horrible for him to know?

I mean, if the tables were turned and he'd done the same to me, I would have found it endearing...

But that's because I like him. It got weird when you didn't have feelings for the other person.

Gah. This was a mess. Because if I wanted to keep hanging out with him, I was going to need to do the number exchange sometime, right?

It wasn't like I could just go out and get a burner phone just for my correspondence with him.

Could I?

No. That was stupid.

I should probably just tell him it was me and explain the whole thing. Right?

But as we drove away from his family's estate and down the road toward the neighborhood where Alessi lived, I couldn't find the words to start that awkward conversation.

And when he began talking about other things, I lost my resolve to be upfront with him and decided to give myself a little more time to come clean.

"So I hear this is actually a frat party," Nash said when we drove past a church on the corner of main street. "I didn't realize it when Alessi first invited me, but that's cool. Hanging out with college kids. I mean, we're technically college kids." He glanced sideways at me and shrugged. "But...you know."

"It should be fun." *And hopefully, not awkward.*

Maybe Tristan and his girlfriend, Brooklyn, were out on a date or something and didn't feel like going to his best friend's birthday party...at the house where he also lived.

I mean, miracles could still happen, right?

We pulled into Alessi's driveway a minute later. While Nash walked to the door to get her, I moved to the back so Alessi could sit in the passenger seat beside him.

Yes, I should basically win the "friend of the year" award.

We drove toward the college campus. Nash parked along the curb a few houses down from the frat house that I'd spent a bunch of time at last summer.

I felt a little jittery with nerves as we walked through the gate to the backyard. I scanned the crowd of college-aged guys and girls bouncing to the loud music, but at first glance, I didn't see Tristan or Brooklyn.

They could just be in the house, but hopefully, they were at the country club Brooklyn's family owned or somewhere else.

"Hey, Kiara!" A deep voice called from near the table where a group of people were playing beer pong. "Long time no see."

When I looked in the direction of the voice, I saw a muscular guy with shaggy brown hair walking toward Alessi, Nash, and me, a red cup of beer sloshing in his hand.

"I'm glad you could make it," Miles said, pulling me in for a side hug when he reached me. "It's been too long."

"It really has," I said, looking up at Alessi's stepbrother who had acted like the big brother I'd never had while I was dating his best friend. "And now you're basically an old man."

"I'm legal to drink this now, at least." He chuckled as he raised his cup higher. "Twenty-one years young."

"Well, happy twenty-first birthday," I said.

"Thank you." He turned to Alessi next, giving her a side hug of her own. "Looks like my little Messy-Alessi couldn't resist coming here, either."

"You know I hate that nickname, right?" she said, hugging him back anyway.

"I know," he said with a half-smile that I knew had made

many girls weak at the knees in his presence before. "Too bad we don't get to pick our nicknames."

"Yes, it's too bad." She rolled her eyes. "If only Miles rhymed with something dumb."

"If only," he said.

Alessi gestured at Nash. "Since we're already on the topic of names, I should probably introduce you to our friend, Nash."

"Nice to meet you." Miles held his hand out for Nash to shake.

Nash took a step forward and shook hands. "It's great to meet you, too. And happy birthday."

"Thanks, man." Miles took a step back, and glancing at the party, he said, "Well, I've got a game to win. You guys should grab yourselves a drink and have fun."

"Oh, I don't dri—" Nash started to say at the same time Alessi said, "Thanks, we will."

I noticed Nash furrow his brow momentarily, like he was confused about something. But before I could figure out what, out of the corner of my eye, I spotted Tristan and Brooklyn walking into the backyard.

No... My stomach instantly dropped when I looked at the guy responsible for ruining my first summer in Eden Falls and the girl responsible for ruining my senior year. As I took in my ex with his dark hair and broodingly handsome face, my neck and chest flooded with an uncomfortable heat.

I shouldn't have come.

If just seeing Tristan made me this much of a mess, how could I make it through the next three hours?

But I couldn't exactly ask Nash to take me home right now, could I?

Sure, he'd said he'd be fine taking me home if I needed...but we'd literally been here for five minutes. I couldn't ask him to leave after we just got here.

Maybe I could hide somewhere before they saw me?

I looked around the backyard for a good place to go. There was a shed that I could probably chill behind while Nash and Alessi enjoyed the party. Or I could always just slip inside the house and see if Will, the introvert of the frat house, was watching a movie in the living room like he always did during these parties.

But when I glanced back at Tristan and Brooklyn, my ex was already looking my way.

Crap!

Recognition soon showed on his face. Then after leaning close to say something to his girlfriend and kissing her on the forehead, he started walking across the lawn toward me.

"Tristan's coming this way," I said to Alessi, panic rising in my chest. "What do I do?"

"Why is he walking over here?" she asked the question I was wondering myself.

"I don't know," I said, my heart beating faster the closer he got. He was only twenty feet away now.

"Just be calm." Alessi touched my arm. "You did nothing wrong. Maybe he just wants to apologize."

Yeah, right.

But I guess I'd be finding out what he wanted in about three seconds since that was all it would take for him to get to us.

"Hey," Tristan said, his voice as rough as I remembered even though I hadn't talked to him since last July.

"Hi," I said.

There was an awkward silence where we just looked at each other, and I wondered why he had come over here. But then he cleared his throat and said, "It's been a while, hasn't it?" He rubbed his hand over his forearm, a nervous tic of his. "Would you mind if we talk for a sec?"

"Um..." I said, not sure what to do.

"I just want to clear the air," he continued, his brown eyes darting back and forth between mine like he was nervous. "We'll both be attending the same school and will probably bump into each other at parties next year, and well..." He swallowed, his Adam's apple bobbing. "I just wanted to make sure we're good."

"Oh, yeah, we're good." I waved my hand, seeing a quick way out of this awkward conversation and deciding to take it. "Like, I don't think we really need to talk about anything."

"You sure?" He furrowed his brow like he didn't believe me. "Because I found out what Brooklyn's friends did to you all last year, and I just wanted you to know that I didn't have anything to do with it. Like, I had no idea any of that was going on until a few weeks ago."

Oh no. I do not want to talk about that right now. Not in front of Nash.

I glanced sideways at Nash to see if he was paying attention to us and was displeased to find him watching us with curiosity in his blue eyes.

I was trying to decide if it would be better to just let Tristan pull me aside and have this conversation away from my friends when Alessi cut in, saying, "Hey Tristan. I don't think you've met Kiara's boyfriend Nash yet, have you?"

My boyfriend?

I looked at Alessi, wondering what the heck she was doing.

But before I could figure that out, my best friend continued, "You've probably heard of his family before since they're kind of famous in this town."

"They are?" Tristan stared at Nash who still seemed to be confused about what was going on.

"He's a Hastings."

"Oooh," Tristan said, recognition dawning in his eyes. After a beat, he asked, "So does that mean you're Joel Hastings' son?"

"Yeah, that's my dad," Nash said, and from the expression he got, I wondered if he was uncomfortable with Alessi basically bragging about how Nash's dad was the local billionaire.

I assumed she'd done it to make Tristan feel intimidated that I was "dating" the son of a billionaire. But...as that wasn't even true, this was just weird.

Tristan cleared his throat. Then holding out his hand for Nash to shake, he said, "It's nice to meet you, Nash."

After looking at Alessi and me like he wasn't sure what he should do right now, Nash shook my ex-boyfriend's hand and said, "Good to meet you, too."

As the guys exchanged pleasantries, Alessi gave me a look that said, *You're welcome.*

Tristan stepped back, seeming unsure of what to do. Then he looked at me and said, "So we're good?"

"We are," I said, still not really knowing what had happened in the past minute. "We're cool."

Now please go back to your girlfriend so I can ask Alessi what in the world she expects me to do now that you think I have a boyfriend here.

This was such a mess.

Tristan walked back to Brooklyn who was filling a cup at the keg. I was about to ask Alessi what she was thinking when one of her friends from work came up and told her there were some people she needed to introduce Alessi to.

"Be right back," Alessi said to Nash and me. Then with a wink, she added, "I'll see you two lovebirds later."

She disappeared into the crowd. Once we were alone, Nash and I both looked at each other.

"Well, that was interesting," he said.

"It definitely was…" I blinked my eyes a few times. "I don't know what Alessi was doing saying all of that."

"Does she do that kind of thing often?" he asked.

"Not that exact kind of thing," I said. "But she does put people in awkward situations for kicks and giggles sometimes."

"Good to know." Nash pushed his hands into the pockets of his shorts. "So are we supposed to pretend like we're dating for the rest of the night?"

"I guess?" I said. "But, like, you don't have to. I mean, I don't want you to feel obligated or anything just because Alessi was trying to make her summer-fling-jealousy plan happen for me."

I shook my head. Seriously, what was she thinking?

"No…it's cool," Nash said.

"Yeah?" I studied his face to see if he actually meant it. I really didn't want this whole night to be weird for him. But since I also didn't want Tristan to think I was lame and that Alessi had lied about me having a boyfriend to help me seem less like a loser, I added, "You could just think of it as practicing for a role—pretending to be my boyfriend. You're just acting on the stage of life instead of an actual…you know…stage."

Ok, wow. That sounded lame. *The stage of life?*

Why did I always say stupid things around Nash?

But instead of looking at me like I was a weirdo, he chuckled and said, "I can totally do that. I've never played the role of fake boyfriend before. But if my brother Carter could do it with Ava last fall, then I'm sure I'll be a master."

"Carter and Ava were fake boyfriend and girlfriend before they started dating?" I asked, surprised that Nash's more serious brother would be into something like that.

"He wanted his ex to think he'd moved on, too, and Ava didn't want people knowing he was her math tutor."

"Interesting," I said. Then after thinking about the pair for a moment, I added, "But it looks like their relationship must not have stayed fake for long?"

"I think they made it maybe two or three weeks." He smirked. "According to Ava, all it took was a fake kiss for Carter to fall in love with her."

"Ah, that's so sweet."

"They had some other drama to deal with, of course," Nash said with a shrug, as if it was just the norm for a good love story to have a little angst along the way. "But they're really happy now, and I wouldn't be surprised if they got married one day."

"That's kind of a crazy love story," I said, only ever hearing of fake relationships in books or movies. "But that's awesome for them."

"It is," he said. "But don't worry. If we end up needing to fake kiss tonight, I promise I won't expect you to be my real girlfriend in two weeks." He winked.

Though I knew he was joking, I was suddenly speechless and found my cheeks growing hot with a blush.

After a few seconds of my brain scrambling, I knew I needed to say something before he would realize how much I would love for a fake kiss to turn into a real relationship with him. But I literally couldn't think of a good response because all my brain was interested in right then was reliving the memory of our kiss last summer.

Oh how I would love to have another kiss like that with him.

Even if it was fake...

"I-I doubt anyone here would expect us to have a fake kiss," I said the first thing that came to mind.

"Well, I bet that's a relief for you." He winked.

Pretty sure it would be more like a dream come true.

But since I couldn't say that aloud, I just said, "I think Alessi *might* have a problem with us fake kissing."

"Well, she's the one who suggested this, so apparently, she's not that territorial of me after our one date."

For a moment, a look of insecurity crossed his face, like he actually thought it was possible for a girl in her right mind to not be obsessed with a great guy like him after a magical date.

But before I could think of a good response, he cleared his throat and said, "Anyway, should we go find some people to practice our fake-boyfriend-and-girlfriend acting skills on?"

"Sure," I said. We started walking in the direction where Alessi and her co-worker had disappeared. As we made our way through the crowd of people, Nash placed his hand at the small of my back to lead me through.

I glanced at his face briefly and found him watching me. And when he mouthed, *Is that okay?*, it took everything in me to simply smile and nod instead of squealing and saying, *Yes!* and *Please oh please keep doing that forever.*

We got halfway across the yard when a guy I recognized as Miles's friend Parker spoke into a microphone. "We're ready to start karaoke. Do we have any volunteers to start us out?"

"Hey, we should sing a song together," Nash said, his face suddenly animated. "I love karaoke."

Of course he did. He was an amazing singer and performer.

Something I definitely was not.

"I think that's a bad idea," I said, glancing over to the karaoke machine under the big oak tree and feeling my mouth go dry. "I-I'm pretty sure I'd need to be a few drinks in before I did something like that."

"Oh..." Nash said, his expression falling. "So do you drink then?"

"Not really..." I said.

"Not really?" He furrowed his brow.

"I mean, I drank at a few parties last summer, but nothing since I broke up with Tristan." I pressed my lips together, suddenly worried Nash would judge me for the few beers I'd forced down to fit in. But when he didn't say anything, I asked, "Um, do you drink at parties?"

"No." He shook his head quickly. "I..." He hesitated, like he was trying to think of a way to put it without seeming judgmental that I had. But then he simply finished with, "I don't drink."

Okay, so now I probably looked like an idiot to him.

Which, yeah, I had been an idiot last summer—so desperate to fit in with my cool college boyfriend when I knew that for me, drinking alcohol was like playing with fire.

I was probably lucky that I'd hated the taste of beer and that Tristan and his friends didn't have fruity drinks at their parties. Otherwise, if I'd had a drink that tasted sweet instead of like cat pee, I might have followed in my father's footsteps and been on my way to becoming an alcoholic.

I'd certainly had a lot of emotions this past year that I would have been tempted to numb.

Stupid Brooklyn and her stupid friends. I sighed.

Deciding to move the conversation back to the karaoke thing, I said to Nash, "You should still do the karaoke, though. I bet you'd be amazing. I saw you in *The Phantom* and you did so well."

"You watched *The Phantom*?" he asked, seeming surprised I'd go to his school play.

"My mom took me. She wanted to support you." *Please don't think I was stalking you since I didn't go to your fancy school.*

"Oh, your mom is the best."

"She is." And there was definitely no reason for me to mention the other two nights that I'd gone to the musical by myself.

Yep. No reason at all.

Nash looked at the karaoke corner then back at me. "Okay, I think I'm going to go up there. Wish me luck."

"Good luck."

Nash went up to Parker, and I watched as he told Parker what song he wanted to sing for all of us. They looked up the song and soon, the intro to one of my favorite songs, "The Search" by NF, started playing.

Was Nash going to rap for us?

For some reason, I'd never pictured Nash as the type to listen to rap music, let alone be able to throw down a beat.

NF was one of the few rappers whose lyrics were clean enough to play around my mom, but still...wasn't Nash more into musicals?

But a few seconds later, Nash started rapping the angsty lyrics that spoke of the search to find peace among the difficulties of life. And even though I'd been worried that he might be about to embarrass himself in front of all of Miles's friends, he was actually really good.

Okay, scratch that, he was *phenomenal.*

He hit every single note—didn't fumble over a single word.

And if I didn't know Nash as an upbeat, outgoing guy from an amazing family, I might have thought he'd written this song himself since he was pulling off the moody vibe of the song in a way only someone who had been through a lot could.

I'd listened to this song a lot when my mom and I had moved here. I'd been angry that she'd made me move all the way across the country right before my senior year. This song had fit my emotional state perfectly at the time.

And even though I doubted Nash had dealt with many demons in what appeared to be a very charmed life, he was somehow able to capture every single person's attention in the backyard.

We were hypnotized by every note.

I'd never seen anyone do karaoke like this. It felt like I was at an actual concert.

"He's so good," Alessi said, coming to stand beside me. "Did you know he could do this?"

"I had no idea," I said, feeling complete awe for the talented boy I had just learned something new about.

I'd known Nash could sing. Knew he was a great performer. But it was something else to watch him just jump into character and sing in a way that made it feel like he had actually experienced the emotions and things the lyrics spoke about.

But Nash couldn't be that angsty in real life, could he?

He was the life of the party. Not the guy who was secretly tortured and had emotional breakdowns.

This had to be him just playing another part.

But whatever it was, I knew one thing: this performance right here had only made Nash more attractive to me. He was powerful and sexy and talented, and if he ever went on tour, I would beg to be his groupie and promise to worship him and make him feel like the rap star that he was every single day.

He finished his song, and the crowd roared with applause. I wanted to go up to him and congratulate him on his spectacular performance, but he was immediately surrounded by a group of girls a year or two older than us.

"Looks like those girls are out to get your boyfriend," Alessi said, raising her eyebrows.

"Yeah, 'cause he's totally *my* boyfriend," I said sarcastically since she was the one responsible for that rumor.

"Are you mad that I told Tristan you were dating Nash?" she asked, concern etched in her green eyes. "Because I was just trying to help make him jealous."

"No, I'm not mad," I said. "It's just a little awkward since, you know, Nash is into you and not me." I shrugged. "I mean, weren't you hoping to further your relationship with him tonight? Doesn't this ruin your plans?"

"No, it's totally cool," she said. "It's not like Nash and I are exclusive or that he's my actual boyfriend or anything. We went on one date."

"But it was a good date, right?" I asked, thinking about what Nash had said about it.

"It was fun." She glanced over at Nash who was still being fawned over by his new fan club. Then looking back at me, she added, "But we'll be in college next year. We should have fun this summer." She gestured to the rest of the party. "Play the field a little."

Play the field a little?

So even though she'd said Nash was the most perfect guy she'd ever been on a date with, she was still interested in talking to other people? Had she already been talking to other guys tonight?

I guess it wouldn't be *that* surprising if she had been, since Alessi was always talking to multiple guys... But I just figured it would be different with Nash because he was, well, Nash.

He was amazing.

Alessi seemed to be reminded of that fact, too, because after a beat, she quickly said, "I do think Nash is a lot of fun. And who knows what the future holds. But it's, like, totally okay if you steal him for the night to make Tristan jealous. We're friends. I know you wouldn't do anything to hurt me."

I glanced back at Nash. When our eyes briefly caught, I remembered how I'd felt listening to his song and couldn't help but feel a little guilty about my friend's obvious faith in me.

Because if Nash took his fake-boyfriend role as seriously as he took his karaoke and decided to fake kiss me in front of Tristan...I didn't think I'd have the willpower to turn down the opportunity.

Even for my best friend's sake.
Not that he would ever fake kiss me.
He wouldn't.
He was a good guy.
Faithful.
But... I imagined what it would be like to have Nash walk straight through the crowd, take me by the hand and pull me behind the shed, and kiss me the way I'd daydreamed about so many times.

To have his fingers slip into my hair. His body pressed firmly against mine as he melded me against the shed wall.

To run my hands along his chest, over his biceps, and the muscles in his back.

And—

"You're really good at the supportive girlfriend role, though," Alessi said, breaking me away from my fantasy. "Just the way you were watching him on stage would have convinced me that you and Nash were together if I didn't know better."

"Really?" I laughed awkwardly.

"Yes," she said, narrowing her eyes like she was wondering why I was suddenly uncomfortable.

I swallowed the lump in my throat. "I-I'm just really determined to make Tristan jealous," I said, hoping it sounded convincing. Then seeing Nash had broken away from his new fan club, I said, "Oh look, he's headed over here."

When he was a few feet away, Alessi nudged me forward. "You should hug him and tell him how amazing he did."

"You think so?"

"You're his girlfriend, right?" Then leaning closer to whisper in my ear, she added, "And Tristan is watching you right now."

Okay. It was showtime, I guess.

So even though I wasn't sure he would be expecting it, I

put on a huge smile and stepped toward Nash, saying, "You did such a great job up there." Then even though it felt somewhat awkward, I held my arms out to give him a split-second warning that I was coming closer and then I wrapped my arms around him in my best "my boyfriend is so amazing" hug.

He went still for a second, like he had momentarily forgotten we were playing fake boyfriend and girlfriend tonight, but then he wrapped his arms around my torso and said, "Thank you. I was hoping to impress you with my song."

We all hung outside for another half hour before Nash said he needed a drink. There wasn't anything besides beer outside, so while Alessi went to talk with some other people, I took Nash into the house to grab some water.

"Wanna sit in there for a little bit?" Nash asked, pointing to the living room where a few people were playing a game of What Do You Meme?

"Sure," I said. It was humid today and I could use a few minutes sitting on the couch in the airconditioned house.

"Are you having fun at the party?" Nash asked, scooting to the end of the couch to make room for me to sit. There were already two other people sitting on the other end, so it was a tight fit but luckily enough room that I wasn't sitting on him.

"It's been all right," I said. "I don't really know anyone well besides Tristan and Miles, though, so it's kind of awkward."

"Yeah," Nash said. "I only know you and Alessi, so it's a little different."

"Because you don't have your freshman fan club to make you feel like a god?" I asked with a smirk.

"The fall from grace is definitely an adjustment." He

chuckled. "But at least I have my girlfriend here to keep me company." He winked.

My cheeks were just beginning to flush when footsteps on the kitchen floor made me look behind us.

"Speaking of being your boyfriend." Nash draped his arm around my shoulder and pulled me closer to him as Tristan and Brooklyn walked into the room and took a seat on the couch kitty-corner from us. Then with his mouth close to my ear, he whispered, "Looks like it's time to amp up our performance."

I didn't know if it was his sudden closeness or the way his hot breath tickled my ear, but I suddenly had tingles racing across my whole body.

He smelled so good, too.

I darted my gaze across the room briefly to check if Tristan or Brooklyn had noticed us yet and found that they were whispering to each other and glancing our way.

Were they talking about us then?

And did they believe this little charade we had going on tonight?

I instinctively scooted closer to Nash and told myself not to worry about what my ex and his girlfriend may be saying about us.

"What happened there, anyway?" Nash asked in a quiet voice. "With you and your ex?"

I sighed. "It's a long story."

"I like long stories," he said. "Plus, I've got nothing else to do."

I bit my lip, trying to decide how much I wanted to let him know.

When I hesitated too long, he bent close to my ear again and said, "Just pretend like you're whispering sweet nothings into my ear and tell me."

"I don't really want to talk about it here," I said as warmth immediately flowed into my chest. Then noticing the staircase behind Tristan, I added, "But maybe we can pretend like we're sneaking away upstairs, and I can tell you about it there."

Nash's eyes lit up, and I wondered if he was used to sneaking upstairs with girls at parties.

With his looks and personality, I was sure he had plenty of opportunities.

But then I pushed the thought away because I really didn't want to think about Nash and any girls he might have spent time with in the past.

So when he said, "Just lead the way and I'll follow," I stood from the couch and led him upstairs.

And even though I knew this was all just for show, as he followed two steps behind me, I couldn't help but hope that all of this might at least get Nash to finally see me as someone he could sneak away with for real sometime.

13

KIARA

NASH and I walked up the wooden staircase and to the third room down the hall on the right that I knew to be Miles's room.

Miles had been playing another round of beer pong when Nash and I first came inside, so I figured he wouldn't be needing his room for at least a little while.

I shut the door behind us, locking it for good measure. After looking around Miles's room and taking in his pile of laundry in the corner, and the open textbooks on his desk that told me he was taking summer classes right now, I took a seat on his messily made bed.

Nash seemed to look for where he should sit before grabbing the wooden chair by the desk, turning it around and sitting down so we were facing each other.

"So what's this long story?" Nash asked, leaning forward and resting his forearms on his knees like he was interested. "How did you end up dating a college guy? Was it pretty recent?"

"It happened last summer," I said. "I was working at The Brew and this guy with dark hair kept coming in each morning." *I'd been so excited to have a cute college guy notice me.* "We chatted a little and things kind of clicked. After talking for a few days, he asked if I had a boyfriend who would be jealous if he caught us talking to each other. I told him that I'd just moved here and was single, and he asked me out on a date."

"Just like that?" Nash asked.

"Yep." I nodded. "I was excited because he was totally the type of guy I usually went for."

"And what's that?"

"Umm..." I looked down at the wooden floor, trying to remember exactly what qualities I'd liked about Tristan. Then looking back at Nash with my cheeks growing warm, I said, "Good-looking. A little older. Had a bit of a player vibe to him. Flirty."

"So basically nothing like me?" Nash asked.

"You're not a player?" I arched an eyebrow.

He sat up straighter and leaned back in his chair. "I've tried, but nope, that player gene seemed to have only gone to Ian in my family."

I didn't know if I believed that since he had totally been flirty and confident when we'd spent time together during his family's garden party.

And the way he'd forgotten about me the next day was something a player would do.

But I still didn't actually know Nash that well, so maybe that had just been a coincidence.

Something that happened because the universe enjoyed making things like that happen to me.

"And your ex has dark hair, so apparently, you go for the tall, dark, and handsome sort."

"I have gravitated toward that look in the past..." I admitted.

"Looks like you would have picked Asher, too, then."

"Huh?" I furrowed my brow, confused by what he meant.

"Never mind..." He shook his head and cleared his throat. "Does Tristan know about your preferences? Did he take one look at my blond hair and know I couldn't actually have a chance?"

"I don't think so." I looked at his dirty-blond hair, which was short on the sides, slightly longer on top, and already highlighted by the summer sun.

I definitely preferred the light-haired guy in front of me over all my exes. They were exes for a reason, weren't they? Because they didn't know how to treat me right.

"Ok, glad the cover might still be intact." Nash wiped a hand across his brow dramatically. Then leaning forward again, he asked, "So what else happened between you two? Why did you break up?"

I thought for a second, trying to remember where I'd left off. I cleared my throat and said, "Okay, so like I said, Tristan ticked the boxes for me, so I was excited to go out with him."

"Which, since you started dating, I'm guessing your date went well."

"It did." I nodded. "We got along great."

"Did he by chance take you to explore a cave?" Nash raised an eyebrow, and a rush of panic flooded over me as I worried he had just figured out that I was the person he'd texted about spelunking last night.

But when I remembered he'd also thought of cave exploring when we'd talked about his date plans for Alessi, I told myself to calm down.

Nash was apparently just really into caves right now.

"Strangely enough, we didn't go to a cave." I smiled, hoping he hadn't noticed my weird reaction. "But I probably would have been a total goner if he had, because cave exploration has always been at the top of my date bucket list."

Nash returned my smile, his eyes lighting up. "Well, it's too bad Tristan doesn't have as good of ideas as I do. No wonder you're here with me now and he's down there."

"If only you'd asked me on that date instead of my best friend," I said, in a light-hearted voice, hoping he wouldn't see how much I wished it were true. "We totally would have had a blast."

"Such a missed opportunity." He sighed and shook his head. "At least we can be fake boyfriend and girlfriend now to make up for it."

Yes, at least there's that.

We were quiet for a second, and I wondered what Nash might be thinking about all of this. But then he gestured to me and said, "Sorry, I distracted you by inserting myself into your story. So your date was good. Not spelunking, but still enjoyable."

"It was." I nodded. "Hanging out with Tristan was fun and kind of filled the void I had at the time. We hung out basically every day after that, and since he and Miles are roommates, Miles introduced me to Alessi and we all just kind of hung out together.

"Things were going really well. We went out on dates. Went to Miles and Alessi's family cabin. Went to parties." I sighed, remembering how happy I'd been last summer, feeling like everything was finally going great in my life after such a tumultuous few years with my dad.

"But then something happened?" Nash asked, guessing the happily ever after I'd been imagining for Tristan and me had soon ended.

"Yeah..." I tried to figure out how to put the next part. When Nash had found me throwing up last summer, I'd told him about the post on the Sherman High gossip page. So if I mentioned that now, it might spark something in his memory.

And even though I wanted him to remember that night, sitting right here in this room, I wasn't sure I was actually ready to bring it up. Because what if he remembered and was disappointed to realize I was that girl at the garden party?

Since that night, I hadn't had any sort of sign that he was even attracted to me. It could have been a fluke, or maybe he just had a thing for pink wigs and renaissance dresses.

What if in the light of day he didn't really find me appealing at all?

So deciding not to go too much into the details, I said, "About six weeks into our relationship, I found out that Tristan already had a girlfriend."

"What?" Nash's eyes went wide, like he hadn't expected that.

"Yeah." I drew in a deep breath, feeling the betrayal I'd felt back then washing over me all over again. "Apparently, she'd been visiting family in Europe for several weeks and Tristan thought it would be fine to sow his wild oats while she was away."

"So you were essentially 'the other woman,'" Nash said, using air quotes around the title I never thought I'd have in a million years.

"Yep." I looked down, my cheeks warming as feelings of shame and betrayal washed over me again. "Which is why his girlfriend hates me."

"But you didn't know she even existed," Nash said. "Like, you didn't know he had a girlfriend who was just out of town when you started dating, right? Tristan was in the wrong, not you."

"I know." I shrugged and met his gaze again. "But she sees me as a homewrecker, and since she didn't want to break up with him, she had to blame someone else."

"And we're at his frat house." Nash looked around the room. "This isn't Tristan's room, is it?"

"No. It's Miles's."

"That's too bad," Nash said. "Cuz I was thinking we should trash it."

"Nash!" I said, not believing such a nice guy like Nash would suggest something like that.

"Kidding but..." He shook his head. "He deserves it."

"I know."

Nash seemed to think for a moment. "Well, if we're not trashing his room, we at least need to make it look like we *really* enjoyed our time up here. Because if he was willing to risk his relationship with his girlfriend to date you on the side, he must have been smitten."

"Or maybe he just wanted to see if he could get away with it," I said. My insecurities over how everything had turned out had made me feel unsure that Tristan had even really liked me. Made me question if any of the sweet things he'd said and done last summer had even been true.

When you had a history of good things always turning out bad like I did, you started to be skeptical of everything.

But Nash shook his head. "You're prettier than his girlfriend. And probably way more fun to talk to. So I doubt it would be just that. He was into you and couldn't resist playing with fire."

Nash thought I was pretty? And fun to talk to?

Well...that was nice to hear. My ego certainly could use a boost after reliving the events that had led to last fall and winter being one of the lowest times in my life.

"So how are we going to make him think we were having lots of fun and not telling my sob story?" I asked.

"Well..." Nash pursed his lips as he considered my question. Then after looking me over, he asked, "Did you ever play with his hair when you guys were making out?"

"Huh?"

Why was he asking about that?

Nash held up his hands. "Before you think I'm too much of a weirdo, I was just thinking that if he knows you like to tousle a guy's hair when you're kissing, that maybe we should make it look like you did the same thing to me."

"Oh..." Yeah...that was way less weird than what I was thinking.

"So hair messed up, or not?" he asked.

"Definitely a little messy," I said. Despite turning out to be a cheater, Tristan did have amazing hair.

Nash walked over to the mirror and started pushing his fingers through his perfect hair to mess it up.

"Does this look right?" He looked back at me.

And even though I thought Nash was gorgeous with his hair the way it had been, this was another look that I liked on him. Probably similar to what he looked like when he first woke up.

But since I really wanted an excuse to touch his hair again, I walked toward him and said, "Maybe a little less tousled than that." And with what I hoped wasn't too noticeable of a shaky hand, I combed my fingers through the hair on the top left side of his head.

And yep, his hair felt as soft as it looked. So apparently, that hundred-dollar shampoo I'd seen in his shower earlier this week didn't just smell really good, but it actually did do amazing things.

I smoothed down a couple of places on top as well, and when I dared meet Nash's gaze, he was looking right at me. Our eyes locked for a split second, and I felt breathless as I wondered if he remembered standing this close to me and breathing each other's breath before. But instead of finding recognition in his eyes, I only found curiosity.

"You have really nice eyes," he said, his voice low.

"Thank you." I met his eyes again, the brilliant blue wowing me like it did every time. I swallowed. "Y-you have really nice eyes, too."

We stood there for a moment, studying each other. But just like you couldn't look at something as brilliant as the sun for too long, I could only look at Nash for a short time before I felt like I might internally combust. So I took a slight step back and, after clearing my throat, I said, "Um, I think your hair looks good now. It should definitely lead Tristan to thinking we were up here kissing."

Nash turned back to the mirror to look at his reflection, and then his mirrored reflection looked at me. "We should probably make it seem like you were my partner in crime too, shouldn't we?"

"S-sure..."

He turned to face me again. Pushing his fingers into the hair at my temples, he combed it out to the sides—basically the opposite of what he'd done when he helped me fix my hair after our drive to Charlie's on Monday.

When he was done, I checked out my reflection. After patting it down in a couple of places so it looked like I'd at least tried to fix it a little after our fake make-out session, I drew in a deep breath then released it. "Should we go take our walk of shame?"

A slow smile spread across his lips at my terminology. "Let's do it."

He held out his hand for me to take. When I slipped mine into his, I reveled in the way the pads of his fingers pressed against the knuckles of my hand.

His hand fit perfectly with mine. Not too big that my fingers were uncomfortably separated, but just right.

We walked downstairs and into the room where Tristan and Brooklyn were still cuddling on the couch together. When Tristan looked our way, I had to fight the biggest smile from taking shape on my face and giving away that this whole charade was for him.

Because as his gaze went to me, and then to Nash, I noticed his jaw flex.

And I couldn't help but think that maybe Alessi was a genius for throwing us into this arrangement after all.

"Think he bought it?" Nash whispered near my ear after we turned into the kitchen to head out back again.

Only when my back was to Tristan did I allow the smile I'd been holding back to take shape on my face.

"He totally did," I said, feeling exhilarated about getting this tiny piece of revenge. "And I might have just been seeing what I wanted to see but...I think he's jealous."

"As he should be." Nash chuckled.

I rested my head against Nash's shoulder for a moment, feeling relieved. "You are basically a fake-relationship genius."

"Why, thank you." Nash released my hand to put his arm around my shoulder and pulled me closer. "All in a day's work."

14

NASH

CARTER AND CAMBRIELLE were sitting in the lounge area at the end of our hall when I got home from Miles's party.

I was tired after the eventful day and needed to head to bed soon, but I decided to sit down on the couch Carter was sitting on to catch up on what they'd done tonight.

"Ava and I went to this art night at the art studio on Milton street," Carter said. "We painted cherry blossoms on a cherry tree, and I learned that I am still not an artist." A slow smile spread across his lips. "But Ava's painting actually looked good enough that I think she was planning to hang it up on her wall when she got home."

"Sounds about right." I chuckled. Carter was definitely the most left-brained of all of my siblings and great with logic and math. "Did you happen to bring your artwork home?" I glanced around the room to see if he'd stowed it anywhere.

"Oh definitely not," he said, like that was a crazy thought. "I threw the atrocity in the dumpster as soon as we walked out to the parking lot."

"It couldn't have been that bad," Cambrielle said.

"It was," Carter said, all serious. "I just feel bad for anyone who goes dumpster diving and tries to figure out what all the pink blobs were supposed to be."

"So what did you end up doing tonight?" Cambrielle looked at me. "Was the party fun?"

"It was interesting," I said, still not sure what I thought about the events of tonight. "When Alessi told me about the party, I originally thought it would be a small get-together with her stepbrother's closest friends. But it ended up being a huge event at a frat house."

"A party at a frat house?" Cambrielle furrowed her brow.

"Yeah." I sighed. "So that was a bit uncomfortable at first."

"I would think so," Carter said, understanding in his expression. "Were Alessi or Kiara drinking?"

"I don't think so," I said. "I wasn't with Alessi the whole time, but I never saw her drinking anything. And Kiara just got water with me."

"That's good," Cambrielle said, relief in her expression, and I didn't miss the brief look she and Carter exchanged.

Which might have offended me last fall when I was new to making different choices at parties, but now I appreciated it because it just showed me that they cared.

"Anyway." I cleared my throat. "I was a bit on edge when we first got there, but after getting on fake-boyfriend duty, I had a good distraction to focus on."

"Fake-boyfriend duty?" Carter furrowed his brow.

"Just trying to follow in my older brother's footsteps." I smirked at Carter. "I guess Kiara dated a guy last summer and it didn't end well," I said, not going into the details since I wasn't sure she wanted her heartache spread around. "Anyway, her ex showed up at the party with his girlfriend, and so Alessi decided to tell everyone that I was Kiara's new boyfriend."

"So everyone thinks you're dating the best friend of the girl you just took out on a date this week?" Carter asked.

"Yep." It had definitely been an unexpected twist in my night. But surprisingly enough, I'd actually enjoyed it. Kiara was fun to hang out with.

"I guess it gave you a chance to practice your acting skills," Cambrielle said.

"It did," I said. "Which is also exactly what Kiara said."

"How was hanging out with Kiara, anyway?" Cambrielle asked. "I always thought it was kind of weird that we lived so close to her but never hung out."

"That is kind of weird, isn't it?" Carter furrowed his brow, like the thought of having a girl our age just across the lawn to hang out with had never registered in his mind.

"I don't know why we never invited her over before." I ran a hand through my hair that was probably still messy from earlier. "But she's cool. Fun. I always assumed she'd be quiet since we never talked much. But I think she's just slower to warm up."

None of the other shy girls I knew dated college guys, anyway.

"We should have her and Alessi hang out with all of us sometime," Cambrielle suggested. "We might as well get to know our neighbor better. Maybe have a pool party?"

"I'm sure they'd be down for something like that."

"Can you bring the Harper and Ash file into my office?" my dad asked from the other side of the line. "We're meeting with them tomorrow, and I want to refresh myself on the details of the merger."

"Will do," I said.

I had been working the front desk today since the woman who worked there, Susie, had called in sick. And after answering calls all morning and dealing with a few walk-ins, I was getting into the groove.

The work I'd done last week had been tedious and I'd dreaded having another monotonous day in the file room. But this job was actually kind of fun. I was a social creature, and getting to chat with people as they came and went had made the morning and early afternoon pass by quickly.

Which had me wondering if Susie would be up for switching jobs when she came back tomorrow.

Yeah...probably not.

"Did you put the Harper and Ash file away yet?" I asked Cambrielle when I walked into the room where we kept all of the client files.

"I don't think so." She tiptoed to look at the stack of files she had sitting on the file cabinet in front of her. After leafing through them, she pulled one out with the words "Harper and Ash" on the tab. "Here it is."

"Awesome. Thanks." I took it from her and carried it down the hall. I turned the corner when I got there and continued until I made it to the end of that corridor where my dad's corner office with its huge walls of windows was located.

"Here's the file you asked for." I stepped across the tile floor to place it on my dad's large modern-style desk. He thanked me, and I asked, "Do you need anything else?"

"Actually, yes." He set the file on his desk that was already covered in the papers he'd been working with today. "Your mom just called in to say she wouldn't be coming back into the office after her meeting with the Jacobsons."

"Is something wrong?" I frowned, wondering why she wouldn't be coming back in. She only ever missed work if she was on vacation, sick, or attending one of mine and my siblings' extra-curricular activities.

"She's not feeling well," Dad said. "She didn't sleep well last night so she might just need to rest."

My mom was a bit of an insomniac sometimes.

"Anyway," Dad continued. "She said she didn't think she'd be up to going to the Yankees game with me tonight, so I wanted to see if you'd be interested in taking our seats."

"Really?" I asked, surprised he'd choose me instead of Cambrielle or Carter who had significant others they could take.

"You've been spending time with some new girls lately, haven't you? I just thought that this might be an opportunity for you to ask one of them out to the game."

"Sure," I said, not expecting him to have known about that since he'd been traveling last week. But my mom and dad talked every night when he was away, so I guess she must have given him an update on what everyone had going on. "I guess I could ask Alessi."

We hadn't actually been able to spend much time together last weekend, so it would be good to get some one-on-one time with her again.

"Sounds great." Dad smiled. Then waving his hand, he said, "In fact, you can go home early if you need to change and pick up your date. I'm sure Cambrielle can manage the front desk for the last hour."

I got to use my dad's VIP tickets *and* leave work early. Talk about a no-brainer.

"Awesome," I said. "I'll tell Cambrielle what's going on."

I headed out of my dad's office, and as I walked down the hall toward the front desk, I pulled out my phone to text Alessi.

Me: **Hey, my dad just offered me his tickets for the Yankees game tonight. Want to be my date?**

I watched as the message went immediately from *delivered* to *sent*. A moment later, her response came through.

Alessi: **That sounds super fun! I have work tonight but let me see if I can find someone to take my shift.**

I walked out of the Hastings Industries building at four. On my way to my car, I checked my texts to see if I'd missed a follow-up text from Alessi. But when I opened my messaging app, the last text I'd received was still the one where she said she'd try to find someone to take her shift.

I drove the twenty-five minutes home, and as I walked through the garage and into the house, I checked my phone again.

But there was still nothing.

Was she already at work then and just busy? She might have said something about the evening shift starting around two or three so it made sense that she might already be there...

I checked the time on my watch. It was four twenty-two. With the commute to New York, we'd need to leave soon if we didn't want to be late.

So I sent her a follow-up text. **Anyone able to take your shift?**

I went up the stairs to change out of my dress shirt and trousers. When I was walking past Carter and Cambrielle's doors, my heart skipped a beat when my phone buzzed. I opened it to find the message: **Sorry, I meant to text. I couldn't find anyone to take my spot, so I'm stuck here.** Followed by a bunch of crying emojis.

"Well, that sucks," I said as I opened my bedroom door.

"What sucks?" a female voice said from beside my bed.

I looked up to find Kiara standing there in her black and white cleaning uniform, pulling the comforter over my bed.

I sighed and tossed my phone onto the couch. Then I sat down on the cushion next to it to remove my dress shoes. "My dad gave me his tickets to a Yankees game tonight, and I asked Alessi but she just told me she can't come."

"Oh, I'm sorry." Kiara grabbed a pillow from my nightstand and started pulling a pillowcase over it. "I bet you guys would have had fun together."

"I think we would have." I pulled off my shoe and was untying the other when my phone buzzed again.

I glanced down at the screen to see another text from Alessi.

I don't have work tomorrow. Maybe we can hang out then?

I picked up my phone and quickly texted back, **Sure. Have a good time at work.**

I dropped my phone back on the couch. Leaning back, I looked over to Kiara and asked, "Know anyone who wants to see a Yankees and Manatees game tonight?"

"The Yankees are playing the Manatees?" Kiara's eyes lit up, like she was actually familiar with both teams.

"Yeah." I studied her for a moment. "Do you like baseball then?"

"I love it." She smiled. "My dad and I used to watch the Manatees games together all the time."

Which, I guess, made sense. She and her mom had moved here from Miami, so of course she'd be familiar with the team.

And without really thinking about it, I was saying, "Do you want to go with me?"

"You don't have another girl you want to ask on a date?"

She glanced sideways as she put a pillowcase on the second pillow. "One of the girls from your freshman fan club perhaps?"

"I'm actually trying to hang out with people closer to my age." I waved the thought away. "And since you actually like baseball, I'd love to go with you."

She looked at her watch. "What time do we need to leave?"

"Fifteen minutes..." I said, making a face that showed her I knew I was cutting it close. "Think you can make that work?"

She put her hands on her hips and glanced around my bedroom. "I still need to vacuum in here and in your closet."

"You can just skip that today," I said, waving the chore away. "I won't tell anyone if you don't."

"You're not going to get me fired?" She arched an eyebrow.

"No," I said. "I'll even keep my door shut so no one can come snooping around for vacuum lines."

"Does your mom check for things like that?" Her amber eyes went wide.

"Of course not." I chuckled. "I promise you won't get in trouble. If anyone does say something, I'll tell them I made you go to the game with me so I wouldn't be sitting alone."

She seemed to think about it for a bit, and after putting the last pillow where it belonged at the head of my bed, she wiped her hands on her skirt and said, "Okay, then let me change real quick and we can go."

15

KIARA

THE STADIUM WAS CROWDED when Nash and I arrived. I kept close to Nash's side so we wouldn't get separated on our way to our seats.

When Nash reached for my hand to guide me down the steps with him, I had to remind myself that this was not a date. Nash was not interested in me the way I wanted him to be.

He was interested in my best friend. He'd asked her first. This was supposed to be *her* date.

I was just the backup plan.

Even if spending all this time with him was making me hope it could turn into something more, it didn't mean Nash saw it in the same way.

"I think these are our seats," Nash said when we made it to the first row, right behind home plate.

"Really?" I gasped.

He nodded. "My dad *might* have some really great connections in the baseball world."

I supposed as a billionaire, he would.

But dang, I thought as I sat next to Nash, *these are the best seats in the house.*

The baseball players came onto the field a few minutes later. As we watched them warm up, Nash had the stadium employees bring us concessions, hats, and jerseys—the whole shebang, which was something I'd only seen in movies.

Definitely not something I'd done with my dad when we'd sat in the nosebleeds two years ago.

Nash and I chatted as we ate our burgers and shakes, and I told him which Manatees players were mine and my dad's favorites.

"Sounds like you two are opinionated about your baseball." Nash chuckled when I told him about the player my dad thought should be traded.

"We just like to see our team win." I shrugged.

"Does that mean you're going to burn this when we get back to your house?" He briefly touched the sleeve of the Yankees jersey I'd put on over my regular clothes.

"No." I grinned, loving that he felt comfortable being more touchy with me. "If my dad was here, he'd probably make me throw it in the trash, but I'm not *quite* that much of a fanatic."

In fact, I'd probably start sleeping in it every night now since it was a gift from Nash.

Not that I'd be telling *him* that.

"Does your dad live in Eden Falls?" Nash asked. "Or is he still in Florida?"

"H-he's still in Florida," I said, glancing down briefly. "My mom and I had to leave him behind."

"Oh." Nash gave me a compassionate look that told me he understood the decision to leave my dad hadn't been an easy one for my mom or me. "I'm sorry to hear that."

I nodded, stifling the wave of emotion that washed over me as I thought about how my mom and I had to slip out of the house while my dad was sleeping. We knew that if he had tried to stop us, it would have made it that much harder to leave.

When I could speak again, I said, "He has some things he needs to work through. Um..." I wiped my eyes and drew in a deep breath. "So it's better for us to be apart right now."

"Sometimes we just need a little time and space to figure things out." Nash put his hand on my knee, giving it a gentle squeeze. "But I hope things can work out for the best there."

"Thanks." I lifted my gaze back up to Nash's face and gave him a grateful smile. "I hope so, too."

The crowd cheered loudly at a play on the field, bringing our attention back to the game. After wiping my eyes that were blurry with unshed tears, I saw two Manatees outfielders collide as they dove for the ball that had been hit by the Yankees player to center field. As a Manatees player chased after the ball, the runner sprinted from first base to second, then from second to third.

Is he going to have an inside-the-park home run?

I hadn't seen one of those happen in forever.

The Yankees runner was already headed for home when the cut-off man caught the ball and threw it toward home plate.

I held my breath as I watched, anxious to see if the Manatees catcher would get the ball fast enough to tag the Yankees player out. But the throw came in high, and number twenty-nine slid in headfirst under the tag.

"Safe," the umpire called as his arms moved for the signal. And the crowd roared louder as the Yankees received a run on the scoreboard. Nash stood and shouted along with everyone, clearly enjoying seeing his team have such an unbelievable play.

"That was so cool," Nash said, turning to me with a huge smile on his face. Then realizing he was talking to a Manatees fan, his expression turned chagrined. "Um, I mean...uh... sorry?"

I chuckled. "No, it was an amazing play. Even I can admit it."

"Whew." Nash dramatically wiped a hand across his brow as he sat down. "Glad you aren't a poor sport."

"Not yet anyway," I said. "We'll see how I'm feeling at the end of the game."

"Should I tell my dad's driver to have a bucket of ice cream ready for you to cry into when we get back to the Escalade?" Nash asked in a teasing tone.

"It might be a good idea..." I said. "For you, of course, since the Manatees are not going to lose."

Nash chuckled. "I guess we'll just have to watch and see."

The next inning started and my favorite Manatees player, Brock Ramsey, took a few practice swings near the plate. As the Yankees' pitcher talked to the catcher, I leaned closer to Nash and said, "These seats are amazing, by the way."

"They really are, aren't they?"

I nodded.

He looked down at me with his blue eyes, and for a moment, the world stood still. And gosh, I could get lost in his eyes all day.

"Thanks for coming with me," he said in a soft voice that made my stomach flutter. "I don't think coming by myself would have been nearly as fun."

"Thanks for inviting me."

We held each other's gaze for a moment longer, but then Nash got a smirk on his lips and before I knew it, he was grabbing the brim of my hat and pulling it down over my eyes.

"Hey," I said, batting his hand away before readjusting my cap back where it was supposed to be.

"Sorry." He laughed, his eyes glittering with amusement. "I

just didn't want you to have to watch your favorite player strike out."

"Ramsey would never." I scoffed and playfully pushed Nash on the shoulder. "He could hit it with his eyes closed." Then because I was suddenly in a goofy mood, I put my hands on both sides of my mouth and called out, "You've got this, Brock!"

Brock looked over his shoulder, seeming confused about who might be cheering him on in a sea of fans wearing Yankees jerseys.

So I waved and said, "I know I look like a traitor right now, but I'm actually a huge fan. That grand slam you had in Atlanta last season was epic. Let's show 'em what Florida is made of."

A grin stretched across Brock's face. Then he touched the brim of his batting helmet and nodded like the true southern gentleman that he was.

"Were you just flirting with Brock Ramsey?" Nash asked once I'd settled back in my seat.

"What? No?" I shook my head, surprised he'd think that.

"Are you sure?" Nash tilted his head to the side, unconvinced. "Because you already told me you go after tall, dark-haired guys who are a few years older than you and..." He gestured at Brock. "There's a really famous guy who fits that exact description standing only a few feet away."

"I wasn't flirting with him." I shook my head as my face grew hot. "I was just showing him support."

"Whatever you say," Nash said, like he still didn't believe me.

Which, sure, I'd had a crush on Brock in the past. I mean, everyone has a few celebrity crushes here and there. But that definitely hadn't been flirting.

Why would I flirt with a professional baseball player when I was already sitting next to the guy I liked?

Brock ended up making it to first base after hitting the ball out to left field, and the Manatees got one more hit during that inning. But sadly for me, no runs.

While the Manatees took the field, upbeat music started playing through the stadium speakers. When I looked up to the jumbotron, I saw that the kiss cam was making its rounds.

While the camera was stopped on an elderly couple wearing Yankees jerseys, Nash said, "Wanna hear a funny story about the kiss cam?"

"Sure," I said, wondering if this story had something to do with him.

"Well, last summer my family came to watch a game. My dad was out of town for work, so it was just my mom, my siblings, and me," he said. "Anyway, the kiss cam came out, just like it is now, and it stopped on my mom and Ian."

"On your mom and your oldest brother?" I asked.

He nodded, his eyes lighting up when he saw my surprise. "I mean, my mom had him when she was nineteen and she looks good for her age. But they must have thought she was a cougar or something."

Mrs. Hastings did look really good for her age.

"Anyway, it was really awkward for a minute since everyone in the stadium was watching them on the huge screen and probably assumed they were there on a date." Nash got a half-smile on his lips. "Pretty sure they thought Ian was just being chicken."

I chuckled, thinking that from what I knew of Ian and all the girls he spent time with, he was the last person who would be shy about kissing.

With someone he wasn't related to, that is.

"Ian tried to tell the camera '*She's my mom*' a few times,"

Nash continued, amusement in his expression. "But when that didn't work, he gave up and ended up kissing her on the cheek. It was funny."

"Did you catch it on video?" I asked, thinking it would be a funny memory to have documented.

"It all happened so fast that we didn't," he said. "But one of Ian's friends found it on YouTube a while later so it's been well documented."

The kiss cam continued making its rounds. When it stopped on a couple a little closer to our age, I said, "Hey, I'm gonna go use the bathroom real quick. Let me know if anything exciting happens?"

"Will do."

I made my way up the steps to find the nearest bathroom. As I waited in the long line, I pulled my phone out of the back pocket of my shorts.

On the screen was a text from Alessi that I must have missed earlier.

Being an adult sucks. I just had to turn down a super cool VIP date to a Yankees game with Nash because I couldn't get off work. Why is the universe so unfair to me?

I grimaced as I read her text, guilt washing over me for benefitting from my friend's misfortune.

Should I tell Alessi that I went in her place?

I didn't want to rub it in or anything. But she was bound to find out about it later, right?

I read her text again. Maybe I should ask Nash what he thinks I should say?

When I got back to my seat, I showed my phone to Nash. "So, I just got a text from Alessi, and I was wondering what you were planning to tell her if she asks you about the game."

"Oh, um..." He sat up straighter, seeming surprised she'd texted me about it. "I haven't really thought about that." He bit his bottom lip, considering my question. "I don't really want to lie but... Do you think she'll be upset to hear that we went together?"

"I don't know. Maybe."

"But she was, like, cool with us hanging out at the party on Friday night, wasn't she?" he asked. "So she shouldn't be bothered by this. I mean, we're here just as friends."

Yeah...just friends...

Thanks for the reminder.

"We should probably tell her, though," I said. "If we don't, she might find out some other way and think we had something to hide."

And I already knew firsthand what it was like to be seen as the other woman.

"You're probably right." Nash rubbed the back of his head. "If she asks, I'll tell her."

I looked at my phone again, torn about how I should respond to her message. If only I'd seen the text in the few seconds between Alessi turning Nash down and him inviting me.

If that was the case, I could have just said, "That sucks," and not have anything else to say...

"Wooohhh," Nash suddenly cheered loudly before jumping to his feet.

I turned my attention back to the game to see that a Yankees player had just got a run.

He sat back down, and when another player went up to bat, I decided to figure out my response to Alessi later and just enjoy the game for now.

"Are you excited for the renaissance fair this weekend?" I asked Nash as we shared a bag of popcorn a while later.

"It should be fun. I have rehearsals tomorrow and on Wednesday right after work, so it should keep me pretty busy." He grabbed a handful of popcorn and popped a kernel in his mouth. After swallowing it, he asked, "What about you? Are you ready to bake up a storm?"

"I am." I smiled at the thought of baking and setting up shop for a few days. "I'll probably need to practice a few of the recipes that I haven't made since last year, just to make sure they come out right. But it should be fun."

"Probably be a great break from cleaning, too." He winked.

"Yeah, that too." My cheeks warmed. "I mean, I'm thankful to have a good summer job. But baking desserts and pastries is just a bit more fun than cleaning toilets."

"I can understand that," he said. "If you need help taste-testing anything, just let me know."

"I will."

Wasn't there a saying about the best way to a man's heart was through his stomach?

Because if so, I might just need to bake Nash something sweet every day until he realized that the girl for him had been living in his backyard all along.

The inning ended with the Yankees scoring a total of two runs, making the score four to two, with the Yankees in the lead.

As the teams swapped places on the field and got ready for the next inning, the kiss cam started making the rounds again.

The first victims were a guy and a girl who looked like they might actually be a little younger than Nash and me.

Nash leaned closer. "Wanna bet it's their first date?" he asked when the guy's cheeks flushed crimson as he glanced between his date and the screen a few times like he was stalling.

"I think it might be," I said. But when the girl leaned closer like she was up for it, he cupped her chin and gave her the kind of kiss that made me think they'd had a few practice sessions before.

I was about to say that maybe they were just camera shy, but before I could get the words out, I watched the image on the jumbotron move from the young couple to focus right on us.

My heart raced as I looked up at Nash with wide eyes—probably resembling a deer caught in the headlights. "What should we do?"

We weren't on a date.

He was interested in Alessi.

"I don't know." He glanced back up at the screen like he was equally flustered. "Should we just..." He swallowed. "Go for it?"

"I guess?" And then because I was bad under pressure, I found myself stupidly saying, "I mean, at least I'm not your mom."

But he didn't seem to register my comment because he was just glancing up at the jumbotron and then back at me, like he was still weighing what to do in this moment.

My heartbeat thundered in my ears as I waited for Nash to make the move.

At least, I hoped he would choose to kiss me since I'd really hate for this footage to end up in one of those "most embarrassing kiss cam moments" on YouTube.

The internet already had enough of my embarrassing moments documented, thanks to Brooklyn's friends.

But thankfully, after only another moment of hesitation, Nash leaned closer and looked at my eyes and lips like he was asking for permission before he closed the gap.

I nodded that it was okay, and a few heartbeats later, he was slipping his hand behind my neck and pulling my lips to his.

Time stood still for a few seconds. My heart pounded so

hard I wondered if I was on the verge of a heart attack, but then I was memorizing exactly how Nash's lips felt against mine.

They were softer than I remembered, and when he let them linger for a second and third kiss, my lower belly flipped and fluttered in a way it hadn't done for way too long.

Probably not since our kiss in the woods.

He pulled away a second later, and when our eyes caught, I thought I saw a look of wonder reflected in his blue eyes.

Like he hadn't expected whatever had just happened.

But the look disappeared as the noise of the crowd cheering for us suddenly broke through the barrier in my mind that had only wanted to focus on that kiss a second before.

Had Nash really just kissed me like that?

I touched my lips with my fingertips, completely awed by that kiss and still not sure it was even real.

As I tried to imprint that kiss into my memory forever, Nash got over whatever daze he'd gone under. Putting his acting hat on, he looked out at the crowd and pumped his fist in the air a few times to ham the moment up for the crowd even more.

As the Manatees player stepped up to bat, all I could think of was, *Wow, I just kissed Nash Hastings again.*

Hopefully, they weren't playing the game on the TVs at Charlie's tonight.

16

KIARA

NASH and I grabbed ice cream from a cute little shop on the way back to Eden Falls. Not because I was a poor sport about my team losing the game—how could you fail me, Brock?—but because it sounded good.

It was close to midnight by the time the driver pulled into the Hastings' garage, but I wasn't nearly as tired as I expected to be after such a big day.

A big part of that was probably due to the fact that being around Nash seemed to keep me hopped up on an endless supply of energy. I was literally always buzzing when I was with him.

Nash helped me out of the Escalade like the true gentleman that he was, and we tossed our ice cream cups into the bin behind the house. As we walked across the slightly damp lawn to my house, I couldn't help but think about the kiss we'd shared and wonder what Nash thought about it.

Had it been as good for him as it had been for me?

Or had it all been part of his act where he was just giving the crowd a good show?

He'd mentioned fake kisses last week at Miles's party, so maybe that was all it was to him?

But then there was that look in his eyes when we pulled apart... The one that made it seem like he was shocked by how good the kiss had felt.

That look couldn't have been for show, could it?

Not when the camera couldn't see that look from the angle it was at.

But he'd asked Alessi out tonight and not you, Kiara.

I sighed. I was just the friend of the girl he wanted.

I'd lived in his backyard for a whole year, and he had lots of opportunities to get to know me, but he hadn't been interested in my existence until he met Alessi.

He was attracted to bubbly, flirtatious girls.

And while I'd always thought a good guy like Nash would be a dream to end up with, I knew from experience that *I* wasn't the type of girl that guys like him went after.

The only guys that had ever given me a second look were the bad-boy type.

The type who cheated. The ones who lied in order to get what they wanted...

Nash and I made it to the steps that led to my front door. With the moonlight on his face, he said, "Thanks again for coming with me tonight. I had a really good time."

"Me too," I said, liking the way he was looking at me. "I'm glad I was at the right place at the right time."

"It worked out great." He nodded. "Speaking about being at the right place at the right time..." He paused for a moment. Then tilting his head to the side and rubbing his neck, he added, "That kiss we had tonight...I..."

He stopped, like he wasn't sure how to let me down gently.

So before things could get too awkward, I hurried and said, "Of course I won't tell Alessi about it. The date and the kiss cam." I shook my head, knowing this was coming out weird. I blinked my eyes shut, trying to get a handle on what I was saying. Then opening my eyes again and meeting Nash's confused expression, I added, "What I mean is, I know that everything tonight—the game and whole VIP experience—was meant for her. So of course things don't need to be weird between any of us."

"Oh..." He shook his head, taking a slight step forward. "T-that's not what..." But then he seemed to think better of whatever he'd been about to say and simply said, "I mean, yes, of course. We wouldn't want that..."

Except, I kind of did.

If having Nash pick me over my friend meant things might get a little tricky between Alessi and me for a while, I was kind of okay with that.

It probably made me a really bad friend...but guys like Nash were one in a million.

Plus, hadn't Alessi told me herself that things weren't that serious between them and that she still wanted to play the field? She couldn't fault me for wanting to be with the guy I'd liked way before she'd even met him, right?

But then again, that would require Nash to actually be interested in me.

Which he probably wasn't.

We stood there awkwardly for a moment, each of us trying to figure out what to do now that we'd established that we wouldn't be making a big deal out of tonight.

What exactly is the proper protocol for a non-date? Should we hug? Give each other high-fives?

Nash pushed his hands into his pockets and took a step back, like he was ready to just leave.

So I smiled and said, "I guess I'll see you later." Then I followed my goodbye with a dorky wave.

Why was I so awkward around him?

But awkward waves were apparently our thing now because he waved back and said, "Yeah. Have a good night, Kiara."

As I was changing into my pajamas, I realized that it was highly possible I'd misinterpreted what Nash had been about to say about the kiss-cam moment before I cut him off.

And now I'd never actually get to know what he was about to say, because going back in time and telling myself to keep my stupid mouth shut so Nash could finish his sentence wasn't exactly possible yet.

Time machines still only appeared in fiction and not real life.

Me and my insecure babbling.

Stupid, stupid, stupid.

I tossed my dirty clothes into the laundry basket and sighed as I dropped into the chair by the window.

I pulled out my phone to do some doom scrolling, but then out of the corner of my eye, I noticed Nash's bedroom light switching on.

I scooted my chair back. If he happened to look through the glass in the French doors that led to his balcony, he hopefully wouldn't be able to see me.

Maybe I should turn off my lamp, just in case?

But before I could get up and switch off the lamp by my bed, Nash was pulling his shirt over the back of his head.

He was undressing? In front of his balcony doors?

Did he not know I could see right into them from my room?

My throat constricted and I wondered what I should do. Should I look away?

Give him some privacy?

But then he walked out of my view, and all I could think of was, *Dang, I really wanted to see that.*

About thirty seconds went by, and I assumed he must have decided to take a shower, but then he appeared in front of the window again. The lighting in his room was just bright enough for me to see that he had changed into gym shorts.

And yeah, he looked good wearing them.

I'd heard that he'd played basketball during his first three years of high school, and I couldn't help but think it was such a pity I hadn't been able to go to any of his games.

He stood in front of the French doors for a moment, and I wondered if he might be thinking about sitting on his balcony like he sometimes did at night.

But instead of opening the doors, he reached for the curtains and pulled them shut.

Which of course he did. It was already past midnight, and he probably woke up early to work out or something.

At least, I assumed he had to work out sometime to have a physique like that.

Not that I'd seen much of it up close. Just the little bit of his chest that I'd tried not to stare at when he'd walked into his closet on Monday.

But even if I hadn't seen too much of him yet, my imagination was *really* good at filling in the details of what his six- or eight-pack would look like.

And the toned muscles in his back.

And the way his biceps would flex when his arms were bent just right.

Ugh. Why did he have to like Alessi? Why did she always get all the guys?

What made her so special that Nash saw *her* as girlfriend material while I was stuck in the friend zone?

17

NASH

"IS ALESSI HERE?" I asked when a middle-aged woman with short brown hair answered the door at Alessi's house.

I'd had my rehearsal with Asher and Elyse and a few other kids from drama club right after work, which had gone smoothly. Then after grabbing a quick bite to eat at a drive-thru, I'd headed to Alessi's house since she'd suggested we watch a movie there tonight.

"I think she went to the storage room to grab some popcorn," the woman whom I assumed to be Alessi's mom said. "But you can just wait for her in our family room and she'll be back soon."

She led me through their bungalow-style home to the back of the house where they had a family room with a wood-burning stove and a couple of couches accessorized with several throw pillows and blankets to make it look super cozy and inviting.

But when I looked at the couch along the wall to my right, I was surprised to find Kiara sitting there.

"Hey," I said when she looked up from her phone.

"Hi." She set her phone down on the cushion beside her.

"I didn't realize you were going to be here," I said. For some reason, I'd assumed it would just be Alessi and me watching the movie tonight. But when I saw Kiara's expression fall, like she thought I was disappointed to find her here, I hurried to add, "But it's good to see you again."

Tonight might just be a little awkward since I was slightly confused about where we stood after what happened last night.

An image of us kissing for the kiss cam flashed through my mind, followed immediately after by a memory of the dream I'd just had last night.

Where had that dream come from?

But I quickly pushed those thoughts away. I didn't need to be thinking about either one of those things right now.

I stepped farther into the room and glanced around at the family photos on the walls. I was looking at a photo of Miles and Alessi, at what I assumed was Miles's high school graduation from the cap and gown he was wearing, when two arms slipped around my waist from behind.

I startled a little at the unexpected hug. When I glanced over my shoulder, I saw it was Alessi who had just snuck up behind me.

"Hey," I said, smiling at the petite girl whose head only reached the middle of my spine.

"Hi!" She giggled a little before stepping back enough to give me the space to turn around and face her better. "My mom said she'd let you in, so I had to say hi real quick before I get back to popping the popcorn."

"What kind of popcorn are you making?" I asked, curious since I hadn't heard any popping yet.

"The microwave kind, of course," she said, a smile in her eyes. "We're super fancy around here."

"Sounds great to me," I said.

She excused herself to go back to the kitchen, and I went to sit on the couch that Kiara wasn't already sitting on.

"So, how was your day so far?" I grabbed a throw pillow from behind me and tossed it to the ground. "Anything exciting happen?"

"Nothing too exciting," she said. "I cleaned the library and music room and things in that part of your house today."

"Thanks for doing that," I said, not really sure what else to say to someone who worked for my family but was also becoming a friend.

"Yeah, no problem."

I glanced toward the door Alessi had disappeared through a moment earlier. After assuring myself that she wasn't close by, I lowered my tone and I asked, "Does Alessi know we went to the game together?"

Kiara glanced toward the doorway, too. Seeing the coast was still clear, she leaned forward and whispered, "I forgot to respond to her text last night." A look of apprehension filled her eyes. "And then today, I didn't really know how to bring it up, so I didn't tell her." She pressed her lips together. "Did you say something to her?"

"No..." I ran a hand through my hair and sighed. "I feel kind of bad that we went without her, but like, you don't think she'll be mad, do you?"

She looked like she was about to respond, but then Alessi's frame approached the doorway. Kiara sat up straighter again and tried to look like we hadn't just been talking about her friend.

Not seeming to pick up on our suspicious vibe, Alessi looked at me when she leaned against the doorframe and asked, "Do you like having extra seasonings on your popcorn?"

"Extra seasonings?" I furrowed my brow, not sure what she was talking about.

Did they just have plain popcorn around here? Without butter or salt?

But then she said, "You know, like those little seasonings they have next to the popcorn in the grocery store?"

I just looked at her blankly.

"Umm." Kiara chuckled, seeming to find this exchange comical. "I don't know if Nash has ever had a reason to go into a grocery store before."

I looked at Kiara. "You don't think I've ever been to a grocery store?"

"Well..." She shrugged. "Have you?"

"Fine." I sighed, leaning against the back of the couch. "So maybe I've never gone to a grocery store. But I've seen people buy popcorn in movies."

"Wait?" Alessi's eyes went wide as if shocked by this revelation. "You've actually never been to the grocery store? Like, ever?"

"Not that I can remember," I said, feeling like my privilege of being a billionaire's son was shining like a big, blinking red sign on my forehead. Because I felt stupid, I hurried to explain, "Our chef does all of the cooking and shopping for us. A-and Kiara's mom also helps us keep everything else really well stocked, so I've never needed to do any of that."

I thought explaining it would help, but from the expressions of shocked disbelief on their faces, I only felt more sheepish.

"Well," Alessi said, pausing like she was trying to figure out what to do with that information. "Do you like ranch-flavored things?"

"I'm a big fan of ranch," I said. "I get those ranch-flavored corn nuts every so often when I stop at a gas station."

"You've been inside a gas station?" Alessi gasped dramatically, putting a hand to her chest. "I can't believe what I'm hearing."

"Har har," I said, making a face. "Believe it or not, but I have stopped for gas a time or two during a long drive."

I just wouldn't mention the fact that our driver, Vaughn, kept all of my family's vehicles well fueled and detailed for us the majority of the time.

Kiara likely already knew about that since her mom oversaw everyone, but Alessi seemed the type to never let me live it down.

"I'm glad you've at least been to a gas station," Alessi said. "I was starting to think Kiara and I might need to take you on an educational tour of all the places commoners like us frequent on a regular basis."

Kiara let out a light giggle, and even though they were clearly enjoying a moment at my expense, I found a smile lifting the corners of my mouth.

"Anyway," Alessi said, standing up straighter. "If ranch popcorn sounds good to you, I can just go add that real quick. But we also have sour cream and onion, caramel-flavoring if you're feeling like something sweet, and this new salt-and-vinegar seasoning that looked interesting."

"Let's stick with the ranch," I said. "We don't want to overwhelm me with too many new discoveries in one day."

While Alessi made her way back to the kitchen, Kiara grabbed the remote off the side table at the corner between our couches and said, "I don't think Alessi picked a movie yet; should we look for something?"

"Sure."

I leaned back against the couch and tried to get comfortable again, but as I watched Kiara scroll past a movie that looked like a baseball romance, a pit of guilt formed in my stomach.

Was it wrong not to tell Alessi that Kiara and I had gone to the game together?

We hadn't been trying to go behind her back or anything. I'd just had an extra ticket and Kiara was right there and liked baseball, so it made sense. Anyone would have taken her in that situation, right?

And so what if I'd actually had a really good time and thought Kiara was cute? Any heterosexual guy would.

Plus, it wasn't like Alessi and I were officially dating or anything.

We'd gone on one date and hung out a few times. And Kiara had been there for most of that time we'd spent together.

If anyone was paying close attention to my social life and saw what I'd been doing this past week and considered me to be dating Alessi because of how much time we'd spent together, they'd also have to think I was dating Kiara since we'd been together just as much...if not more.

And it wasn't my fault that I'd dreamt about her last night.

Dreams didn't come from a place that we could control.

I sighed as the dream from last night crept back to the forefront of my mind.

In my dream, I'd just gotten to my bedroom after dropping Kiara off for the night, only to receive a text from her asking me to come back over and watch a movie with her in her room because she couldn't sleep.

And since you didn't question things like that in dreams, I'd padded across the yard and slipped into what I assumed was her bedroom window. Once I was inside, I found her standing near her bed wearing a silky, blue cami top and shorts. I'd gulped, not expecting her to be wearing sweet yet sexy pajamas, but instead of just staring at her curves the way the caveman part of my brain wanted to, I made my gaze focus on her face and at her hair pulled up into a messy bun.

She asked if I wanted to watch *The Mindy Project,* and I agreed since watching something funny would help keep my thoughts from wandering about how beautiful she was and how strange it was that I'd never really noticed it before.

She turned on the show. And even though I thought I'd gone over there with the purest of intentions, once we were sitting side by side on her bed, things suddenly took a less innocent turn.

I'd started lazily kissing her, tasting her lips carefully like I had at the baseball game. But it wasn't long before the heat turned up, hands started roaming, and I was pulling her on top of me and kissing her in a way that was much different from the innocent kiss we'd shared in real life.

I'd woken from the dream before things could get steamier, but yeah...I might have been distracted by "dream Kiara" all day at work.

"What do you think about this one?" Kiara asked, startling me.

When she glanced over her shoulder to look at me, all I could hope was that she couldn't read my thoughts.

Based on what she'd said about the kiss-cam moment when I'd tried to bring it up last night, she didn't see me in a romantic way. She didn't think we needed to talk about it because it was nothing, and she thought I should be with her friend.

Which was how I'd seen things, too...right up until the moment we'd actually kissed and something stirred inside me that I hadn't felt in a long time.

A feeling of *rightness.*

Which was weird. Because how could a simple ten-second kiss with my neighbor girl awaken something that my previous crushes hadn't been able to?

I hadn't even been that nervous during the kiss, which was

another strange occurrence on its own. I was always anxious when I was around someone I liked.

"Is everything okay?" Kiara frowned when I was still apparently in a daze. "Was it a long day or something?"

"Yeah, sorry." I shook my head. "I think I'm just tired. I didn't get a lot of sleep last night."

"Same." Our eyes locked, and when something seemed to spark in her gaze, I briefly wondered if she'd had any dreams similar to mine.

Had her subconscious been trying to confuse her about our kiss, too?

I shook the thoughts away. Then I looked at the screen so I could see the movie she was asking about, a psychological thriller I'd been wanting to see. I cleared my throat. "That one looks great."

"Cool," she said, clicking on the movie cover to get it loaded and ready to go.

"Does Alessi like psychological thrillers?" I asked, just in case Alessi didn't like this kind of movie.

"She usually likes to watch scary movies with guys," Kiara said. "So this should fit her goals for tonight."

"Her goals for tonight?" I frowned, unsure what she meant by that.

Kiara shrugged. "She likes scary movies because they give her an excuse to cuddle."

"Oh..." I said, not sure how I should respond as she was obviously hinting that Alessi would be cuddling up to me. "I guess that works then."

Which must mean that if Kiara was choosing this movie, knowing that about her friend, then she really must not care if I ended up cuddling with Alessi tonight.

So maybe that kiss-cam moment really hadn't been as memorable to her as it was to me.

Guess it was good I'd found that out before I'd let my temporary confusion run on for too long.

A minute later, Alessi came back and handed Kiara and me our popcorn bowls before sitting next to me on the couch.

While the opening credits played, Alessi nudged Kiara's leg with her foot and said, "Hey, so I was talking with Miles this weekend about his party and how it reminded us of how much fun we all had together last summer."

"Yeah?" Kiara furrowed her brow like she wasn't sure where this was going.

Alessi nodded. "Anyway, we decided that we all needed to hang out again."

"That would be fun," Kiara said.

"I thought so," Alessi said. "Plus, you guys have always been so cute together."

She thought they were cute together?

What did that mean? Did Kiara have a thing for Miles then?

He *was* someone who would fit her usual preferences, I guess...

"You think so?" Kiara asked.

"Of course!" Alessi said. "Which is why I was thinking it would be fun to go on a double date this weekend." Alessi angled her face toward mine. "What do you think, Nash? Wanna go on a date with me so Kiara can start a summer fling with my stepbrother?"

"Oh, um..." I said, not sure I could really turn down the idea if I wanted to. "T-that sounds fun."

Kiara's gaze met mine briefly, and I was momentarily worried that the twinge of jealousy I suddenly felt might be obvious on my face.

So I tried to maintain an unbothered expression while I

searched for any signs that she was interested in having a summer fling with Miles.

But since I hadn't known her long enough to have a good read on her emotions, it was hard to discern what she might be thinking.

After considering the proposed double date for a moment longer, Kiara shrugged and said, "If Miles wants to hang out, then we should do it."

18

KIARA

WELL, *that was an uncomfortable movie,* I thought as I stood up from the couch to leave Alessi's house.

I'd tried to not keep looking at Nash and Alessi from the corner of my eyes throughout the movie, since I didn't want my jealousy to be too obvious...but when I picked up my popcorn bowl from the cushion, I allowed myself one more look.

And just as they'd been for the last hour of the movie, they were sitting close with their hands still entwined.

Did I feel slightly better knowing that it was Alessi who had been the one to scoot closer during an intense part of the movie and slip her hand into his?

A little.

But Nash was still holding her hand, and I was still definitely a third wheel tonight.

They hadn't made out in front of me or anything—thank goodness. (Alessi and her boy toys hadn't been afraid to do that in front of me in the past.)

But since I hadn't ever liked any of the guys she'd kissed in the past, this was more painful than that.

And now I get to watch them while we hang out with Miles this weekend.

Yayyy.

I still wasn't interested in a summer fling. But at least Miles was fun to talk to.

And hot.

Having a pretty person to distract me from the pretty person my best friend would be flirting with would hopefully help me not look too jealous all night.

Nash and Alessi still weren't moving to get up from the couch yet, even though the credits had been rolling for a couple of minutes. So even though I really didn't want to leave them alone and make it easier for more sparks to ignite between them tonight, I said, "Well, I'm gonna head out now. Thanks for the movie."

"Is your mom already on her way to pick you up?" Alessi frowned, sitting up a little. "Because Nash could probably give you a ride. He said he had to leave by ten."

"No, I have the car tonight," I said. Which I'd thought was a convenient thing…right up until two seconds ago when I was offered a chance to ride back with Nash.

Was it too late to pretend I'd actually walked here?

"Okay, well, thanks for coming over," Alessi said. "I'll tell Miles you're up for something this weekend."

"Sounds good." I turned to leave. But then, because I still had hope for something happening with Nash once Alessi got distracted by the next flashy guy, I turned back to them and said, "Just don't tell Miles I'm hoping for a summer fling, okay? I know you think it's a fun idea, but I'm just not interested in something like that right now."

"You could be, though," Alessi said with a wink. "And Miles already told me how hot you were looking on Friday."

Nash cleared his throat. "If Kiara doesn't want a summer fling, we really shouldn't try to force it on her."

"Thank you," I said, appreciating him backing me up. Alessi could be so insistent sometimes.

"Fine." Alessi sighed dramatically and shook her head. "You guys are no fun sometimes. But I guess the summer-fling plan has kind of lost its luster now that Tristan already thinks you two are dating."

"Thanks to your genius idea," I reminded her just in case she tried to turn me into the bad guy for having a fake relationship with the person she was still cuddling with. "And Tristan knows me well enough to know that I wouldn't switch to another guy after a few days. Not after the convincing performance Nash gave on Friday night, at least."

"It's true." Nash's eyes lit up at my mention of the antics we'd gotten up to at Miles's party. Then putting a hand to his chest, he added, "It was probably one of the most epic performances of my career so far."

"You could have won an Oscar for it," I said, grinning back at him.

"I could say the same for you," he said.

Our eyes caught for a second, and I couldn't help but think from our banter that maybe he had actually enjoyed sneaking up to Miles's bedroom and messing up each other's hair as much as I had.

Would it be too obvious if I suggested we hang out at Miles's frat house for our double date? Because if Tristan happened to show up, I really wouldn't mind being forced to play Nash's girlfriend again.

"Well, we better let you go," Alessi said. And from her expression, I worried that she was annoyed at the exchange Nash and I just had.

Did she feel threatened?

Had she seen something between us that was making her feel territorial?

Because if so, then maybe the sparks I'd felt with Nash this week weren't all in my head.

"Thanks for inviting me," I said politely, knowing I needed to leave before I irritated her any further. Alessi was my only real girlfriend in Eden Falls, so it was best not to get on her bad side. "I'll see you guys later."

"You're sure they're okay with me using their kitchen?" I asked my mom for probably the third time this morning.

"Mrs. Hastings said it was just fine," Mom said as she used her key to unlock the back door to the Hastings' house.

"But what about Marie?" I asked, peering through the window in the door to look at the dark kitchen. It was five-thirty a.m., so Marie most likely wouldn't be here for another thirty minutes. But the kitchen was her domain, so I didn't want to intrude just because the oven in the cottage had quit working yesterday.

Why did the oven's computer system have to take a crap the day before the renaissance fair? We'd just gotten the new oven last fall.

"Marie uses the chef's kitchen," Mom said. "The main kitchen won't have anyone using it this morning unless Cambrielle or Nash suddenly have the desire to pick up baking in the middle of the night."

"Okay." I sighed, even though I was still anxious that someone in the family may walk in while my strawberry cream cheese croissants were baking and call security.

Mom led me into the house and turned on the light to reveal the Hastings' beautiful kitchen. It was mostly for show since they usually ate out or ordered in when Marie had her days off.

Did it make me sad that a kitchen this breathtaking rarely ever got used?

A little, since it really was a work of art with its white cupboards, marble counters, and state-of-the-art appliances.

But that was the way of the top one percent. They had the luxury of their houses being for show and visual appeal—even if certain areas weren't completely put to use.

Mom and I carried in the baking sheets I'd already prepped with pastries this morning. After helping me figure out how to get the double ovens preheated, she left to finish getting ready for her workday.

The house was quiet for the next thirty minutes as I worked. Around six a.m., when I was making the batter for my Black Forest brownies, Marie walked in through the door at the side of the house. After giving me a friendly wave, she headed into the chef's kitchen to make breakfast for the family.

I was just pulling my first batch of croissants from the ovens when the faint thud of footsteps sounded on the stairs. A moment later, Nash appeared in the kitchen, wearing salmon-colored swim trunks with a beach towel draped over a shoulder.

"Oh, hi," he said, taking a step back like I'd startled him.

"Hey," I said, worried from his reaction that he hadn't been warned that I would be working in here today.

Nash glanced around the kitchen and dining room area with his brow furrowed. To me, he said, "Did Marie call in sick and ask you to make breakfast this morning?"

"Oh no." I pointed to the doorway behind him. "She's in the other kitchen." When he still looked confused, I said, "The oven went out in the cottage yesterday, so your mom said I could cook the food for my booth in here until it gets fixed."

"Okay, that makes sense." He looked down at the baking

sheets I'd just set on the stove to cool. Seeming to finally understand what was going on, he said, "So I don't get to have one of those for breakfast?"

"Not unless you want a sugar rush to start off your day," I said, a grin stretching across my cheeks. "But I think Marie is already whipping up something a bit healthier for you."

"She does like to keep us well fed." He patted his stomach, and I had to resist the urge to check him out.

What was he thinking walking around shirtless like that? Did he think I was immune to his good looks?

Because yeah...I wasn't immune at all.

But to keep myself from staring at his six-pack and chest muscles and making my attraction to him more obvious than it already was, I grabbed the next pan of croissants and turned to put them in the oven.

After setting the timer, I turned back to the counter to mix the brownies I'd been working on before Nash walked in.

"Well, I better get to the pool," Nash said. "But I'm definitely going to have to stop by your booth this evening for one of those." He pointed at the pan of pastries.

"And a scotcharoo, right?" I asked, referring to our previous conversation when we'd talked about my booth the first time.

"Of course." A slow smile spread across his lips. "In fact, I'm pretty sure I'll want to try everything since that brownie batter smells amazing, too." He glanced toward the doors that led to their pool. "And then I'll just have to swim extra laps in the morning to make up for the sugar binge."

"Pretty sure you can handle a few desserts," I said. "I mean, don't people with a lot of muscle tone burn more calories anyway?"

"Have you been checking out my muscles then, Kiara?" Nash asked, an amused look in his eyes.

"Umm…no?" My stomach dropped as soon as I realized what I'd just said. "W-why would I do something like that?"

Why was I so good at saying embarrassing things to Nash? Why did the self-preserving part of my brain just disappear whenever I was within ten feet of him?

"I have no idea." He chuckled. Then hooking his thumb over his shoulder, he said, "Anyway, I'm gonna go get that swim in. If you feel like checking out my amazing calves as I walk away, I won't tell anyone."

"Since it's totally your calves that are the most distracting thing about you right now," I said, figuring I might as well banter back now that I'd already made my ogling obvious.

His grin stretched wider. And even though I felt like a dork, I couldn't help but return his smile.

"I'll see you at the fair tonight," he said. "Good luck with your sales today."

I was restocking the scotcharoos at my booth when Nash and his friends took the stage in the northeast corner of the park on Main Street.

I'd been waiting all day to see his skit and was excited to see what he'd prepared. His costume consisted of a flowy, cream peasant-type shirt, brown trousers, and boots from the renaissance era.

Would I think he looked a little dorky if I was to see him around town dressed like that?

Sure.

But after watching him interact with a few little kids who had gone up to him when he'd first arrived this afternoon, I couldn't help but think he looked kind of adorable today.

I finished loading the scotcharoo platter and put the container with the extras back in the cooler behind me. Then I sat back down on the camp chair I'd brought to relax in during the slow times.

Nash and Asher were just pulling out their wooden swords to fight for the fair maiden's favor, played by Elyse, when Miles showed up at my booth wearing a ball cap with his fraternity's symbols on the front.

"I see your fake boyfriend is fighting for another girl's heart right now." Miles nodded toward the stage; his brown eyes filled with mirth. "He certainly gets around, doesn't he?"

"He's acting right now," I said, even though the comment niggled at my insecurities since from what I'd overheard, Nash had feelings for Elyse earlier this year.

But instead of focusing on who Nash may or may not have dated in the past, I asked, "How did you know he was pretending to be my boyfriend last week?" I'd thought for sure our performance had been convincing.

"Alessi told me." Miles shrugged his broad, football-playing shoulders. "Said it was your way of getting back at Tristan."

"Yeah, that was all Alessi's brilliant idea, by the way." But since I was curious, I found myself asking, "Do you know what Tristan thought about that whole thing?"

"I don't think he liked the idea of you moving on with a billionaire." Miles chuckled, finding the situation amusing. "He was asking me if I'd known you were going to bring Nash to my party. Poking around for more details."

"You didn't tell him it was all fake, did you?" I asked, hoping he hadn't blown my cover and made me look like an even bigger loser for needing to fake a relationship.

But Miles said, "No." And then shooting me a wink, he added, "I got your back."

"Okay, good." I sighed, feeling like I could relax again. "That's the last thing I need right now."

Nash let out an exaggerated wail from the stage, and I looked back to see him stumbling around with Asher's sword tucked under his armpit like he'd just been stabbed.

The children in the crowd all giggled at the funny spectacle he was making, and I found myself smiling as well.

"He's stabbed me in the heart," Nash called out in an English accent. As he fell to the ground, he said to Elyse, "Wilst thou bestow me with a kiss, fair maiden? I fear I shall perish without it."

Elyse looked at him. And then to the crowd, she mock-whispered, "What say ye? Shall I bestow this knight with a kiss?"

Shouts of "yes" and "no" and "if you won't do it, I will" immediately sounded from the audience.

"Perhaps just a kiss on the forehead will help heal him," Elyse said. Then she was bending down on her knees to give him a gentle kiss on the forehead.

Once she'd given Nash the forehead kiss, she sat back on her haunches to watch and see if anything happened.

When nothing did, she looked back to the crowd with a concerned expression and said, "Perhaps it was too late for true love's magic to work its miracle."

"Or perhaps the fair maiden's true love is still alive and standing right here." Asher stepped up beside her. After taking her hand to help her stand, he pulled her into his chest and rubbed her back, saying, "There, there, my love. Fate has spoken, and it seems we are destined to be together instead."

"I believe you are correct." Elyse pulled back to look up at Asher's face. "Fate has named you the better man."

They moved as if they would kiss, but before they could, Nash suddenly sprang back to life with a growl. Then brandishing the sword that had been tucked under his arm, he said,

"Hands off of her, you scoundrel. I am not dead. 'Tis but a scratch that thou gavest me."

Several children laughed and cheered, and before long, Asher and Nash were dueling again.

"I think I know which of the two guys you'd give your favor to," Miles said, after another thirty seconds of dueling went on.

"What?" I asked, feeling my face suddenly grow hot. "W-why do you say that?"

"Because it's obvious from the way you're watching them that you totally think Nash is hot."

"What?" I said again, apparently not knowing what else to say when being accused of thinking the guy I secretly liked was attractive.

A knowing smile stretched across Miles's face. "The question is, did you like him before he played your fake boyfriend or after?"

"That's a silly question," I said.

"So you don't like him?" Miles arched a dark eyebrow.

"He's interested in Alessi," I said, attempting to sidestep his line of questioning. "Th-they've been hanging out a lot."

"Ah." Miles nodded slowly. "My stepsister sure gets around, doesn't she?"

"She's never had trouble finding a guy to flirt with."

"That is very true." Miles stepped behind my table, and when he went to reach for the last strawberry and cream cheese pastry, I touched his arm and said, "Sorry, I'm saving that."

"Who are you saving it for?"

I pressed my lips together, knowing my answer would definitely make my denial of liking Nash less believable.

But Miles could apparently read my mind because he grinned and said, "It's for Nash, isn't it?"

"Fine." I rolled my eyes. "So maybe I'm saving it for him."

"But I thought you didn't like him."

"I—" I started. But since I really couldn't just outright lie, I sighed and said, "He told me this morning that he wanted to stop by and try one of these tonight. So I'm saving one for him. That's all."

"Okay." Miles raised his hands in the air. Then going to reach for a brownie, he asked, "Am I allowed to have one of these? Or are you saving all of them for blondie, too?"

"You can have one of those," I said. "But it will be five dollars."

"Five dollars?" He coughed.

"It's a gourmet brownie." I gestured at the cherry chocolate topping. "No one else has had a problem paying five dollars."

"I'm sure it's worth it," he said. "But isn't there, like, a friends-and-family discount?"

"Not for you," I said. "I'm trying to save up for college. Not all of us are smart or athletic enough to get full-ride scholarships." Lucky for Miles, he was both a genius *and* had a football scholarship.

"You're plenty smart, Kiara."

"I know..." *I just read slow, which makes it hard to get through those timed standardized tests that colleges love to base everything on.*

Okay...and my B average didn't exactly scream "star student" either.

"Well, I bet pretty billionaire boy won't have to pay for his treat." Miles handed me a five-dollar bill.

I put the bill in my cash box and closed it. "I guess you just need to be prettier to get the pretty-boy discount."

Miles smirked at me. "We already know I'm pretty enough."

I let my gaze run over his handsome face, looking at his dark eyebrows, dark-brown eyes, and strong jawline.

Miles *was* extremely attractive. And if I didn't already have a crush on Nash, I'd probably be thrilled about going on the double date with him this weekend.

So deciding to cater to his ego just a bit, I said, "You probably are pretty enough—"

"Finally, you speak the truth." He winked.

I resisted the urge to roll my eyes. "Which is why you'll probably get that discount you're looking for at the snow cone shack when you flirt with the owner."

"Nah, I'm good." He waved his hand before taking a bite of his brownie. "I think I'd rather stay here with you and see what happens when Nash comes to get his pastry."

He took the camp chair beside me that Alessi had been sitting in this afternoon before her set.

A couple more customers dropped by during Nash's skit, but when I wasn't dishing out desserts, my eyes were trained on Nash.

The skit was entertaining, and it was fun seeing him in a comedic role after watching his more serious performance as The Phantom this winter.

Soon the skit was wrapping up with a few girls dancing around a maypole as Nash played the fiddle that I didn't know he could play until this moment. Miles leaned closer to me and said, "Based on the way you're watching billionaire boy, I can guess that you're *super* excited for our double date on Saturday."

My cheeks flushed instantly, and all I could say was, "You know I always have fun with you."

"Just as a friend though, right?" he asked.

"Probably just as a friend," I said, meeting his gaze. Then worried I might have hurt his feelings for liking someone else, I added, "I haven't told Alessi, or really anyone else this, but..." I paused, wondering if I should really tell Miles about my secret crush. But since Miles had always been a good friend and had my back through all of the Tristan mess despite being Tristan's friend first, I said, "I've kind of had a thing for Nash for a while." I fiddled with the sea glass charm on my necklace. "Basically, since Tristan and I broke up."

"Really?" Miles's eyes widened.

I nodded. "I haven't really done anything about it since he's well..."

"A billionaire?" Miles guessed.

"Yeah," I agreed. "And living in his backyard would be so awkward if things didn't work out."

"I can see that."

"And Alessi has never been super great at keeping secrets, so I just never said anything to her when she met Nash and liked him."

"And now they're going on dates and you have to just watch."

"Basically."

I glanced back at the stage where Nash and the other actors were taking their final bows. Nash walked off the stage, and when he started looking around the park like he might be searching for my booth as he'd promised to, my heart raced.

His gaze scanned the edges of the park where the different vendors had set up their pavilions and tents, and soon, he was facing my direction. He seemed to smile when he recognized me under my pavilion and started walking toward me.

"I think he's coming over here," Miles said in the sing-song voice he used whenever he teased Alessi. "If you have some love potion hiding in that cooler, you better hurry and put a few drops on his croissant."

"Shhh," I said, gently shoving him in the arm. "Is it really going to be like this now?"

He laughed. "Hey, if you're not interested in dating me,

then the only other option is for me to treat you like a little sister instead."

"There's no middle ground?" I asked.

He shrugged. "I'm all about living in the extremes."

I looked back at Nash, just in time to see him stop about twenty feet away with what appeared to be a disappointed expression on his face.

"What do you—" I started to ask Miles before Alessi appeared behind Nash and tapped him on his shoulder. He glanced behind him to see who was there, and instead of continuing toward my booth like I had hoped, he turned to talk to her.

Just lead him this way please, Alessi, I urged her in my head as I watched her speak animatedly to Nash. She laughed at something he said, and then with a big smile on her face, she gave him a hug.

They chatted for a moment before Nash cast a quick glance back at my booth. His gaze went to Miles. After seeming to consider something, he shrugged and turned back to Alessi.

Before I knew it, Alessi was looping her arm through his and they were walking toward a food truck in the opposite direction.

What the heck?

"Can you tell me what just happened?" I asked Miles who had watched the same thing that I had. "Didn't it look like he was going to come over here?"

"Maybe he's just really hungry and he'll come back later?" Miles scrunched up his face with the suggestion.

"Which this pastry could have helped with." I gestured at the plate I'd been saving for him.

Miles gave me a sympathetic look that told me he pitied me for thinking I had a chance with someone like Nash.

So I picked up the croissant and offered it to Miles. "Well, I guess someone might as well eat this."

"It looks delicious…" He looked at the pastry and then up at me. "But I feel kind of bad eating it now."

I sighed, handing it to him. "Better you than me."

19

NASH

"WE SHOULD all hang out together after everything ends tomorrow," Asher said to Elyse and me when we were in the performers' tent after our skit on Friday evening. "It could be like our wrap parties in high school."

"That would be fun," I said, wanting Asher to know I appreciated him putting forth the effort to hang out together. "I'd totally come if I didn't already have plans with some new friends tomorrow night."

"You have new friends?" Asher frowned. "Are you trying to replace us?"

"I'm not replacing anyone," I said, not wanting to hurt the progress Asher and I had made after the feud we'd kept going for several years. "I'm just trying to not be the only single guy in the group."

What looked like a flash of guilt passed across Elyse's face at my mention of not wanting to be single anymore. But she smoothed her expression, and with a look of interest, she asked, "Who have you been hanging out with? Anyone we know? Those girls you were with at the graduation party?"

Elyse had noticed that?

Of course she did. She was observant.

It definitely was not because she had any sort of residual feelings for me.

I was over her, anyway.

Even if she looked amazing in her dress right now...

I allowed my gaze to run over her peasant dress with the brown corset over it. Then out of nowhere, a sense of déjà vu suddenly washed over me as an image of a girl locked in the recesses of my memory jumped to the forefront of my mind.

A girl with flowing pink hair and a peasant dress like Elyse's.

Wait...

Was that real?

That girl hadn't been a figment of my imagination, had she? A hallucination brought on by the demons I'd been dealing with at the time?

The memory flash faded away as quickly as it had come. When my eyes focused back to the present, I realized I'd just zoned out in front of Asher and Elyse.

"Sorry," I sat up in my chair, clearing my throat. "What did you ask me?"

Elyse glanced at Asher briefly before asking, "Have you been hanging out with those girls from the party?"

"Oh yeah. I've been hanging out with Alessi and Kiara."

"Oh, I know Kiara," Elyse said. "Well, we wave to each other anyway whenever I see her walking her dog past my dad's house. She seems nice."

"She's fun," I said, even though I was feeling a bit confused about my feelings toward her.

After my dream, I'd thought I might have been chasing after the wrong girl...thinking that maybe I was more compatible with Kiara than Alessi.

But then I'd seen Kiara flirting with Miles in her booth last night, and knowing they had a date planned for tomorrow, I had decided it was probably best for me to forget about that weird dream and focus back to the girl who had made her feelings more obvious.

Chasing after a girl who was already interested in someone else wasn't something I wanted to do again. So I finished my reply to Elyse by adding, "Kiara's friend Alessi is pretty cool, too."

Most of the time, anyway.

The little jabs she'd made last night about me wearing my costume out in public and making her look like she was attracted to the eccentric sort hadn't made me feel the best, though.

If she'd been so embarrassed to be seen with me in my costume, she shouldn't have dragged me away from the park in the first place.

"Well, let us know if you want to hang out sometime." Asher leaned back in his chair and stretched. "I think Cambrielle mentioned something to Elyse about having a pool party sometime."

"She said that to me, too," I said. "I'm sure we can figure out something soon."

"When you do," Asher said, "just shoot me a text and I'll try to make it all the way from my new place to your pool." He smirked.

I chuckled. "Since you'd have to literally just take twenty steps outside of your bedroom to be there."

Asher had moved into the pool house for the summer to live with my older brother Ian and Asher's brother Owen.

A loud group of kids walked past our tent. When I glanced through the tent's opening, I saw that most of the booths were closing up for the day.

If I wanted to visit Kiara's booth before she closed, now was my chance.

I just hoped she wouldn't be busy flirting with Miles again today.

I grabbed my water bottle from the folding table near my chair, and looking at Asher and Elyse, I said, "I better go. I'll see you guys tomorrow."

"See you then." Asher nodded. "Be prepared for the duel of a lifetime."

"Of course." I waved goodbye and then jogged off toward the back of the park and up to Kiara's booth.

"Hi Nash," Kiara said as she pulled out a plastic food storage container from a cooler and started to load the few fancy-looking brownies she had left into it.

"Hey," I said, taking in a deep breath after my short jaunt across the park. "How are things going? Did you get a lot of sales?"

"They've been going pretty good," she said. "I've sold out of most things both days so far."

"That's awesome."

She went back to putting things away, and I might have been reading into my own nerves, but it almost seemed like she was mad at me.

Had I said something wrong?

Or was she embarrassed to be talking to a guy in a peasant costume, too?

"Um." I swallowed. "Do you happen to have any of those amazing croissants left today?"

"I sold out of those a couple of hours ago."

"Dang. Those looked so good when you pulled them out of the oven yesterday," I said, trying to tiptoe around her weird mood.

"I tried to save one for you yesterday but..." Her words

tapered off, and even though I hadn't come over because I didn't want to interrupt the good time she'd seemed to be having with Miles yesterday, my stomach twisted with guilt.

Had I interpreted things wrong there?

Had she been hoping I'd come over after all?

"Sorry I didn't stop by yesterday," I said, rubbing the back of my neck anxiously. "I had something else come up."

"It's okay." She shrugged, like it was no biggie.

But even though she was acting like things were cool and chill between us, it felt like they might not be.

Which meant I needed to fix this awkwardness between us somehow. Regardless of who she may or may not be interested in, I still enjoyed hanging out with her and wanted to at least keep building on the friendship we'd started growing the past couple of weeks.

So I gave her an earnest look and asked, "Will you be making any more croissants tomorrow?"

"I'm planning on it." She snapped the lid down on the plastic container. "But they've been going fast so..."

"So I might need to help you set up tomorrow morning, so I can be your first customer?"

A smile played on her lips, and when she said, "That's probably the best plan," a whoosh of relief filled me because maybe we were still going to be cool after all.

"Awesome," I said. Then looking around at the chairs, table, cooler, and other display items she had under the pop-up pavilion, I asked, "How have you been getting all of this here every day anyway?"

"My mom's friend, Traci, has been letting me store the table and shade in her garage." She set the container on one of the coolers and started folding the white tablecloth. "Her house is just down the street. And then my mom dropped me and the food off today since she needed the car tonight."

"Well, if you want," I said, stepping to the other side of the table so I could help her fold the tablecloth, "I could probably trade Carter vehicles tomorrow and we could haul everything over in his truck. Then when it's all over, we can take all the things back to your house afterward. It could save your mom a trip."

"You think that would be fine?" Her gaze darted back and forth between my eyes as we walked toward each other to put the two ends of the tablecloth together.

"Of course." I handed my end of the tablecloth to her, letting her finish folding it the way she liked.

"Then that would be great."

When she smiled, it gave me another idea. "Is your mom coming to get you now?" I asked as I picked up one of the camp chairs and started stuffing it into its storage bag.

"I told her to come around eight-thirty." She checked the time on her watch. "So she should be leaving soon."

"Well, I'm here now and going the same way." I shook the bag so the chair would drop down better. "I think we could fit all of this in my car, and you can call her and tell her she doesn't need to come."

"I'm sure she would love to not have to come all the way over here tonight," she said. "Thank you."

She called her mom, and we worked together to put the things she needed to take back home into the trunk and backseat of my car. Then we carried the table and shade across the street to Traci's Victorian-era house.

As we made our way back to my car, a girl with long, pink hair walked past. I immediately stumbled and before I knew what was happening, another flash of memory passed through my mind.

Instead of walking toward my car, I was suddenly standing at the edges of one of my family's garden parties, watching a girl with light-pink hair carry a tray of pastries through the crowd.

I couldn't picture her face or anything in the flash, so it could have just been a really vivid memory of a dream since I didn't always see faces in my dreams. But for some reason, this flash, like the one I'd had in the tent, seemed like it had actually happened.

Were these flashes coming from somewhere?

"Nash, watch out!" Kiara's voice entered my consciousness. A split-second later, she was grabbing my arm and yanking me away from a car that was backing out of a parking spot along the curb.

The driver hit the brakes when she realized she'd almost hit me, and through her open window, she called out, "I'm so sorry. I didn't see you."

"It's okay," I said as I got my footing under me. "I'm okay."

Thanks to Kiara.

I looked down and found Kiara inspecting my face with a worried expression.

"Is everything okay?" she asked, concern etched in her eyes.

"Yeah." I sighed and ran a hand through my hair. "I just..." I started, not sure how to explain. Then I said, "There was a girl with pink hair that reminded me of something."

Kiara went still for a moment. Then narrowing her eyes, she asked, "A girl with pink hair?"

"Yeah." I glanced around to make sure I hadn't imagined that girl, too. When I found her on the other side of the road, I pointed to her and said, "It was that girl over there."

Kiara's gaze went to the girl with light-pink hair. Seeming to think for a second, she asked, "What did it remind you of?"

"I'm not really sure." I rubbed my cheek as I tried to bring back the memory and see if it brought anything else with it. When nothing else came through, I said, "I just think I must have met someone with pink hair at one of my family's parties that I forgot about last summer."

I hadn't had a recollection of a party where the servers were dressed up in renaissance costumes until just tonight...but...was it possible I'd met a girl with pink hair last summer?

Someone my subconscious was trying to get me to remember?

20

KIARA

"I HAVEN'T HAD anything to eat since lunch," Nash said as he pulled out of his parking spot. "Do you mind if I stop somewhere to grab some food before heading home?"

"Oh, sure." I pulled the elastic from my wrist to put my hair up in a ponytail. "You can grab something."

"Do you want something, too?" He glanced sideways at me after stopping at a red light. "Or did you already eat?"

Dinner sounded amazing. But since I didn't want to eat into any of my profits for the day, it would be smarter to wait and make something at home.

"I had a late lunch, so I'm fine waiting until I get home."

But then, of course, my stomach decided to growl at that exact moment.

Nice.

Nash glanced down at my stomach briefly, like he'd heard it. And with a half-smile on his lips, he said, "I'm getting you something, too." The light turned green, so he proceeded through the intersection. "What do you feel like? American? Mexican? Italian? Vietnamese?"

"I'm really fine just grabbing leftovers," I said, not wanting to seem like I was mooching off of him since he'd already bought my dinner at Charlie's last week and taken me on the VIP baseball date on Monday.

"Well..." he said, glancing at me as he switched on his blinker to turn left onto Main Street. "I kind of have this thing where I don't like people just watching me eat when I know they're probably hungry, too. So...you would actually be doing me a service by allowing me to buy you dinner." He winked and gave me a charming smile that melted my insides.

I was apparently unable to resist him when he smiled at me like that, because I found myself saying, "Okay, then I think Italian food sounds amazing."

"Great. I feel like Mexican so...The Italian Amigos it is."

A few minutes later, we walked into the quirky restaurant that was decorated with a mixture of traditional Italian and Mexican decor. We waited a moment near the small replica of Michelangelo's *David* statue that had been dressed in a sombrero and swim trunks with little Mexican flags. A woman, whose name tag said "Rosa," greeted us shortly. While she was telling us that it would be about a five-minute wait, I spotted Tristan and Brooklyn sitting a few tables away.

"*Seriously?*" I groaned under my breath.

"What?" Nash asked. "Five minutes isn't too bad."

"I know," I said, realizing he thought I was reacting to what Rosa had said. I shook my head and lowered my voice. "Tristan and his girlfriend are sitting in a booth." Nash seemed to scan the room, so I added, "Wait a second to look, but they're right over there." I pointed to a booth to our right just as Tristan looked my way.

And because I was super awkward sometimes, I forced a smile on my face and waved to my ex.

He froze, holding his fork mid-air, and seemed to do a

double take like he wasn't sure it was me at first. Then as recognition dawned on his face, he sent a slight head nod in my direction. His gaze went to Nash next, and as he took him in, his expression became unreadable.

"Mind if I hold this for you?" Nash moved closer, taking my hand in his.

"Of course," I managed to say as goosebumps raced up my arm from his unexpected touch. "Thank you."

He bent close to my ear. "Anything for my *girlfriend*." Then he glanced down at the costume he still wore from earlier. With an apologetic expression, he said to me, "Sorry I look like a medieval peasant on our date night out. If I'd known I needed to put on a different type of performance tonight, I would have brought a change of clothes."

I looked at his baggy cream shirt, brown trousers, and boots. He was probably the best-looking medieval peasant I'd ever seen. But I refrained from telling him that and simply said, "You look fine. Cute."

"Cute?" His shoulders slumped. "That's something you'd say about a puppy."

"Were you hoping I'd say you look super sexy in that costume tonight?" I teased.

Was he fishing for compliments, or did he actually not realize how attractive he was?

"I wouldn't mind hearing you say that..." He shrugged. Then he opened the baggy shirt where it was loosely tied at the collar, revealing his defined collarbones and a good amount of his bronzed chest. "I mean, this is a super sexy look, right?"

I couldn't help the smile that lifted my lips. "That peek at your chest is definitely helping your case."

"I knew you had a thing for man chest." He chuckled. "I caught you checking mine out in the kitchen yesterday morning after all."

"You saw me checking out your chest?" My voice raised an octave as my eyes went wide.

He studied my face, his smile broadening as he seemed to realize something.

He leaned closer. "Were you actually checking me out in the kitchen then?" His eyes looked me up and down. "Because I was just teasing you about the calf thing yesterday...but..."

My whole body was flooding with heat now. What was I supposed to say? Did I admit to it? It was super obvious now...

"Nash?" Rosa interrupted my scattering thoughts. "Your table is ready."

"Awesome. Thanks," Nash said.

We followed Rosa into the dining area, toward a booth at the back.

As we passed Tristan's table, Nash placed his hand at the curve in my lower back, right where my skin was exposed beneath the hem of my crop top. Then in a way that would make it seem like he was whispering sweet nothings into my ear, he said, "It's okay if you were checking me out. I tend to get lost in my reflection in the mirror, too."

If it wasn't for the fact that I was overwhelmed at the way his hand was currently bringing all of the blood in my body to that one place, I might have teased him for being as cocky as you'd expect a hot billionaire's son to be.

But I couldn't exactly form words right then because Nash Hastings was touching my skin and flirting with me and—and I might need to sit down before I fainted.

And Nash was apparently in flirty, fake-boyfriend mode right now because when we took our seats, he scooted onto the bench right beside me instead of across from me and said, "I need to make sure everyone knows that you're *my* fake girlfriend tonight and that I think you're as gorgeous as you apparently think I am."

He thinks I'm gorgeous?

Or was that just him taking his fake-boyfriend duties seriously and offering me compliments that no one could hear?

"I see that I've stunned you into silence," Nash said with a half-smile as he picked up the menus Rosa had left on our table and handed one to me.

Say words, Kiara!

I cleared my throat. "No, sorry. I'm just..." I made myself look up into his handsome face. "I wasn't expecting your comment about you getting lost in your reflection and then um...anything else from the past few minutes really."

"Well, for what it's worth," his eyes crinkled at the edges as his smile broadened, "I don't actually get lost in my reflection."

"Well, that's probably good," I said. "You'd get stuck in your bathroom a lot if you did."

You'd get stuck in your bathroom if you did?

What kind of stupid sentence was that?

I should have probably stuck with staying starstruck and keeping my mouth shut.

He chuckled. "You're fun to flirt with Kiara."

"Yeah?" I asked, my heart going still in my chest at the thought that he might actually have been intentionally flirting with me.

"Yeah." He studied my face for a moment, his eyebrows knitting together as he seemed to realize something.

And I was reminded of a time when our faces had been this close before. The night I'd replayed in my mind a hundred times.

Was he remembering it right now?

Could being this close to me have triggered some sort of memory? Like seeing that girl with pink hair?

I held my breath, waiting...hoping...wishing that he'd remember.

Do you remember me, Nash?

He narrowed his gaze and curled his bottom lip between his teeth like he was considering something.

But then he looked down, and with a slight shake of his head, he said, "We should probably figure out what we want to order before we get lost in each other's gazes even more."

"Yes." I cleared my throat and shook away the memories from last summer. "Good idea."

21

NASH

"IF ANYONE HAS BEEN PAYING any attention to me this past week," I mumbled into Kiara's hair as we walked toward the restaurant's exit hand-in-hand, "they might think I was like your ex over there."

"Why?" She glanced back at Tristan's table, and then at me like she was confused.

"Just because it probably looks like I have two girlfriends," I said, telling her about something I'd thought about before.

Her eyebrows knitted together. "What do you mean?"

"Well, just thinking of all the things I've done with you and Alessi the past couple of weeks. The parties, dinners, and ball games..." I shrugged. "It's just been a lot of one-on-one time with two different girls my age."

"I guess so," she said, like she hadn't considered it. "If anyone is paying attention, they may wonder if Alessi and I are your sister-wives."

"But it would seem like you're my favorite wife." I pushed the exit door open, pulling Kiara through to the humid summer night. "Since I think I've actually hung out with you more."

"I guess so." She looked down at the sidewalk like she was uncomfortable. Then after a beat, she peered up at me in the moonlight and asked, "How are things with you and Alessi anyway? You asked her on two dates, so it seems like you must be pretty interested, right?"

"Yeah..." I sighed. "I guess it would seem like that?"

"You guess?" A pucker line formed between her eyebrows.

I looked at the parking lot ahead as I thought about it.

Alessi was cute and I had a lot of fun with her.

But I could probably say the same things about Kiara, couldn't I?

When I was hanging out with both of them together, things went well. We all laughed and had fun together.

But when it was just Alessi and me on a date, or hanging out like we did after the fair last night...there were always a few awkward moments—little hiccups in the way we communicated.

As if we were sometimes speaking different languages and it created awkward misunderstandings.

She was a more high-maintenance girl, and while me being the son of a billionaire probably made it seem like I would act a certain way: proper and poised and cool—much like how my brothers Carter and Ian were—I was definitely not like that. In fact, I had a hard time just relaxing and being myself around her.

And when she'd suggested we eat our food in the car so she wouldn't have to be seen with me dressed like a peasant in public, that hadn't felt great either.

It was basically the opposite of tonight where Kiara was fine with me pretending to be her boyfriend and holding my hand while walking through a parking lot.

You shouldn't date someone that you couldn't be yourself

around, right? People needed to get each other's own version of weird.

And I was the weird Hastings' son.

I shrugged. "I don't know if it would work out long term between us."

"Really?"

Yeah.

Kiara seemed surprised, and I worried I shouldn't have said that. So I said, "Do you think Alessi thinks we're more serious?" I swallowed, suddenly nervous that Kiara might be thinking about slapping me across the face and accusing me of leading on her best friend. "Am I as bad as Tristan then?"

Kiara chuckled. "I don't think so. I mean, you haven't asked Alessi to be your girlfriend or anything, have you?"

"No." I shook my head. "I mean, I haven't even kissed her. She can't be thinking we're super serious if I haven't even done that yet, right?"

"No..." After considering something for a moment, she asked, "You really haven't kissed her yet? I thought for sure..."

"No." I wiped at my forehead, suddenly feeling flushed with nerves. "I mean, I know I've been putting on this amazing show as your fake boyfriend and everything but...in real life, I'm kind of a chicken when it comes to making a move."

"You're making that up..." She narrowed her eyes, like she couldn't believe what I'd just said.

But I shrugged and said, "Sadly, I'm not. That is...unless I'm playing a part." *Or a few drinks in, like I was most of last summer.* "I'm like the most uncool date."

"But you can't be." She shook her head. "I literally don't believe you."

"You've never actually seen me on a date."

"But you're so cool anytime we're hanging out."

"Because those haven't been dates. That was just us hanging out and doing fun things."

"Right..."

"Like right now," I continued, needing her to believe me for some reason. "This isn't a date. Sure we had dinner and sat close, so it's a date-like activity, but like, there's no extra pressure because I know you're not interested in me." She was interested in Miles. "Or looking for this to turn romantic, so there's no pressure to be cool or hot or intriguing." I looked down at my clothes. "I mean, I can wear a medieval peasant costume and you're totally fine with me pretending to be your fake boyfriend because you know we're just hanging out. Like, after this I'm not going to get back to your house and stand there on your doorstep wondering if I'm supposed to give you a goodnight kiss and possibly read the signals wrong and get your cheek instead."

She gasped. "Have you gotten someone's cheek before?"

And the way she gasped made me realize I'd just revealed way too much about my failed dating life.

"Yeah..." I looked down at the sidewalk as the memory of one of my dates last fall passed through my mind again. "Which I probably shouldn't have just admitted out loud."

"I'm not going to judge you." She touched my arm "But, like, how?"

"Because I'm the worst at reading signals." I sighed. "Even just this winter, I was all hung up on this girl and asked her out and took her on a dream date. And I thought things were going well. But then before I knew it, she was telling me she liked another guy and that she just wanted to be friends."

"That sucks."

"Yeah." I released a deep breath. "So I think something is wrong with my date radar. My instincts suck." I thought about when things always seemed to turn on me. It was always right after the first kiss. I sighed. "Or maybe I'm just a really bad kisser."

"No... that can't be right."

"I think it is. That's where things always go south for me," I said. "I mean, that's why I dodged Alessi's goodnight kiss last night."

"You turned her down?" Kiara's jaw dropped.

"I didn't give her my cheek or anything. I just kind of went in for the hug before it could get there."

"Wow...that's..." She didn't seem to know how to respond to the level of awkwardness I could bring to a situation. "I just don't think Alessi has ever had a kiss rejected before."

"I figured." I sighed. "I just didn't want her to know how bad I am. That way I could leave it a mystery and not ruin the mystique I've got going."

"Nash..." Kiara said, her tone almost scolding. "You are way too hard on yourself. Like, there is literally no way that you're actually a bad kisser."

"So that peck I gave you for the kiss cam was life-changing then?" I nudged her with my elbow, hoping it would come off lighthearted and not reveal how curious I really was about how she felt about it.

Her eyes went wide, like she hadn't even been thinking about that kiss. But then she sidestepped my question by asking a question of her own. "It was a little more than a peck, wouldn't you say?"

"I guess," I admitted, remembering how my usual self-consciousness had somehow disappeared in the exhilaration of the moment and I'd gone in for a second and third kiss. "But if you say there's no way I'm a bad kisser, does that mean the kiss cam actually changed your life?"

Okay, I was probably being totally obvious about how interested I was in her reception of that kiss. But for some reason, I just really needed to know.

She bit her lip, seeming to consider her answer. Then with a playful look in her eyes, she said, "It completely rocked my world."

A grin stretched across my cheeks. "Rocked your world, you say?"

"You know it. I mean, those ten seconds that our lips touched... Boom. *Fireworks.*" She made a fireworks gesture with her hands. "I'm surprised the kiss-cam screen didn't burst into flames."

"I bet." I chuckled, appreciating that even if I knew she was exaggerating, she was having fun with me still.

But when I glanced sideways at her, she was staring blankly ahead with a serious expression.

Was she going to tell me the truth now?

Had she had a little fun, telling me she'd felt fireworks, only to reveal that she'd actually scrubbed her lips with a wire brush that night because kissing me had been pure torture?

That the only reason she was still holding my hand as we walked to my car was because she was just really invested in convincing her ex of this fake-relationship thing we had going?

I braced myself for the words I knew were coming. But instead of saying anything like that, she cleared her throat and said, "Anyway, I think that maybe your experiences in the past have nothing to do with you or how good of a kisser you are." She angled her face toward me, her brown eyes meeting mine in the darkness. "Have you ever considered that maybe you just haven't been kissing the right girl?"

With those words, another flash of a memory popped into my mind: a moment when I was dancing with a girl wearing a renaissance dress.

I couldn't see the girl's face in the memory flash, but everything else was so vivid and realistic.

The way it had felt to hold her close.

The feel of her dress on my fingertips.

The way she'd let me tilt her chin up so I could kiss her.

Had that happened?

And was the reason I hadn't remembered that night was because the kiss had gone so badly that my subconscious had tried to protect my ego from such a disastrous memory? And since we all had an evolutionary need to reproduce, my subconscious probably knew I'd swear myself to celibacy if I remembered how badly it had gone.

I sighed as the memory flitted away. Focusing my gaze back on Kiara, I said, "Maybe I haven't kissed the right girl. But I'm kind of thinking that I might need to find some kind of kissing coach before I get up the nerve to try that again. Just so in the future I'll know if it's me or just the wrong partner."

We made it to my car, and as I opened the door for Kiara to climb in, I briefly thought about how I'd have to be really comfortable with someone to even take lessons like that.

Where would I even find someone who would teach something like that?

As Kiara stepped into the passenger side of my car, I found myself asking, "Do you think that's an actual job?"

"What?" She looked up at me.

"A kissing tutor." I leaned against the open car door. "Like, there are coaches for sports and school and business. Do you think there are people out there who teach about dating, kissing, and that kind of thing?"

Hadn't Mack joked about being Cambrielle's kissing tutor at one point?

I pushed that thought away. I didn't need to think of my good friend kissing my sister.

"I think there are, like, tutorials on the internet," Kiara said.

"Yeah. I've watched those..."

As soon as the words were out of my mouth, I cringed.

Before she could think I was even weirder than she already thought, I hurried to say, "Um, it wasn't recently or anything. I only watched those because I was doing a scene for a play my freshman year and didn't want to look like I didn't know what I was doing."

Why did I always have to reveal so much about myself to pretty girls? She had to think I was a complete idiot now.

But then she said, "No, it's totally cool. I also looked into that kind of thing back in the day."

"Really?"

"Yeah..."

"You must be pretty good, though. You had a college boyfriend for a while," I said. "Only the coolest, most experienced girls date college guys in high school."

She chuckled.

I closed my eyes, shook my head, and said, "Okay, I think this conversation has definitely taken a weird and revealing turn that I did not expect. Just pretend like you didn't get this much of an inside look into my failed dating life."

I needed to stop talking.

Just stop saying stupid things, Nash.

So to shut myself up, I closed the passenger door and walked around the back of my car to climb in the driver's side.

After buckling in, I sat up straight and tried to appear more confident as I said, "In case it wasn't obvious already, I'm totally a Casanova in real life. It's just these peasant clothes that are making me want to seem more relatable."

Kiara grinned, the sparkle in her eyes telling me that she found me more entertaining than dorky. Then she said, "I saw you in *The Phantom of the Opera*. And I know you couldn't see yourself on stage, but..." She drifted off, and the veins in my arms throbbed with anticipation over what she was going to say.

After making me wait for two heart-pounding seconds, she said, "But that *Point of No Return* scene pretty much cemented in the audience's mind that Nash Hastings is the most casanova-ing Casanova to ever grace the town of Eden Falls."

"Well, that's a relief." I wiped my hand across my brow as a whoosh of relief flooded me. "I was hoping it came across that way."

22

NASH

I HELPED Kiara carry her things into her house when we got back to my family's estate. After confirming with her mom that I could drive Kiara and her things to the fair the next morning, I headed across the lawn to my house.

When I walked through the family room, my parents were in there, cuddling on the couch and watching a movie. They asked me how my day was, and after telling me they were excited to see my performance tomorrow, I headed up the stairs.

After switching on my bedroom light, I walked into my closet to change. I sniffed my costume before hanging it on its hanger. And while it still smelled okay after two days of sword fighting in the Connecticut summer heat, it would definitely be ready for Belinda to wash when she did my laundry on Monday.

I considered going right to bed, since I normally showered after my early morning swims, but knew that if I didn't shower off the slight stickiness from the day, I wouldn't sleep well.

I walked back into my bathroom and turned on the shower.

While it warmed up to the temperature I liked, I filled the cup I kept in my medicine cabinet with water and took my meds for the night.

About ten minutes later, I was clean and dressed in my boxer briefs.

I'd skipped my meditation session this morning in my haste to get to work on time, so instead of climbing in my bed and risk messing up the good habit I'd been building over the past several months, I slipped out onto the balcony I shared with Carter.

There was a slight breeze that made the leaves rustle on the trees, but overall it was a really calm night tonight. Just the crickets and the occasional owl making sounds to let me know I wasn't the only one enjoying the late June evening.

I took a seat on the meditation cushion I had out there. Once I was in a comfortable position, I closed my eyes.

I was still new to the practice and definitely not the best at clearing my mind. But I'd found that taking a few moments to focus on my breath each day did improve my mood and helped my brain respond to stress and anxiety in a better way.

I was able to focus my attention on my third eye for a minute or two, but before long, my mind wandered back to the events of tonight and my dinner with Kiara.

I winced as I remembered all of the stupid things I'd said.

Why in the world had I brought up being a bad kisser?

That was not something you brought up to a girl you may or may not be interested in.

But she had stayed instead of running away, I told myself.

So maybe she didn't think I was too crazy?

And maybe she'd be okay staying friends and hanging out again sometime?

Which would be nice, since I really did have a lot of fun

with her. I hadn't really thought much about it before, but she had super pretty eyes—light brown with really thick eyelashes.

And her little giggle. It was so funny and cute.

And the way she'd looked in her crop top tonight...

I pushed that thought away. I was supposed to be meditating. Not fantasizing about the girl next door.

I looked up at the clouds that were slowly making their way across the moon. The sky looked really beautiful tonight, and I couldn't help but feel grateful to be here and in a better place than I was this time last year.

A place where things had gotten fuzzy and blips in time just didn't exist, thanks to the huge amounts of alcohol I'd consumed on the nights I just didn't want to feel anything.

Which reminded me, I should probably ask my parents if they knew anything about a server at their summer garden party with pink hair.

Or if they had any photos from that night that I might find a girl like that in the background?

Hmmm... I thought as I patted where my phone would be if I was wearing my shorts. *Maybe I had some photos from that night.*

I made to stand up when I remembered I'd already stuck my phone on my charger, but before I could get up, a light from the cottage across the way switched on.

I looked in the direction of the light and saw Kiara standing in the middle of what must be her bedroom.

The curtains were open, and while I couldn't see a whole lot from this far away, I could make out a dresser in the background and maybe the foot of a bed.

The curtains were usually closed when I sat out on my balcony at night, so this was the first time I remembered being able to see into her room ever since she and her mom moved there.

And now that I could see through the window, I was curious if my subconscious had gotten any of the details of her room right when I'd had my dream Monday night.

I still couldn't believe how intense that dream had gotten before I'd woken up, especially because we were just friends and had only done anything remotely romantic for the kiss cam or when I was pretending to be her boyfriend.

She definitely hadn't given me any hints that she was even slightly interested in me before that dream had come.

But yeah…it sure had been something.

I let my mind wander back to it again. Back to how she'd kissed me and climbed on my lap, straddling my legs with hers and guiding my hands so they were on her hips.

How I'd pulled her down closer so there was no space left between us and…

Kiara moved across the window, bringing my attention to her and away from the dream. After taking a few steps toward her dresser, she began pulling her top over her head, revealing a black sports bra beneath.

I held my breath and my body flooded with warmth as I watched her drop her shirt to the side, like she was putting it in a laundry basket. When she loosened the button on her shorts next and started pulling them down to reveal her black panties, I knew I really needed to look away.

I needed to go inside and close my curtains instead of sitting here like a creeper.

Even if black underthings have always been my favorite…

She bent over to toss her shorts into the laundry basket and—

Get up and go inside, Nash.

I made a move to stand like a good boy, but Kiara must have realized the curtains were wide open at the same time because she suddenly turned toward the window and moved to pull them shut.

She stood in front of the window with her hands on both sides of the curtains. For a heart-pounding moment, it seemed like she was looking right at my balcony.

I hadn't turned on my balcony light when I'd come out here, so it was possible she couldn't see me in the darkness, but...did our eyes just meet?

I promise I wasn't waiting out here for a peep show, I thought as I sat there frozen on my cushion.

Another moment passed as I imagined her opening her window and yelling at me to quit being a Peeping Tom.

But she pulled the curtains shut instead, leaving only shadows visible behind them.

And before anything else could happen, I jumped up and went inside.

If she brought it up, I'd tell her it was a complete accident and I had only seen her in the amount of clothing most girls went to the pool in.

It would be fine.

23

KIARA

"THINK you still want to have your own bakery after all of these early mornings?" Mom asked when she unlocked the Hastings' back door for me Saturday morning.

"I think so," I said, following her through the back door with the tray of croissants I'd already prepared in our kitchen. "It's definitely more fun than cleaning toilets."

"That's probably true." Mom chuckled as she switched on the lights in the kitchen. "Smells a lot better, too."

"You can say that again."

I set my baking sheet on the kitchen island then turned to the double ovens behind it to get them preheated.

Marie had offered the prep kitchen to me today since she didn't work for the Hastings family on the weekends, so I got the ovens in there preheating as well so I could have the brownies baking at the same time.

Saturday was always the biggest day at the fair, so I planned to bake two extra trays of each dessert to ensure I had enough to make it through the long day.

Mom brought over the rest of the supplies while I made my

brownie batter. Then since she didn't have work today, she said she was going back to bed.

"Good luck with your sales," Mom said as she stood at the back door. "I'm really proud of how hard you've been working to make your dreams come true."

"Thank you," I said, warmth spreading throughout my chest.

I had already saved up enough money to pay for my first semester of college, so hopefully with my job cleaning for the Hastings, I'd have enough saved for the second semester soon.

These early mornings and long days would all be worth it.

Would it have been wiser for me to go to bed by nine o'clock last night so that this morning's four a.m. alarm wasn't quite so painful?

Probably.

But when faced with the opportunity to have dinner with Nash or get seven hours of sleep in, I'd probably choose to forfeit sleep any day of the week.

I added the eggs to my batter and smiled when I thought about the conversation Nash and I had on the way to his car last night. When looking at him and knowing how talented and awesome he was, I never would have guessed that he had insecurities about dating. He always seemed so cool and confident. But it had felt nice that he'd trusted me enough to share some of his insecurities with me.

Even if they were way off.

Like, he thought he needed a kissing tutor? How in the heck was that even a thing in his mind?

The girls he went after in the past must have really been wrong for him or something, because I knew firsthand that Nash was an amazing kisser.

And not just from the kiss-cam experience that he'd teased

me about. No, there was a much different kiss that I hadn't been able to stop thinking about for a year.

How could he not remember it?

Had he hit his head right after? Been in an accident?

Was he suffering from some sort of amnesia? Short-term memory loss?

I had initially thought that our moment must have just blurred in along with all of the other amazing flings he'd had last summer, but it sounded like he actually didn't have moments like that as often as I had assumed someone as attractive and talented and fun as he was would.

Maybe he'd only had a moment like that with me.

My arms and hands went tingly with the thought.

Why did he have to forget about it?

I was just putting my second batch of brownies in the prep kitchen ovens when I caught a glimpse of Nash and Carter out the window, chatting with Asher in the pool house.

They'd come downstairs about thirty minutes ago wearing swim trunks, saying they were off to have a race with Asher in the pool this morning. Apparently, Asher had been bragging about how his "senior class voted 'best physique'" could wipe the floor with them in an athletic competition any day.

They'd asked me if I wanted to come watch and be the unbiased judge, which had been extremely tempting since what eighteen-year-old girl wouldn't want to watch three extremely good-looking guys show off their athletic dominance?

But I was in a time crunch with the extra baking, so unfortunately, I had to turn them down.

I know...responsibility sucked sometimes.

They waved goodbye to Asher, and he headed back toward the pool house. Nash and Carter walked out the doors that led into the enclosed walkway connecting the pool house to the main house.

When I caught a glimpse of their profiles as they walked side by side, I couldn't help but think that the half-brothers resembled each other quite a bit from this angle. And for a split second, I worried that maybe it was me who had the bad memory.

Was it possible it had actually been Carter who had comforted and danced with me last summer and not Nash?

He had just broken up with his ex, Sofia, right around that time. Had he been rebounding and just never said anything to me about it because he knew it was a mistake?

I put a hand to my chest as I worried the darkness of the woods had made things more confusing than I'd thought.

But then Nash seemed to notice me through the window, and when our eyes met and he smiled at me, I was reassured again that it had been Nash.

I wouldn't have gotten the two brothers confused.

I hope.

I set the timer on the oven and then went back to the main kitchen to check on my croissants that should be about done. They were a beautiful golden-brown color, so I grabbed my hot pads and pulled the trays out to set them next to the batch I'd cooked earlier.

Carter and Nash strode into the kitchen and filled some glasses with water from the fridge.

"So, how did the race go?" I asked. "Did one of you prove to be the better swimmer than your friend?"

Nash and Carter both glanced at each other. After exchanging a look I didn't understand, Carter said, "The results were inconclusive."

Nash lifted his glass to his lips, appearing like he was trying to hide a smirk behind it.

Okay, I think I understand what's going on here. Two egos might have just been a little bruised by the competition.

I raised an eyebrow. "Would it be more accurate to say that the results of your race were inconclusive because Asher finished first?"

Nash sent a furtive glance to Carter, and with a shrug, he said, "It's hard to tell."

I chuckled. "I bet."

Nash set his water glass on the island and distracted me with a question. "Hey, do you think I could actually just buy one of these from you now and then get another after I help you set up this morning? Because these look and smell amazing."

"They do smell really good," Carter said, looking at them, too.

"Sure," I said, my cheeks glowing from their compliments. "You can each have one. I made extra today."

"Oh, but we can pay you," Nash said, patting his swim trunks like he was looking for his wallet. "I know you're saving up for college and—"

"No, it's okay." I grabbed my spatula to dish up a croissant. "I'm using your kitchen. We'll just call it the friends-and-family discount."

"Are you sure?" Nash asked.

I nodded.

Nash grabbed two small plates from the cupboard behind him and stepped up beside me so I could dish them up.

"Thank you. These really do look so good," Nash said as I slid a pastry onto his plate. "I promise I'll pay for my next one, though, when we're at the park. I wouldn't want anyone thinking I'm getting perks just because I'm a huge Casanova."

And when he winked at me, I just hoped my face wouldn't turn red and give away how much I liked it. Or how standing so close to him was making my mind hazy.

I dished up Carter next and then watched both boys as they took their first bites.

This was the first time either of them would have a taste of my baking, so I hoped it didn't disappoint.

Nash's eyes lit up, and a second later, he was saying, "Okay, this is sooooo good." He lifted the croissant higher. "Like, I'm pretty sure I'm having a spiritual experience in my mouth right now."

"Thank you," I said, giggling at his enthusiasm.

Carter narrowed his eyes at Nash, like he thought he was being slightly dramatic, but then he took a bite and a look of unexpected surprise lit up his eyes. "Wow," he said, clearing his throat. "I thought Nash was exaggerating, but...it is really good, Kiara. In fact, I'm pretty sure you could give Marie a run for her money with these."

My chest warmed at his comment. Unlike Nash, Carter was the more serious brother and didn't seem the type to hand out praise to just anyone. If he said something was impressive, he really meant it.

"Well," I said, "since Marie taught me how to make this recipe herself, I think she'll be okay."

"I do still need a personal chef for when I'm at Yale," Nash said after taking another bite. "You sure you don't want to tag along? Skip out on your own education and just make delicious croissants for me every day?"

"As tempting as that sounds..." I chuckled. "I think I may need to learn a few more recipes before you'll want me there. You can only have so many croissants and brownies before you'll want something else."

"Okay, fine," Nash said, waving his hand. "Don't let my sweet tooth derail you from going after your hopes and dreams." After giving me another wink, he added, "But once you've finished culinary school, don't be too surprised if I try to hire you."

He wanted to *hire* me?

"I'll start working on my résumé." I tried to say it lightly, even though his comment stung a little.

I was probably being too sensitive since he meant that as a compliment but...it kind of bothered me that he still obviously saw me in a supporting staff role.

Like, even though we'd become friends and I thought we were making progress, he still had apparently put me in a box in his mind as the estate's Head of Staff's daughter.

We were still in different social classes.

I cleaned his room and baked him desserts.

And he complimented me and thanked me for my service.

He didn't seem to notice that my feelings got hurt though, which was probably good.

He finished his croissant. After setting his plate in the dishwasher, he brushed the crumbs off his fingers. "I'm gonna go get ready now. I'll be down in a bit to help you get everything to the park."

He ran upstairs then, leaving Carter and me alone in the kitchen.

Since I still wasn't super comfortable with Carter yet, I made myself busy by getting the ingredients for the cherry chocolate topping that I'd be putting on the brownies.

Carter watched me for a moment as he finished his croissant, and I wondered what he might be thinking about.

He was the more studious brother, and while my feelings for Nash had seemed to slip under Nash's radar the past couple of weeks, I wondered if Carter may have noticed something in the way I'd been watching his brother this morning.

But instead of saying anything about it, he looked over the different things I had out on the counter and said, "I'll have to bring Ava by your booth when we're watching Elyse and Nash at the fair today. She loves brownies."

"Does she like cherries to go along with her chocolate, too?" I asked, gesturing at the cherries I had sitting on the counter.

"I'm pretty sure she does," Carter said.

"Then I'll make sure to save her one of these."

An hour later, Nash and I were setting up my booth. He asked, "Did Alessi ever say anything to you about what we'll be doing tonight? I haven't heard anything from her since Thursday."

"I haven't heard anything, either," I said, realizing that we hadn't nailed down any particulars aside from who we'd be going with and that it would be tonight. "But I can text her right now and ask."

When I opened my messaging app and saw the message thread I had going with Nash near the top, I quickly angled my phone away from him just in case he happened to peek at my phone screen as he pulled the pop-up pavilion from its bag.

I really didn't need him discovering that I was the "Wrong Number Girl" he'd been texting.

In fact, I should probably find a way to get ahold of his phone and delete the message thread and contact info if he still had it on there. That way, if he ever did try asking for my phone number again, I could give it to him and not have any incriminating evidence on his phone to make him realize I'd already been messaging him.

I sent my text to Alessi. Then after helping Nash with the pavilion and the table, I put my tablecloth on the table and started getting my display set up just right.

I had just placed the scotcharoos on the glass cake plate with gold-rimmed edges when my phone vibrated with a text.

Alessi: **I completely forgot we had plans for tonight! Miles invited me to go to New York for the**

day with some friends and I don't think we'll be back until late. So sorry!

"Looks like Alessi and Miles forgot about our plans," I said, turning to Nash and explaining what the text had said.

"They both forgot?" Nash furrowed his brow.

"That's what she said..."

He looked up at the trees above us like he was trying to decide what to make of this. Then after sighing, he said, "That kind of sucks, doesn't it?"

"It does," I said, even though I wasn't sure I actually felt too bad about the turn of events.

Because while I did enjoy hanging out with Miles and Alessi, I was okay with Nash not hanging out with Alessi anymore right now.

Not when he'd said a few things last night that made it seem like he was confused about what he wanted with my friend.

I texted Alessi back that it was fine and that I hoped she and Miles would have a good day with his friends. Then I grabbed the container with the croissants from the cooler. While I set them on a rectangular platter, I said, "I'm sure we can reschedule something for next week, if you want."

Nash pursed his lips as he seemed to consider it. Then he said, "We'll have to do that."

He looked at the time on his watch and startled a little, like he didn't realize how late it had gotten.

"I'm supposed to be on stage in ten minutes." He sighed, running his hands through his blond hair that looked golden in the morning sunlight. "I better get over to the performers' tent."

"Thank you for your help," I said. Then as he started to walk away, I called after him, "Break a leg."

He turned around. Walking backwards, he put his hands

on either side of his mouth and called back, "Good luck with your sales today."

My booth had a big rush around eleven o'clock, which kept me busy and made the time go fast.

It's a good thing I made extra today, I muttered to myself as I restocked and made sure my display looked good. I had already sold half of my desserts by noon, and if this afternoon went in a similar way, I might sell out completely and be ready to close shop by six instead of eight.

Once my display was set just right, I decided to eat my packed lunch while scrolling through social media. I tried not to get on social media too much, since opening the apps usually sent me into either an anxiety attack or a depressive spiral after all of the things Brooklyn and her friends had posted about me. But now that I'd made my account more private and unfollowed the accounts that had a negative impact on my mental health, it was usually safe to scroll for a few minutes each day.

I mean, who wouldn't love having a feed that was mostly pug videos and baking tutorials?

I opened my preferred social media account. When I checked my notifications, I saw I had a message request from someone named Nash Hastings.

I frowned and clicked on the message.

@nashhastings: **Hey, I didn't have your number so this seemed like the next best way to contact you. Your profile pic looks like my backyard neighbor anyway and you have the same name.**

I leaned forward and glanced around the park to see if I could see him. But there were no tall guys with blond hair wearing peasant costumes in the part of the park that I could see, so he must have been in the performers' tent or grabbing lunch or something.

So I messaged him back.

@kiaramatheson: **This is your housekeeper, future chef, and fake girlfriend.**

Conversation dots showed up on the screen right away. Then my phone buzzed.

@nashhastings: **Whew. That's a relief. I made this account just so I could contact you and I'd hate for that to have been a waste.**

@kiaramatheson: **You signed up just to talk to me?**

I had tried to find his social media accounts in the past without any luck, but I'd figured he might have just used a random name or something.

@nashhastings: **I used to have an account. Last year. But it was messing with my mind, so I deleted it.**

I clicked on his profile photo—a selfie that he must have taken this morning because he was wearing his costume and it looked like he was sitting on a chair in the performers' tent—and sure enough, Nash had zero followers and was following no one.

A notification popped up at the top of my phone.

@nashhastings is requesting to follow you.

I tapped on the confirm button to approve his request.

Then I went back to our message thread and typed, **I see I'm the first to make the cut of people cool enough for Nash to follow.**

@nashhastings: **I only follow the coolest people.**

He sent another message.

@nashhastings: **Anyway, I was thinking that even if**

Alessi and Miles can't hang out, that doesn't mean we can't still go have fun. So I was wondering if you wanted to play laser tag with me once this is done.

I grinned, loving that he still wanted to hang out with me.

@kiaramatheson: **That sounds fun! I love laser tag!**

Yay for more one-on-one time with Nash.

I was just thinking that it would almost be like a date when another message came through.

@nashhastings: **Asher and Elyse have been wanting to hang out with us. Mind if I invite them too?**

My heart sank as I read it.

So much for having Nash to myself.

I sighed as I thought about how to respond, weighing whether I dared tell him I wanted it to be just us tonight.

But then I realized that laser tag really was more fun with more people. Plus, hanging out with Nash's friends could be a bonus, right?

Like a rite of passage, since getting his friends' approval could just move us closer to the next step.

So I messaged him back, saying, **That sounds fun. I'd love to hang out with your friends.**

Hopefully, we'd all have lots of fun together.

24

NASH

I WENT BACK to my house after helping Kiara put away all of the things from her booth. After showering real quick and changing into some more normal clothes—there was no way I'd force Kiara to be seen in public with me wearing my peasant clothes two days in a row—I sprayed on some cologne and took a few minutes to try and look good.

Not because I was trying to look good for *her* or anything silly like that. It was, you know, just in case Kiara's ex happened to be playing laser tag and we needed to put on our fake-relationship charade again.

Okay, and yeah, maybe I also wanted to prove to Kiara that I wasn't a *complete* theater dork.

Especially after all the embarrassing things I'd said last night.

At least she hadn't said anything about seeing me watching her from my balcony.

That would have been awkward.

Once my hair was the way I liked it, I went downstairs and

found Carter and Cambrielle hanging out with Ava and Mack in the family room.

"I just heard from Elyse that you invited her and Asher to play laser tag with you and Kiara tonight," Ava said, turning to me with her eyebrows raised.

"Oh, you did?" I frowned, wondering why she looked disappointed.

She nodded. "And I just have to ask, why weren't any of us cool enough to get an invite?" She gestured at the four of them on the couch.

"Ummm." I hesitated, trying to figure out from her expression if she was actually hurt or just teasing me. I was pretty sure she was joking, but just in case she wasn't, I explained, "I was just with them when I was making plans. But yeah, you guys should totally come. It's way more fun when there is a bigger group."

"Oh good." Ava smiled, like that was all she needed. "I'd hate to think you were embarrassed by Carter." She nudged my brother with her elbow and Carter just rolled his eyes.

"It is good you invited us," Mack said, coming up behind me and putting a hand on my shoulder. "Because we were going to show up anyway."

"I bet you were," I said, smiling.

"Should we invite Addison and Evan, too?" Cambrielle asked me before looking around at the group. "We haven't all hung out in way too long."

"Sure," I said. "Do you want to text them and just have them meet us there?"

"Sure," Cambrielle said, already pulling out her phone.

"Are you already set on taking your car?" Mack asked me as Cambrielle typed on her phone. "Or do you think we should all load in my Land Cruiser? I think we'll have enough seats since there will be eight of us, not counting Addison and Evan."

"I think that would be fun," I said, before realizing I probably should have asked Kiara if she was okay with all of these extra people.

My friends and siblings could be a lot sometimes.

Hopefully, she'll be okay with it...

"I'm gonna grab Kiara real quick," I said, deciding I should at least give her a heads up before she walked in here. "Then we can head out."

"Someone smells good," Kiara said as we walked across the lawn a few minutes later.

"You think so?"

She nodded, and I liked that she seemed to be blushing a little. Kiara had beautiful skin normally, but the slightly pink hue made her even more beautiful somehow.

"I decided it might be a good idea to shower real quick," I said.

"And use the Creed Aventus cologne that I've seen on your bathroom sink, I'm guessing," she said.

"Yeah, how did you...?" I started to ask before realizing that Kiara *would* know exactly what kind of cologne I kept next to my sink among all of the other things I kept in my room, closet, and bathroom.

In fact, she probably had way more insight into my private life than most people.

But I had other colognes in there, too. Had she been curious enough to smell each of them and memorize them?

Or was she just a fragrance connoisseur as well as a baker?

Seeming to understand what I was thinking about, Kiara got a bashful look on her face and said, "I might have been curious one day and sniffed the nozzle to see what it smelled like."

"Does it smell the same?" I asked. "Because I've heard scents smell different with the wearer's body chemistry mixed in."

"It's a little different," she said. "I liked it before, but...I think it smells even better on you."

My lips stretched up into a smile. It felt nice hearing that—having her notice something like that.

I didn't know if anyone had ever cared to know something so personal about me before.

As we made it to the steps that led up to the terrace, I couldn't help but glance back at her and ask, "What other things have you learned about me from cleaning my room?"

"Just that you don't like making your bed." She looked up at me and shrugged. "And that you leave the drawers in your bathroom half-open most days. I'm guessing it's because you're in a hurry, not because you're testing me to see if I'm actually cleaning your room." She laughed that adorable little giggle of hers then added, "Oh, and you have a stash of Twix bars hiding in your closet and a huge container of peanut M&Ms hidden behind the blanket on your couch."

"Looks like you know all my darkest secrets and could totally blackmail me if you wanted."

"I totally could." She grinned, her brown eyes sparkling. "But I promise I don't have plans to tell everyone about your secret candy-bar-hoarding tendencies."

I wiped my brow. "That's a relief."

We made it to the terrace, and I realized I still needed to prep her for the crowd waiting for us inside.

I turned around to face her. But when she met my gaze in the early evening light, I was instantly hit with how beautiful her eyes were.

Like, wow, they were unlike any brown I'd seen before.

They appeared to be more amber-colored at first glance, but with the way the light was hitting them right then, I could suddenly see little flecks of lighter gold that I hadn't noticed before.

They were mesmerizing.

And with her super long and thick lashes, she really did have the kind of eyes that I could get lost in.

She narrowed her gaze, like she was confused at why I was just staring at her. And so I searched my memory to try and recall why I'd turned to face her in the first place.

It came back to me a second later, so blinking a few times to get rid of my daze, I said, "H-hey, so do you mind if Cambrielle and Carter and a few other friends join us tonight?"

"Oh, um..." Her expression showed surprise for a second, but then she said, "Sure. That could be fun."

"I was hoping you'd say that," I said, looking at her sheepishly. "Because they're all inside and planning to all drive in Mack's SUV together."

"You prep-school kids like to carpool?" she asked.

"Gotta make up for my dad using a private jet somehow." I winked.

"I never thought of it like that." She chuckled. "But yeah, all the celebrities cutting down on using private jets to go to lunch across the country would really do a lot more for the planet than me riding my bike to work at the coffee shop all of last summer."

"You rode your bike to The Brew?" I asked, not sure that I'd ever seen her bike anywhere.

"I rode it most days," she said. "When the weather was good, anyway."

"Have you ever ridden on the trails we have out back?" I asked, pointing past the stone path and line of trees behind it that held the different dirt trails my siblings and I usually rode our ATVs on. "Or do you just have a road bike?"

"I have a mountain bike. But I haven't ridden any of the trails."

"Well, you totally should," I said. "You live here, too. You can use the trails anytime you want."

"Thanks, maybe I will." She looked down at the lower half of her body and said, "I need to stay in shape somehow."

And before I knew it, I was giving her a good look over.

She did have a really nice shape.

Not overly thin or athletic, but healthy and fit with toned legs that could definitely fit in with someone who cycled a lot.

Or wear short pajama shorts like she'd worn in that dream.

I blinked my eyes shut then brought my gaze back to her face when I realized I was about to slip into fantasyland after totally checking her out.

When she gave me a smile, like she knew I'd just been enjoying the view, it was my turn to blush.

"Anyway," I said, fighting a smile as I gestured at the back doors. "Everyone is just waiting inside, so we should probably get in there."

She followed me in the house, and when I introduced her to everyone, she seemed really cool and not at all uncomfortable, which was a relief.

"You still okay with us all squishing in the same vehicle?" I asked, just in case, as we walked out the front doors and to where Mack's SUV was parked in his driveway next door.

"It sounds fun," she said, seeming like she actually meant it. "Your friends—especially Ava and Mack—seem like a riot."

"They are," I said. "Never a dull moment with any of them really."

When we pulled into the parking lot of the fun center a few minutes later, Cambrielle said, "Addison just texted back.

She says that she and Evan are just finishing something up at their apartment, but they'll try to get here in time for the second round."

"Perfect," Mack said, putting his Toyota in park. "That will give all of you time to warm up before Evan and I dominate."

"So we're doing guys against girls again?" Ava asked.

"I think so," Carter said.

"Great," Ava said, a competitive glint in her eyes. "I love winning."

Everyone chuckled at that since the girls had yet to win a round so far this year.

"I think you said you've played laser tag before?" I said to Kiara as we walked toward the entrance of the fun center.

"I haven't played since moving here," she said. "But I played a few times back in Florida."

"Okay, good." I opened the tinted glass door for her to walk through. "Because I was hoping I wouldn't have to go easy on you."

"You think you'll have to go easy on me?" She gasped and put a hand to her chest as she walked through the door.

"I just don't want your first hangout with my friends to be a bad memory all because I play to win."

"I don't think you'll need to worry about that," she said. Then stepping closer and patting my chest, she added, "Because I also play to win."

And as she turned and sauntered up to the counter, all I could do was swallow and think, *Wow, that's kind of hot.*

25

KIARA

"WHEN YOU SAID you played to win, you weren't kidding," Nash said, coming up behind me. He was still wearing his laser-tag gear after the first twenty-minute round had ended. "Are you sure you've only played a few times before?"

"I *may* have been downplaying it just a bit," I said, trying not to smile too big.

"You think?" he asked, an impressed look on his face. "Because I'm pretty sure you got more kills than Mack. And no one *ever* beats Mack."

I glanced ahead of us to where Mack was looking at the screen with all of our scores. After scanning down the list for a moment, he stared at me with his mouth hanging open.

"You're going down next round," he said. Then to everyone, he called out, "Watch out for Kiara, guys. She's a crafty one."

I just grinned, loving that I had been able to make a good impression.

Nash chuckled beside me. "Mack is going to be on your butt all of next round now."

"Only if he can find me," I said.

Nash let his other friends walk ahead of us to check their scores. Then leaning his shoulder against the wall, he asked, "Did you happen to count how many times you snuck up behind me?"

"Probably at least a dozen times," I said, unable to hide my grin as I looked up at him.

"Stalker." He pushed against my shoulder playfully.

I pushed him back. "You're just not as sneaky as you think."

I watched everyone else check their scores. When Cambrielle, Ava, and Elyse all saw the final team scores, they turned back to me with shocked expressions on their faces as Ava said, "We won! The girls actually won this time."

"All thanks to Kiara," Elyse said, looking at me with a friendly smile.

I smiled back, proud of my performance.

As Cambrielle taunted Mack about losing to a bunch of girls, Nash slipped his arm around my waist and squeezed me against him as he said, "Who knew you were such a bad A."

"I have a few tricks up my sleeve," I said, trying not to blush too hard from his praise and the way he'd pulled me close.

Man, he smelled so good.

And it might be the fact that I'd grown up on various army bases, but Nash looked somehow even hotter in his laser-tag gear.

Hot in the "my man can protect me from the bad guys" sort of way.

You know…if I wasn't already able to protect myself, that is.

A tall guy with brown hair and a petite girl with blonde hair walked into the laser-tag area a moment later. And when the girl went up to Cambrielle and gave her a hug, I had to do a double take because I could swear it was someone I knew.

"Hey, let me introduce you to Addison and Evan," Nash said, seeing the couple.

But I stood there frozen in my spot when the guy looked my way and I recognized him, too.

"Come on," Nash said, tugging on my hand. "Don't be shy. Evan may look intimidating, but I promise he's really nice."

Yeah, how he looked wasn't the problem.

Though, he did have a very intimidating look. He was at least six-foot-four with huge biceps and a build similar to what I imagined Hercules would look like if I stepped into the world of Greek mythology.

But the real problem was that I knew Evan from Florida and he was standing with a girl who could be a doppelgänger for my friend, Adriana, if it wasn't for her blonde hair.

Had Adriana bleached her hair?

The girl who looked like the best friend I hadn't seen since moving away from Miami noticed Nash and me coming their way. And when our eyes locked, she gasped, and the color drained from her face.

"Kiara?" she asked, her voice exactly as I remembered. "What are you doing here?"

26

KIARA

"WAIT, YOU ALREADY KNOW ADDISON?" Nash frowned as he looked at me and then at Adriana.

"Yeah," I said, looking into Adriana's eyes. Was she wearing contacts to make her eyes look blue instead of their natural brown? Because this was kind of freaky. "We were friends back in F—"

"Arizona," Adriana cut me off. "We were friends back when Kiara lived on an army base in Arizona with her mom and dad."

Huh?

What the heck was going on? Why was she lying to Nash about where we knew each other from?

Why was she in Eden Falls with her brother's best friend?

And why was everyone calling her by the wrong name?

"So you met Addison and her stepbrother when you lived in Arizona?" Nash asked like he hadn't known I'd lived in Arizona before moving to Florida. And why would he? I hadn't had a reason to tell him that my family moved every few years because my dad used to be in the Army.

Wait... I went still as something else registered in my mind.

Had Nash just said that Evan was Adriana's *stepbrother*?

How the heck did that happen?

Had her parents divorced and remarried one of Evan's parents? Adriana had complained about her dad being distracted in the months before I moved away. Had he been involved in a secret affair with Evan's mom?

I noticed Adriana and Evan watching me with anxious expressions and realized I still hadn't answered Nash's question.

So even though I didn't know why Adriana was lying about where we'd become friends, I told Nash, "Yes, we all met when my dad was stationed in Arizona."

And when I said that, I noticed Adriana and Evan both seem to relax.

Mack walked over to us. Putting a hand on Evan's shoulder, he said, "You two need to suit up. We have an epic battle to get to."

And before I could ask Adriana what was going on and why she was lying about who she was, she and Evan followed Mack into the room where the laser-tag gear was stored.

I was barely able to concentrate on the next game. And when we all checked the final scores at the end, my score was significantly lower than it had been the previous round.

"Looks like they actually registered my hits this time," Mack said to me when he saw his name at the top of the list. "Hopefully, you weren't just going easy on us all."

"We'll just pretend like I was," I said, sending him a half-smile.

"Is something wrong?" Nash asked when he came up

beside me after checking the scores for himself. "You've been off since Addison and Evan showed up."

"I think I'm just shocked to see them," I said, glancing over to where they were standing with Asher and Elyse. When Adriana looked my way and our eyes caught, she mouthed what looked like, *I'll explain soon.*

We decided not to play another round since there was another big group waiting to use the laser-tag room.

"Do you guys want to head back to our house for a pool party?" Cambrielle asked when we all stood in the lobby of the fun center. "It's only nine, so the night is still young."

"I'm in," Elyse said.

"Me too," Ava said.

"What do you think?" Nash asked me. "You up for a pool party with everyone?"

I glanced around the group. Deciding that it might give me a chance to talk to Adriana and figure out what the heck was going on with her, I said, "That sounds fun."

"Perfect," Nash smiled. "A pool party it is!"

We started walking back toward Mack's Land Cruiser, but when we were about halfway there, Adriana appeared at my side and asked, "Do you want to ride back with Evan and me?"

"I'm not sure..." I met my old friend's gaze, still thinking it was weird to see her with blonde hair and blue eyes. "I came with Nash and everyone so..."

"Nash can ride with us, too," she said. "It's better than being squished in Mack's SUV anyway."

I considered her offer. She and Evan wouldn't do something sketchy with me if Nash was there too, right?

After studying Adriana for another moment and checking in with my gut, I said, "Okay. Sure."

We had to stop at Adriana and Evan's condo so they could grab their swimsuits and towels. It was in one of the newer subdivisions in Eden Falls where a lot of the younger families and college students lived.

"Wanna help me pick out my swimsuit?" Adriana asked once we stepped into the minimalistic yet cozy living area.

"Sure." Glancing back at Nash, who had just sat on the couch near the front door, I said, "I guess we'll be right back."

With my eyes, I tried to say: *If you hear me scream, please come save me.*

But from the way he looked around at the decor without a care in the world, I figured he didn't get my telepathic message.

I followed Adriana into the bedroom at the very end of the hall. Once we stepped inside and she shut the door behind me, Adriana instantly threw her arms around my shoulders in a hug.

"I can't believe you live here," she said, sounding emotional and like she was trying not to cry. "I never thought I'd see you again."

"I was so surprised when I saw you, too." I hugged her back, finally feeling like I was with my old friend for the first time since seeing her today. "But I'm also confused." I pulled away and looked into her watery eyes. "Why is everyone calling you Addison and think you're from Arizona?" I touched her blonde hair. "And why do you look so different?"

"It's a long story." She sighed, her shoulders dropping as if just thinking about the reasons behind the lies took everything out of her. "Do you remember how my dad had some new guys doing some business stuff at the coin shop last spring?"

"Kind of," I said. Adriana's dad owned a rare coin shop in Miami that had a lot of interesting people come in. "Was it the guys who were always wearing suits?"

The ones Adriana and I had been leery of whenever they came in because they looked like they could be in the mafia.

I swore they had their fingerprints burned off.

But Adriana shook her head and said, "No. These guys dressed more casually. Just T-shirts and polo shirts most of the time. My cousin Gabriel was always with them."

At her mention of her cousin Gabriel, I immediately knew who she was talking about.

"So, what do those guys have to do with why you're here with Evan?" I asked, still confused about what was going on.

She looked down. Then after taking a deep breath, she met my eyes with a solemn expression and said, "They killed my parents."

"What?" I covered my mouth with my hands as my stomach dropped, not believing what she'd just said.

"Turns out Gabriel had joined the drug cartel and he and his friends were running drugs through my dad's shop," she explained. "And when my dad figured out what was going on, he tried to get them out and threatened to call the cops if they didn't take their business somewhere else. But..." Her words drifted off as she stared at the mostly empty bookshelf in the corner.

"Oh Adriana." I stepped closer and pulled her into a hug.

She let me hold her for a moment, but then she pulled back again and said, "Anyway, the cartel came back and shot my dad one day while I was at school, and when my mom came out of the back room to see what was going on, they shot her, too."

"Oh no!" My insides twisted and tears instantly filled my eyes. "That can't..." I shook my head, feeling like I was going to throw up. "I'm so sorry. That's so horrible."

"I found their bodies when I got home from school," she said, wiping at the tears that had sprung to her eyes at her mention of the horrific experience. She glanced around her room like she was looking for something. Then grabbing a tissue from a box on her dresser, she dabbed at her eyes and continued, "Anyway, Tomás found out what happened and decided to go after Gabriel and his friends. He ended up killing one of them, but then he ended up getting shot, too."

"Tomás is gone?" I gasped, not believing this could actually be true. Her parents and brother were all gone?

"Yes." She drew in a shaky breath and dabbed at her eyes again. "Things were pretty scary the next few days, and I wasn't sure what to do since I didn't know if the cartel would come after me next. It seemed like they wanted to silence anyone who knew what was going on. And then, I also didn't know the first thing about planning a funeral or figuring out all the financial stuff from my parents' business."

"I wouldn't, either," I said.

And if this was a little over a year ago, Adriana would have still been just sixteen when the tragedy happened since her birthday wasn't until August.

"I didn't know what to do, but Evan…" She pointed to her closed door, like she was pointing to the guy she now lived with. "Evan found me. He figured I might be in danger, so he got me out of Miami so that I wouldn't end up like the rest of my family."

"Thank goodness he knew you'd need help," I said, not wanting to think about what might have happened if she'd stayed.

"So we moved to Nebraska for a little while as we figured out a good place to go long term. After doing some research, Evan found Eden Falls Academy, and since it fit our needs, he made all of the arrangements so we could come here last fall."

"You didn't want to do online school?" I asked, curious why they'd choose to live in a boarding school surrounded by other people when there was a different option.

"I was already really depressed and knew that spending so much time alone and hiding would only make things worse." She tossed her tissue into the trash can by her desk. "So Evan found a school that had really amazing security, and we changed my name and forged some documents so he could stay close and attend as well."

"Were you able to use your parents' money to pay the tuition and other fees?" I asked, knowing that the price of attending the prestigious academy was something only the wealthiest people could afford.

"That money is tied up until I'm eighteen," she said. "But Evan had a small inheritance from his grandpa and had been investing in tech startups since he was eighteen. One of them took off in a big way a few months before my parents died, so he's basically taken care of everything while my money is tied up."

"You're lucky Tomás had such a good friend," I said. I hadn't known Evan very well back in Florida, but he'd always seemed smart and nice, even if his muscles were somewhat intimidating.

Adriana nodded. "I don't know how I'll ever repay him for what he's done. He's literally sacrificed everything he had going for him to take care of me."

"Is he kind of like your undercover bodyguard then?" I asked, thinking he definitely looked the part.

"Basically. He's literally always with me," she said. "Like, the only time I'm not in his sight is when I'm in the bathroom or when I was in the girls' dorms at the academy since they had such great security there."

"And everyone thinks he's your stepbrother?" I asked, remembering how Nash had mentioned that earlier.

"We told everyone our parents got married last year and

sent us to school here because their jobs kept them really busy with travel these days."

"And they think we met in Arizona?" I asked, still not sure what our story was supposed to be. Though from her name change and the blonde hair, I assumed we weren't telling the truth now.

"I told everyone that I'm from Arizona, since I remembered you talking about moving from there when we first met, and it's the first warm place that came to mind. So if you can just keep telling everyone that we met when your dad was stationed there instead of Florida, that would be amazing."

"I'll say whatever you need." Her safety was more important than small details. "I think the Hastings family knows that my mom and I moved here from Florida. But I don't think she mentioned any of the other bases we've been stationed at. And I don't see a reason why she might have ever mentioned where and when I would have met a friend named Adriana." I paused and shook my head. "I mean Addison."

"It takes some getting used to," she said. "Evan just calls me Addie most of the time since it could be a nickname for either name."

"I'll try to do that, too," I said.

"Thank you." Adriana—*Addie* hugged me tight. When she pulled back, she had fresh tears in her eyes. She wiped at them and said, "I just can't believe you're here and that you've been here all along and I didn't know it."

"I know," I said, thinking that of all the boarding schools she and Evan could have chosen, it was crazy they'd picked the one I lived by. "And I'm so sorry about your parents and Tomás. So, so, sorry."

Addie nodded and breathed in a double breath, like she was trying not to cry. "It's been a nightmare."

Another wave of emotion passed over me as I thought about the whole Garcia family being gone.

Everyone but Adriana—*Addie*.

I needed to get the name change right before we were in public.

Addie wiped her eyes, and after looking at her watch, she said, "The guys are probably wondering what we're doing in here. I better grab my swimsuit and get myself together so we can get to the pool."

I gave her one more hug. When we walked out of her room a minute later, I noticed a look pass between Evan and Adriana, as if Evan was silently checking in to see if everything was okay.

Addie gave a slight nod. Then putting a smile on, like she hadn't just told me the completely horrific story of her whole family's murders, she said, "Should we get out of here?"

"So, what are your plans now that you've graduated?" I asked Addie as we walked down the steps into the Hastings' gorgeous indoor pool.

The guys and Ava were already playing a game of pool basketball when we got here, and while Nash and Evan had decided to join the game, Addie and I preferred to watch from the other end of the pool since we had so much to catch up on still.

"We're just going to stay in Eden Falls for now." Addie turned around to face the game once we were chest deep in the water. "We have no idea if I'm still in danger or if the cartel is looking for me. I'm hoping they're focused on other things since it's been a little over a year now. But I don't really want to risk going back to Florida. Eden Falls is a great place, so as long as I'm safe, I'll probably stick around."

"What about Evan?" I glanced over to the other side of the pool. "You said he put things on hold to help you. Was he in college? Or did he have a job besides investing in tech startups?"

He had to be close to Tomás's age, so that meant he had to be around twenty-two or twenty-three.

"He was able to finish his bachelor's degree online," she said. "But I'm not sure what will happen with him." Addie sighed and looked at Evan who was holding the basketball close to his chest and looking like he was trying to find a way to get it past Mack.

Evan was strong and seemed to be holding his own pretty well against the future Columbia basketball player, but when he lifted up the ball to pass it to Asher, Mack ended up getting it away from Evan.

Mack immediately passed the ball to Nash, who was under the net. A second later, Nash dunked it. And wow. The way he did that was super hot.

I knew he had to be a good swimmer and he was amazing on the stage, but I didn't realize he'd be so great at pool basketball either.

Addie must have noticed how I was staring at Nash because she leaned close, and in a lowered voice, asked, "Is there anything going on between you and Nash?"

"What?" I startled, a rush of tingles racing across my shoulders. "Um, I mean, of course not. W-we're just friends."

"Really?" Her dark eyebrows knitted together like she didn't believe me.

"Well…yeah," I said, my face growing hot. "I mean, we've been hanging out a lot. But he asked my friend out a couple of times already, so I don't think he's interested in me."

At least...it was hard to tell where we stood since things were always so confusing.

"Then why are you here tonight instead of your friend?" Addie arched an eyebrow.

"She's hanging out with her stepbrother. We were supposed to go on a double date, but they both forgot."

Somehow.

Was it possible Miles had arranged things on purpose because I told him I'd liked Nash first?

Probably not...but...Miles did like to get his kicks and giggles in eccentric ways sometimes.

"But you like him, don't you?" Addie asked, nodding toward Nash.

I followed her gaze over to Nash. When he smiled back at me like he'd just looked over here at the same moment, warmth flooded over me from my head to my toes. And I had to say, "I like him so much."

So much it sometimes hurts. Because the more I got to know him, the better he turned out to be.

He was funny and smart and dorky and cute, and when I was with him, I was in a permanently good mood.

He just made me happy.

And spending time with someone who made me so happy after a rough couple of years was so nice.

Even if our friendship never turned into more than that, I'd still feel lucky.

Though, of course, I still hoped there was a chance for more.

So I told Addie all about the unrequited crush that I had on the boy next door, and everything that had happened over the past year. Then I explained how we'd recently started hanging out—sometimes with Alessi and sometimes alone—and how he'd taken on fake-boyfriend duties and everything.

"That's so crazy," she said when I finished my most recent life story. "And he hasn't done anything more than take your friend on one date and cuddle with her during a movie?"

"That's what he said."

"Then you should go after him. See if you can make something happen," she said. "I mean, if your friend didn't even remember your double date, Nash obviously isn't as big of a priority to her as he should be if you're going to stand on the sidelines. You've given her a chance, but it's okay to live for yourself, too. Go after what *you* want."

"I know," I said, watching the game again. "I want to. I know a guy like him won't stay on the market forever."

Ava rebounded the ball and cheered loudly. Then Carter grabbed her from behind and she yelled, "Foul, foul," giggling right until Carter dunked them both in the water.

Man, I wanted someone to be like that with.

I sighed and turned back to Addie. "It's just scary to put yourself out there."

"Ain't that the truth." Addie let out a long sigh of her own and looked at Evan.

"Wait," I said, putting two and two together. "Is there something going on between you and Evan?"

"Shh..." Addie shushed me.

My eyes went wide, and I couldn't help but whisper-shout, "Oh my heck!"

"I know!" Addie got a pained look on her face before saying in a hushed tone, "And everyone thinks he's my stepbrother. Plus, we're roommates now. So I literally can't say anything about it."

With her mention of liking the guy she was roommates with, I was reminded of an email I'd seen in Hunter's advice column earlier this month. It was such a big coincidence that I had to ask, "Did you happen to write to *The Confidant* about your predicament?"

Addie covered her face with her hands at my guess. Then after slowly sliding them down until they rested on her chest, she said, "I'm totally the girl who wrote about her crush on her best friend and future roommate."

"Dang..."

"I know." She blew out a long breath. "It's hopeless. I mean, if I did something and he rejected me, it could go so bad. Like, how could I face him every day for who knows how long after something like that? At least with you, you don't live across the hall from him."

"Living across his backyard and cleaning his bedroom isn't much better."

"I guess that's true," she admitted.

"Yep," I said. "Which is also why I just keep waiting and hoping he'll make the first move."

"Same."

I glanced at Evan again, and after looking over his chiseled face and body, I asked, "Do people actually believe that he's our age, though?"

Because seriously, he was way too built to look like he just graduated from high school.

I mean, the rest of the guys in the pool were all super fit and looked like they put in their time at the gym—Asher's arms were huge. But Evan was just a bit more of a man and probably had to shave every day.

But Addie didn't get a chance to answer my question because Cambrielle walked through the door that came from the main house then, carrying a tray of meats, cheeses, and crackers, followed by Elyse with a tray of veggies and dip.

"Who wants food?" Cambrielle called out to everyone before setting her tray down on one of the tables.

"That looks good," I said to Addie. "Wanna grab some?"

"Of course." We walked toward the pool steps to climb out. Before I could get on the first step, Addie touched my arm and said, "I can't tell you how good it is to see you. It's like having a bit of home with me again."

I looked at the girl who had been my best friend for the three years I'd lived in Florida and couldn't help but feel the same. "It's kind of unreal that you're actually here. But I agree. And we'll have to hang out all the time now."

We filled our plates with the late-night snack as the guys and Ava climbed out of the pool to join us.

Once everyone was sitting around in a circle on the lounge chairs, Cambrielle said, "Hey, so I was thinking that while most of us are here, we should talk about our trip to the Hamptons next week."

"Should we see if Hunter and Scarlett want to FaceTime for the chat?" Ava asked. "I can just grab my phone."

When she stood to get her phone from a chair on the opposite side of the pool, I leaned close to Addie and said, "I'll just head out so you guys can plan your thing."

She looked at her friends around the circle, seeming unsure what to do, but then she nodded and gave me a quick hug. "Call me tomorrow and we can set up a time to hang out."

"I will."

I stood and looked at everyone awkwardly before saying, "Well, I better get home. Thanks for letting me hang out with you all tonight. It was fun."

"Wait, you're leaving?" Nash stood and touched my arm before I could get two steps away.

"Yeah." I tucked some hair behind my ear as I looked back at him. "It's getting late, and you guys have your weekend to talk about so—"

"Oh you should totally come," Nash said before I could

finish my sentence. Then looking at everyone else, he asked, "We have room for Kiara, right?"

"Of course," Cambrielle said. "You should totally come. You and Addison can share a room. She doesn't have a roommate yet."

"Are you sure?" I asked, glancing around at everyone anxiously. "I don't want to intrude on your fun weekend just because I'm here tonight."

Nash put his other hand on my arm and stared into my eyes. In a serious tone, he said, "I want you there. I'm going to need someone to hang out with while everyone else is buddied up. Please come."

"You said it's next weekend?" I asked, trying to figure out if I'd even have the time off. It was the Fourth of July weekend, so I wouldn't have work Saturday, Sunday, or Monday because of the holiday.

Nash nodded. "We're leaving Friday morning then coming back on Tuesday."

Oh...that was a bit longer than I could manage.

I bit my lip.

"What is it?" Nash asked, noticing my hesitation. "You don't think you can stand to be around me for that long?"

"No, it's not that," I said. I didn't think that would ever be a problem since I never seemed to get enough time with him. "I'm just not sure I'll be able to get that many days off work."

"I'm pretty sure my family will be okay with you taking the long weekend off," Nash said.

"Especially since we'll all be gone that weekend, anyway," Carter added.

Nash nodded. "And if your boss has a hard time with that, I'll ask my parents to talk to your mom."

So I sighed and said, "Okay. If I can get the time off, then I'd love to come."

27

KIARA

"IT SHOULD BE PRETTY fun having you at the beach house with us," Nash said as we walked on the path that led from the pool house back to the cottage. It was close to midnight now, so we walked under the light of the moon with the solar-powered garden lights illuminating the way.

"It sounds like it will be a blast," I said. "If I can get off work, that is."

"You can get off work," he said, like it was already a done deal. "And what a coincidence that you and Addison know each other already. What a small world we live in."

"I know. I was so shocked when I saw her since I never thought I would after I moved away."

When my mom and I left Florida, we hadn't known where we'd end up long term. We'd only come to Eden Falls because my mom's friend, Traci, had told her to come stay with her while we figured out our next steps.

It was merely an amazing twist of fate that the job at the Hastings' estate became available the week after we got here and that the position included housing on the estate.

So as far as Addie knew, we were just going to live with a friend for a while and move on. There hadn't been any details to tell beyond that.

And since Addie also apparently had a lot of chaos and heartache to deal with at the same time, we'd just never gotten back in touch.

Until tonight.

I just wished Addie hadn't had such nightmarish circumstances bring her here.

Poor Addie.

Nash and I walked past the bench, and when he did a double take at the place he'd first kissed me, his expression went blank.

Was he remembering something? My heart raced with the thought.

Last night he'd mentioned that seeing a girl with pink hair had reminded him of someone he met last summer... Could being here with me have made him recall something else?

When he stopped and stared at the bench, as if looking at it would fix his memory, I asked, "Is something wrong?"

"I don't know." He sighed and ran a hand through his dirty-blond hair. "I've just been having these weird memory flashes this week. Like I'm remembering something."

"You have?" My breath caught in my throat.

What were these flashbacks showing him?

Did he remember me? Or the time we spent back here?

But instead of seeming to gain clarity from whatever he'd just remembered, he shook his head and said, "But maybe I'm just imagining things."

You're not. It was real, Nash, I wanted to tell him so badly.

But how was I supposed to go about that? Was there anything I could do to help him?

Maybe if we talked about it he might remember more?

I swallowed the huge lump in my throat and asked, "What's in these flashes? Do you know what made them start? Maybe I can help you figure out what they mean."

"Well..." He licked his lips and looked back at me. "They started yesterday at the renaissance fair, when I was talking with Elyse."

When he was talking with Elyse?

She hadn't been at the garden party, had she?

"It wasn't because of Elyse, I don't think," he said, seeming to guess what I was thinking. "But the dress she wore for our performances brought back a memory. And then there was the flash I already told you about last night. The one that happened when I saw that girl with pink hair."

I nodded.

"Hmm." He bit his lip and looked up like he was remembering something else. "And this wasn't an actual flash of memory," he said. "But when I first sat next to you in the booth at The Italian Amigos, there was a second where I felt a weird sense of déjà vu."

I'd thought there might have been something.

"But I don't know," he said with a shrug. "It might have just been a dream I had once instead of a memory. I have pretty vivid dreams. Like earlier this week I—" He stopped suddenly, his cheeks flushing. "Um, never mind. We don't need to go into the details of my weird dreams. But yeah, it could have just been a dream that I'm remembering. Of a night with a pink-haired girl in a renaissance dress."

My heart was beating everywhere now—thundering in my veins and pulsing in my arms and face and chest.

He remembered.

Not enough to know it was real, or that it was me whom he'd spent the evening with.

But there was a flicker of that memory locked in there.

A start.

Should I tell him it was real? That it had been me?

Or would he think it was weird that I would remember a night like that with him and pretend for all this time we'd been hanging out that it hadn't happened?

It probably wouldn't go over too well if I just called out, *Surprise! I'm the girl with the pink wig and peasant dress. I've just been sitting in your backyard this past year, waiting for you to remember me.*

"Anyway..." He cleared his throat and started walking toward my home again. "I wasn't in the best place at the time. And um..." He rubbed the back of his neck. "I was trying to escape my feelings by medicating with enough alcohol that there were a few nights I don't remember at all."

"Really?" My breath caught in my throat as a feeling of dread flooded me.

Nash had a drinking problem?

The reason he couldn't remember the garden party was because he'd been blackout-drunk at the time?

My stomach hollowed out with the thought.

This was serious.

It might not be a big deal to some people but...I'd already had to leave someone I loved because of his struggle with alcohol.

If this was still something Nash was dealing with, I didn't know if I could go down that road again. It was too hard.

Nash must have sensed my sudden wariness because he gave me a pained look and said, "It's not something I've really told anyone besides my family about."

I nodded, not sure what I should say.

But I needed to know more if I was going to keep spending time with him. I had to ask, "Do you still drink sometimes?"

Were blackouts still something he experienced? Would there be more nights he'd forget?

How had I not been able to tell that he'd been drunk that night?

I must have been really distracted by the drama with Tristan and the gossip site or something to not even have an inkling that I was dancing with someone who had been drinking.

I'd always been able to smell the alcohol on my dad.

Then I remembered something. *The mouthwash.*

Had he been carrying it with him to cover up the alcohol on his breath?

Or even worse, was that what he'd gotten drunk on?

I'd thought he'd just been prepared to have kissably fresh breath at a moment's notice, but...did that bottle have a different purpose?

Nash pushed his hands into the pockets of his swim trunks. With a hesitant expression, he said, "I don't drink anymore."

With those four words, a whoosh of relief passed through me.

"I haven't drunk alcohol since right after school started," he continued, angling his gaze at me as we passed the patch of peonies. "So it's been just over nine months."

"Yeah?" I asked, needing him to confirm it again for some reason.

"I almost slipped up this winter after *The Phantom* was over since I always go through a bit of a grieving period between shows." He spoke the words carefully, like he was self-conscious to be sharing these private details with someone he was still just getting to know. "And, um...I was slightly heart-broken over a girl I really liked." His gaze darted to mine. "Believe it or not, I'm not always an irresistible Casanova."

That made me smile.

He shrugged. "But I resisted enough times before that, and so I didn't want to ruin my clean streak. So I pushed through, using some tools my mom and my doctor had taught me."

"I'm glad you were able to push through," I said. "I know from my own experience with my dad that it can be rough to stay sober."

"Your dad had a drinking problem?" Nash furrowed his brow, like this was the first time he'd heard about it.

"He still does, as far as I know." I sighed and looked back at Nash's face, grateful that it was dark and he couldn't see my face very well. "I haven't really been in contact with him since...well, I think he stopped paying his phone bill when we moved here. The person on the other end said I had the wrong number, anyway."

Wrong-number girl strikes again.

"That sucks," Nash said, his voice rough and sympathetic. "From what you've told me, it sounded like you were close."

"We were." I blew out a deep breath, trying not to cry. "He was my best friend."

When my voice broke with those words, Nash put his arm behind me and pulled me closer.

We walked in silence for a moment, his arm still holding me against his side. But when my house came into view, I knew I needed to get myself back together so I could say goodnight without having tears in my eyes.

I used the insides of my wrists to wipe at the tears that had trickled down my cheeks. "Sorry to turn into a downer."

"You're not a downer." Nash stopped and turned so he was facing me. With a soft look in his eyes, he reached out to wipe my remaining tears away with his thumb and whispered, "You just showed me that you're a human who's dealt with hard things but has still managed to bring lightness into the world."

I smiled tentatively, letting my head lean into his hand as I searched his eyes in the darkness.

He seemed to swallow, and then he tucked the hair that had fallen from my top knot behind my ear. And when he whispered in a rough voice, "You've definitely brought a lot of happiness into my life these past couple of weeks," I felt like I might just float away and up to the stars.

When his gaze dipped down to my mouth, I suddenly found it hard to breathe.

He licked his lips. When his eyes met mine again, they had a look I hadn't seen in them before.

Excitement and nerves exploded inside me at the same time. Was he thinking about kissing me? Right here on the same path where we'd shared our first kiss?

Because the way his gaze was suddenly intense and smoldering made me wonder if he might be thinking of doing just that.

His lips parted, and when he looked at my mouth again, my heart started thrumming faster than I ever thought it could.

Is this really happening? Was Nash finally going to kiss me again?

He was just dipping his head down when an owl hooted loudly from a tree branch above us. And that dumb owl totally ruined the moment, because just as my heart felt like it might explode, Nash froze and the look in his eyes instantly shifted.

"Sorry," he said, dropping his hand from my face like I'd just burned him. "I got—" He shook his head. "I didn't realize how late it was."

Noooo! I thought. *Even if I've been up since four-thirty a.m., it could never be too late for you to kiss me.*

Don't leave yet.

But when he took a step back, I knew that the moment we'd almost had wouldn't be coming back.

So before he could bolt away, I said, "Thanks for trusting me enough to tell me about what you were going through last summer."

"You make it easy," he said. "And I promise I'm sober now. I know you've been hurt in the past by someone with a similar problem. But I don't want you to worry that it will be a constant thing with me."

"I appreciate that." I looked down at my sandals briefly before meeting his gaze again and saying, "I'll admit that when you mentioned it, my first instinct was to run."

"I get that." He nodded. "But I really am in a better place now. And while I know there will always be ups and downs in life, I've learned to stay away from certain environments that could make things harder to resist."

"Is that why you seemed uncomfortable when Miles said we could grab drinks at his party?" I asked, only just remembering the insistent way Nash had said that he didn't drink.

At the time I'd thought he might be judging me for the choices I'd made in the past, but maybe he'd just been reminding himself of the boundary he'd set for himself.

"I haven't really been in an environment where everyone is drinking since getting sober, and so, yeah, I was a little nervous."

"I wish you'd said something," I said, feeling bad he'd been in an uncomfortable position without me even knowing it. "We could have left. I mean, you knew it wasn't at the top of my list of things to do that night, right?"

"I know." He sighed and leaned against the little white picket fence that surrounded the cottage. "But I didn't want to be a party pooper."

"You wouldn't have been." I set my pool bag down on the ground since my shoulder was getting tired of holding it. "Were you uncomfortable the whole time?"

"Just at the beginning." He shrugged. "Doing the karaoke and pretending to be your boyfriend helped keep my mind off of it."

"Well, I'm glad that pretending to be my boyfriend brought you some benefits, too." I smiled.

"It would seem it was a pretty great trade off." He returned my smile and winked, which made the butterflies in my stomach come back to life. "Plus, playing a part is something that's on my pick-me-up list anyway."

"Your pick-me-up list?" I frowned, not sure what he was talking about.

He nodded. "I do best when I have something to look forward to and am active. So I have a list of quick pick-me-ups on my phone that I can tap into when I'm in a bad mood or slipping into a funk," he said. "It's something my mom recommended since her own list has helped her whenever she's depressed or anxious."

His mom dealt with anxiety and depression? For some reason, that surprised me. Mrs. Hastings always seemed so vibrant and put together.

"That's really smart."

"My mom's the smart one."

I knew it was past midnight and he'd said a minute ago that it was probably time for him to head back. But since I might literally be addicted to talking to Nash, I tried to delay his departure as long as I could by asking, "What are some of the things on your list? Do you have any of them memorized?"

I hoped he did. And that it was a really long list.

Because I could stand against my fence with him for hours and hang onto his every word.

"I have a few of them memorized," he said, his half-smile telling me he liked that I was interested in this. "So first is exercise. Those endorphins are real."

"Is that why you swim every morning?"

"It's one of the most important things for my day." He nodded. "Other things on my list are four-wheeling, playing basketball with my family and friends, and getting outside in the sun. Also, looking at old photos to bring back fun memories. Meditating. Journaling. Saying positive affirmations that I connect with. Playing with Duchess."

Duchess was their family's little dog that spent a lot of time lounging on one of the couches in their family room when I was cleaning it.

"Watching a really good movie," he continued. "Hugging someone..."

"Hugging someone?" I raised an eyebrow. "Are we talking, like, a random person on the street?"

"That would probably get me a restraining order if I just hugged people as I walked down the street." He chuckled. "Usually, it's my mom. Or Duchess. They're usually happy for a cuddle. But some of my friends are more huggy than others."

"I bet your freshman fan club was always eager to get a hug from the Casanova known as Nash Hastings."

"That is my nickname." He smirked. "But I was actually referring to my bro-cuddles with Mack and Hunter..."

I pulled my head back. "Really?"

"No." He laughed and shook his head. "We just give the three-slaps-on-the-back when we're greeting each other because we're all tough and manly like that."

"Oh you totally are."

He grinned, and I liked the way it made his eyes crinkle in the corners. "So maybe I get most of my hugs from my mom and Duchess...and yeah, my freshman friends, too."

"I knew it."

"But now that they're gone for the summer, I might have to start hugging random people on the streets for my oxytocin boost." He sighed dramatically. "My mental health is worth the possible restraining order, right?"

I imagined Nash walking down the streets of Eden Falls, giving hugs to random strangers.

I bet a lot of people actually wouldn't mind getting a hug from the most lovable son of the local billionaire.

But since not everyone had the same weakness for him as I did, I said, "If it keeps you from getting a restraining order, I could always try to fill your *freshman fan club*'s shoes."

"You think you could handle that?" he asked.

"I think so."

The way his eyes lit up made my stomach do funny things.

Did the idea of hugging each other sound as good to him as it did to me?

A huge part of me really wanted to suggest a practice hug with the excuse that we should probably make sure I knew how to fulfill my new duty.

But Nash must have been on the same wavelength because before I could figure out a normal way to say it, he took a slight step closer and asked, "Would you think I was weird if I suggest we have a practice hug right now?"

It took me a moment to loosen my tongue, since I hadn't expected to actually be on the same wavelength as him. But when I froze for too long, he added, "I was just thinking it would be good to have evidence to back up my decision to add 'hug Kiara' to my pick-me-up list."

Okay. We were literally thinking the same things.

And since I really didn't want to miss my chance, I tried to seem really chill and not at all nervous as I hurried to say, "That's a good idea. We really should have some data to back up the hypothesis."

"Someone paid attention during science class." A half-smile lifted his lips. "Are you a science nerd, Kiara?"

"That's pretty much the only thing that stuck from science class." I couldn't keep the grin from my lips because it was literally impossible not to smile when Nash was looking at me like that. Man, he was so cute. "That and the experiment where you put Mentos in Coke to make it explode."

Which was actually a good image for what was happening inside of me right now.

Since when did the idea of hugging someone make me feel so giddy?

Since I had the option to hug Nash Hastings, apparently.

"So I guess we should test that hypothesis now?" Nash took another step closer until we were nearly chest to chest.

"Y-yes, we should." I nodded and tried to keep a calm exterior as I looked up at his face.

Hopefully, he won't be able to tell how jittery I'm feeling when he hugs me.

There was a split-second where we both tried to figure out whose arms were up and whose were down, but then Nash bent forward and wrapped his arms around my torso, and I stood on my tiptoes to be tall enough to wrap my arms behind his neck.

When he pulled me close and said, "Now we just need to hold this for a few seconds to see if this is the kind of hug that could be added to my pick-me-up list," all I wanted was to melt into him forever.

He felt taller than I remembered from when we'd danced last year. Had he grown a few inches since then?

When we first started hanging out, I'd thought he might have, but having to be on my tiptoes so much told me it might be even more than I thought.

And I liked it.

Sure, it was superficial to have a height requirement for

guys you dated since how tall a person got was literally out of their control.

But ending up with a guy who was six inches taller than me was not something I would ever complain about.

Pair that with the fact that Nash had the body of a Greek god, ocean-blue eyes, and a personality that I could easily become obsessed with, he was basically perfection in human form.

He was solid and strong, and when I drew in a deep breath, I caught the scent of his cologne which still smelled amazing on his T-shirt, even when mixed with the smell of chlorine that clung to him from the swimming pool.

"Do you think this will do the job?" I asked, making myself break out of my daydreaming fantasies before he could pick up on the fact that I was not seeing him or this hug in the platonic way he probably did.

"I think so," he said. "I just need to check one more thing." Before I knew it, he was squeezing me a little tighter against his chest and playfully twisting us from side to side. Then he stood up a little straighter and loosened his embrace. "Yep. I think this might work."

"Yeah?"

He nodded. "In fact, it might be better than any of the hugs my other friends gave me."

"Even better than the little red-headed fan I saw following you around at the renaissance fair this morning?" I asked as butterflies flapped around in my belly.

He chuckled. "You saw that?"

"I might have been paying attention to your show when my booth wasn't hopping."

"Well then, yes, your hug may have been better than that." Then lowering his voice like he had a secret, he added, "But don't tell her because she traveled all the way from Maine just to see my performance."

"Really?"

"That or she came to see more of Asher and Elyse together on the stage one last time."

"Well, I'm glad my hug might make the list then."

"It's pretty much a sure thing." He chuckled. "In fact, I think this was possibly even better than the cuddles from Duchess."

"But not your mom?"

"That's still up for debate." He shrugged. "I'm a momma's boy. I can't let her feel threatened." He winked.

While some girls would probably see that as a red flag and that a guy would always be running to his mommy or having her as a third wheel in their relationship, I knew Nash and Mrs. Hastings well enough to know that they were a lot different from that.

So really, him saying that was just cute.

Though...there was part of me that hoped to find a way to make it to the top of his list someday.

"Anyway, I really better let you go now," Nash said after checking his watch. "You probably don't want to stay awake for a full twenty-four hours."

"I have been up for a long time," I admitted, feeling a yawn coming on.

Nash must have noticed how I was trying to hold back a yawn because his lips quirked up into a smile. "Have a good night, Kiara," he said in a low voice. "I'll see you soon."

"Good night, Nash."

We both waved goodbye to each other, and then he turned to head back to his house.

I watched him for a moment, committing the broad shoulders I'd just hugged to my memory. Then I lifted my pool bag back on my shoulder and walked up the porch steps and into my house. Duke was already waiting for me by the door, his black ears flopping back as he tried to jump up on me.

So I set my bag down and sat on the couch with my excited puppy. As I ran my thumb along the soft wrinkles of Duke's forehead and thought back over the night, I was reminded of what Nash had said about how doorstep scenes usually went for him after a date. How he always got super nervous when he was at the doorstep with the girls he liked.

Was that why he'd decided not to kiss me when the owl interrupted us? Had he just been nervous? Or worried it would go badly like his more recent kisses?

I hoped that was the case.

Because if it was, then maybe I just needed to make it more obvious that I liked him, too, and help him become more sure of himself.

I had always been thankful for having the ability to seem cool and calm on the outside when with a guy that I liked. You were less vulnerable to getting hurt when people didn't know how much you actually cared.

But maybe it was time for me to put myself out there a little more. To stop hiding so much and try to make something happen.

If the feelings were reciprocated, then yay, that would be awesome. I'd know the one magical night we had last summer wasn't just a fluke, a one-time thing that would have never happened if he'd known it was me.

And if I discovered that Nash really couldn't see himself ever having romantic feelings for me, at least I'd know and be able to shut that door for good and not be tempted to crack it open every time we crossed paths again.

"I'll just have to make the best of next weekend at their

beach house," I said to Duke as I rubbed the top of his head. "Think I should try that?"

Duke just looked at me with his big brown eyes, his tongue flopping out to the side as I scratched the spot behind his ear.

"I'm going to take that as a yes," I said, knowing I might be a lunatic to ask for dating advice from my pug. "But if it crashes and burns, I'm blaming you, okay?"

Duke just kept panting and enjoying the attention I was giving him.

I patted him on the head one more time and then put him back on his bed in the corner so he could get back to sleep.

I made sure the doors were locked, and before going into my room, I poked my head in my mom's door to tell her I was home for the night.

I went into my bathroom to shower off the chlorine before climbing in bed, but before I could turn on the water, my phone lit up with a notification.

@nashhastings has sent you a message.

My heart thumped against my ribcage as my mind raced over what he might have to say.

I quickly opened my notification to the message thread we'd started this afternoon and saw a new message that said, **Thanks for letting me feel safe to open up about my "stuff." I haven't really talked about it with anyone outside of my family, so it was nice to have it go so well. You're the best, and I'm glad we started hanging out.**

My chest filled with warmth. *He's glad we're hanging out.*

I'd hoped it might be the case since we'd spent so much time together lately, but it was nice to have him confirm it.

And because our feelings were definitely mutual, I

messaged him back with, **I'm glad we started hanging out, too.**

I waited a few seconds and was about to climb in the shower when he sent a photo that looked like a screenshot of the Notes app on his phone.

When I touched the screen to enlarge the photo, I saw it was his list of pick-me-ups. And right there in the middle, next to the words "hug someone," I could see that he'd added *Mom, Kiara, and Duchess give the best hugs. (Plus, Kiara already told me I could get a hug whenever I want so I can avoid getting a restraining order.)*

I laughed out loud when I read that part and got the biggest smile on my face.

@kiaramatheson: **Thanks for sending over this list. I'll have to type up a version for myself.**

@nashhastings: **Since you were so generous to let me add your name to my list, I'll be happy to return the favor and let you add my name to yours.**

A few seconds later, another message came through.

@nashhastings: **That is, only if you want. I guess you never told me if hugging me was a positive experience for you.**

Did he actually believe it would be possible for anyone to not want a hug from him?

Because I was pretty sure I would pay to hug him for an extended period of time if hugging booths were a thing like the kissing booths at the fair this weekend.

And because it was time for me to take a tiny risk, I messaged back, **It's definitely going on my list.**

28

NASH

MESSAGING Kiara about my pick-me-up list right before bed was probably the reason for my dream. Because around five-thirty in the morning, I was suddenly transported back to the night before.

The moon was high in the sky, and I was back in the hot tub after our planning session for the Hamptons had wrapped up. Everyone had vacated the pool a few minutes earlier, but I was tired after the long day and didn't have the energy to walk up to my room quite yet. So I just laid myself back and looked through the glass ceiling above me to gaze at the night sky.

The stars and moon were brighter than usual, taking on a glittering quality that was too stunning to be real. I was just trying to figure out which constellations were above me when the sound of a glass door closing startled me.

Mind if I join you? Kiara's voice sounded from above me.

I blinked my eyes, not expecting her to still be here, but then I sat up straighter and scooted over to make room as I said, *O-of course.*

She stepped down into the hot tub. As I watched her, I realized she looked different than she had earlier. Her dirty-blonde hair was still up, but the bun was messier and she had soft tendrils of hair framing her face in a way that made her look even sexier than she'd been before.

She was also wearing a different bathing suit. She no longer wore the blue floral two-piece with a high waist; instead, she sported a black one that resembled the sports bra and panties I'd seen her wearing through her window last week.

It wasn't as revealing as the bikinis a lot of the girls had worn to the beach last summer, but I kind of preferred that. It showed just enough skin to get my blood pumping but left enough mystery to pique my interest.

Basically, she looked good. Really, *really* good.

She stepped into the hot tub and took a seat next to me. When she leaned in closer to whisper something in my ear, my heart took off to the races.

So I was thinking... She scooted close enough that her chest brushed against my arm. *That for my pick-me-up list, I might want to add something a little different than hugging.*

You do? I asked, the dream version of me feeling tongue-tied and overwhelmed with anticipation over what she might be about to suggest.

Yes. She glanced down at the water before meeting my eyes with a shy look. *I remember you saying something about wanting a kissing tutor, and I figured this might be a mutually beneficial arrangement.*

Y-you do? I swallowed.

She nodded, her gaze tracking down to my lips for a second before moving up to my eyes again. *You see, dating an older guy has helped me learn a few things when it comes to kissing, and I'd be happy to teach you everything I know.*

I gulped.

Instead of adding "hug Nash" to my list, she continued, *I* would, in exchange for the lessons, be able to kiss you any time I need comfort or to feel better.

You think kissing me would make you feel better? I asked, the dream version of me doubting my little experience in that arena would draw someone as mature and experienced as her.

I think it would make me feel very good. She traced her fingers across the water droplets on my chest. *And I think it would make you feel good, too.*

I wasn't doubting that.

Do you want to have the lesson right here? I asked, already feeling slightly overheated from the hot tub and the warmth of her body next to mine.

I think it's the perfect place, she mumbled in my ear, sending chills racing down my spine. *Moving somewhere else would take too much time.* Her hand slipped across my chest and upwards until she was cradling my neck. *And with how hot you're looking right now, I don't think I can wait any longer...*

And then, she was suddenly kissing me.

Her lips were softer than I expected, and when her teeth caught on my bottom lip, goosebumps raced down my neck. Even though this was supposed to be a kissing lesson where she was teaching me how to kiss more confidently, the dream version of me apparently didn't need such lessons because I was suddenly sliding my hand along her hip and down the outside of her leg to guide her onto my lap for a closer kiss.

But since dreams didn't make sense, instead of still sitting beside me, she was suddenly on my lap with her knees straddling my hips.

My hands were on her back, my fingers digging into the skin beneath her shoulder blades and then sliding down her sides until they rested on her waist to pull her closer to me.

I've been waiting so long for this, she murmured against my lips before kissing me again. *Ever since I caught you watching me through my bedroom window.*

You saw me?

Yes. She nodded. *I was watching for you, too. I watch for you every night.* She pressed a kiss to my neck, my temple, and then my lips again. *And when you're not there, I dream about you.*

My lower belly pooled with heat, and I said, *I dream about you, too.*

The realization that I was talking about dreams within a dream jarred me, and I teetered on the edge of consciousness. But I kept my eyes shut, not wanting to give up this dream quite yet.

After a moment, I slipped back in.

I can't believe we went all this time without kissing each other, a sweet, feminine voice said.

But instead of sitting in the hot tub with Kiara, I was suddenly standing in the woods behind my house with my back against a tree and an unfamiliar girl in my arms.

A girl with long pink hair, wearing a dress like the one Elyse had worn at the fair. When I tried to pull back enough to get a look at her face, I couldn't.

How could you forget about me? she whispered in my ear. *Why don't you remember this night?*

I tried to look at her face again, but when I did, it was completely blank.

29

NASH

I WOKE UP WITH A START, my heart hammering in my chest and my bed sheets twisted around my legs.

Before I was fully awake, a series of memories started flashing through my mind.

Memories of a girl with pink hair walking through the crowd at my parents' garden party, a tray of pastries in her hand.

The way she smiled and waved at me across the yard made me feel seen for the first time all night, and I wanted to walk up to her so I could introduce myself.

Then the way my stomach twisted with nerves as I realized I wasn't nearly drunk enough to introduce myself to the most alluring girl I'd ever seen.

Another memory of me slipping into the prep kitchen when no one was looking and sneaking a few watermelon margaritas from a serving tray.

The tiny bottle of mouthwash that I always kept in my pocket and which I would quickly down so no one would notice the alcohol on my breath.

The warm, fuzzy feeling that was with me as we flirted and talked and got to know each other a little better.

The way the girl's eyes lit up when I asked her to dance on the stone path behind my house.

The moment at the end of the night when she said she needed to go home, and I didn't want to let her go. And how I'd used the liquid courage coursing through my veins to give her a goodnight kiss.

The way her soft lips had felt against mine and how I'd asked her to meet me again the next night—at the waterfall on the edge of my family's property—so we could continue to get to know each other and find a chance to further our spark.

I sat up in my bed, my skin clammy, as I realized that this dream—the flashes—were actually real.

They weren't just coming out of nowhere or made up by my vivid imagination.

My siblings had been able to walk me through the events of several nights that were just blank spots in the timeline of my life. But had this one stayed forgotten because the only other person who could remind me of it was this mystery girl?

Had I stood that beautiful girl up?

Had she gone to the falls and waited for me? Only to have me forget all about it?

I wiped a hand across my brow as I tried again to picture the girl's face. But it was still fuzzy.

Who is she?

I went for my morning swim, hoping the repetitive movement of my arms and legs would help me get back into the meditative state that might bring back more memories.

But when my laps were finished and my legs and arms were exhausted and heavy, I had no further enlightenment.

I made quick work of getting ready and had an idea to scroll back through the photo app on my phone to see if I had any with the pink-haired girl in the background of my parents' garden party. But the only photos I'd taken that whole night were the ones from before the party. Me posing in my navy-blue Armani suit that I'd quickly posted to my old social media accounts with hopes that I'd look like a thirst trap and at least get a few DMs from cute girls.

Yeah, it was a good thing I'd shut down my accounts shortly after that. Seeking constant validation for how attractive or talented strangers thought I was had not been great for my self-image.

And the things some of the internet trolls felt empowered to say from the comfort of their homes were so vicious sometimes it made me wonder how any of the other kids my age were handling the digital drug.

Maybe I'd received more attention than the regular teen, since my parents were semi-famous and people assumed the son of a billionaire could use his dad's money as an armor against the hate that was spread online.

But it definitely hadn't helped shield me. As a tradeoff for the thousands of followers that I had on my social media accounts who told me I had gorgeous eyes and they would be using my latest photo as the lock screen for their phone, I also had trolling voices pointing out the flaws keeping me from being a "perfect ten" or comparing how my brothers and I might make up the perfect specimen for a man if only we traded a few different body parts and personality traits.

Like the account some stranger had created to track the digital footprint my brothers and I had that said, "Ian has the perfect jawline and 'come have my babies' smolder. Carter's mind is sexy and at six-foot-three, he has the perfect physique. Nash has the best hair, eyes, and addictive personality."

Had it felt good to have three good traits mentioned when my brothers only had two? A little. But after the initial rush, it only made me more obsessed with making up for the ways the trolls had deemed me lacking and even more jealous of my brothers for being better in ways I couldn't compete with.

Things I couldn't even control.

And it definitely didn't help that I'd always compared myself to Carter, since we were born only seven months apart and in the same grade.

All of that became even more magnified under the microscope of social media.

I closed the photo app and tossed my phone back onto my bed, needing physical distance from the digital world to keep me from circling back to old thought patterns.

"*I am a valuable human being.*"

I started speaking my affirmations aloud.

"*I am at peace with myself.*"

"*I show up every day and do my best.*"

"*I don't need external validation to know my worth.*"

I closed my eyes as I drew in a deep breath, held it for eight seconds, and then let it out.

I couldn't always control my thoughts, but I could control the ones I focused on and the things I told myself. Thoughts created our reality, and it was important for me to remain proactive in feeding myself the type of thoughts that would be beneficial to me.

If I wanted to have a future career as an actor and open myself to public criticism again, I needed to build a thick skin and use the tools that would put me in a better place to handle the attention better than I had last year.

And yeah...probably having someone else handle social media accounts for me in the future would help, too.

I shook my head and decided I needed to get on with my day since ruminating too much on my thoughts and feelings sometimes put me in a funk. Action and forward momentum always put me in a better mood.

And I had a mystery I needed to solve.

The mystery of what happened last summer and who was the girl who kept popping up in my mind.

I grabbed a breakfast sandwich from the fridge and heated it up in the toaster oven before taking it to the table where my mom and dad were having their weekly couple's planning meeting.

I ate my breakfast silently as I listened to my parents discuss their plans for the holiday weekend. They were flying to Alaska on Friday morning and brainstorming any information they thought my siblings and I may need to know before we left the same day for the Hamptons with our friends.

"Do we really trust Ian and Owen to keep all those kids in check?" Mom asked Dad as she pulled her long, brown hair back into a ponytail. "Because I overheard him talking about the girls he's already planning to meet up with, and I'm starting to think he'll be more than a little distracted."

"So he's not dating Selma anymore?" Dad asked, his blue eyes going wide.

Selma was the model from Norway whom Ian had been lovestruck over for the past two weeks.

Mom fluffed the top of her ponytail and shook her head. "He told me they ended things on Wednesday."

Dad sighed. "I guess the apple doesn't fall too far from the tree, does it?"

As in, Ian had a lot in common with my own father who had been a walking fling before he married my mom.

Though, since Ian wasn't actually my dad's biological son—coming from my mom's first marriage—the sentiment of the apple not falling too far from the tree didn't actually really fit here.

And even then, my dad had at least had some long-term relationships during his early dating years. Ian, on the other hand, seemed to suffer from shiny-object syndrome, and I couldn't remember him dating anyone for longer than three weeks.

He loved the chase too much.

Dad rubbed the back of his neck with his hand. "Even if we can't necessarily count on Ian to act any more mature than all the eighteen-year-olds, I think we can at least rely on Owen. He's a high school teacher. He should be reliable enough to make sure there isn't too much trouble."

Mom bit her lip as she thought over my dad's assurance that Asher's older brother would make a good chaperone. Then turning to me, she asked, "What do you think, Nash? Are we incredibly naive to send our almost seventeen-year-old daughter and eighteen-year-old sons off to the beach house with their friends and significant others while we go to the opposite end of the continent?"

"I can't speak for anyone else," I said. "But I promise I'll behave."

"Oh, I'm not worried about you." Mom reached over and patted my hand. "You've always been a gentleman."

I was also one of the few people there who wouldn't have a girlfriend or boyfriend to tempt me into sneaking into a bedroom that wasn't mine...

But we didn't need to shine a light on my permanent single status.

Which reminded me.

"Hey, do you think you can make sure Regina gives Kiara the whole holiday weekend off? We were all hanging out last night and invited her to come."

"One of the girls you've been spending a lot of time with is going with you?" Mom arched an eyebrow. "Do we need to worry about you after all?"

"Nah. We're just friends." I waved my hand. "Plus, she usually dates older guys, and I don't think she's interested in me that way."

Or at least, I didn't have any concrete evidence that she was interested. My dreams weren't exactly based on reality.

Sadly.

"I can ask Regina to give all of the staff the long weekend off," Mom said. "They deserve to have a few days off like the rest of us."

"Awesome. Thanks," I said.

I took a bite of my sandwich and as I chewed, I tried to think of a way to bring up the other thing I'd been wondering about.

When my dad got up to refill his mug with coffee from the pot on the counter, I asked, "Do either of you remember any of the girls my age that came to your garden party last summer?"

"Girls your age?" My dad frowned as he poured his coffee. "I don't think so."

"What about you?" I looked back to my mom.

She pursed her lips as if trying to remember, but then she shook her head and said, "I was busy chatting with the Armstrongs or dancing with your father for most of the night, so I'm afraid I don't recall anyone specifically. Why do you ask?"

"I just remembered something from last summer that I

think might have happened during one of my well...you know..."

"During a blackout?" Mom said the word for me.

I nodded. "There was a girl wearing a renaissance dress with pink hair. Do you remember seeing anyone dressed like that?"

"Isn't that what the servers were wearing?" Dad asked my mom as he walked back to the table.

"Yes." Mom nodded. "I don't remember the pink hair specifically, but we did have the servers dress up in costumes like that. So this girl could have been one of the extra servers Regina hired for the event."

"So maybe Regina will know?" I asked, hopeful.

"I don't know if she kept that kind of record," Dad said. "But you can always ask."

It *would* be a lot to keep track of all of the servers we had at our parties.

Regina usually reached out to a local temp office with college students looking for weekend gigs, so unless the pink hair had stood out to her as much as it had to me, it would be like trying to find a needle in the haystack.

"Is there a reason why you're interested in this girl specifically?" Mom asked.

Because I think I kissed her and then left her waiting by the falls the next day.

But instead of saying that, I tried to play nonchalant and said, "Just trying to fit some puzzle pieces together."

An hour later, I was sitting on a lounge chair next to Cambrielle in the backyard, going through my texts and deleting the messages I didn't need anymore. I was about halfway through when I came to the message thread with "Wrong Number Girl" that I'd all but forgotten about.

We hadn't texted anything for a while, so I should probably just delete the thread along with her contact information.

She was fun to joke around with when I was bored, but I really didn't see a reason why I'd need to message her again.

I scrolled up through the texts and gifs we'd passed back and forth, just to see if there was anything worth saving. But it was mostly us just joking about parties we'd never sported our colorful hair at and dates we'd never actually gone on.

Wait...

I scrolled up to the top as tingles suddenly raced down my scalp.

With my hands starting to shake, I read the second text she'd ever sent me.

We do know each other. We met at a party last summer.

And then the third text.

It was a party at this really big house last summer. Near the end of July. People were dressed up in costumes.

My heart thudded against my ribcage so hard I thought it might beat out of my chest.

Was this a huge coincidence or...was this girl the one I kissed at that party?

30

NASH

SHOULD I JUST TEXT HER? I sat up straighter as I tried to figure out what my next move should be.

Should I just ask her if we'd actually met for real?

We kept making eye contact during dinner. Then when dinner ended, you found me again and we talked and danced.

"That's exactly what I remembered," I said aloud to myself after reading another text she'd sent.

She hadn't mentioned the part where I'd drank a bunch of margaritas, but those were the exact things the flashes showed me doing with the pink-haired girl.

There was another message where she'd claimed to be really tall with blue hair and a humpback. But maybe she'd just decided to say those things and pass everything off as a joke when I didn't seem to remember any of it.

If someone had no recollection of a night they spent with me, I'd probably do something similar in order to save face.

Had I given her my number that night, too? And she'd just finally decided to text me after almost a year?

Or maybe it really was a wrong number and some stranger had made up some scenarios that were very close to my real life.

Since there was only one way to know, I typed the question I needed this "Wrong Number Girl" to answer.

It was a much longer text than I usually sent, so I read it over to make sure it said what I wanted.

Hey, so this may be kind of random. But I'm wondering if what you said about meeting me at a party might actually be true. You see, my parents had a big party last summer and I forgot a lot of details from that night, thanks to some other things I had going on.

If this was just a random stranger, she didn't need to know all the details of my drunken past.

Anyway, I recently remembered meeting a girl along a path in the wooded part of my backyard and we talked for a while. When you mentioned us meeting at a party last summer, you made it sound like you were making it up completely. But...did that actually happen? Are you the girl with pink hair? Was that moment in the woods real?

Deciding that the text said what it needed to, I held my breath and hit the send button.

Then because I suddenly had too much energy pulsing through my system, I stood from the lounge chair and started pacing across my back lawn as I watched my phone screen.

Please be available. Please don't make me wait.

I was walking past our blueberry bushes for the third time when the message went from *delivered* to *read*.

My breath hitched in my chest as I waited. Then finally, after what seemed like an eternity, the three dots showed at the bottom of the screen.

I quit my pacing and stood by the blueberry bushes with my hand to my chest. The dots had stopped moving, and I worried she'd changed her mind about responding.

But then they showed up again.

Just tell me.

She needed to say something so I could breathe again.

A second later, a gray text bubble pushed up on my screen with three little but powerful words: **It was real.**

31

KIARA

WHAT DO I DO NOW? I wondered as I sat on the rocking chair on my back porch, staring at the text I'd just sent Nash.

The text that confirmed we had indeed met at the garden party.

He seemed to remember a lot more than he had last night.

Did he remember it all?

Did he remember talking and dancing and kissing?

Did he remember asking me to meet him the next day and that he'd stood me up?

I knew he remembered the renaissance dress and the pink wig from what he'd told me about his memory flashes, but did he remember more than that?

How tall I was? The color of my eyes?

Had he already figured out it was me and was just waiting for me to admit it?

The conversation dots showed up on my screen, and a second later, a text pushed through.

Nash: **Do you know who I am then? Did you know it when you texted me?**

Ahhh, what should I tell him? Do I admit to it? Make him think I'm a total stalker?

Maybe I should just feel things out a little bit. Then I'll know better how to answer.

Me: **Do you know who I am?**

I held my breath as I waited for his answer.

Did I want him to know who I was?

Would that be a good thing or a bad thing?

Would he want *me*—Kiara Matheson—to be the girl? Did he remember that night fondly—you know, now that he actually had some recollection of it?

Nash: **I asked you first.**

Ugh. Of course he'd say that.

And since it was probably obvious with everything we'd already talked about and the fact that I had his number and approached him in the first place, I texted, **I know who you are. And I knew who you were that night.**

But you didn't know who I was. That night wasn't as life-altering for you as it was for me.

He'd completely forgotten about it. Hadn't even recognized me the next day.

I'd felt so invisible.

Until last night when he'd told me the reason for his forgetfulness.

Nash: **Why wait a whole year to reach out?**

I looked up from my phone and sighed.

After watching the clouds slowly float across the bright blue sky for a moment, I decided to go with the truth.

Me: **I figured you forgot about that night, so I tried to move on. The text I sent a couple of weeks ago was meant for someone else.**

Nash: **You text random people about that night?**

Of course this didn't make sense to him.

I tried to think of how to explain.

Me: **I thought I was texting my friend and asking how her date went that night. But I accidentally sent the message to you. Once I realized I was chatting with you, I couldn't resist bringing up that night to see if you remembered me.**

I wasn't sure if I wanted him to figure out that the friend I'd tried texting had actually been on a date with him that night, since it would lead him to realizing who I was. But I was determined to be as honest as I could and hope things worked out for the best.

Please work out in my favor.

Somehow.

Nash: **Were you one of the servers that night? My parents said the servers were dressed up in those renaissance costumes.**

Me: **Yes, I was working that night.**

A minute passed and I wondered if he would say anything else, or if he'd decide to end the conversation now that he'd had his questions answered.

But then another message came through.

Nash: **I'm sorry I forgot about that night. From what I remember, I thought you were gorgeous and I had to get drunk before I could get the nerve up to talk to you. I know how stupid that was now, but I wasn't in the best place.**

He'd really been that nervous to talk to me?

I didn't love the way he'd dealt with it but hearing that he thought I was beautiful made some of the insecurities I'd felt this past year lessen.

Me: **I should probably tell you that the pink hair**

was actually a wig. So if that was your favorite thing about me, I'm afraid it's not real...

I heard a deep laugh from the Hastings' back lawn. When I stood from my rocking chair to peek around the corner of my house, I found Nash standing near their blueberry bushes with his phone in his hands.

And I felt giddy over the fact that he was smiling like that because of his conversation with me.

I stayed close to the corner of my house so I could watch him. He started typing on his phone again and my phone buzzed a moment later.

Nash: **From what I remember, I don't think I could pick just one favorite thing about you. So I think we're good.**

Me: **Well, the only thing I didn't like about you was how you forgot I existed the next day. So... yeah, thanks for remembering. You're pretty much a perfect 10 now.**

I watched Nash check my message. When his grin stretched wider than I'd ever seen it before, I suddenly wanted to send him a hundred compliments a day to keep him smiling like that all the time.

How could he ever think he wasn't anything but amazing and wonderful and everything a girl could ever dream of?

It was like what the bartender said to Topher Grace's character in my mom's favorite movie *How to Win a Date with Tad Hamilton*.

Everyone had someone who was *Tad Hamilton* to them—someone who took their breath away and made their world turn around.

And Nash was Tad Hamilton to me.

He was everything.

Nash started walking across his lawn again, moving out of my view. Even though I really wanted to walk to the other side of the house to keep looking at him, I decided to not be creepy and sat back on my rocking chair again.

Nash: **Have we met in person since that night without me knowing?**

I stared at his question, anxiety building in my chest.

Should I tell him we'd seen each other almost every day since then?

I let my fingers hover over my keypad as I tried to decide how much to reveal.

I still wasn't sure where we stood in real life. And since I was feeling just a little chicken with the prospect of spending the weekend in the same house with him and all of his friends, I decided to keep it less obvious. **I've run into you a few times since.**

Nash: **How could I have seen you again and not know who you are?**

Me: **I blend in a little better without the wig and renaissance costume.**

There was nothing super remarkable about me, really.

Nash: **I wish I remembered your face. Everything else has become more clear…but your face is still blank in my mind.**

Me: **Sounds like you're actually remembering me pretty clearly. I have a really rare genetic condition that made my face a blank slate. No eyes or nose or lips to give it any definition.**

Nash: **You have lips. I might not be able to picture them, but I recently remembered how much I enjoyed kissing them.**

Eeeeeek! I put a hand to my chest and squealed.

Then realizing Nash wasn't too far away and might have just heard me, I jumped up and ran inside the house to hide.

I took a few deep breaths, hoping to calm my racing heart, then I walked into the living room to peek through the windows and make sure my squealing hadn't just helped him figure everything out.

But when I pushed the curtains to the side, instead of walking toward my house to confront me, he was sitting on a white cushioned lounge chair next to Cambrielle.

Whew. I pressed my back against the wall, sagging with relief.

Obviously, I was *just a little* on edge now that Nash remembered that night.

And he remembered the kiss.

And liked it!

I let my head rest against the wall and squealed again.

I managed to calm down a moment later and, suddenly feeling emboldened by what Nash had said, I texted: **I enjoyed that kiss quite a bit too. Which is why I was hoping for another kiss at the falls.**

Seriously, I needed to kiss Nash again. The kiss at the baseball game wasn't nearly enough to satisfy the cravings I'd had for him this past year.

Nash: **Hopefully we'll get another chance to do that soon.**

Did that mean he wanted to meet me again?

Before I could figure out how to respond to his last message, another text came through.

Nash: **Do you think you'll ever try to meet me again? I promise I'll show up this time...**

I stared at the text. I did want to meet him again.

But how was I supposed to do that when he thought I was someone else?

Knowing I'd need a little more time to figure out how to go about this, I said, **Just don't ghost me again and we might be able to arrange something.**

Nash: **Okay. Just promise you won't keep me waiting as long as I made you wait.**

Me: **I promise.**

Just let me get through the week ahead and I will hopefully know what to do.

32

KIARA

NASH and I texted back and forth until we made ourselves go to bed at eleven forty-five on Sunday night.

This took more self-control than anyone could know. If he didn't have work early in the morning and I didn't need to be awake to clean his and his siblings' bedrooms the next day, I probably would have stayed up all night.

Because it was so fun.

We texted about the most random things: our favorite movies, foods we loved and hated, and things we had on our bucket lists. One minute we would be joking around and sharing our favorite memes, and then suddenly, the conversation would shift to more serious things like when we last cried in public and what our favorite childhood memory was.

My mom walked into the living room around five-thirty and asked why I had a permanent smile on my face all afternoon, and I just had to tell her the guy I liked had finally given me the time of day.

Nash and I texted here and there on Monday when we had

breaks during work, and the conversation was just as fun as it had been the day before.

I'd always been a sucker for movies like *You've Got Mail* where strangers fell in love through email, but I'd never expected to actually experience something similar for myself.

But yeah, if I hadn't already been head-over-heels for Nash, these few days of nonstop texting would have definitely made that happen.

I just hoped he was falling for me as much as I was falling for him.

I didn't get to see Nash on Monday or Tuesday, since I went to Addie's condo on Monday night and Nash went with his family to dinner in New York the next day. But having the constant texts almost made me feel like I was still with him.

We finally bumped into each other on Wednesday afternoon when I was vacuuming the beautiful, oriental rug in the entryway of his home. He wore a navy-blue suit that made the blue of his eyes pop, and when I saw that his tie was already loose around his neck with the top button undone to show a hint of his tanned chest, I had to work hard not to stare. Nash wearing a suit at the end of a workday might be one of my all-time favorite looks.

And even though he said he didn't want to take over the family business, I was pretty sure he needed to play the part of a hot boss or have some kind of role in a movie where he had to wear a suit like that all the time.

"Hey Kiara," he said when I switched off the vacuum to chat for a moment. "How have you been the past few days?"

"I've been good," I said. "Working a lot, as usual."

"Same," he said, gesturing to his suit. "Have you been hanging out with Alessi after work this week?"

"No. She's had work the last two nights, so I've been hanging out with Addie and Evan."

"Oh, that's good," he said. "I'm sure it's been fun catching up."

"It has been," I said. "How was d—" I started to ask how his dinner in New York had been, only to remember at the last second that it was "Wrong Number Girl" whom he'd told about that dinner and not me. So after a moment of panic, I quickly switched gears and asked, "Um, how have you been?"

Yeah, keeping track of what I was and wasn't supposed to know was going to be tricky.

At least until I figure out how to tell him that the girl he'd kissed at that party and had been constantly texting with is me.

"I've been really good, actually," he said. "It's been an eventful past few days." Then seeming to think of something else, he asked, "Hey, do you actually have a minute to chat?"

"Um, sure," I said, a flash of nerves suddenly washing over me as I wondered what he was about to ask.

Did it have anything to do with the texts we'd been sending? Had he figured things out already?

But instead of saying anything about that, he said, "Okay, so…I know you're best friends with Alessi and know her way better than me. But I guess I'm wondering if you think she'd be disappointed or upset if I just kind of stopped pursuing her since there's this other girl I'm interested in now."

"You met someone else?" I asked, hoping I sounded surprised by this.

He nodded, and a look of guilt crossed his face when he said, "Yeah." Then looking down at his shoes like he was worried I'd be upset by this, he added, "Um, like I said, it's been an eventful few days."

It was eventful because of our texts, and not because he'd hooked up with a girl in New York, right?

I pushed the thought away, telling myself to stop being so insecure. Then I said, "I'm not sure what Alessi will think. But

I'm sure she'd appreciate a conversation about it at least. Just so you're both on the same page." When he suddenly looked more nervous, I quickly added, "But I'm sure it will be fine. Alessi is always going on dates with new guys."

"Okay." He breathed out a low sigh. Then nodding, he said, "I'll probably text her later to see if we can chat."

"Sounds like a good plan," I said. "I don't think she has work today, so I'm sure she could talk tonight."

And then he would officially be unclaimed by my best friend and able to pursue me.

Once I tell him everything, that is.

Next week.

Yes, I'd tell him everything next week.

Surely I'd find a good way to go about it by then.

Nash excused himself to go upstairs, and I finished my last few minutes of vacuuming.

About an hour later, when I was loading the dishwasher after dinner with my mom, I got a text from Alessi.

Alessi: **Well, looks like Nash has moved on. I just got a text from him where he basically said he just wants to be friends.**

Me: **He broke things off through text?**

I'd thought he'd at least call her... I mean, they hadn't been officially boyfriend and girlfriend or anything like that. But still.

Alessi: **I took a shift for Natalie so I was working and couldn't answer when he called.**

Well, that was a little better.

He was probably just in a hurry to break things off and move on without any guilt hanging over his head.

Which made me feel pretty good because it meant that Nash really must be excited about me.

But since I knew it would be inappropriate to throw a party

when my friend was probably hurting, I quickly texted her back.

Me: **I'm sorry he did that. If you want, I can come hang out at your work in a bit so we can talk.**

Her message came through a moment later.

Alessi: **You're the best. But I'm actually okay. We weren't hitting it off as well as I'd hoped. But if you want to come hang out…I might have a lot to tell you about this guy I met when Miles took me to New York last weekend.**

Me: **What!? You met a guy???**

Alessi: **I did!! His name is Bash and he just graduated from NYU and he's soooooo hot. We're going to hang out again this weekend.**

Well, I guess I didn't need to feel too guilty about Nash breaking up with her then.

In true Alessi fashion, she was already five steps ahead of us all.

She sent me a photo of her and Miles standing on a street in Manhattan with a dark-haired guy with glasses and a tall, athletic build.

Me: **Wow! He is super cute! Way to go!**

Alessi: **I know! Basically, Nash has perfect timing. Now we just need to find out who this other girl is!**

Yeah…so does he.

"Nash just pulled up," Mom called from the living room on Friday morning as I was packing the last things for the Hamptons.

"I'm almost ready," I called back from the bathroom where I was grabbing my curling iron.

I didn't curl my hair super often, but Cambrielle mentioned we'd be going out most nights, so I figured I should pack a few things to make myself stand out among the crowd of other beautiful girls that might try vying for Nash's attention while we were there.

I added my makeup bag to the suitcase, grabbed my phone charger from the wall, and was just zipping up my light-pink suitcase when Nash knocked on the front door.

"Good morning, Nash," my mom said in a cheerful voice when she opened the door a second later. "Come on in."

I set my suitcase down on the floor and pulled out its handle. Then after putting my backpack over one shoulder, I wheeled my suitcase out of my room and into the living room.

"Ready to go?" Nash asked when he saw me.

"I think so." I glanced behind me just to make sure I'd grabbed everything off my bed. Then turning back to him, I asked, "Should I bring my own pillow?"

"Only if you're more partial to your own," Nash said. "But we have some pretty nice ones at the beach house and on the yacht."

"Okay, I'll just leave mine here then."

"Want me to take your things to the car for you?" he offered, stepping forward and already reaching for my backpack and suitcase.

"Uh, sure," I said, not used to having someone helping me like that. "That will be great."

I passed my things to Nash, and as he took them outside, I allowed myself to admire his broad shoulders for a moment.

Mom cleared her throat. "Do I need to worry about you going away with my boss's son this weekend?" she asked, her eyebrows raised like she'd definitely noticed the way I'd just watched Nash.

"Shhh," I whispered, looking at her with wide eyes. "He's literally right there."

Mom chuckled. "Well, you have fun this weekend, okay?" She held her arms out for a hug.

"I'll do my best," I said, going into her embrace.

I hugged her for a second then stepped away when I heard Nash shut the trunk of his car from just outside.

"Now where's my little buddy?" I glanced around for Duke so I could say goodbye to him, too. "Are you here somewhere, Duke?"

A second later, Duke came running out of my bedroom with a black piece of clothing hanging from his mouth.

"Oh no, Duke," I said, running toward him when I realized what he had stolen from my laundry basket.

But this was the little menace's favorite game to play, so instead of coming toward me and letting me steal my black bra back from him, he darted to the side and around me and then ran straight out the front door.

"Duke, come back here," I called as I chased after him. He stopped at the end of the porch and looked back at me, but as soon as I tried reaching for my bra to snatch it away, he bolted down the steps and toward the driveway at the side of the house.

Nash was just coming around from the back of his car, and when he saw me running after Duke, Nash started chasing after him, too.

Duke ran all the way around Nash's lime-green BMW with Nash jogging right behind him. As the dog circled my mom's car next, I just prayed that Nash would be so focused on grabbing Duke's chunky, fawn-colored body that he wouldn't realize what Duke was holding in his mouth.

Why hadn't I remembered to shut my bedroom door behind me? I knew Duke couldn't ever be trusted in there.

"Maybe if you go the other way we can head him off," Nash called out when Duke started his second lap around my mom's car.

"Yeah, good idea," I said.

So I turned and started running around my mom's car the opposite way. Duke came around the passenger side at the same time I did, and seeing he was about to be blocked, he turned back around to go the other way.

But Nash was right there and quickly picked up the little troublemaker before he could dart away again.

I came around the back of the car just in time to see Nash tugging on my bra to get it from Duke's locked jaw.

And man, that was not the way I imagined Nash becoming acquainted with the type of bras I wore. I thought for sure we'd at least make it to second base before that happened.

Nash was able to get my bra away from the naughty little monster after twisting it just right. But it was only after the intimate piece of clothing was in his hand that he inspected it closer and seemed to realize what he was holding.

"Um, here you go," Nash said, holding the bra out for me to take back, his cheeks flushing just a little.

"Thanks," I said, quickly taking it from his hand and folding it so it was small enough to tuck under my arm and somewhat out of sight.

Nash and I both looked at each other awkwardly for a moment, like we weren't sure what to say after the undergarment exchange. But then I held out my hands for Duke and said, "Here, I can take him inside."

Nash handed Duke over to me and I carried him back to the house, scolding him all the way up the stone path for being a naughty boy and embarrassing me.

Why'd he have to do that when Nash was here?

I dropped Duke inside the living room. When my mom looked our way, I held up my bra and said, "Nash just had to help me get this from Duke. So yeah, I might as well just die now."

Mom looked at the bra and laughed before saying, "At least it wasn't your panties?"

I shook my head as I thought about that.

"Always looking on the bright side, aren't you?" I rolled my eyes.

I took my bra back to my room and tossed it back in the laundry basket. Then after making sure my bedroom door was shut this time, I went back to the living room and said to my mom, "Have fun with the little gremlin this weekend. I'll see you in a few days."

33

KIARA

"SO DOES Duke get into trouble a lot?" Nash asked when he pulled out of our driveway a few minutes later. "Because it seems like I've seen you chasing him around the property several times since you got him."

"Yeah, he's my little terror." I shook my head. "My mom says it's like having a toddler all over again."

"How old is he?"

"He'll turn one in August."

"Oh, so he's still a puppy then." Nash pushed the button on his car visor to open the front gates as we approached them. "Duchess is seven, so she's like a middle-aged lady who likes to lie around all day."

"Yeah, not Duke. He's basically crazy all the time."

Nash pulled through the gates once they were opened. Putting his visor back up, he said, "And here I always thought pugs were lazy."

"My mom and I thought so, too," I said, thinking of the roly-poly pugs I'd seen in all the reels on Instagram. "But I guess we should have realized he'd be a terror when we rescued him from the pet store and he just ran circles around us."

"You *rescued* him from the pet store?" Nash furrowed his brow as he pulled onto the road that led out of the cul-de-sac we lived on.

"That's what we call it, anyway." I shrugged. "When we called the pet store and asked them to send us photos of the pug they had, we realized he was the same pug I'd tried to convince my mom to buy three months earlier. And once we got to the store and saw the tiny cage he'd been kept in, we just had to get him out of there."

"And now he's wild and free and stealing your underwear." Nash chuckled.

"Ah, don't remind me." I covered my face with my hands. "You really weren't supposed to see that."

"Hey, I just got to know a little more about you is all." Nash grinned. "Do you always wear black sports bras then?"

"Umm, usually..." I said, not sure why he'd said it like that. "How'd you know? Was that not the first time you've caught Duke running outside with my underthings?"

"Oh, uh." Nash's eyes widened. Then he cleared his throat and said, "I mean, no. I just...I just thought I may have seen you wearing a black sports bra some other time. Maybe when you were exercising outside?"

I furrowed my brow, confused as I tried to figure out when Nash would have seen anything like that. I didn't usually walk outside the house in my sports bras.

He seemed to notice my confusion and then said, "Oh you know what." He snapped his fingers like he'd just realized something. "I think that was just a dream I h—" He stopped and his face blanched as he shook his head. "Actually, never mind. I don't know what I'm talking about right now."

A warm feeling cascaded down my shoulders. *Did Nash have a dream about me?*

Was that what he'd almost said?

"So what made you want to get a pug, anyway?" Nash asked the question quickly, like he was trying to change the subject. "Have you always wanted one?"

"Not always," I said. "I've always thought they were cute. But it wasn't until we moved here and things got kind of rough that my mom thought it might be nice for me to have a comfort animal."

"To keep you company since it was hard to move away from your dad?" Nash guessed.

"Partly because of that," I said. "But also because of some things that were happening at school after Tristan and I broke up."

"Oh, yeah. Breakups are rough. I definitely cuddled with Duchess a lot when Elyse picked Asher over me."

"If only our breakup was the only thing that happened."

Nash glanced sideways at me with a curious expression. "There was more?"

"It's kind of a long story so I won't bore you with the details." I waved my hand like it was a trivial story.

"We have over two hours before we get to the Hamptons. Think that's long enough?"

"Probably." I sighed and tried to figure out where to start. Then I said, "So it all started a few days after I found out that Tristan already had a girlfriend. Alessi sent me a link to the Sherman High gossip page. And someone—I'm guessing it was Brooklyn or one of her friends based on what happened later on—had taken a bunch of photos of me and posted them on there with a scathing introduction post that basically called me a homewrecker."

"What?" Nash's jaw dropped as he looked at me.

"Yep," I said, exaggerating the "p" at the end of the word. "I was pretty shocked by the post at first since I really didn't even know anyone at my new school aside from Alessi."

"When was this posted? Didn't you say you and Tristan broke up during the summer?"

"We broke up in the middle of July," I said. "The post went up a few days later."

On the night of the garden party.

I studied him for a moment, wondering if my mention of the post would spark a memory of what I'd told him about it during the party. But he didn't seem to have any reaction to it, aside from surprise.

Maybe he didn't remember that part of the night? He'd said he couldn't remember my face and that his memories of that night were kind of patchy.

"You said some other things happened during the school year?" Nash asked. "Was there another post?"

I wish it had only been one. Because just *one* more post wouldn't have sent me into the depression that I'd gone into last fall.

I blew out a low breath as we passed the sign that said *Thank You for Visiting Eden Falls.* Then I turned back to Nash. "Brooklyn and her friends ended up making a whole social media account dedicated to mocking me."

"Wait. What?" Nash's voice rose in pitch.

"Yeah," I said. "The handle was @edenfallsskank, and they'd basically just take really bad photos of me during school or at The Brew. Just in really unflattering positions. And then they'd post them on this account with snarky captions." I shrugged. "It was kind of like the 'People of Walmart' pages, but just focusing on me as the star."

"I can't believe—" Nash shook his head and gripped the steering wheel tighter. "Like, why would anyone take the time to even do something like that? You literally did nothing besides date a guy you thought was single. They should have been mad at Tristan."

"I know." I held my hands out. "I still don't understand why they did it really."

"Probably because they felt threatened by you since you were the gorgeous new girl in town, and they knew a bunch of old bitties like them couldn't compare."

"I doubt that's why they did it," I said. Though it was nice to hear Nash say that I was gorgeous.

I could really use the ego boost at this point.

"I can almost guarantee that it is," he said. "I mean, I was—" He shook his head. "Um, I mean, if I was a girl, I'd be intimidated by you."

"Well, I appreciate you saying that," I said. "Whatever their reasoning, things got pretty bad." I thought back to how it had felt at the time. "So bad that after it kept happening week after week, I ended up having panic attacks every time I had to leave my house to go to school or work."

Nash turned onto I-95 which would take us to the Bridgeport-Port Jefferson ferry. We passed a semi-truck, and once we were a safer distance from it, Nash relaxed into his seat again. He asked, "Did you tell your mom or the teachers about the online bullying?"

"Not at first," I said. "I guess I kind of hoped it would stop if I ignored it. Plus, I wasn't sure exactly who was running the page at first. I had a few guesses, of course, but not enough evidence to claim I knew who was behind it."

"Did ignoring it work?"

"I wish." I sighed. "But my mom noticed me withdrawing in December and finally got me to tell her what was going on."

"And it had been going on for four or five months at this point?" Nash asked.

"Almost six months, if you count the first post in July," I said. "The posts didn't happen every day or anything, so after a while I'd start thinking that maybe they'd decided to give up. But then a week or so would go by and I'd see people whispering about me in the halls once more. And I'd know that something had been posted again."

"Geez." Nash shook his head. "I don't know how you kept going to that school. I would have begged my mom to let me transfer or go online."

"I probably should have. It would have been better for my mental health to get some distance," I said. "But growing up with my dad in the army and having the mindset that we never quit things or give up, I just didn't see it as an option."

"You're a lot stronger than me then," Nash said.

"Or just dumber."

"Definitely stronger." His eyes locked with mine momentarily, and I liked that he seemed to really believe I was strong.

I certainly hadn't felt strong at the time.

"So what did your mom do when you told her?" Nash asked. "Because I can kind of picture Regina going all gangbusters on the girls."

"She definitely went into mama-bear mode." I chuckled, remembering my mom's reaction. "She went to the school the next morning to talk to the principal, and they were able to figure out which girls were responsible for the account and suspended them."

"Only suspended?"

"For a week."

"Seriously?" His eyes widened like he thought that was a minimal punishment.

Which, compared to the emotional turmoil I'd experienced for months on end, was tiny.

"They had cheer competitions coming up and it was the middle of basketball season, and since most of the girls were involved on those teams, the school let them off easy."

"Lame."

"I know."

Nash put the top down and turned on some music after the heavier conversation was over, and I just sat back and listened to him sing along to his playlist as the wind blew through my hair.

"You have a lot of NF songs on here," I commented after he'd belted out the song "Happy."

"I listened to his music a lot last year," he said, turning the music down a little so we could talk.

"Me too," I said. "That one you sang at Miles's party was basically my anthem when I moved here."

"Really?" he asked, his eyes lighting up.

I nodded.

"Well, it looks like we were on similar wavelengths then because I basically played it on repeat all summer."

"Which is why you sang it so well."

"You thought I did okay?" he asked like he really didn't know how amazing he was.

I nodded. "It felt like we were at your private concert."

His lips quirked up into a huge smile. "Does that mean you won't mind if I belt out the next song on this playlist?"

"Is it 'The Search?'" I asked, hoping I was about to get a second performance of that song from him.

"You know it." Instead of waiting for the current song to finish playing, he tapped the next button on his dash and then turned the music up again. As Nash rapped for me, I couldn't help but feel like the luckiest girl in the whole world to be sitting in his car with him right then.

We drove onto the ferry dock a few minutes later, and once we were in our spot where we'd be parked for the hour-long ferry ride, Nash put the convertible's top back up and turned off the engine.

I'd never been on a ferry with cars before, so I wasn't sure what we were supposed to do now. But when I saw Nash move to climb out, I unbuckled and followed him up to a lounge area on the deck above.

There were various chairs up there for the passengers to sit on and relax as we floated across the seventeen-mile stretch of the Atlantic Ocean.

"Do you want something for lunch?" Nash asked when we approached the concessions area. "It's my treat."

"That would be awesome." I smiled. "Thank you."

We got in the line before it got too much longer, and I scanned down the menu for something that sounded good. We made it to the front of the line about five minutes later. After Nash ordered a BLT platter for himself, I ordered a chicken wrap and a cup of water.

"Wanna find us some seats while I wait for the food?" Nash asked when the cashier handed him the receipt.

"Sure," I said. "Do you care which level we eat on?"

"Anywhere is good for me."

"Okay, I'll look around and then message you where I end up."

I glanced around the lounge area for a bit, then deciding that fresh air and a view sounded amazing, I headed up the stairs to the top deck. I sat on a bench that faced north, since I preferred having the sun to my back and I figured it would give Nash's more sun-sensitive blue eyes a bit of a break.

Nash joined me about ten minutes later, and we ate our food as the waves rocked us back and forth.

"I'm really glad you don't get motion sickness," Nash said after swallowing a bite of his sandwich. "Because traffic would have sucked today. I guess Addison and Evan left an hour before everyone else to make sure they got to the beach house on time."

"Oh yeah. Addie gets motion sickness really bad," I said. "She only made it like five minutes the last time we went out on her dad's boat before begging him to take her back to shore."

She never would have lasted the hour-long ferry ride.

"Did you guys go boating a lot in Arizona then?" Nash furrowed his brow. "Are there many places to do that there?"

"Umm," I said, remembering too late that Nash thought Addie and I knew each other from a completely different state than we actually did. "There are a few lakes."

"Which one did you guys go boating at?"

Off the coast of Miami.

"Patagonia Lake," I said instead, since it was the lake closest to the army base I'd lived on. I hadn't actually gone boating there, but I'd heard of people doing it before.

I didn't love lying to Nash, but hopefully, he'd forgive me if he ever found out about it someday.

Hopefully, Addie would be out of danger someday and wouldn't have to hide the truth from everybody forever.

"Do you know what this reminds me of?" Nash asked when we were standing near the railing at the front of the boat a while later.

"What?" I asked, curious.

"That scene from *Titanic* where Jack helps Rose fly."

"Such a good scene," I said, thinking of the iconic scene from the movie that had launched Leonardo DiCaprio and Kate Winslet into super-stardom.

"It really is," Nash said. "If only I could have James Cameron write another scene like that and cast me as the lead someday. That would be a dream."

"That would be so cool," I said, thinking about the possibility of seeing Nash on the big screen someday. "You're definitely talented enough."

"Ah, now you're just flattering me," he said with a chuckle. "First you tell me I'm a good singer, and now you tell me I can act. What's next? I'm really good at basketball?"

"You did slam-dunk the ball in your pool last week, so..."

He smiled. "Okay, so I'm just amazing."

"You totally are."

Nash looked at the railing, and after biting his lip and thinking about something for a moment, he said, "Do you want to do something silly with me?"

"Depends on what it is," I said honestly.

"It will be fun." A charming half-smile lifted his lips. "I promise."

"Can you tell me what it is first?" I asked. Knowing Nash, he might try to rope me into doing karaoke in front of all the people on the ferry.

Which would be bad since with the way he was smiling at me, I was tempted to say yes to anything he asked.

"Okay, fine." He sighed. "So, ever since I watched *Titanic*,

I've always thought it would be fun to recreate the scene where they're at the front of the boat."

"You have?"

He nodded. "And...since I'm all about visualizing my goals, I think that if we reenact it right here, then maybe the universe will send some sort of message to James Cameron that Nash Hastings needs to be on his radar." He winked. "I mean, that's how it works, right?"

"Totally," I said. At least I hoped all the times I'd daydreamed about owning my own bakery would help make it a reality. "So you want me to pretend to be Rose and you'll be Jack?"

"Unless you prefer the gender-swap version."

"No." I chuckled. "I think we'll stick with the way it was written."

"Awesome."

I glanced around the area to make sure we didn't have too much of a crowd watching us.

I wasn't exactly ready to make an on-deck debut quite yet.

Thankfully, there was only a middle-aged couple on this end of the boat. They were both looking at their phones though, so I figured that as long as we weren't yelling or making too big of a scene, we shouldn't have an audience.

"Okay, so in the movie, Jack helps Rose step onto the bottom rung of the railing," Nash said, taking my hand and pulling me closer to the rail. "But since this is a different kind of rail, we'll just have to pretend we're doing that and keep our feet safely on the deck instead."

"I think I like that idea better, anyway." I definitely didn't want to fall overboard.

Nash guided me to the spot he wanted and stepped up behind me. Then going into character, in his best Leonardo

DiCaprio voice, he said, "Okay, now if you trust me, you can let go of the rail."

"O-okay." I doubted we were quoting the exact words Rose and Jack said in the movie, but this was more about the actions than direct quotes.

I slowly released the railing and pretended to wobble a little like Rose did in the movie, but just like Jack had done, Nash put his hands on my waist to steady me.

"Am I supposed to put my arms out now?" I asked, feeling somewhat breathless.

"I think so," he said before helping me raise my arms out like they were wings.

I looked out at the blue waves in front of us, and with the wind whipping against my face, I said, "It feels like I'm flying."

Nash chuckled near my ear, and taking a step closer, he said, "It's like you've watched *Titanic* as many times as I have."

"My mom watches it every year." I glanced back at him, meeting his eyes which were so close and so blue right now. I could only hold his gaze for a moment before I had to look back out to the ocean as I said, "I've probably seen the whole thing at least twenty times."

"Twenty times?" he asked, like he was surprised by that number. "Really?"

"Yep." I met his gaze again. "You know, except for that drawing scene that my parents always told me to cover my eyes for."

"My mom made us do that, too." Nash grinned. "I'm still not sure I've actually seen that whole scene yet."

"Me neither."

Nash looked ahead again. After seeming to think for a moment, he glanced back at me and said, "I think I'm supposed to sing a little song for the next part of our reenactment. But I don't really know what it is."

"I think 'Row, Row, Row Your Boat' might do," I suggested.

He chuckled, but then he said, "I think we'll just pretend like I did that."

"Okay." I closed my eyes for a moment and bobbed my head like I was bouncing it to the beat of a song. Then opening my eyes again, I said, "Wow, that was really good, Nash. Who knew you had such a hypnotizing voice?"

He grinned, and with a shrug, he said, "It's a gift."

He removed his hands from my waist. And just like in the movie, he entwined his fingers with mine and slowly moved my hands down until they rested on my stomach.

As his arms tightened their embrace, my heart suddenly raced as I remembered what happened next in the movie.

This was when Jack and Rose would have their iconic kiss.

Nash took a step closer and pulled me more snugly against him, so his chest was pressed against my back. But instead of continuing the reenactment we'd been doing, he rested his chin on my shoulder and looked straight ahead instead.

"Isn't the water so beautiful?" he asked in a soft voice that made my insides twist in knots.

"It is," I managed to say, even though I was practically on the verge of a heart attack from having Nash so close. "It reminds me of home."

"Did you go to the beach a lot in Florida?" he asked, looking at me.

"Every chance I could."

Nash turned his gaze back to the water again, and I tried my best to get my heart rate and breathing under control. He was so close that it had to be impossible for him not to notice how shallow my breaths were.

And since I could feel my heart beating everywhere, it was also likely that he could feel it, too.

Around my waist where his arms still embraced me.

Or where his cheek rested against mine.

He tilted his face toward my neck, and after seeming to breathe me in, he said, "You smell really good."

"Th-thank you." My voice was coming out all breathy.

When the tip of his nose brushed against my jawline, the hair on my head stood on end and tingles immediately raced down my neck.

What was happening?

Was Nash planning to finish the scene we'd started?

Was that something we could do?

I looked at him from the corner of my eye. His gaze traveled from my collarbone to my jaw and farther up until our eyes locked, and there was a heated look in his dazzling blues that I hadn't seen before.

And even though I was scared to death that I might be reading the signs all wrong, I knew that if I let this moment pass without taking a chance, I would regret it.

And I didn't want to have any more regrets where Nash was concerned.

So digging deep for some courage and pushing down the fear building inside my chest, I leaned my head farther back and whispered, "Should we finish the scene?"

I might have just been seeing what I wanted to, but it seemed like a hint of desire sparked in Nash's eyes at my suggestion. His gaze darted down to my lips. After a moment where I held my breath and thought I might faint, he nodded and mumbled, "It's only right that we finish what we've started."

His gaze met mine one more time as if he was checking to make sure I was really okay doing this. Then he slipped his hand to the nape of my neck and pulled my face closer to his.

And the instant our lips touched, I melted.

His lips were so soft, the kiss careful and slow. When his

hand that still rested around my waist squeezed me tighter, my lower belly clenched and jumped at the same time.

He kissed me again, and I turned around in his arms, stumbling into him a little because I was suddenly lightheaded and dizzy at the same time. As our lips melded and moved together, I let my fingers comb into the soft hair I'd been watching him comb his fingers through all summer.

I'm kissing Nash! I squealed in my head.

Holding him.

And he was kissing me back.

And it was such a good kiss.

Not too fast. Not too slow.

Just right.

So very right that I wished I'd been brave enough to make this happen sooner.

"I've been waiting so long for this," I mumbled, unable to keep a smile from my lips.

But something about those words seemed to jar him because he suddenly froze. When I opened my eyes to see what had startled him, his eyes had gone wide and he had a look of horror on his face.

When he lifted his hands in the air and took a step back like I had a communicable disease, a feeling of dread coursed over me.

"Sorry," he said, "I-I don't know what I was doing. I—we shouldn't have—" He shook his head. "We shouldn't have kissed. That shouldn't have happened."

"Wha—?" I started to say, but the word got stuck in my throat because I literally couldn't comprehend what was happening right now.

Was this real?

Or had I somehow slipped into a nightmare?

Why was Nash looking at me like I'd just made him commit a crime?

He must have seen the confusion on my face because he said, "I like someone else. I'm sorry if I gave you the wrong idea and made you think—" He shook his head like he needed to start over.

Please start over.

Please go back to thirty seconds ago when you were kissing me, and I thought you wanted it as much as I did.

But then he said, "Did you think I was talking about you when I told you about another girl being the reason I needed to break things off with Alessi? Because I know we kind of had a moment by your house Saturday night, but...I was actually talking about someone else..."

I wanted to die. I wanted to jump off the side of the boat right now and die in a watery grave like the people in *Titanic*.

But, of course, my legs were suddenly made of cement, and I couldn't do anything except stare stupidly at Nash as he continued to explain why he would never in a million years want to kiss someone like me.

"I mean, I think you're great and everything and we have a ton of fun together..." he said. "But I—I've already fallen for someone else. And—"

"It's cool," I said, cutting him off when my tongue finally decided to work. "Of course you weren't talking about me. I just got caught up in the moment."

"Oh good," he said.

He looked like he was going to say more, but since I literally couldn't stand here a second longer and listen to all my hopes and dreams regarding Nash and me being crushed to teeny tiny pieces and thrown into a garbage disposal, I ran.

I ran away from Nash and straight for the stairs, and when I got down to the next level, I did everything I could to keep the tears from escaping out my eyes as I searched desperately for a dark corner or a private bathroom where I could hide.

I saw a restroom sign across the way, and when I heard Nash call out, "Kiara, wait!" from the top of the stairs, I darted toward that bathroom like my life and dignity depended on it.

The door on the last stall opened as soon as I walked in there, and even though there were two other women waiting in line, I rushed past them and locked myself in the stall.

And then, with my hand clutched to my chest like it might keep it from ripping apart, I finally let out a loud sob.

34

KIARA

I STAYED in the bathroom stall for the rest of the ferry ride. When a voice came over the speaker system to announce that we had arrived at Port Jefferson and could return to our vehicles, it was the last thing I wanted to do.

Maybe I could call Addie and see if she and Evan could pick me up at the port and take me home?

But when I walked out of the bathroom, Nash was standing right there.

"We should probably get to my car," he said, the look of guilt on his face telling me my puffy, red eyes were as obvious to him as they were to me.

Yay. And now he knows I was in there crying.

Not that he probably hadn't already guessed that from how I'd run away from him earlier.

We drove in silence for the next hour: Nash looking ahead at the road and traffic, me staring out the passenger window, wishing I could disappear into oblivion.

But when the GPS on the car's dash showed that we'd arrive at the beach house in three minutes, Nash said, "I really am sorry about earlier. I shouldn't have suggested we reenact that scene."

"It's fine," I said quickly, hoping he'd just drop it.

But he apparently thought I needed more closure than that because he continued by saying, "I know things were kind of shifting in our friendship and we've been spending a lot of time together lately. Which has been really fun." He glanced away from the road to look at me briefly. "I've really had so much fun with you, Kiara. But..."

Of course there's a "but."

"But I actually met this other girl last summer in a really cool way and we recently reconnected and..." He sighed, like he didn't actually want to continue. But then he said, "And I really like her. It probably doesn't make sense to you, but I just feel like there's something special about her and she wouldn't have come back into my life again if it wasn't for a reason."

He cleared his throat like he was preparing to tell me even more reasons why he couldn't date me.

Which yes, I understood that this *other girl* he was talking about was actually me.

And that he was telling me all of this because of the very real interaction we'd had last summer and the text conversations we'd had since then.

All the things that had made me fall for him, too.

But since he knew me in real life and decided I wasn't worth pursuing because of this fictional version he'd hyped up in his head...everything he was saying was just a big ol' slap in the face.

He really must have filled the blank spots in his memory of me with a supermodel or something.

And I couldn't compete with a fantasy like that.

I hadn't even been able to compete with Brooklyn West.

Because just like with Tristan, I still wasn't the type of girl the guy I liked wanted. Not when he could have someone else.

I wasn't even good enough for my dad to try and get sober.

Or heck, even call on my birthday when my grandma said she'd helped him get a new number.

Maybe I was being overdramatic about everything, but was it so bad that I wanted someone to choose me for a change?

Choose the real me who was standing right in front of them over a partially made-up daydream?

"I hope things won't be weird between us this weekend," Nash continued when I didn't say anything, like he felt the need to fill the silence now that he'd broken it. "Because I really want to be friends. I think we'd make better friends in the long run, anyway. This girl is just..." He paused, as if he needed to think about how to describe this dreamed-up version of myself to me. "She's just the type of girl that only comes around once in a while and I need to see it through."

So basically I, Kiara Matheson, was chopped liver. And this other girl was a goddess.

I got it.

How disappointed he would be when he discovered that Wrong Number Girl was chopped liver, too.

Nash turned onto a private driveway surrounded by tall shrubs a minute later, and we were soon parking in front of a sprawling, three-story, shingle-style beach house.

If I hadn't just had all of my confidence crushed by Nash, I might have asked him to tell me more about the house and if they had a separate staff to maintain the mansion while they were away. But since I literally didn't know if I could ever speak to him, let alone face him again after today, I just gawked at the gorgeous behemoth before me and prayed my bedroom would be on the opposite end of the house from Nash.

Best-case scenario would be that I slept in the west wing and he slept in the east wing, and I wouldn't have to face him the whole time we were here.

So as soon as Nash popped the trunk, I grabbed my backpack and wheeled my suitcase to the front door.

"You can just walk inside," Nash called after me when he saw me waiting on the front porch. "I think most everyone is already in there."

I pressed the button on the handle down with my thumb and pushed the huge door open. And yes, just taking two steps inside I could already tell that this house was just as impressive as the Hastings' mansion in Eden Falls.

Only, instead of having modern traditional decor like that one, this house was decorated in whites and blues to fit the coastal vibe.

Addie and Evan were seated on a white couch with light-blue pillows in a sitting room just to the right of the entryway. My eyes must have still been puffy or something even after the hour drive because as soon as Addie looked my way, she instantly jumped up from the couch and rushed toward me.

"What happened?" she asked, her voice laced with worry. "Are you hurt? Did something happen on your way here?"

Something happened all right.

But since I didn't trust my voice and I didn't want everyone else coming in here and seeing me like this, I just asked, "Can you take me to our room, please?"

"Of course." She nodded. "Let's get you upstairs."

She took my suitcase from me. After glancing at Nash who had just walked through the door and giving him a confused expression, Addie led me up the staircase to the left.

I barely saw the hall as we walked down it, but I was sure it was beautiful like everything else the Hastings' family owned.

Addie led me through a white door at the end of the hall. Once we were inside, she shut the door.

"What happened, Kiara?" she asked, her blue eyes filled with empathy. And it was that look from my friend that had my emotions bubbling right back up to the top again.

"It's so humiliating," I whispered, my voice shaking. "Like, I literally can't face Nash ever again."

She frowned like she didn't understand. "Why can't you face him?"

"Because—" I shook my head and felt tears welling in my eyes again. "He doesn't want me. I kissed him and..." I sighed and covered my face with my hands. "I kissed him, but he told me he doesn't like me like that." And with those last words, the sobs I'd been trying to keep inside this past hour broke free.

"He doesn't want you?" she asked, her voice tinged with confusion. "Did you tell him that you're the girl he's been texting then? And he felt betrayed or something?"

"No, that's not it." I looked back at my friend through my tears. "He doesn't know that part. I didn't—" I sighed. "I couldn't tell him."

"So he still thinks he met some other girl last summer?"

I nodded.

"Then why don't you tell him the truth? Wouldn't that make everything better?"

"Not when he only sees me as a *friend*." A bitter laugh escaped my lips. "You should have heard him, Addie. The things he was saying about this fantasy version of me in his head. She's perfect. Gorgeous. Fun. They have this wild connection that only comes around once in a lifetime."

"He thinks all those things because of you, though," Addie

said, not seeming to understand how it had felt to have the guy I'd crushed on for over a year reject me to my face.

Not two seconds after an earth-shattering kiss.

So I told her everything he'd said on the boat and then just barely in his car.

"He doesn't see me as girlfriend material," I continued. "He likes the fantasy version in his head, but he doesn't like the real me that was standing right there in front of him." I was quiet for a second as I thought. Then in a more subdued voice, I said, "I couldn't tell him the truth and have him reject me all over again. My heart just can't take another blow like that after everything that's happened this year."

I couldn't have Nash reject me at the same level that my dad and Tristan had.

Because at least without telling Nash everything, I could cling to the glimmer of hope that maybe he would have wanted me if only he'd known.

Because even after everything, I still wanted to tell myself that fairytale.

Addie stepped closer. "But he likes you, Kiara." Her eyes searched mine, a glimmer of determination shining through. "Maybe he doesn't recognize the amazing girl living right under his nose all this time because you haven't given him the opportunity to truly see you." She took my shoulders in her hands and looked into my eyes with an intensity I didn't usually see in Addie. "He deserves to see the confident girl I knew back in Florida. The one who had all the boys tripping over themselves to get to her."

"But what if I'm not that girl anymore?" I murmured, a surge of pain and vulnerability coursing through me. "What if I've changed too much? What if too much has broken me down that I can't be that girl again?"

"You're amazing, Kiara." Addie cupped my face in her

hands, her thumb caressing my cheek. "I know I've lied about a lot of things this past year, but I'm not lying about this." Her eyes held a depth of understanding that pierced through the walls I had built around myself. "You're my best friend. You're beautiful, smart, talented, a hard worker, reliable, fun." She pressed her lips together as she let those words sink in. Then with a faint smile, she said, "You're one of the best people I know. And yes, I don't know everything that's happened to you this year—the things that have made you afraid to shine like the sun. But I know all the things I love about you are still in there. And if you really care about Nash as much as you say you do, then he deserves to know what he's missing out on by chasing after some fantasy girl he's cooked up in his mind."

"But how do I do that?" I asked, a flicker of hope struggling to break free from the chains of self-doubt.

"You *show* him." Her voice was firm, her gaze unwavering as it locked with mine. "You can lick your wounds this afternoon. But tonight, when we all go out, you're going to get all dressed up and show Nash exactly what a powerful and beautiful woman Kiara Matheson is. You're going to do exactly what Nash *thinks* he wants—treat him like a platonic friend—and then you'll have the time of your life dancing and talking with other guys."

"I have to dance with other guys tonight?" I asked, the thought making me want to bolt.

"Yes." She nodded. "The hottest, most confident guys there."

"So you want me to play the jealousy game?" I asked, not sure this was a good idea.

"I just want you to go out and have a good time tonight," Addie said. "If Nash gets jealous, then I guess that's his problem."

35

NASH

I STOOD on the edge of the club's dance floor on Friday night, fatigue seeping into my bones after an unexpectedly emotional day. Going out and dancing with strangers was the last thing I wanted to do after the awkward interaction with Kiara this afternoon. But since Cambrielle and Ava had basically dragged me out to Mack's SUV earlier and promised we'd have a good time, here I was.

Was I having a good time so far tonight?

Not exactly. But thankfully, dinner hadn't been as awkward as I'd expected. Kiara had sat at the opposite end of the table from me, but at least she'd seemed to be in better spirits while talking with Addison and Evan.

So that made me feel slightly better.

Maybe she'd just had other things going on this afternoon and the emotional reaction had nothing to do with me or anything I'd said after that kiss.

It definitely wouldn't be the first time I'd interpreted something wrong with a girl.

"Thinking about asking someone to dance?" Evan asked, coming up to my side with a glass of water in his hand.

"Not really," I said, wondering if I'd looked like I had been watching someone when I'd actually just been lost in my thoughts. "I have a headache so I'm not really feeling up to it. What about you?"

"I'm not really feeling it, either," he said. Then gesturing at the dance floor with his hand, he added, "But it looks like Kiara and Addie are having a blast."

I looked in the direction he'd pointed and right there in the middle of a group of college-aged guys were Kiara and Addison. They were dancing to the beat with huge smiles on their lips, appearing to be having the time of their lives.

"Looks like they're having enough fun for the both of us," I said.

"Addie has certainly found her element," Evan said. But from the look on Evan's face as he watched his stepsister dance with another guy, I got the feeling that he wasn't a fan of the attention she was getting.

Was that just his overprotective-brother side kicking in?

Or was there something else going on there?

I definitely had my overprotective-brother moments with Cambrielle...but I didn't think I'd ever looked at her the way Evan was watching Addison.

Like, if the guy she was dancing with so much as let his hand slip an inch lower on her waist he would go off on him.

"Do you think Addison likes that guy?" I asked Evan, hoping it would help me figure their weird dynamic out. "Is he her type?"

"I don't know," Evan said, his gaze still intense as he watched Addison and her dance partner. "She told me that she and Kiara were planning to dance with as many guys as they could tonight, so he's probably just the first of many." He watched both girls for a moment, then nodding toward Kiara, he asked, "You've been hanging out with Kiara a lot lately, though. Did she ever tell you what her type was?"

"Tall. Dark hair. A few years older," I said, remembering what she'd told me in the past.

"So just like the guy she's dancing with?" Evan raised an eyebrow.

I studied the guy who currently had his hands on Kiara's waist as they danced to the beat. He had black hair, was one of the taller guys on the floor, and from the scruff on his face, he was definitely a few years older than us.

So maybe she really had just gotten caught up in the *Titanic* scene, too. Maybe I'd been projecting my own feelings onto her because I'd felt some sparks during that kiss. Maybe she'd felt nothing, and she'd actually been telling me the truth when she said we were cool.

And the reason I'd heard her crying in the ferry's bathroom was because...?

Well, I didn't know. The timing and circumstances had pointed to what had happened after the kiss. But who knows, maybe it had nothing to do with me. Girls had their own sets of hormones that I couldn't even begin to understand.

Living with my mom and Cambrielle had taught me that there were some days where certain things just didn't make sense to my male mind.

"I think I'm gonna grab a table for when everyone wants a break from dancing," I said to Evan, deciding I might need to put Kiara out of sight so I could stop ruminating on where we currently stood. "You can join me if you don't feel like standing all night."

"Thanks," Evan said, pulling his gaze from Addison for a moment. "But I think I'll stay here to keep an eye on Addie for now."

"Okay." I shrugged. If he was going for the most-overprotective-brother award tonight, I wouldn't interfere.

There was a small group of people standing up from a table close by, so I waited a moment for them to clear out. Once they were gone, I sat in the seat farthest from the dance floor but where I could still watch what was happening out there.

When a waitress came by, I asked her to wipe the table down and clear off the glasses the other people had left. After she was done and asked if I needed anything else, I had her bring me a virgin margarita for myself and a few waters for when my friends needed some hydration after all their dancing.

Just because I didn't drink alcohol these days didn't mean I couldn't still enjoy the citrusy drink with a salt-rimmed glass.

The drinks came a few minutes later, and as I lifted the margarita glass to my lips, they puckered just thinking about the taste.

And it was good. Slightly different from the alcoholic ones I'd charmed a college-aged girl into buying me last summer when I'd come here with my friends, but still a refreshing drink.

And hey, by the time morning came, I wouldn't have a hangover or blank spots in my memory.

Yay for sobriety.

I sipped on my drink as I watched the people on the dance floor for a few minutes, then I pulled out my phone to see if Wrong Number Girl had responded to the text I'd sent her this afternoon.

But when I opened our text thread, the last message in there was the one from me that said: **I hope you have a great weekend. It's been an eventful day so far with some tricky conversations. I'd love to chat about it with you if you have the time.**

The text was still marked as *delivered* but not *read*, so she was probably just busy.

Still, it was a bit weird to not hear back yet because she had always been really quick to respond before.

Hunter and Scarlett dropped by the table a little while later and brought me up to speed on what they'd been doing in New York the past few weeks.

"I've been staying at my mom's for the most part, since things are still a bit tricky with my dad," Scarlett said.

Her dad was the pastor of a church in the heart of New York, and it had taken some pretty crazy stuff happening to get him to accept that Scarlett and Hunter were going to date whether he liked it or not.

"But since my mom's place is in the same building as Hunter's family," she continued, "it's actually pretty great."

"So no secret rooftop rendezvous anymore?" I asked, remembering what Scarlett had once told me about the secret make-out spot they'd often escaped to the first time they'd started dating.

"Oh, we still go up to the rooftop a lot." Hunter chuckled, his eyes lighting up. "Gotta keep things exciting."

"Of course." I laughed.

Maybe Wrong Number Girl and I needed a secret rooftop of our own.

Or a waterfall...

I knew she'd said she wouldn't make me wait a whole year to meet up with me and tell me who she was. But if I was going to have to keep running into Kiara, she was eventually going to notice if this girl I'd told her about didn't ever materialize.

And then she'd think I had been making the story up to get out of an uncomfortable situation.

So when Scarlett stood and pulled Hunter back onto the dance floor, I texted Wrong Number Girl again.

Do you think you're any closer to letting me meet you? I'd love to finally put a face and voice to the girl currently known as Wrong Number Girl.

I watched my phone for the next minute or two, hoping the text would go from *delivered* to *read* this time. But when a new song started playing through the speakers and it still hadn't changed, I put my phone back in my pocket and tried not to think that I'd just made a mess of everything with Kiara for a girl who didn't actually exist.

Hopefully, this wasn't actually some kind of prank.

The night dragged on, and even though I really shouldn't have been paying attention to Kiara, I'd noticed that just as Evan had predicted, she had gone from one dance partner to the next, each guy seemingly more attractive or muscular than the last.

And yep, they all had dark hair, too.

She really does have a type, doesn't she?

Not that I cared.

That much.

I shook my head and told myself to stop watching her as she laughed and danced, but regardless of what I'd told her earlier today and what I'd been telling myself all night, I couldn't seem to look away.

"Why don't you just ask her to dance?" Cambrielle asked a while later after apparently noticing my interest in our neighbor. "It has to be better than just staring at her and those guys with that irritated expression you've been wearing all night."

"I don't want to dance with her," I said, the words sounding unconvincing to my own ears.

"Do you think she'll say no?" Cambrielle asked. "Is that why you've been pouting at this table all night?"

"No," I said. But since that too sounded unconvincing, I added, "I have a headache and just don't feel like dancing."

"I'm sorry you have a headache," Cambrielle said, seeming to decide not to poke the bear.

I checked the time on my watch. It was a few minutes past eleven, so I asked, "When do you think everyone will be ready to leave?"

"Not sure." Cambrielle shrugged. "Probably when they're tired of dancing."

"So when they kick us out at, like, two?" I asked.

"I'm pretty sure that's what Ava was planning on at least," Cambrielle said.

I sighed. "Well, maybe I should just get an Uber."

"Just stay until midnight, okay?" Cambrielle said. "I'm sure a few of us will be ready to go home by then."

"Okay."

I glanced back at Kiara—out of habit, *apparently*. And when the guy she was dancing with slipped his hands just a little too low on her butt and a sudden look of discomfort crossed her face, I leaned close to Cambrielle and asked, "Do you think she's trying to get away from that guy?"

Cambrielle narrowed her eyes and looked in the direction I was pointing. When the guy forced Kiara's hips closer to his, her look of discomfort turned to panic as she tried to put more space between them but couldn't.

"Yes, she needs help," Cambrielle said. "Let me get Mack or Evan..." Like it would take the biggest guys in our group to save Kiara.

But instead of wasting time waiting for Mack to come back from the bathroom or for Cambrielle to find Evan, I scooted my chair away from the table and said, "I've got this." I was two steps away before I turned back and added, "But if that guy starts beating me up, please send Evan over to save me."

As I strode toward them, I tried to figure out the best way to go about this. I'd never been very intimidating or one to pick fights—my previous rivalry with Asher had always involved words more than anything physical.

Could I just slide in between Mr. Handsy and Kiara like I was there to steal a dance and hope this guy would back off?

Should I offer him money to leave her alone?

Or would bringing back the charade Kiara and I had already used a couple of times this summer work? If I pretended she was my girlfriend and that I was just late getting here, would the guy believe it?

I was only a few feet away now and no other brilliant ideas seemed to be coming my way, so I decided that was probably my best plan.

This could totally backfire on me, I thought to myself, as the anxiety bubbling up in my stomach became more intense with each step.

The guy could get aggressive, or Kiara could look at me like I was insane for assuming she'd prefer my company to this guy's after everything that had gone down today.

But when Mr. Handsy started grinding on her and she glanced around like she didn't know what to do, I knew I had to at least try to help.

"Hey babe," I said, stepping right next to Kiara and tapping her on the shoulder. "Sorry I'm so late. Traffic was a nightmare."

Kiara and the guy both looked at me, and for a few gut-wrenching seconds I worried I had read everything wrong from across the room and that Kiara was going to tell me to leave her alone. But after the initial confusion, her expression turned to one of relief and she said, "You finally made it!"

And the guy was surprised enough by my sudden appearance that the grip he'd had on her loosened so that she was able to get away from his grasp and jump into my arms for a hug.

I was just hugging her back and trying to figure out what I was supposed to do next when Mr. Handsy seemed to realize what was going on. Then with a baffled look, he said to Kiara, "Wait, you have a boyfriend?"

Kiara looked back at the guy, still keeping her arms wrapped behind my neck like I was her lifeline as she said, "Yeah, sorry. I-I thought you saw my ring."

Her hands moved behind my neck like she was adjusting something in them. A second later she held her left hand out to the guy and said, "He's actually my fiancé. We just got engaged so it's kind of new."

The guy looked at the sparkly ring that she must have just swapped onto her left ring finger. Then he put his hands out to his sides, like he felt guilty for feeling up another guy's fiancé against her will, and said, "Sorry I didn't pay closer attention. Uh..." He shook his head, looking somewhat dazed. "Congrats on your engagement."

"Thank you," Kiara said, the cheerfulness in her voice sounding somewhat forced to my ears. "Thanks for keeping me company while I waited for him to get here."

The guy nodded, still acting confused by the recent turn of events. But thankfully, he didn't seem to want any drama and stepped away to search for another dance partner.

"Thank you." Kiara sighed, her body going slack with relief once the guy had gone. "I was kind of panicking there for a minute."

"I'm glad I noticed what was happening and could help," I said, rubbing her back to comfort her. Then after a beat, I added, "Good thinking with the engagement ring, by the way. I think that really helped sell the story."

"I'm just glad he bought it." She shook her head, like she

was still in shock. "And glad the ring my dad got me for my sixteenth birthday could pass for an engagement ring."

"Your dad got that for you?" I took her left hand in mine to inspect the ring more closely. It was silver with several little diamonds encrusted in the band.

"I don't know if the diamonds are real or anything." She shrugged; her expression suddenly self-conscious. "But diamonds are my birthstone, so he thought I should have sixteen diamonds for my sixteenth birthday."

"Oh that's perfect," I said, thinking how the dad she had so many good experiences with sounded so different from the one she was now estranged from. How confusing that must be.

"I thought so." She shrugged and let her hand drop back down to her side when I released it.

And when a sudden sadness seemed to sweep over her, I wanted to take it away from her.

She said she hadn't had contact with her dad in a year. That she didn't even have a way to contact him anymore.

That sucked.

But since I didn't want her dwelling on sad things right now, I asked, "What month were you born then?" I'd only ever paid attention to my own birthstone—which was emerald for May.

"April."

"You're older than me?" I raised my eyebrows, surprised.

"I guess."

When I met her brown-eyed gaze again, I suddenly remembered where we were. And I realized that just because she was happy to get away from that guy, it didn't necessarily mean she wanted to stand here and chat with me. So I cleared my throat and said, "I should probably let you get back to your night."

"Wait." She reached for my arm when I took a step away. "Aren't you going to dance with me?"

"Y-you want to dance with me?" I asked, a swell of nerves suddenly filling my stomach again.

"We just told that guy we're engaged." Her gaze darted to Mr. Handsy who was watching from the edge of the dance floor with Evan suddenly standing close by. "Don't you think it would look weird if we didn't?"

"Yeah, I guess you're right..." I rubbed the back of my neck. "So, uh, you don't mind dancing with me after all the stupid things I said earlier?"

"If I could sit in the car with you for an hour after all that, I think I can get through a few dances."

My cheeks burned at the way she said that. And because I really did regret how things had gone, I said, "I'm sorry I acted like an idiot. I shouldn't have assumed you wanted that kiss to mean anything. I think it just surprised me and I didn't know what to do."

"Are we really going to talk about it again?" she asked, her voice and eyes wary.

"No, sorry." I shook my head. "I think we should just dance and then never talk about that again."

"Deal."

36

NASH

THE NEXT DAY, as we all gathered near the back gate that would lead us to the beach where we'd be attending a bonfire, my eyes couldn't help but be drawn to Kiara as she walked across the grass. She wore a red top with white shorts today, and with the way her curls bounced in the light breeze and how the setting sun glinted in her beautiful amber eyes, I had to admit that she looked absolutely stunning.

She sent a shy glance my way as Addison pulled her through the gate, and as my gaze followed her, memories of dancing with her last night flitted through my mind.

How was it possible that a day that had gone so wrong could suddenly shift into a magical night, all from a few dances with a beautiful girl?

I followed behind Kiara and Addison to the sandy beach below. When I caught a whiff of Kiara's familiar perfume in the air, I couldn't help but remember the way it had felt to hold her in my arms for those few dances. Or how the warmth of her cheek pressed against mine had felt so right—bringing almost a sense of déjà vu with it.

"Think you'll actually enjoy this party tonight?" Cambrielle asked when she and Mack stepped up beside me as we walked across the sand on our family's private beach. "Or are you planning to sit out on all the fun again like you did last night?"

"I'm not sure," I said, glancing at the group of people already gathered on the beach behind Ky Miller's house. Ky was a famous pop star who had bought a beach house a couple of plots down from ours last year. "I don't have a headache at least, so hopefully, I'll be more fun."

My sister smiled. "That's good to hear."

Though, since I'd seemingly swapped a headache for confusion, how much fun I'd be able to have tonight was all still up in the air, really.

Had I been wrong about which girl to pursue? Had I been completely stupid to tell Kiara that the girl I'd only met once last summer was the one I wanted, when the connection we shared was still very much there?

When the attraction I felt for Kiara was at a level I wasn't sure I'd ever experienced before?

I sighed and shook my head. Had I just gotten wrapped up in the idea of a crazy cool love story with a mystery girl that I'd ruined my chances with a girl who was actually real?

A girl who had been living in my backyard this whole time?

The girl you met last summer is real, too, the confusing voice in my head told me. *Just because she hasn't texted you in two days doesn't mean she doesn't exist.*

Ugh. Why did this have to be so confusing? Why wasn't there a guidebook to this kind of thing?

We were about ten yards away from the group of people who were already standing around the fire pit when Asher seemed to recognize two guys with identical faces and statures pretty similar to his. Asher started running across the sand, yelling, "Logan? Jace? What the heck are you two doing here?"

And when the twins both looked our way, I recognized them as the cousins Asher was with at the debutante ball we'd all attended in December.

"You guys all know my cousins Jace and Logan, right?" Asher said to our group after giving his cousins each a hug.

"How could I forget Elyse's first boyfriend?" Ava said, a smirk on her lips as she walked toward the twin on the left to give him a hug. "It's good to see you again, Logan," she said. Then moving to the next twin and giving him a hug, she said, "Good to see you, too, Jace."

The twins both nodded and seemed happy to see Ava who, now that I was piecing things together, had probably gone to school with Asher's cousins in Ridgewater, New York before moving to Eden Falls this past year.

Then Elyse went to greet the twins as well. With the Cohen twins coming face to face with Asher's twin cousins, it really was like seeing double.

Now that was kind of freaky. Two sets of identical twins standing side by side.

"Do you guys know Ky Miller then?" Asher asked, nodding toward the blond-haired, blue-eyed singer who was chatting with a few people on the opposite end of the fire pit from us.

"We met him when we came here last summer," Jace said. "Our grandma's beach house is right next to his."

"Oh cool," Asher said, his gaze following Jace's hand that gestured at the blue-and-white beach house to the right of Ky's white one.

"Yeah," Logan said, putting his arm over Asher's shoulder. "It's so crazy you're here this weekend, too."

Asher introduced the rest of us to his cousins, and after we were all acquainted with one another, he and Elyse followed

Jace and Logan to the other side of the fire pit where the twins' girlfriends—a blonde and brunette—were sitting on beach chairs.

"I heard that you're the one who invited Kiara to join all of us this weekend," Hunter said about an hour into the bonfire as he sat in the chair next to me. "Is that right?"

"Yeah. We've been hanging out this summer," I said, wondering why he was bringing it up.

"Cool." He nodded and looked up at the night sky above, like he was trying to get up the nerve to ask another question. Hunter had always been one of my more observant friends, so I was curious what he might have picked up on. After a moment, he looked sideways at me with his green eyes and asked, "But if you guys are friends, why have you been avoiding her the whole time we've been here?"

And there was the question I was trying to figure out myself.

"I saw you dance to a few songs last night," Hunter continued. "But aside from that, you're basically like repelling magnets." He gestured to where Kiara was currently playing a game of Mafia with a big group on the far end of the party. "Always staying at the opposite ends of the group."

So apparently, Hunter hadn't yet been told about my huge kerfuffle yesterday. I'd told Cambrielle and Carter all about it when I arrived at the beach house. I'd expected them to tell everyone else about it, too, since the others were probably curious why Kiara had hidden upstairs most of the afternoon. But since Hunter didn't seem to know anything about it, I guess I really could trust my siblings to keep my more humiliating moments on the down-low.

Hunter was someone I could always confide in, though, and he usually had pretty great advice, so I told him everything. And as I unloaded on him about everything that happened last summer—the drinking, the party, the blank spots in my memory—and then told him about everything from this past month—hanging out with Kiara, the texts with Wrong Number Girl, and the flashes that led me to remembering what had happened—it felt good to get it all out.

"So you think you have a better connection with this other girl?" Hunter asked. "That interaction last summer and this past week of text messages have helped you decide she's a better fit for you?"

"Yes... I mean, no..." I shook my head and sighed. "I mean, I guess I don't really know." I shrugged. "I just want to know who she is. If she'd just tell me who she actually is and agree to meet me in person, then I could make up my mind." I watched the sparks rise from the fire in a cloud of smoke as I tried to find a way to explain it better. But when nothing substantial came, I looked back at Hunter and said, "It might make me a jerk, but if things worked out with Kiara—if she even wants to be with me —I wouldn't want to have any 'what ifs' in the back of my mind."

"I get that." Hunter nodded thoughtfully. Then he met my gaze, like he was about to impart what I'd always called his "Hunter Wisdom," and said, "But in life, we can't always dwell on 'what ifs.' Sometimes, we have to make a decision, commit to it, and stop searching for what might be coming around the corner."

"I know." I dropped my head into my hands and gripped my hair. "I guess I also worry that whoever I choose will change her mind later. I haven't exactly been successful in making a girl stick around for long."

"Love always carries risks," Hunter said, glancing toward

Scarlett who was sitting across the fire with Kiara. "But it can also be amazing."

"That's what I hear," I said. "I'm just really great at messing it up."

Hunter patted me on the back. "Not many people get it right the first time. Just look at me and Scarlett. We've been best friends for three years, but we weren't able to make it work until a couple of months ago."

"But do you think Kiara would even give me a second chance after making her feel like a second choice?"

Hunter glanced at Kiara who looked our way at the same time. After mulling my question over for a moment, Hunter said, "I think Kiara is more understanding than a lot of people. So, if you were really serious and knew what you wanted without being wishy-washy, I think you could make it work. I know you're still curious about this other girl, too, but I'm rooting for things to work out for the best."

"If only the other girl would message me back, I might get out of limbo," I said.

I pulled out my phone and checked the message thread with Wrong Number Girl again. There weren't any new messages, but there was one small change. Instead of saying the messages were simply delivered, the status had marked them as *read*.

Was she ignoring me now?

I stood from my seat, anxiety suddenly pulsing through me at the thought that I really might have ruined everything with a sweet girl for someone who was ghosting me.

"I'm gonna go for a little walk," I said to Hunter.

Hunter furrowed his brow. "Is something wrong?"

"I don't know." I sighed. "I just—I need to be alone for a bit."

"Okay," he said, concern etched in his eyes. "Just let me know if I can do anything."

"I will."

I left the party and headed back toward the beach house. As I walked along the wet sand, I typed out a text to Wrong Number Girl.

Me: **I'm probably making a big deal out of nothing, but I'm starting to worry that I'm being ghosted or catfished. Which would really suck since I really liked you and have kind of put some things on the line for what I hoped was an authentic and amazing connection. Please message me back. I don't want to scare you off, but I really think we need to meet.**

37

KIARA

"HE'S LEAVING THE PARTY?" I mumbled to myself as I watched Nash walk away from the beach around ten.

Really?

I'd assumed we'd gotten on better terms last night, and then there was the little moment we had on our way to the bonfire that made me hope we were done avoiding each other.

I'd thought that after he chatted with a few other friends and after I finished my game of Mafia we would have a chance to hang out and take some steps toward getting back to normal.

But if he was leaving now, how were we supposed to fix anything?

Did he just not care then? And if he didn't care, what was I even doing here this weekend?

Sure, I had Addie—thank goodness she was here—but when I'd made all the plans for this weekend and pictured how it would go in my head, a lot of it had centered around furthering my friendship with Nash.

"Hey, I think I'm gonna grab something to drink and just sit out this next round," I told Scarlett as the group got ready to draw their roles for another round of Mafia. "If someone wants to take my spot, that's fine."

"Okay," Scarlett said. She glanced at the table with the drinks and refreshments and added, "I heard someone talking about how amazing the pineapple juice was. I guess Ky brought a bunch of pineapples back from Maui last week and made it fresh. If you try it, let me know what you think."

"Will do," I said, thinking fresh pineapple juice actually sounded really good.

I walked up to the table with the drinks, and just like Scarlett had mentioned, there were two big glass dispensers full of the yellow juice.

"Do you know if there's a difference between the two of these?" I asked a couple of guys who were standing next to the table with red plastic cups in their hands.

"One of them is just plain pineapple juice," a guy with red hair said. "The other is also pineapple juice...just a little more fun."

And when he winked, I knew what he meant by the "fun" part.

"Which one is plain pineapple?" I asked, not interested in getting drunk.

The redhead turned to the short blond guy beside him and asked, "It's the one on the left, right?"

The blond guy looked at both dispensers. After a beat, he nodded. "Yeah, that's the one my mom would want me to drink tonight."

"Okay, cool."

I grabbed a cup from the end of the table. And since I wanted to be safe just in case the guys were playing a trick on me, I poured just a small amount of juice into my cup to test it.

It tasted like regular pineapple juice. *Perfect.*

I filled my cup the rest of the way and sipped on it as I

walked over to where Addie and Evan were talking to Nash's older brother, Ian, near the fire.

Ian and Evan were talking about some business stuff and Addie seemed to actually understand what they were talking about, so I just stood quietly next to Addie in their little circle and listened.

"Did Evan major in business or something?" I whispered to Addie after several minutes had passed and Evan and Ian were still deep in their conversation about portfolios and acquisitions and other things I didn't understand.

"Shh." Addie looked around the area, suddenly paranoid for some reason. Then leaning closer, she whispered, "You're going to blow our cover if you say things like that out loud."

"What?" I furrowed my brow, confused.

"You're just talking really loudly," she said in a hushed voice. Then stepping closer, she added, "No one is supposed to know that Evan already graduated from college."

"Oh." I nodded slowly even though I didn't quite understand why she was so worried. I looked at my cup, and seeing it was almost empty, I said, "Their conversation is kind of boring. I'm gonna get some more juice. You want some? Or some water?"

Addie glanced back to the drink table. After looking it over, she said, "No, I'll be okay. I had some water while you were playing Mafia."

"Okay, cool."

I trudged back up to the table. And moving away from Florida really must have made my legs weak on the sand or something, because I ended up wobbling a few times on my way back.

"Back for more?" the redhead I'd talked to earlier asked when I made it back to the table.

"Yep." I nodded as I stuck my cup up to the juice

dispenser. "This stuff is so good. I'm gonna have to tell my mom to order pineapples from Maui the next time her bosses have a party. They're billionaires so they're, like, super fancy."

"Billionaires, really?" The guy arched his eyebrow like he was intrigued.

I nodded, liking that at least one guy here seemed to find my conversation interesting. "I'm friends with their—" I stopped, realizing that might not actually be true anymore. I shook my head. "I mean, I came here with their kids. They're pretty nice. Not as stuck up as you'd think super rich kids would be."

"Well, that's cool," he said, an amused look in his eyes. "I'm glad you don't think all rich people are stuck up."

"Oh are you rich, too?" I gasped, suddenly realizing I was probably at a party with a bunch of rich kids since we were in The Hamptons after all.

"My parents do okay," he said. "Not billionaires or anything, but close."

Close to billionaire status?

Wow.

Yeah, I probably stuck out like a sore thumb to all these prep school kids.

"Well, I hope you have a good night," I said, not knowing what else to say to this stranger now that my cup had been refilled. "I'm gonna go back to my other rich friends."

"Enjoy that drink." He smiled.

"I will." I held it up, smiling back. "It's delicious."

I took a few steps away, but apparently, I'd filled my glass a little too full because with each step, a little juice sloshed over the top and onto my hand.

Well, that's going to be a sticky mess.

I stopped for a moment to lick my hand clean, and then for

good measure, I took a few more sips before continuing back down the beach to Addie and Evan.

But as I walked down the hill, I ended up tripping over someone's purse and shoes and the momentum of that made me fall forward to my hands and knees.

"I'm okay," I called out when a few people looked my way. Then leaning back on my haunches, I held up my cup and said, "I spilled some of Ky's special pineapple juice, but it's okay. I can get some more."

A few people snickered, and seeing that I'd made people laugh, I suddenly started laughing, too.

Man, I was in a silly mood right now. This was fun.

Who cared if Nash wanted to be a party pooper this weekend? I was going to have fun without him.

I managed to get myself back to standing with a little effort. When I made it back to Addie and Evan, they were thankfully done having their boring conversation with Ian.

"You guys ready to party now?" I stepped up beside Addie, suddenly buzzing with energy. "Because I was thinking we should all play Limbo or something. Wouldn't that be fun?"

"You want to play Limbo?" Addie frowned. "Right now?"

"Of course." I nodded. "Limbo is the best. I know you could never beat me back in the day, but I think that's just what this party needs."

I turned to face the crowd that was still playing Mafia and yelled, "Do you guys want to—"

But I didn't get to finish my sentence because Addie was suddenly taking my cup from my hand and sniffing it.

"Hey," I said, wondering what she was doing. "That's my juice. You said you didn't want any."

But instead of handing my cup back to me like I wanted, she gave it to Evan who sniffed it, too, before asking, "Do you know what's in here?"

"Oh, it's just pineapple juice," I said, reaching for my cup. "It's from Maui."

"Pineapple juice?" Evan asked, sniffing the cup again before taking a sip. He shook his head and looked at Addie. "I bet it's loaded with booze. Guys at my fraternity used to make something like this when hazing our new recruits."

"You think she's drunk?" Addie asked.

"What?" I furrowed my brow, confused about how I could get drunk when I hadn't tasted any alcohol.

"Kiara, how many cups of this have you had?" Evan's tone grew more serious, a tinge of worry in his eyes.

"This is my second," I said, not understanding why he was so serious all of a sudden.

I couldn't get drunk off a cup and a half of pineapple juice, could I?

But Evan's concern seemed to only deepen because he said, "You need to stop. If you have any more, you'll be blackout drunk." Then to Addie, he said, "I'll get her some water. Can you help her sit down before she falls again?"

Evan walked away to dispose of my drink. A minute later, when I was seated in a beach chair nearby, Evan returned with a cup of water in hand.

"Here, drink this," he said. "You need to hydrate now."

So even though I was still confused about how I could get drunk with the juice that the redhead had said was fine, I did as he said.

"We're just going to play a game of cornhole," Addie said a while later when the world was spinning. "Will you be fine?"

"Of course," I said cheerfully. "I'll be fine. You go have fun with your *stepbrother*." I winked and then giggled because it really was so funny that everyone thought Evan was Addie's stepbrother.

And I was the only one who knew their secret.

I pretended to zip my lips with my fingers in a "my lips are sealed" gesture then giggled to myself again.

This was all so fun. I loved bonfires. Parties were my favorite.

Pineapple juice was my favorite.

I leaned back in the chair and looked up at the sky, feeling so happy and lucky that I'd found Addie again. She really was the best. I loved her so much.

She was my bestest friend in the world.

"Just don't tell Alessi I said that," I said to the empty chair next to me. Then I giggled because I was talking to a chair.

Man, I was so silly tonight.

I watched Addie and her super hot "stepbrother" toss bean bags back and forth and thought that I should probably tell Evan how Addie feels. He was such a nice guy to take care of my friend. He wouldn't have been so nice if he didn't like her back, right?

But no, no, no, I shook my head. I couldn't tell her secret.

Nope.

I couldn't do that.

I sighed. Secret crushes were tricky.

I sat for a couple more minutes, just smiling and giggling at random thoughts as they flitted through my mind. This was so relaxing. I really needed to come to the beach more.

I also need to pee. The thought came to me when a sudden pain pushed against my bladder.

Yeah, I needed to pee.

But I couldn't do that here...

I looked around, wondering if there was a bathroom nearby.

But this was a private beach, so they didn't have things like that.

A couple of girls walked past my chair, so I asked, "Do you know where the bathroom is?"

"It's just up in Ky's house," a girl with black and pink braids said, pointing behind me. "Just walk through the back door. It's right there."

"Just in the back door?" I nodded. "Thanks."

It took me a moment to get myself up on my feet since the chair was so low to the ground. When I tried to walk, I realized I must be even drunker than I thought because I was wobblier than a baby taking her first steps.

"Hey, do you need help getting there?" the girl with the braids asked, taking my arm in her hand to steady me.

"If you don't mind," I said. "I guess I had too much juice tonight."

"It happens to the best of us," the girl said, patting my arm.

The girl walked me up the steps to Ky's house. When we got to the bathroom, she asked if I wanted her to wait for me, but I said, "No, I think I'll be fine now. Thank you."

I shut the door and gave my bladder some relief. Once I was done in the bathroom, I was feeling pretty tired and decided I should probably just head back to the Hastings' beach house.

It should probably be pretty easy to find from here. Just two or three houses down, right?

I made my way through Ky's house, keeping my hand against the wall for support. When I found his front door, I stepped outside and onto a huge porch. After looking around and deciding his house was probably set off the road like the Hastings', I started walking down Ky's long driveway.

38

NASH

MY WALK along the beach ended up taking me farther than I'd originally planned. But since I had so many conflicting thoughts running through my mind tonight, I'd needed some extra time alone to sort it out.

Or to stop feeling so anxious, at least. I didn't really figure anything out since I still hadn't heard back from Wrong Number Girl, and I hadn't been able to decide what to do about Kiara.

I walked around the bend near my family's beach house and the bonfire came back into view. It looked like the party was still going strong, so hopefully, I hadn't missed too much.

I still wasn't sure it was fair for me to have feelings for two different girls and not know what to do next. But I did know that I regretted telling Kiara that we were better off as friends.

I just didn't know if I should tell her exactly where I was right now, or if I should wait until I actually knew.

It probably wasn't fair to ask her to wait around for me when I was so wishy-washy, right?

I made it back to the party and stood on the edge, trying to see if I could find her and just hang out. But while I was able to spot my siblings and the rest of my friends scattered around the party, I couldn't see Kiara anywhere.

Did she leave?

Deciding I should check inside Ky's house before I headed home to look for her, I walked up the stairs. But when I was about halfway across Ky's back lawn, my phone dinged with a text.

I pulled my phone out, and my heart did a flip-flop when I saw who had just texted me.

It's Wrong Number Girl.

I swiped up on my phone to read her text, hoping for an answer to why she'd been MIA the past two days.

Wrong Number Girl: **Wres are hose Im lost.**

I frowned as I read the text. *What?*

Did Wrong Number Girl have a younger sibling who had stolen her phone?

Me: **Sorry, I didn't understand your text. What did you ask?**

The message dots showed up on the screen. I watched them for what seemed like a long time, but when the text finally came through, all it said was, **Im looking for yr hose.**

She was looking for my hose?

Like a garden hose?

Was she trying to water plants this late at night?

Me: **You need a hose?**

Wrong Number Girl: **np I cant fond your hose!**

This was so bizarre.

Wrong Number Girl: **Im lot! And drink!**

Okay, this had to be a little kid.

Me: **Did you steal your sister's phone?**

Wrong Number Girl: **I don't had a sister.**
Okay...
Me: **Are you butt texting me?**

But instead of sending another jumbled text back, the person on the other end of the phone called me.

I furrowed my brow, confused by what was going on and who I might be about to talk to. But since I was so curious and would love to finally put a voice to the girl I'd been messaging for weeks, I swiped my finger across it and said, "Hello?"

"You thought my butt was texting you?" a feminine voice said from the other end, her words slightly slurred. "You're so silly, Nash."

And when she giggled like this whole interaction was hilarious, I went still.

Completely still because I recognized that cute little giggle.

I'd been listening to it all summer.

"Kiara?" I asked, my voice rising in pitch. "Is that you?"

"Of course it is," she said, not seeming to notice that I was completely shocked to hear her voice calling me from *this* number.

I shook my head, my mind reeling from this discovery. *Kiara is Wrong Number Girl?*

"Where's your house?" she asked. "I tried to walk there but I think I lost it."

"Oh, you're looking for my *house,* not my *hose.*"

"Why would I want a hose?" she said, sounding as confused about the hose as I'd been.

"Never mind," I said, thinking I knew what was going on. "Have you been drinking tonight?"

"Yeessch." She giggled again, like she thought her pronunciation of the word was hilarious. Then in a softer voice, she whispered, "But it was an accident."

She'd gotten drunk by accident?

"Where are you?" I asked, concern flooding through me as I remembered the guy from last night. "Are you safe? Did someone take advantage of you?"

"I wish you'd take advantage of me," she said in a flirtatious tone.

I didn't know if I understood what she meant by it, but before I could respond, she continued, "But you'll never do that because you don't like me in that way. Which is why you should have let me dance with that guy last night. Maybe I should go talk to him again."

My heart sank at her words, and I wanted to reassure her that I did like her. But since I needed to make sure she was safe first, I asked, "Where are you? I need to help you get home."

"Umm..." She paused as if thinking. Then she said, "I'm by the bushes in the darkness."

"What?"

But instead of explaining, she said in a sing-song voice, "Oooooh. Nash wants to know where I am."

"Yes, I want to know where you are," I replied firmly, not finding this situation as comical as she apparently did.

"But it's just me," she said. "Your fantasy girl isn't here."

My fantasy girl?

Was she talking about Wrong Number Girl? She thought I'd turned her into a fantasy?

"Can you just share your location with me?" I said, deciding that getting to her was more important than sorting all that other stuff out. "If I walk you through the steps, do you think you can follow my directions?"

"No promises," she said lightly before giggling again.

"Okay, just put me on speakerphone and we'll figure this out."

It took a couple of minutes, but I eventually got Kiara to send me a pin with her location.

When I saw it come through and that she was only a one-minute walk away, I said, "Okay, just find a spot on the sidewalk and sit down. I'll be there soon."

I found Kiara sitting on the sidewalk near Ky's front gates. Apparently, she'd walked up to them, couldn't find the button on the left side that would have opened them, and then gave up.

Which was probably good. Who knew where she might have wandered off to in the confused state she was in.

"Ready to go home?" I asked when she looked up at me in the moonlight.

She nodded and put her hands up in the air in the way kids usually did when asking a parent to carry them. And now that I wasn't so worried about her and where she might be, I had to admit that drunk Kiara was kind of cute.

I took her hands in mine and helped her get to her feet. Since she was pretty wobbly, I put my arm around her waist to help guide her home.

As we walked past the house that separated my family's beach house from Ky's house, Kiara leaned her head against my shoulder. Then in a more subdued voice than she'd used on the phone, she said, "Do you wanna know what I found out tonight?"

"Yes," I said, wondering if it was as shocking as the thing I'd just discovered.

That Kiara was the girl from last summer.

Kiara was the girl I'd been falling for through text at the same time I was falling for her in real life.

But instead of saying anything about that, Kiara said, "I found out that I'm a happy drunk." She tilted her head back so she could look up at me. "I thought I'd be an angry drunk because that's what my dad was. But I'm a silly, happy drunk."

"You are very silly," I agreed, rubbing her arm with my hand. "I, on the other hand, am a very stupid and forgetful drunk."

"You're not stupid," she said, like she thought she needed to console me. "But you are forgetful."

Was this her way of telling me that I'd forgotten her? Did she even realize that I knew exactly who she was now?

I couldn't tell.

But when she looked up at me and our eyes met in the darkness, it felt like she was trying to say something to me.

Trying to give me a hint that the girl I'd met last summer had been right in my backyard all along.

This beautiful girl with the kindest soul was the girl I'd forgotten.

No wonder she hadn't told me who she was. I'd probably run into her at least a hundred times since last summer and I'd never once tried to get to know her until I was interested in her friend.

I'm such an idiot.

We made it to the gates of my family's property, and I typed in the code for them to open. We were about halfway down the private drive when Kiara stopped suddenly and said, "Oh, I don't feel so good."

A few seconds later, her drunkenness suddenly took hold and she vomited in the bushes.

When I saw her looking around for something to wipe her mouth with, I quickly pulled my shirt over my head and handed it to her.

"Thank you," she said weakly, wiping her mouth with my shirt.

"Let's get you inside," I said, taking her arm in mine and guiding her up the drive once again.

We made it inside the beach house, and I took her straight upstairs to the room she shared with Addison.

I helped her sit on the bed, and she promptly laid herself flat on it. Then I said, "I'm gonna grab you some water, okay?"

She lifted an arm lazily in the air. "Okay."

I walked to the door, but then I remembered something else. So I turned back and said, "I think we might have some pizza left over from dinner. I'll heat some up for you, too. It might help soak up some of the alcohol."

"Okay," she said, lifting a floppy arm in the air again.

I smiled. She really was funny this way.

I stopped by my room on the way down and tossed my dirty shirt in the laundry basket before putting on a fresh T-shirt.

Once I'd washed my hands and grabbed the pizza and water, I hurried back up the stairs.

I'd almost expected Kiara to be zonked out from how tired she'd seemed, but when I stepped into her room, she was sitting up with one arm stuck in her shirt like she was struggling to get out of it.

"Are you trying to change into your pajamas?" I asked, setting the pizza and water on the dresser and going to her side.

"Yes." She nodded, her head drooping forward. "This is too tight."

Uncertain of what to do, I quickly grabbed an oversized T-shirt from her suitcase and assisted her, pulling her red top over her head and guiding her arms through the sleeves of the big T-shirt. She didn't say anything about her shorts, so I figured I'd leave them alone unless she said something later.

I grabbed the pizza and water from the dresser. After handing her the cup and asking her to hydrate, I helped feed her the first piece of pizza.

"Do you think you could eat another slice?" I asked, holding up the second piece. From my experience, eating two slices of greasy pizza really did help soak up alcohol and reduce the risk of a hangover.

Depending on how much she'd drank, that was.

"I don't know," she said sleepily. Then clutching a hand over her stomach, she groaned and said, "Ohhh, I don't feel so good."

Worried she might vomit again, I grabbed the garbage bin nearby and held it up to her chin.

She vomited again, and when she was done, I helped her clean up with a wet washcloth.

Once that was done, I gave up on the pizza, deciding my trusty pizza trick might not work for Kiara tonight.

"Do you want to go to sleep?" I asked her in a gentle voice.

She nodded.

So I pulled back the covers on her bed and helped her lie on her side to sleep in case she got the throw-ups again.

I grabbed a clean bowl from downstairs to set on the nightstand by her head, and I was about to leave when Kiara looked up at me with her big amber eyes and said, "I'm scared."

"You're scared?" I asked, wondering what she might be afraid of.

She nodded, and after licking her lips and swallowing, she whispered, "What if I'm an alcoholic now?"

I furrowed my brow and sat on the bed beside her. "You're worried you might be an alcoholic after accidentally getting drunk one time?"

She nodded. "It can run in families, right?"

"That's what I've heard." I shrugged. "But I think a lot of it has to do with our emotional state and the reason we're drinking in the first place."

Her eyebrows knitted together, making little worry lines on her forehead.

I reached out and smoothed my thumb across her frown lines, not wanting her to be worried. Then I said, "For me, I drank to escape my feelings. They were strong, and instead of feeling them and trying to work through them, I thought numbing them was better. I drank so I didn't have to deal with them anymore."

She nodded, like she understood.

"I think addictions come mostly when we're trying to avoid feeling a certain way. They provide a 'quick fix' or a 'band-aid' as my therapist told me," I continued, recounting some of what I'd learned. "But until we actually deal with the real issues behind those emotions, they'll never actually go away. Sure, numbing them with alcohol, drugs, food, gambling, shopping, or whatever vice we have might feel good in the moment. But it only buries the issue for a time until it resurfaces again and 'future us' has to figure out how to deal with it the next time."

"Future me is probably going to have a headache to deal with tomorrow." Kiara sighed sleepily.

"I think you're probably right," I said. And because I couldn't resist, I allowed myself to smooth the hair back that had fallen over her face, combing my fingers through her silky locks. "But I'll be here to help you."

Her lips curved up into a sleepy smile, and I could tell she was drifting fast. Her eyelids closed for longer and longer with each blink.

As I watched her creep closer and closer to the realm of slumber, I had to think that even when she was tired and drunk and not feeling well at all, she was beautiful.

But then, she'd *always* been beautiful, hadn't she?

I'd just been too blind to really see her.

She closed her eyes, her head relaxing even more against her pillow, and I knew she was entering dreamland.

I bent forward and gently pressed my lips to her cheek before mumbling, "Sleep well, Kiara." Then because I needed to, I ran my hand across her hair once more and whispered, "I'm not sure what you'll remember in the morning or how brave I'll be by then, but I just want you to know that you are the most amazing girl I've ever met. I just hope I'm lucky enough to get another chance with you."

39

KIARA

"KNOCK, KNOCK," Nash said from the open doorway to my bedroom on Sunday morning with a large sports drink bottle in one hand and a cup of what looked like tomato juice in the other. "Mind if I come in?"

"Sure," I said groggily, sitting up against the pillows at the head of the bed I'd shared with Addie.

I'd been awake for a few minutes, but even though the light filtering through the cracks in the curtains told me it was late morning, I had yet to climb out of bed because of the splitting headache and nausea assaulting my senses.

What had I done last night?

Because I was pretty sure this was what death felt like.

"I brought you some tomato juice, electrolytes, and ibuprofen," Nash said, coming up to the side of the bed and setting the supplies on the nightstand. "I don't know if you've ever had a hangover before, but these were my best ammunition when I drank too much and needed to be human the next day."

"Thanks," I said, giving him a weak smile. "I have to admit I'm a first timer."

And hopefully, a last timer, too.

"I thought that might be the case." Nash picked up the sports drink and untwisted the cap. "I know this pineapple-coconut-flavored drink might be a bit on the nose since it was pineapple juice that got you here, but coconut water is also good for hangovers so I figured it was worth a try. I can get something different if you don't like it, though."

"So I'm guessing I picked the wrong pineapple juice last night?" I asked, remembering that part of the night at least.

"It would seem that you ran into Ky's cousin at the drink table and were unfortunate enough to fall for one of his pranks."

"He gets people drunk for fun?" I asked.

"He did last night, anyway." Nash shook his head as he handed the drink and ibuprofen to me. "Which is why Ky had to officially ban him from the rest of his parties this summer. Underage girls getting drunk at his parties is apparently a no-no in Ky's book."

"Well, that's good," I said.

I didn't really know much about Ky Miller aside from recognizing a few of his songs on the radio. But he seemed like a good guy.

Unlike his prankster cousin, it would seem.

I put the ibuprofen in my mouth and then washed it down with a few sips of the pineapple-coconut-flavored drink. I followed that with some tomato juice and then had to call it good for a bit so my stomach could settle.

"I know you left the party early," I said to Nash once I'd leaned against the pillows again. "But do you happen to know if I did anything embarrassing while I was drunk?"

Or possibly said something I hadn't wanted to?

I'd heard alcohol could be like truth serum for some people and it would be really bad to be under the influence while around Nash's friends, especially when I had a particular secret.

"According to Addie, you just talked kind of loudly and giggled a lot," he said with a shrug. "So I don't think there was anything too embarrassing."

"That's good." I sighed, relief washing over me.

But then he got a smirk on his lips as he added, "You were pretty entertaining as I walked you home, though."

My heart halted to a stop and a feeling of dread slipped over me.

Nash had walked me home?

How did I not remember that?

"What did I do?" I asked, fear suddenly tightening my throat. "Or say...?"

Please don't be what I think it is.

Please don't tell me I drunkenly confessed that I've been in love with you for a year and secretly texted you all summer.

Please oh please don't tell me I'd done any of that.

"You giggled a lot with me, too," he said. "And then you were really happy about the discovery that you were a happy and silly drunk instead of an angry one."

"Well, that's not too bad," I said, feeling relieved again.

But then his lips quirked up into a half-smile and I knew I needed to brace myself.

What had I done?

He thankfully didn't drag the suspense out too long. "And then there was the moment when I asked if you were safe or if anyone had taken advantage of you, and you said that you wished *I'd* take advantage of you."

"I said that?" My voice rose an octave as I covered my face with my hands.

"Yep." He chuckled. "And I think you were also mad that I'd interrupted your dance with that guy at the club."

"Sounds like I'm more of an idiot drunk than a happy or silly one."

"You were entertaining and full of surprises, that's for sure." When he winked, I worried that he was hinting that something more had happened.

But he'd tell me if I'd done something really embarrassing, wouldn't he?

I studied him for a moment, trying to gauge what he may or may not know. But since my hangover hadn't given me any magical mind-reading abilities, I just shrugged and said, "I still can't believe I got drunk off a cup of pineapple juice."

"Evan said it was almost two cups," Nash said. "But yeah, you definitely got pineappled."

"Have you been pineappled before?" I asked, curious if it was actually a thing.

"No." He shook his head. "Sadly, my drinking was always done on purpose."

"You *chose* to feel like this?" I asked as my head pulsed with another pain, like someone had put a thick rubber band around my head and snapped it. "Multiple times?"

A self-conscious look filled Nash's eyes at my comment. With a shrug, he said, "'Present-day us' doesn't always care enough about what 'future us' will have to deal with."

"Huh?" I frowned, confused why he was talking in riddles when my mind was already spinning.

He seemed to get that I was lost because he added, "What I mean is, *choosing* to get a hangover is pretty stupid."

We were both quiet for a moment and I worried I may have hurt his feelings, but then he said, "I think most everyone is planning to play spikeball and a few other games on the beach today. Do you think you'll be up to it?"

"I don't think going in the sun is the best idea for my headache," I said, remembering how my dad had always kept the curtains shut when he was hungover. "I'll probably just stay in bed and rest."

"That's probably a good plan," he said. "Would you like me to bring you some breakfast? Maybe some toast?"

"I think I could handle toast."

"I'll make some for you then." He patted my leg where it rested under the quilt before standing. "Hopefully, we'll get you feeling better before too long. It would be a shame to miss The Hamptons on the Fourth of July."

Nash came back a few hours later with some lunch and asked if I'd like more pain medication, too.

"That would be awesome," I said. "Thank you."

My headache had subsided a little with the ibuprofen from earlier, but I wanted to stay on top of the pain as well as I could.

He came back a minute later with Tylenol and a tumbler full of water. As I took the pills, he glanced at the TV on the wall across from my bed and asked, "You like watching baking shows?" Then with a smile in his eyes, he added, "How did I not guess this?"

"I like what I like, I guess." I set my tumbler on the nightstand. "This one has the added fun of a competition and British accents, so it's not your typical cooking show."

"I noticed that," he said, nodding as he watched the guy on the screen add piles of buttercream frosting on top of a seven-layer, red velvet cake. "It's kind of mesmerizing, isn't it?"

"It is," I said, liking that he seemed to enjoy it, too. "It's one of my comfort shows."

The screen switched from the guy and the red velvet cake to a woman in her sixties who was creating a sunset on the beach scene out of frosting on a cookie cake.

"Ever considered making something like that in your future bakery?" Nash asked, pointing to the screen as the woman piped a palm tree onto the beachy scene.

"I don't know if I'm quite that good," I said, doubting my artistic talent. "But it would be fun to learn how."

We watched the show in silence for a moment. I was considering inviting Nash to sit down and watch the rest of the episode with me when Addie peeked her head in the door and said, "Hey, Evan and I are going to grab some stuff from the store for lunch tomorrow. Did you want us to grab anything for you?"

"I was planning to bake a dessert to bring with us on the yacht tomorrow night," I said, remembering the great plans I had to win Nash over with more baking before I'd gotten myself sick. "Would you mind getting the ingredients for me?"

"Sure." She smiled. "Just text me what you need, and we'll make sure you have it."

"Perfect."

I grabbed my phone from off the quilt beside me and searched for the photo I'd taken of my grandma's tres leches cake recipe so I could send it to Addie.

As I did that, Addie asked Nash if he was heading back to the beach or if he wanted to come with them to the store.

"Actually, if Kiara doesn't mind," Nash said, briefly glancing sideways at me, "I was hoping I could stay here and finish this show with her."

I looked up at him, surprised he'd want to stay here when he could be having fun with his friends. "You want to stay cooped up here with me?"

He nodded, and there was a hint of insecurity in his eyes as he said, "If you don't mind the company, that is."

"Oh I don't mind," I hurried to say. "I'd actually love the company."

"Sounds great," Addie said. And when our eyes met, she gave me a look that told me she was rooting for something good to come from this.

I finished sending her the recipe. After her phone buzzed with my message, she said, "Got the list." Then looking back to Nash and me, she added, "Enjoy your baking show. I'll see you later."

When she disappeared down the hall again, Nash and I looked awkwardly at each other for a moment like we weren't sure what to do next. Then remembering he'd said he wanted to watch my show with me, I scooted to the other side of the bed and said, "You can sit here if you want."

He looked at the mattress that had a slight indentation from my body. Seeming to be okay with the suggestion, he shrugged and said, "Thanks," before climbing in beside me.

We watched the show quietly for the next few minutes. Though honestly, I wasn't able to focus on it nearly as well as I had earlier since my brain and body were much more interested in the fact that I was sitting on a bed with Nash Hastings and there were only a few inches between us.

We weren't touching or anything, but if I moved my arm or leg slightly, they would probably bump against him.

"Think you'd ever be open to giving me a baking lesson?" Nash asked a minute later as Mario, a guy with blue hair, added some rose buds on top of his cake.

"Y-you want a baking lesson?" I asked, licking my lips. "From me?"

"Yeah..." He nodded, his gaze briefly dipping down to my now moist lips. "I think it would be good for me to learn how to bake. Especially since I'll be living on my own soon."

"True," I said, suddenly overheated from the way he was looking at me.

Which was silly.

He was looking at me the way he'd looked at me a hundred times before.

But for some reason, having him look at me this closely while we were sitting on a bed made it more intimate.

The image that flitted through my mind of him sliding his arms over mine as I whipped the topping wasn't helping with my hot flashes, either.

But now I suddenly wanted to recreate that pottery scene from *Ghost* with Nash, only using heavy whipping cream, powdered sugar, and a mixing bowl instead of a pottery wheel and clay.

Geez, who knew a baking fantasy could be so hot.

When an image of Nash lifting me onto the counter and kissing me came to my mind next, I quickly pushed it away.

"Um..." I tried to think, knowing I needed to focus on this conversation more than a kitchen make-out scene. "Y-you could help me make my tres leches cake tomorrow. It should be a pretty simple recipe for a first-time baker."

"That sounds amazing." Nash smiled, not seeming to pick up on my weird thoughts. "It's a date."

And when he winked, I wondered if he actually meant it that way.

Was it possible I'd found my way back to flirty Nash again? Did he change his mind about focusing only on Wrong Number Girl?

Had he realized the real-life version of me was worth pursuing something with, too? Something more than friendship?

I knew I should probably have my guard up high since he'd literally turned me down to my face not two days ago and told me there was another girl he liked more...but it was hard to know what to do about that when that other girl was literally me.

Having him torn between both versions of me would be kind of perfect.

You know, in a twisted kind of way.

We started another episode of *The Great British Bake Off* when the first one ended, but my hangover really must have taken all my energy out of me because about ten minutes into the show, my eyes became heavy and I soon found it impossible to keep them open.

I woke up sometime later with my cheek pressed against something solid and warm. The lighting in the room had changed, telling me a couple of hours might have passed since I'd last been awake.

When fingers lightly traced along my left arm, I realized the solid and warm thing I was lying on must be Nash.

Had I cuddled up to him in my sleep then?

I was pretty sure I'd been on my pillow when I'd drifted off.

Voices from the TV screen registered in my mind a second later, telling me Nash was still watching the show. And when his fingers traced along my arm again, I closed my eyes and wondered if he'd keep doing that if I pretended I was still asleep.

It felt so good. And until this moment, I hadn't realized how much I'd missed cuddling up to a guy during a movie.

Sure, Duke was good for lots of puppy cuddles. But this... This was just really nice.

Yes, better. Way better than puppy cuddles because it was with the guy I liked.

It was with *Nash*.

I was cuddling with Nash, and he wasn't running away.

Was it possible he might like being close like this, too?

I allowed myself to rest against Nash for another minute or two, but when the show ended, I knew I should probably get up.

So I opened my eyes and stretched a little, like I'd just woken up.

"You awake?" Nash asked, his voice soft and deep as he looked down at me.

I nodded and tilted my face up toward him, and with a sheepish look, I said, "Sorry if I kind of trapped you here for a while."

"I didn't mind," Nash said, his thumb rubbing against my arm. "It was actually kind of nice."

"Yeah?"

He nodded. "I haven't cuddled with anyone in a long time. And you know how important cuddles are for my pick-me-up list."

"I haven't cuddled with anyone for a while, either," I admitted.

But since it was probably weird for me to just lay myself against him now that he knew I was awake, and I actually kind of needed to pee, I got up to a sitting position.

Nash paused the show. Then he turned toward me and studied my face, asking, "Are you feeling any better after your nap? Has the headache or nausea improved at all?"

I thought about it, checking in with how I was feeling.

The headache was barely there now, and I felt like I might actually be able to eat a real meal. So I said, "I think I'm about over everything. Thanks for taking care of me and keeping me company."

"Anytime." He gave me a gentle smile as he rested the side of his head against the cushioned headboard.

We held each other's gaze for a moment. And I might have

just been imagining things, but it kind of seemed like Nash was looking at me differently today.

Like something had changed between yesterday and today that made him see me in a different light.

It could have been that he just knew a little more about me now that he'd seen me drunk and sick. But I wasn't sure...there was a look in his eyes that just went deeper. Like we had somehow grown closer over the last twenty-four hours.

Maybe taking care of girls after they'd thrown up was just his thing?

He *had* asked me to dance after the first time he'd seen me throw up.

He sighed and opened his mouth like he was going to say something, but then Addie appeared in the doorway at the same time.

She seemed to realize she was interrupting something because she took a step back. But since Nash was already looking at her expectantly, she cast me an apologetic look and said, "Sorry to interrupt, but we were thinking of heading out to dinner in thirty minutes or so. Do you think you're up to going out? Or do you want me to have food delivered for you?"

"I'm feeling a lot better now," I said. "So I'd love to go with everyone."

"Awesome." She seemed to hesitate for a moment, like she wasn't sure what to do next. Then looking at Nash who was still sitting comfortably on the bed, Addie said, "Actually, I think I'm gonna change before dinner so..."

"I should probably leave the room so you can do that," Nash said, sitting up straighter, taking that as his cue to leave.

He climbed off the bed and was almost to the door when Addie said, "Evan and I were going to be taking his car to the restaurant. You guys can ride with us if you want."

"Sure," Nash said, briefly glancing my way. "That would be great."

"Sounds great to me, too," I said.

With that decided, Nash left, and Addie shut the door behind him as I climbed out of bed.

40

KIARA

AFTER GOING pee and taking a quick shower, I changed into one of the dresses I'd brought—a white, ruffled mini dress that tied in the back. Then I pulled my hair up into a high ponytail and swiped on some mascara and blush to make me look a little less like death.

Nash was standing at the bottom of the stairs when I got there, wearing a sage-green button-up that hit his biceps at just the right spot.

And dang, his arms looked so good today.

And his hair.

And his legs.

And his face.

And okay, basically everything about him was attractive to me.

Even the fine, golden hair on his muscular forearms was hot.

So yes, I was enchanted by Nash to an almost ridiculous degree.

And when he looked up at me and smiled, an overwhelming rush of happiness washed over me. Because he was smiling at *me*.

When I made it to the bottom of the stairs, I expected him to walk toward the door. But instead of doing that, he stepped closer and slipped a hand behind my waist. Then bending down so his breath was hot on my ears, he whispered, "You look absolutely stunning tonight."

Shivers of pleasure spread through me and my cheeks instantly warmed with a blush. When I met his blue-eyed gaze, which was only inches from mine, I found nothing but admiration in them.

"Thank you," I managed to say even though part of me felt like I was floating away into the clouds of some fantasy.

He nodded. Then rubbing his hand across my back, he said, "Evan and Addie are already in the car. Should we head out?"

"S-sure," I said, feeling lightheaded and like I might melt into a puddle from the way the pads of his fingers seemed to linger on the exposed skin of my back.

Had Nash ever touched me like this before?

Because this felt different from the times he'd been pretending to be my boyfriend.

More intentional.

More like I was actually *his*.

Nash guided me out the front door. And since we were the last people out of the house, he turned to lock it before stepping off the front porch with me.

When he joined me again on the short sidewalk that led to the driveway, his hand brushed against mine, his pinky lingering for a second and causing my heart to skip a beat.

Did he do that on purpose? I dared a quick glance up at him to see if he was looking at me. But he was looking straight ahead with a neutral expression so I couldn't tell.

We reached Evan's car a moment later. I didn't know if Addie was trying to help me out or what, but when Nash opened the door for me to climb inside, I found a big, white cooler sitting on the other end of the backseat.

"Sorry about the tight fit," Addie said, swiveling around in the passenger seat, her expression apologetic. "Evan volunteered to pick up some ice on our way home from the restaurant and the cooler wouldn't fit in the trunk."

"I-it's okay," I said, glancing at the small space left on the seat and trying to gauge whether a Nash-sized butt would fit there next to mine. Deciding it looked about his size, I said, "I think we can still fit."

I scooted over to the middle seat to make room beside me. Then Nash slipped into the seat behind Evan.

And the cooler really must have been a big one, because once Nash was in and had shut the door, there was literally no extra space back there.

"Is this okay?" Nash asked, glancing down at the way our legs and hips were pressed together. "Because if it's too tight, I can take my car instead."

"No, it's good," I hurried to say. Then clearing my throat, I added, "I mean, I really don't mind."

"Okay, cool."

I barely breathed on the way to the restaurant, too aware of the way every point of contact I had with Nash burned and zapped with energy.

Nash helped me out of the car when we got there, and as we walked into the restaurant to meet everyone else, his hand brushed against mine again.

I peeked up at him like I had before, but this time instead of having his gaze trained straight ahead, he was looking at me. And when our eyes met, he winked.

What is going on?

Had Nash decided to bring his Casanova side out to play tonight?

I sure hoped so because I really, really liked the little touches and looks and how affectionate he was being.

The host led us to the huge table in the back where the rest of our party was already seated. Evan chose to sit at the end of the table—probably for some sort of bodyguard safety reason—so I sat on the other side of Addie while Nash took the seat between me and Cambrielle.

Even though I was feeling quite a bit better than I had earlier in the day, when the waitress came to take our orders, I decided to stick with the trusty soup of the day—AKA, chicken noodle soup with extra saltine crackers.

"Smart choice," Nash said, bumping his leg against mine under the table.

"It looked pretty good," I said.

I expected him to move his leg away from mine after the quick exchange, but instead of moving it away, it remained pressed against my leg.

And I liked it.

I liked it so stinking much.

If it was appropriate to ask him to smother me with his body right now, I would. Because I craved him and his touch so much.

Dinner arrived a while later. As we all ate, Nash and Asher told everyone about the various pranks they'd played on each other during their "feuding years" as they called them. And as Nash told everyone about the time he snuck onto Asher's laptop during play rehearsal and programmed the word "the" so that it autocorrected to "Nash Hastings is my hero and way more talented than I'll ever be," my cheeks started to hurt from smiling so much.

Who knew Nash could be so devious? I loved it!

"How long did it take for you to fix your laptop?" I asked Asher, who sat across the table from us.

"A while," Asher said, amusement in his brown eyes as he remembered the encounter. "I tried avoiding it at first. But it's surprisingly difficult to write a ten-page research paper and not use the word 'the' a dozen times on each page. So after a few hours of deleting 'Nash Hastings is my hero and way more talented than I'll ever be,' I went and found a classmate who was really good with computers and paid him twenty dollars to fix it."

I tilted my face toward Nash. "I never would have guessed you'd be so good at computer hacking."

"I have a few tricks up my sleeve." He grinned, his blue eyes crinkling in the corners.

"Speaking of Nash hacking into computers..." Carter said, looking at Nash from the other end of the table. "Ava and I almost didn't make it through our first tutoring session, thanks to what he did to my tutoring contract."

"I totally forgot about that," Nash said with a deep laugh. And man, I loved his laugh. It was the kind of laugh that just warmed your whole heart up.

The kind I could spend my whole life listening to and never get tired of.

"So what's the story behind the tutoring contract?" I asked, hungry for all the stories I could get about Nash and his endearing antics.

And as Ava and Carter recalled the story from the first day of school when Carter discovered Nash had put a "no dating clause" into his tutoring contract and had to think fast for how to make it seem like a necessary addition, I just leaned back in my chair and grinned as I learned about a side of Nash that I hadn't known before.

After another hour filled with lots of stories and laughter,

Carter asked the waitress to put everyone's meals on one check, saying tonight's dinner was on him.

Once the check had been paid, Nash's friends—who I was beginning to think were also becoming my friends—started clearing out from the table to head back to the beach house for a game night.

"Mind if I squeeze past you?" Nash leaned closer as I was reaching for my crossbody bag on the floor, resting his hand on my knee. "I need to use the bathroom before we head out."

I was momentarily distracted by how good his warm, masculine hand felt on my knee, but once his words registered, I said, "Sure. I-I should probably stop by the restroom, too."

"Sounds good." Nash squeezed my leg and let his hand slide up an inch or two, gazing deeply into my eyes for a moment like he was gauging my reaction to his advances.

And oh my heck, I loved how comfortable he suddenly seemed to be with me.

Casanova Nash was *sexy*.

I might need to splash myself with water when I get to the bathroom.

"Should we go then?" he asked.

"T-to the bathroom?" I asked, my mind short-circuiting as it suddenly fantasized about finding a maintenance closet or a private dining area where we might explore this new side of Nash a little further.

"Yes," he said. Then letting his gaze dip to my lips for a split second, he added, "Unless there was somewhere else you think we should go."

Breathe, Kiara, breathe.

But then I remembered that Addie and Evan would probably come looking for us if we didn't make it to the car, so I blinked the daydream away and said, "Um, yeah. We should probably stop by the bathroom first."

But if you feel like skipping out on the game night with your friends, I definitely wouldn't mind going somewhere else with you.

I followed Nash down the hall where the bathrooms were located. When I saw a private, unisex bathroom, I briefly considered grabbing his hand and pulling him in there with me.

But I thankfully came to my senses a second later and realized that a public bathroom was not the most romantic place for a make-out session—especially with a guy who had turned me down the last time we'd kissed.

So instead of initiating a bathroom rendezvous, I watched him walk into the men's bathroom while I got in the line outside the women's.

While I waited for the line to move, I pulled out my phone to see if I'd missed any messages over the last twenty-four hours.

I had a message from my mom where she asked if I was having a good time. So I texted her a quick update, telling her things were great. Then I moved down to the next unread message.

It was a text from Alessi, where she asked how the Hamptons was going and then talked about her plans to go to a Fourth of July party on a fancy yacht with Miles and her new crush, Bash, tomorrow night.

Me: **You're going to a party on a yacht? That's so crazy because I'm totally doing the exact same thing tomorrow!**

She texted me right back.

Alessi: **Really? That's so crazy! Where's your yacht?**

Me: **Somewhere off Long Island. Yours?**

Alessi: **Same!! Maybe we'll be on the same one?? Bash and Miles said some of their friends from high school invited us. I think their names are Ian, Owen, and Ky.**

What the heck?

Me: **Looks like Bash and Miles went to school with Nash's older brother and his friends.**

Alessi: **Small world!**

Me: **Seriously! Guess I'll get to meet your new crush tomorrow!**

Alessi: **Yay! See you then! Just try not to faint when you see how hot Bash is in person.**

I laughed.

Pretty sure I'll be trying not to faint from the fever dream Nash currently has me in.

I exited out of our message thread and scrolled down through the other messages to see if there was anything I'd missed.

A second later, my heart jolted when my eyes caught on a message that I didn't remember receiving from Nash. It said, **Are you butt texting me?**

41

KIARA

WHAT THE HECK?

I opened the message thread with Nash to see if it would give any insight behind the message that was sending me on the verge of a heart attack.

And when I saw there were several unreadable texts from me above that, mixed with confused messages from him, I realized I'd texted Nash while I was drunk.

No...*Wrong Number Girl* had texted Nash when *she* was drunk.

On the same exact night that *I'd* accidentally gotten wasted.

My veins surged with adrenaline as the realization of how bad things could actually be set in.

Had he figured things out then? Had he put two and two together and realized I'd been secretly texting him all summer?

Because what were the chances that he believed the two *different* girls he was talking to were both drunk at the exact same time?

Was there any chance that something like that was possible?

Oh crap, oh crap, oh crap!

I put my head in my hands and tried to think as my mind swirled in panic.

Was this why he was suddenly a lot more flirty?

Because he'd solved the puzzle and knew the girl he'd met last summer was me?

And if so, was he happy about that? Or was he just going with it because he had no one else to distract him at the moment and it was convenient?

I didn't want to just be convenient, though.

I wanted him to flirt with me because he actually wanted *me*.

Not because I was the only option this weekend.

Maybe he doesn't know, though.

Maybe...just maybe...he didn't even know Wrong Number Girl had been drunk.

I looked up at the other texts we'd sent last night. He'd thought it could have been a butt text or a younger sibling.

Maybe he hadn't connected any dots past that...

I scrolled up even farther until I saw that he'd sent another longer text that I had also missed.

Nash: **I'm probably making a big deal out of nothing, but I'm starting to worry that I'm being ghosted or catfished. Which would really suck since I really liked you and have kind of put some things on the line for what I hoped was an authentic and amazing connection. Please message me back. I don't want to scare you off, but I really think we need to meet.**

Well...that was a pretty big message, length-wise and content-wise.

I read it over again to pick out the important details.

He thought Wrong Number Girl was catfishing or ghosting him.

Which...it couldn't really be considered catfishing when I hadn't actually sent a photo or given him a specific name different from who I actually was, right?

And as for the ghosting part, I'd definitely been ignoring his messages before that because I didn't want to continue this Wrong Number Girl thing anymore after he'd rejected me for a fantasy.

I read the next sentence of his message where he mentioned that he thought we had an amazing connection, but he was putting some things on the line because of it...

Did him putting "some things on the line" refer to our interaction on the ferry and how he'd put our relationship on the line for Wrong Number Girl?

And if so, did that mean he'd felt regret after doing that?

It was hard to know.

The bathroom line moved again and there was only one person ahead of me now.

So I studied the last part of his message and tried to decide what to say.

Should I just ignore him? Let Wrong Number Girl disappear again and hope he'd forget about her?

Or should I do what he asked and arrange a time where we could meet face to face and see what he really thought about the girl who cleaned his toilets being the girl he felt an *"authentic and amazing connection"* with?

The woman in front of me walked into a stall that had just opened.

I'd be back in Evan's car with Nash soon.

Making a split-second decision, I texted him back.

Me: **Meet me at the falls Wednesday night at sunset. I'll be the girl with pink hair.**

I held my breath as I watched the text go immediately from *delivered* to *read*.

And I realized belatedly that whatever Nash said next would give me some insights into whether anything had changed on his end.

I'd know if all the flirting he'd done today was genuine. Because if he'd changed his mind about Wrong Number Girl, he could easily just text back and say he didn't need to meet her anymore, right?

And then we could walk off into the sunset tonight and he'd never have to know...

My phone buzzed just as a stall opened up and I nearly jumped out of my skin.

I waited to read the text until I'd walked into my stall and shut the door.

Nash: **I'll be there. I can't tell you how excited I am to finally meet you.**

I leaned against the stall door and sighed, releasing a shaky breath as both disappointment and nerves crashed over me at the same time.

He still wanted to meet his fantasy girl. He was *excited* to meet her.

So, nothing big had actually changed between us today.

And now, in just three nights, all my secrets would be out in the open and I'd come face to face with how Nash Hastings really felt about me.

42

NASH

"I THINK I'm just going to head upstairs," Kiara said when we made it back to the beach house after dinner. "I don't think I'm feeling up to a fun game night after all."

"Do you want company?" I asked, not wanting the night to be over just yet. Not after how much closer we'd seemed to get today. "We could watch another episode of your British baking show..."

I definitely wouldn't mind some more Kiara cuddles.

Or possibly even a kiss.

But instead of seeing the sparkle in her eyes that she'd had all night, she gave me a wary look and said, "I think I'm just going to go to sleep."

"Okay..." I furrowed my brow as I studied her face, wondering what might have happened to change her mood so suddenly.

Was she actually not feeling well?

Or did this have something to do with her plans to finally meet me as Wrong Number Girl?

Was she regretting setting up a time so soon? Or was she

just nervous about it—worried I'd be surprised when I saw her by the falls and possibly not be excited that it was her?

Because that was a non-issue for me at this point.

I knew exactly who she was. And for me, Kiara being the same girl I'd met at that party last summer was kind of the best way for all of this to turn out.

Because now that I'd actually gotten to know her, I didn't want *anyone* else.

She was the girl for me. And the only reason I'd been single this year while all my other friends got coupled up was because I'd been looking in all the wrong places for the girl of my dreams.

So before she could go upstairs and possibly worry that I didn't care about her, I held my arms out and asked, "Can I get a hug before you go upstairs?"

She looked up at me, her eyes still seeming unsure about where we stood.

So I added, "I could use a pick-me-up, and I'm starting to think Kiara's hugs might be the best at doing that."

"Even better than your mom's?" she asked hesitantly.

"Yes, even better than those." Then lifting the corner of my lip, I added, "Just don't tell her, okay?"

"I won't."

She stepped forward tentatively, and when I pulled her against me, she almost clung to me like this might be the last hug we'd ever have.

Was she really that scared that I'd be disappointed to see her at the falls? Because that was the only reason I could see for this sudden nervousness in her.

So I rubbed her back with my hands, and with my chin resting near her temple, I tried to reassure her by saying, "I'm so glad you came with me this weekend."

"Me too." She nodded and then burrowed even closer to my chest.

We stood there for a moment longer and she seemed to relax a bit. But then Ava walked into the entryway and asked, "Are you guys coming? We're about ready to start Secret Hitler."

"I'm actually gonna sit tonight out," Kiara said, pulling away from our embrace to look at Ava. "I'm still not feeling that great yet."

"I'm sorry to hear that," Ava said, compassion in her brown eyes. "We'll have to play the game another time when you're feeling better. I think you'll really like it since you enjoyed Mafia so much last night."

"Yes, some other time." Kiara nodded.

"What about you Nash?" Ava looked up at me. "You still planning to play or are you gonna keep Kiara company?"

"Kiara said she's going to bed," I said, looking sideways at Kiara briefly. "So I'll be there in a bit."

"Great, I'll make sure to deal you in."

Ava left us to head back into the kitchen where everyone else was waiting around the table.

"I hope you can get some good rest," I told Kiara, giving her a gentle smile. "And that you'll feel better in the morning."

"Thanks," she said. "Me too."

She gave me a weak smile, waved goodnight, and then turned to walk up the stairs.

The next morning, I helped Kiara make her tres leches cake with blueberries and strawberries on top. But instead of it being the romantic adventure I'd hoped for when I asked for a baking lesson—a chance to stand close and flirt with each other—Kiara just seemed more stressed than anything as we worked in the kitchen.

Around three o'clock, we boarded the tender that would ferry us to where my family's superyacht was anchored. And when Alessi showed up and introduced Kiara to the new guy she'd been hanging out with—who turned out to be Hunter's older brother Bash—Kiara seemed to relax a bit more.

Addie and Evan had decided not to risk inducing Addie's seasickness and had opted to head back to Eden Falls after lunch. So maybe Kiara had just needed a more familiar face in the group today to help her feel more at ease.

I always felt better in new situations when I had my friends or family close by, at least.

Alessi, Kiara, and I all chatted with Miles and Bash as we cruised across the water, and when Kiara realized we were having our dinner on the 377-foot boat anchored a few miles off the coast, instead of the fishing yacht we were in the process of passing, her jaw dropped.

Turning to me with wide eyes, Kiara asked, "We're spending the night on *that*?"

I nodded, unable to keep a smile from my lips. "Let me introduce you to the birthday present my dad gave my mom a few years ago."

"That was a birthday present?" Alessi asked, her eyes as wide as Kiara's.

"Yeah," I said, tilting my head to the side and shrugging. "My dad might have gone a *little* overboard for her fortieth birthday."

"Did he happen to name it 'Birthday Present' too?" Kiara asked, looking back at the yacht.

"Like the guy in *Overboard*?" I laughed, guessing the movie reference.

"Yeah," she said. Then meeting my gaze with her amber eyes, she added, "Such a good movie, by the way."

"It really is," I said, smiling at our shared opinion. "But sadly, my mom wasn't so on the nose with naming this beauty. Instead, she named it 'Omorfiá ton Thalassón,' which is Greek for 'Beauty of the Seas.'"

"She is a beauty," Kiara said, sighing as she looked at the white luxury vessel ahead.

"That she is."

We were able to board the yacht a short time later. Cambrielle and I gave a tour of the four upper decks to our friends who hadn't been out here with us last year—showing them the various staterooms, sitting areas, gym, and IMAX theater.

"So this is basically like a really big house on the water?" Kiara asked when we walked into my parents' suite.

"Essentially," I said. "But my parents entertain clients out here quite a bit during the summer and charter it out the rest of the year, so they rationalize having such an extravagant thing by calling it a business investment."

"Nice."

We finished our tour, and everyone decided to hang out at the pool while Ian and his buddies worked to impress their dates with their grilling abilities.

"Didn't feel like getting in the pool?" I asked Kiara when I found her sitting on one of the seats overlooking the water, still wearing the same tank top and jean shorts she had on earlier.

"I just needed a few minutes of quiet time." She moved her gaze away from the water to look at me, her eyes briefly running over my bare torso and swim shorts. "It would seem I'm a bit of an introvert and need to recharge before I get in party mode tonight."

"Am I bothering you then?" I asked. My mom and Carter

were introverts so I knew how essential downtime could be after a lot of "peopling."

"No, you're good. I never mind talking to you." She smiled at me.

"Well, that's good," I said, taking the seat across from her. "Because I always like talking to you, too." I draped my arm across the railing, and as I pulled my phone out of my pocket and set it on the bench between us, an idea suddenly popped into my mind.

An idea that might help us get all the secrets out in the open right here and now instead of waiting another two days.

"Speaking of not minding talking to me," I said, deciding to follow my impulse, "that reminds me that I still haven't gotten your phone number."

"My phone number?" Her voice went higher. "Um, y-yeah..." she stammered, sitting up straighter as a look of panic filled her face. "You're right...I-I didn't realize that."

"We've been hanging out so much that I didn't think about it, either," I said, using some of my acting skills to make it seem like I was clueless about how she was scrambling to get out of this without revealing her secret. I quirked my lips up into a half-smile. "But it would be nice to be able to just text or call you instead of messaging through social media or knocking on your door, right?"

"Yeah...that would be better..." Her eyes tightened and she bit her lip like she was concentrating really hard on figuring out how to sidestep giving her number to me. Something I was just now realizing she'd actually done before.

Man, she'd been so good at this.

Then something changed in her eyes, and I knew she had an idea brewing.

What had she come up with this time?

But instead of changing the subject or distracting me with a sudden shark sighting in the water, she surprised me by actually reaching for her phone.

Was she going to tell me then? Was she actually giving me her number and letting me see it was the same as Wrong Number Girl's?

My heart raced with anticipation over the idea that we might finally be laying all our secrets out right here and now.

"Just tell me your number and I'll text you," she said.

But as she was lifting her phone from her pocket, she appeared not to know her own strength because it came out with much gusto, and before I knew it, her phone was flying over the glass railing beside us and dropping right into the Atlantic Ocean.

"Oh, no!" She gasped, covering her mouth with her hands as if shocked. "I-I can't believe I just did that." She kneeled on the bench and bent over the rail as if looking for it in the water below. "I'm *such* a klutz."

And man, if I didn't know better, I might have actually believed this was an accident because Kiara was a surprisingly good actor.

And apparently determined to not let this Wrong Number Girl thing out of the bag until the very end.

So I decided to play along with her little stunt for now and looked at the water for a moment with her, as if in shock, before shaking my head and saying, "The universe really doesn't want me to get your phone number, does it?"

"It would seem not," she said way too innocently.

Man, someone needed to sign this girl up for the next Eden Falls community play!

But since every good actor deserved to be challenged every once in a while, I narrowed my eyes and said, "Unless you just did that on purpose."

Come on, Kiara. Just tell me!

What do you think is going to happen?

Because I'm pretty sure the only thing I want to do right now is kiss you for your amazing ability to stay in character during this performance of yours.

"You think I dropped my eight-hundred-dollar phone into the ocean on purpose?" she asked, her jaw hanging open.

"I don't know." I shrugged. "Did you?"

"Only an idiot would do that," she said.

"Well, you're definitely not an idiot, so it must have been an accident." Then deciding it was time to really test her spur-of-the-moment performance, I picked up my own phone and said, "But no worries. You can just give me your number and I'll text you mine when you get a replacement phone."

"Ohhh, yeah..." she said, drawing out the words as she bit her lip. "I've actually been thinking about going with a new provider. Um, you know, get on my own plan now that I'm eighteen and will be moving out soon."

"So you'll probably be getting a new phone number, anyway." I nodded slowly, seeing where this was going.

"Yes, probably." She nodded. "I mean, and it will probably be a while before I can even afford a new phone since all of my money is going towards tuition and housing soon, so..." She shook her head. And then, a shadow crossed her face, as if she was only just realizing how expensive and inconvenient it was becoming to avoid telling me she was the girl from last summer.

Should I just tell her that I knew? Tell her the game was up and we could just go buy her a new phone in the morning and laugh about this?

"Hey, Kiara!" Alessi called from the pool. "Miles needs someone to play chicken with against me and Bash. Come play with us!"

Kiara looked toward her friend who was already standing in the middle of the pool with the two guys. Seeming to see this as her way out of our conversation, she turned back to me and said, "I better go help Miles."

As I watched her walk to the pool, pulling down her jean shorts and taking off her tank top to reveal a blue bathing suit, I had to smile to myself.

Because never in a million years did I think a girl would throw her phone in the ocean just to avoid giving me her number.

Kiara was definitely one of a kind, wasn't she?

But since there still seemed to be a part of her that doubted I'd be excited to see it was her at the falls on Wednesday night, I knew I needed to do what I could to remove all of those doubts.

I'd never been successful in getting a girl to be my girlfriend before. But I was determined that after tonight, there would be no doubt in Kiara's mind that I wanted her to be mine.

43

KIARA

ANTICIPATION BUZZED in the air as everyone gathered on the lower deck of the yacht, preparing to watch the Fourth of July fireworks display. I scanned the area, searching for Nash among the group of his friends and family.

Where did he go?

I'd seen him disappear on one of the upper decks about twenty minutes ago, expecting him to come right back. But he was still nowhere to be seen.

Had he decided to watch the fireworks from up there?

By himself?

Even though I was still unsure of where we stood since he was still excited to see Wrong Number Girl, I had been hoping to at least share this magical moment with him.

Watching fireworks with the guy you liked always seemed so romantic, and I wanted to experience at least one more romantic moment with him before my secret came out.

"Kiara, come sit with us," Alessi said, patting the lounge chair beside her. "The fireworks are about to start."

I checked my watch. It was just a few minutes before nine-thirty, and I knew the fireworks would begin any moment. Resigned to the idea of watching them without Nash, I walked over to sit with Alessi, Bash, and Miles.

"One more minute," Ava called from a few seats to my right. "Happy Independence Day, everyone!"

"Happy Independence Day," I said back with everyone else, slightly less enthusiastically.

Where is Nash?

I was just looking over my left shoulder to scan the crowd and see if he'd slipped into a seat near someone else when a tap on my right shoulder startled me.

When I turned around, Nash was standing right there, a mischievous grin playing on his lips.

"Want to watch the fireworks in a more secluded place?" he asked, his eyes sparkling with excitement.

"Where?" I asked, anticipation warming me.

He pointed to the deck above. "My parents have a private deck just off their suite."

I looked up to where he was pointing and excitement bubbled inside me as I said, "Let's go."

Then leaning closer to Alessi before I stood, I whispered, "Guess I'm going somewhere else."

Alessi looked at Nash and then at me, and with a knowing smile, she said, "Have fun up there, you two."

"We will," Nash said, and when he took my hand in his to lead me up the stairs to the deck above, a rabble of butterflies took flight in my stomach.

Nash led me through his parents' suite and opened the sliding glass door to reveal what he must have spent the last twenty-five minutes setting up.

There was a cozy daybed adorned with blankets and an array of soft pillows. A tray sat nearby, with chocolate-covered strawberries and fizzy drinks.

"Wow!" I gasped after taking it all in. "You did all this for us?"

"For you," Nash said, his eyes sparkling. "I wanted to do something special for you."

"Really?" My throat was suddenly tight with emotion as tears stung my eyes.

He nodded. "I wanted to find a way to show you how special you are to me" He studied my face with a gentle look. "And how thankful I am that we've gotten to know each other this summer."

"This is so sweet," I said, looking around at the setup once more before meeting his eyes in the moonlight. "No one has ever done something like this for me before."

"I'm glad you like it," he said, using his thumb to gently sweep away a tear at the corner of my eye. He gestured at the daybed. "I think the fireworks are about to start. Shall we?"

"Yes."

So we both climbed onto the daybed, nestling ourselves against the plush pillows. And even though the daybed was quite large, I loved how close Nash scooted next to me. Close enough that our arms rested against one another's.

We gazed up at the starlit sky, and within moments, the first fireworks exploded in a colorful spectacle in the distance. And when Nash slipped his hand over mine and intertwined our fingers tighter, it felt like fireworks might just start exploding inside of me, too.

"Is this okay?" he asked, running his thumb over mine.

"Yes," I said, looking up at him and studying the way the light from the fireworks lit up his face. "It's more than okay."

"Good."

We watched the fireworks like that for a few minutes. The loud booms in the distance rumbling in my ears, the colorful splashes of lights creating a sense of awe.

"This is perfect," I said, turning to Nash and resting my head beside his on the pillow.

"It really is," he said, giving me a boyish grin that was contagious. "I'm glad you came up here with me."

"I'm glad you invited me."

When he tucked his arm around my shoulders, I allowed myself to scoot even closer, resting my head against his chest as I'd done in my sleep yesterday.

His heart beat steadily against my ear, and I liked the feel of it. It was soothing. Peaceful.

"Did Cambrielle ever show you which room you and Alessi would be staying in tonight?" Nash asked, drawing slow lines along my arm with his finger.

"We're sharing the one with the cherry blossoms all over it."

"Oh that's a nice one."

"Which room is yours?" I asked, wondering if his was on the same deck as mine or anywhere close to it.

"I'm staying in there tonight." He pointed to his parents' suite behind us.

"Really?" I tilted my head back to look into the huge bedroom we'd come through to get to the deck. "Ian didn't claim it for himself?"

"We were supposed to share it," Nash said. "But he and the girl he brought didn't quite hit things off, so he's planning to take her back to shore after the fireworks show is over."

"So now you get the biggest room on the boat all to yourself?"

"Yep." Nash smiled. "Ian's loss is my gain, I guess. Though, I'm sure he'll find another girl to bring here later this summer. He's pretty good at that."

"I kind of gathered that about him," I said, thinking of all the other girls I'd seen Ian bring home with him this past year.

"Yeah, Ian hasn't really figured out how to focus on one girl for very long."

"And what do you think about that?" I asked, curious if Nash was similar to Ian in that respect since he was still planning to meet with who he thought was a girl he hadn't seen in a year, just two nights after doing this sweet thing for me.

Would Nash ever want to be the boyfriend type? Or did he like the idea of playing the field a lot first?

"I think he's having fun." Nash shrugged. "But I don't think I could ever date as much as he does. When I'm invested in a girl, I can't really pay attention to anyone else."

"Really?" I furrowed my brow, unable to keep the skepticism from my voice since he was literally texting who he thought was another girl right now.

Or, at least he probably would be texting her if her phone wasn't at the bottom of the Atlantic Ocean at the moment.

"I'm a one-woman man." He turned slightly to study my face. "But it kind of sounds like you don't believe me. Have I done something to make you doubt that?"

"Um...kind of..." I said, my voice going higher. "I mean, I guess I'm just a little confused since you did all this for me tonight after telling me three days ago that you liked someone else."

"Oh...yeah..." He scrunched up his nose, a flash of guilt filling his eyes. "When I said all those things on the ferry, and in my car...that was just me being really stupid and confused."

"Stupid and confused?"

He nodded. "I acted like an idiot on Friday and..." He sighed, his blue-eyed gaze sincere as he searched my eyes. "I actually feel horrible that my confusion hurt you. You didn't deserve any of that."

"Yeah?" I asked, my pulse thundering in my ears as I hoped he'd continue to explain what had changed between now and last night when he'd told Wrong Number Girl that he was excited to meet her.

"I honestly wish I could go back and tell myself to shut up and just keep kissing you on the ferry," he said, turning on his side and propping himself up on his arm to look at me better. "Because it really was the perfect moment." He licked his lips and looked down briefly. "I think I was just so caught off guard by how much I liked you and that kiss. So I got scared and...I don't know...I guess my first instinct was to sabotage the moment since I wasn't used to things ever being so perfect with a girl."

"Really?" My heart was melting at his explanation.

He nodded. "I know I probably tricked you with all that fake boyfriend and Casanova stuff...but I'm literally just fumbling my way through all of this." He reached out to tuck some hair behind my ear. "Sometimes it just takes me a while to figure things out."

When his eyes met mine in the firework-studded night, I was suddenly hit with the thought that Nash might have figured things out.

Maybe he'd been more affectionate the last couple of days because he'd somehow figured out I was Wrong Number Girl.

And he hadn't been mad or disappointed or anything like that. Maybe he was actually happy about it.

"I really like you, Kiara," he whispered, dipping his face down so his forehead rested against mine.

"You do?" I asked, not daring to ask him my other questions in case I was wrong.

I didn't know exactly where this moment was going, but it kind of seemed really good and I didn't want to possibly mess it up.

"I like you a lot," he said, looking deeply into my eyes.

And it felt like I was dreaming because this couldn't actually be happening right now, could it?

I couldn't actually be lying on this daybed with the guy of my dreams, hearing him say the exact words that I'd dreamed of hearing since last July.

That he liked me.

That the girl from everywhere could mean something to the boy with the whole world at his feet.

But this was happening. And he was looking at me like he actually thought I was something special.

So I found the courage to admit the words I'd been holding inside for almost a year and whispered, "I like you too, Nash." I swallowed, letting my gaze dart back and forth between his ocean-blue eyes. "So much."

So much it hurt sometimes.

So much and for so long that it would probably scare him if he knew just how long I'd liked him for.

He smiled, seeming to like hearing those words from me. He ran his knuckle across my cheek, causing a trail of heat to glow everywhere, and said, "Then I think there's just one thing we need to do." His thumb gently ran over my bottom lip. "Something I regret stopping when we were on the ferry."

"Yeah?" I asked, unable to say any other words from the anticipation currently pulsing through my limbs.

"Yes," he said. "This..." And before another moment could pass, he slipped his hand behind my neck then gently pressed his lips to mine.

It took a second for my brain to catch on to the fact that this was actually happening. That Nash was actually kissing me, and this wasn't just another one of my daydreams. But once my brain caught up with the fact that Nash's lips were actually moving against mine, I put my hands on either side of his face and kissed him back.

The kiss was slow at first, unhurried as we allowed our lips to get to know one another. He tasted of mint and ChapStick, and he smelled of his intoxicating cologne. And when he slipped his hand behind my waist to pull my hips closer, I gasped as my pulse went haywire.

"Is this okay?" he asked, pausing the kiss for a moment to check in with me.

"Y-yes." I panted, looking down at how close our bodies were now pressed together. So close that all the space between us had been completely erased. Then meeting his eyes again, I breathed the words, "I like being close to you."

His lips curved up at the corners. He leaned his face closer so his lips were mere centimeters away from mine, and then he mumbled, "I like being close to you too," before kissing me again.

Our lips met again and again. And it was so crazy to me that this was only our fourth kiss—because instead of feeling clumsy or awkward like the early stages of kissing usually felt like with a new person, this moment just felt right. So unbelievably right.

Like we were meant to be doing this all along.

And as the world around us faded away, all my worries and insecurities did, too.

Because Nash liked me. He'd said those words himself.

And even if he was surprised or shocked when he'd see me at the falls two nights from now, I had a feeling that he would also be happy. Happy that his fantasy girl was actually just... me.

Nash's hand slipped up the side of my ribcage, his touch both gentle and possessive. When he deepened the kiss with the slightest flick of his tongue, my insides swirled with heat before lighting on fire.

And oh my heck, I liked the way that felt. Deciding to be a

bit daring myself, I deepened the kiss again. When he let out a soft groan, I knew he liked it, too.

"How does this feel so good?" Nash asked, his voice full of wonder as if he had never experienced a moment like this before.

"I don't know," I said, not sure I had the presence of mind to really theorize about that at the moment. "But I can't believe you ever thought you needed a kissing tutor."

"Maybe it's like you said," he mumbled breathlessly between kisses. "Maybe I was never kissing the right person before. Maybe all along I should have been kissing the girl in my backyard."

"I think you're probably right," I said as his lips trailed a path from my mouth to my jawline, leaving a trail of fire in their wake.

We should have been doing this since the moment we danced in your backyard.

He kissed me again before sucking gently on my neck. When his mouth found its way back to mine and he rolled on top of me with his six-foot-two-inch frame, it felt like the fireworks were going off in my body along with the sky above.

"You okay with this, too?" he asked, looking down at me with desire and want in his eyes.

"Yes," I said, finding it slightly harder to breathe with the delicious weight of his muscular body on mine. "This is perfect."

So perfect.

44

NASH

WHO IS THIS GIRL? I wondered as Kiara pushed me onto my back until I was inclined against the pillows. I watched in awe as she climbed on top of me and straddled my hips with her knees. *Because this is kind of insane.*

And hot.

Like, I knew Kiara had to be better at all of this than me, but dang...this was so incredibly hot.

It was like the girl I'd had that hot-tub kiss with in my dream a couple of weeks ago was actually real. Like I'd been dreaming about a moment that could actually exist with Kiara.

"How is this even my life right now?" I muttered as she pulled her hair over one shoulder and leaned in closer to me. "Are you even real?" I asked, reaching up and brushing her cheek with my thumb.

"I think so," she said, a slow smile lifting her lips at my question.

She leaned the rest of the way down, and when she started kissing me again, her tongue parting my lips, I knew I had to be the luckiest guy in the world tonight.

I let my hands graze across her hips, loving how soft she was right there. When she whispered my name against my lips followed by a single word, "Closer," a surge of desire I'd never felt before coursed through me.

The fireworks gave their final bursts in the sky, painting it with their vibrant colors for the last time. And when everyone cheered and clapped on the deck below, Kiara seemed to remember where we were.

"Do you think they can see us up here?" she asked, panting breathlessly as she turned her head to look in the direction of their applause.

"I don't think so," I said. "I think the daybed is far enough back that they can't see us."

"Could they accidentally walk up here though?" she asked.

"No." I shook my head. "This is a private deck. The only way to get here is through the bedroom door."

Which...I'd locked.

I hadn't been sure something like this would happen when I'd brought her up here, but I'd certainly hoped it might.

"Good," she said.

Then before I knew what was happening, she was sitting up again and unbuttoning my shirt.

"Is this okay?" she asked, peeking down at me through her lashes when she'd worked through half of my buttons.

"Y-yeah," I said, trying to sound cool even though every touch of her fingertips sent shivers down my spine. "Th-that's fine. Nice."

"Good," she said. "Because I've wanted to do this for so long."

But when her lips brushed against my neck and collarbone, and she smoothed her hands across my chest, a twinge of nerves started to tingle at the back of my mind.

I had never done anything like this with a girl before. Never had someone unbutton my shirt and explore. So in the midst of pleasure, the intensity of the moment and the connection I felt with Kiara overwhelmed me.

Was kissing all we were doing here?

Or was she hoping this would turn into something more?

Something I wasn't sure I was ready for, regardless of how much I liked her.

"R-remember when I mentioned that I thought I needed a kissing tutor?" I managed to say, my voice breathless and uncertain.

"You're trying that lie on me again?" Kiara paused, her eyes meeting mine, her touch still lingering against my chest. "Because there is absolutely no way I can believe that after the past twenty minutes."

"I know..." I gulped, looking down. "It's just—" I blinked my eyes shut, needing to close them as I got up the nerve to be painfully vulnerable with her. "I-I really like this, Kiara. Like... a lot." I opened my eyes again so she could see in my gaze just how much I liked everything that was happening between us right now. "But I—" I sighed, not believing I was actually about to admit this. "I'm a virgin, and I'm sure you have a lot more experience than me, but I just...I don't think I'm ready to, um, you know, not be a virgin quite yet."

"Oh." Her movements halted as the weight of my confession registered. "Sorry, um...I was just unbuttoning your shirt." She removed her hands from my chest like I'd suddenly burned her, lifting them in the air like I was the police and this was a hostage situation. "I-I wasn't planning to do much more than that. I'm a virgin, too." She swallowed, her tone tinged with embarrassment. "Sorry if I pushed things too far. I thought it was okay..."

"Oh," I said, my voice embarrassingly high for some reason as I realized I had gotten ahead of myself. "No, that's...that's fine," I stammered. "Um, actually, that's great. In fact, let me help you." I sat up and pulled my shirt the rest of the way off. Then tossing it aside, the action more hurried than smooth, I said, "Is this better?"

"This is great." Kiara smiled as she took in the sight of my bare upper body, thankfully seeming to find my awkwardness more endearing than a turn-off.

"Okay, good." I blew out a low breath. Then since I knew I wasn't coming off as cool as I'd hoped, I gave her a bashful look and said, "Sorry I'm so awkward." I shook my head. "I just really like you and I don't want to mess things up."

"I really like you too, Nash." She bit her lip like she was considering something. After a beat, she looked bashfully down at me and said, "And since we're being honest here, I should probably tell you that I've kind of had a crush on you for a long time."

"Really?" I asked.

She nodded, a hint of nerves in her eyes as she added, "Like, I don't want to tell you how long I've had a thing for you since it will probably make you freak out, but um, it's been a while. Which is why I'm totally fine taking things slow. Just being like this with you is already more than I could have hoped for."

She wasn't admitting to being the girl from the garden party yet. But somehow, this felt better.

I leaned forward to kiss her once more, and as our lips met in another passionate exchange, the weight of the world melted away. Kiara's hands roamed across my shoulders, squeezed my biceps, and traced down my sides. And since I wanted to also be a giver and not just a taker, I allowed myself to do some exploring of my own.

I smoothed my hands along the fabric at her waist then ran them up the ridges of her sides. And when she arched into me like she wanted more, I couldn't help but grin against her lips.

I had never dared do anything like this with a girl before—my nerves had always gotten the better of me. But even though this was as exhilarating as all get out, I only became more and more sure of myself as the minutes passed because her happy sighs and soft moans told me she was enjoying this moment as much as I was.

I kissed my way down her jawline then sucked gently on the skin just beside the hollow of her neck, enjoying the feel of her steady heartbeat beneath my lips.

"I like that..." she said breathlessly as her head tilted back.

I moved the strap of her tank top aside to kiss her collarbone. But when the black strap of her bra came into view, I was suddenly distracted by the tempting sight.

Black again. This was the third time I'd seen a black bra of hers.

Once through her window. Once when I'd retrieved the bra from her pug. And now.

I tucked my finger beneath the strap, then smoothing my thumb down the fabric an inch or two, I found myself asking, "Black really is your favorite, isn't it?"

It took her a second to snap out of a daze and register my words. But then she said, "Pink is my favorite color but, yeah, I like the way black looks on me."

"I like the way it looks on you, too," I said. It really did look amazing next to her bronzed skin.

And I suddenly wanted to see more...just to see if my memory was accurate.

"How would you know how I look in it?" she asked, unaware of the thoughts running through my mind right now. "I don't think I've worn anything black all summer."

"Oh, um..." I said, trying to think of a time I'd seen her

wearing black that didn't include when I'd seen her through her window.

There had to be another time. Especially if she liked the way she looked in the color.

"Weren't you wearing a black apron a couple of weeks ago?" I asked, knowing full well that her apron had been pink when she'd been working in my kitchen.

"Try again." She grinned.

"Um..." I said, trying to think of another time. Any other time.

Come on, brain. Work!

"Does this have anything to do with that dream you had?" she asked, running her fingers playfully up my chest when I didn't say anything. "The dream you mentioned on Friday when we were driving here."

"M-my dream?" I gulped. I hadn't actually gone into detail about the dreams I'd had about her, had I?

"Yes, your dream." She nodded, a mischievous spark in her eyes. "You mentioned that you must have seen me working out in one of my black sports bras in a dream before."

I had slipped up and said that, hadn't I...

That was a pretty innocent type of dream to have though, right?

At least a workout dream was way more innocent than the real dreams I'd had about her and me.

And definitely more innocent than the night I'd actually seen her through her window...

Deciding to go along with her assumption, I said, "Um, sure. Let's go with that."

"Let's go with that?" She narrowed her gaze. Then covering my hand with hers, she asked, "What are you not telling me, Nash? Was it actually not a dream then?"

"Okay, fine..." I sighed, deciding to just come out with it.

"There might have been a night where I accidentally discovered that your bedroom window faces my balcony."

Please don't think I'm a creeper.

But instead of calling me out like I expected, her eyebrows arched in amusement as she said, "You *just* figured that out?" She laughed. "Because I'm pretty sure I've known that for a while."

"What?"

She lifted a shoulder and gave me an innocent look. "Don't worry. The most revealing thing I ever saw was when you walked onto the balcony wearing your boxer briefs one night."

I shook my head and chuckled. "So is that when you first decided you liked me? Because I tempted you from my balcony?"

"That's not exactly what did it." She laughed. "But it certainly didn't hurt."

45

KIARA

NASH and I walked hand in hand back to my room a little after midnight. The last two and a half hours had been magical and everything I'd hoped for. And after spending the better part of that time kissing and laughing and just having a really great conversation, I was even more certain that he'd be excited to see me at the falls two nights from now.

"I better let you get some sleep," Nash said after he'd pressed me against the wall beside my door and kissed me again for a few minutes. "Even though I really don't want to leave."

"I don't want you to leave either," I said, taking his hands in mine. Then raising an eyebrow, I added, "We could always go back to your room...I know how much you like to cuddle."

"Always tempting me, aren't you?" he said, a half-smile playing at his lips.

"I just have good ideas, that's all."

"It is a good idea," he said. And for a second, it really looked like he was considering it. But then he sighed and said, "But I need to prove that I still have at least a tiny bit of a gentleman inside of me tonight. So I better sleep alone."

"I guess you're right," I said, even though part of me didn't actually want him to be such a gentleman.

But I wouldn't push my luck. If things kept going the way I hoped they would, we'd have plenty of nights in the future where we'd simply have to say good night instead of goodbye.

Because Nash liked me.

Wanted me.

I could barely believe this was even real. That he was actually looking at me like I was special and beautiful and like it really was hard for him to leave me here instead of taking me back to his room.

"Good night, Kiara," he said before pressing a soft kiss to my forehead. "I'll see you in the morning."

"Good night."

I watched him walk down the hall to the room he had to himself for the night. When he made it to his door, he turned back to look at me one last time.

And when he blew me a kiss, I melted.

I expected Alessi to be asleep when I walked into our room since most everyone else had cleared off the main deck an hour ago. But when I stepped inside, I found her sitting on the edge of the queen-sized bed we'd be sharing, with a look that said I had a lot of explaining to do.

"So..." she said after I shut the door. "When exactly were you planning to tell me that you and Nash have the hots for each other?"

"Um..." I scrunched up my face and lifted a shoulder. "How about right now?"

"Yeah, I think right now sounds like a good time," she said. But instead of seeming annoyed or betrayed, she had a huge grin on her face that told me she was excited to hear my story.

So I told her everything, starting with the garden party to the ridiculous amount of pining I'd done over the past eleven months, to the accidental text then to the sparks I'd felt and hoped were reciprocated every time Nash and I hung out.

I even admitted to kissing him at the Yankees game, because once Wednesday night had come and gone, I didn't want to be keeping any more secrets.

"I can't believe you didn't tell me you liked Nash!" Alessi said once I finished telling her everything. "You must have hated me when I was flirting with him."

"I didn't hate you," I said, relieved that she didn't seem upset after hearing my story. "I knew you wouldn't have gone after him if you'd known how I felt." I shrugged. "But yeah...I'd be lying if I didn't admit to being insanely jealous when he asked you out instead of me."

"I don't blame you," she said. "I'd be jealous, too."

"And when you texted me to say you had the most amazing first date, I kind of regretted telling him to take you to a fancy restaurant instead of exploring the cave he wanted to take you to."

"He almost took me to a cave?" Her eyes widened.

"Apparently, he has a thing for them," I said, remembering all the times he'd brought caves up in conversation with both me and my alter ego. "But when I told him you were more of a dinner-and-a-movie kind of girl, he changed his plans."

"Wow, you're a way better friend than me," she said, chuckling. "Because if you were going on a date with the guy I'd liked for a year, I totally would have let him take you to a cave and then done everything I could to sabotage you if the cave didn't already do the trick."

I laughed, knowing she wasn't exaggerating. "Good thing Miles introduced you to Bash so we could still be friends after this summer."

"For real."

Nash and I drove back to Eden Falls together the next day. He held my hand most of the way, and to my relief, the ferry ride back thankfully went *much* better than the one to the Hamptons.

I hung out with my mom that night and told her all about my weekend as we took Duke on a long walk. Then when we got back to the house, I went into my room to search for the perfect outfit to wear to the falls the next night.

Nash seemed to have a thing for black...and I did have a black romper that was pretty cute.

But would that go well with the pink wig I'd be wearing?

I pulled the romper and the wig from my closet and stood in front of the mirror with them to see how they looked together.

As I inspected my reflection, a thrill of nerves washed over me.

So much had happened since I'd made the impulsive decision to wear a pink wig to that party last year. I had gone through a lot and changed so much.

And now, in less than twenty-four hours, I would find out if that dance and the stolen kiss in the woods had actually been as life-changing as they felt.

I went to work the next day. I didn't know if Nash had told his mom about the way things had shifted between us over the holiday weekend, but when she saw me on her way out the door, she seemed even friendlier than usual, telling me she was so thrilled that Nash and I had gotten to know each other better this summer.

My mom had me work on the family's bedrooms that day, even though I usually cleaned the kitchen and other rooms on the main level on Wednesdays. I went through the bedrooms in my usual order: Carter's, Cambrielle's, then Ian's old room, and finally, Nash's.

I'd gotten faster in the past few weeks, so instead of starting his room around three-thirty like I had the first week, it was only two o'clock in the afternoon when I stepped into the beautiful yet masculine bedroom that was decorated in blues, whites, and yellows.

I grabbed a clean dust cloth from my cart and got started on the dusting first. When I was dusting the bookshelf near his couch, I noticed a white slip of paper that seemed out of place.

I picked it up, and when I looked more closely, it was a note written to me in Nash's handwriting.

K,

Sorry you have to clean up after me. It feels wrong somehow now that you know how much I like you. (You really know all my secrets now, don't you?) But...since you're here and you do such an amazing job at making my room a peaceful haven to come home to, I thought it might be fun to send you on a little treasure hunt. I hope you know how these go...

So, without further explanation, I think you should look under my pillow.

Happy hunting!

-N

I smiled after I read his note. Nash was sending me on a treasure hunt?

How fun!

I hadn't been to one of these in years. Not since I was little. But I used to do them all the time because my dad was always bringing fun little treasures home from work and made giving them to me into a game.

Which was something Wrong Number Girl had mentioned to Nash in one of our late-night texting sessions last week.

So Nash *had* to know Wrong Number Girl was me, right? He wouldn't do something for me that a different girl had mentioned loving, would he?

"Guess I'll find out that answer tonight, won't I?" I said to myself, deciding to stop worrying about that and go on this fun treasure hunt instead.

I walked across the room to his bed and looked under the pillow. And right beneath it was another slip of paper with a note.

K,

You have the most captivating smile I've ever seen. I hope I have many more chances to see you smile.

Look under my couch cushion.

-N

I smiled as I raced toward his couch, interested in what the next clue might say. Because if it was another compliment, I might just want this to last all day.

K,

Your kindness and compassion toward others inspire me to be a better person. You have such a beautiful soul.

Look in the second drawer on the far left in my closet.

-N

I went into Nash's closet, curious which drawer he was sending me to since I'd never dared open any of the drawers before. Inside the drawer he'd indicated, I found another clue sitting on top of his neatly folded T-shirts.

Thank goodness he hadn't thought to be funny and send me to his underwear drawer. That would be awkward.

K,
I admire your ambition and drive. You have the determination to achieve your dreams, and I have no doubt you'll succeed.
Look on my bathroom counter.
-N

I put my hand over my heart as I read his words again, not knowing until that moment just how much I needed someone besides my mom to tell me they believed in my dreams.

The next several clues went much the same. Each started with a meaningful compliment that made me smile, followed by another clue.

As his clues led me to various hiding places around his room, I learned that Nash thought I was beautiful, smart, fun, and sexy—which he said he meant "in the most gentlemanly way" so he didn't scare me off—and he loved my "beautiful and genuine heart."

By the time I made it to the eighth or ninth clue, I literally didn't care if there was anything besides another note at the end of this because hearing Nash thought all of these things about me was a treasure all of its own.

It was all I'd ever dreamed but didn't dare hope a guy would feel about me someday.

The tenth clue led me to his desk. When I opened the middle drawer, there was a rectangular box inside wrapped in white wrapping paper with an elegant eucalyptus-stem print. There was a note with my name tucked under the twine that had been tied in a bow around the gift.

What's in the box? I wondered as I lifted it from the drawer. It wasn't too heavy, only a pound or two.

I carried it over to the couch so I could open it and see what was inside.

But I made myself read the note first.

Kiara,

Thanks for indulging me by going on this little treasure hunt. I wanted to find a way to show you a little of how I feel about you. You are such an amazing girl and I'm so glad that we got to know each other this summer. I know it's only been a month, but it seems like I've known you much longer than that. Being with you feels like coming home. You make me feel safe in a way no one else ever has before and your presence is always comforting. (Kiara cuddles are my favorite for a reason!)

So, in case it wasn't obvious yet, I really like you, Kiara. And I can't wait to continue to get to know you better.

Yours,
Nash

"Oh Nash..." I said, feeling choked up as I ran the tips of

my fingers over the sweet words he'd written. How was he even real?

I read through his note once more, knowing I'd probably read his words again and again. Then I set the note beside me on the couch and opened the gift.

I knew exactly what was inside the box as soon as I saw the image printed on top.

He'd gotten me a phone!

And not just any phone, but the latest model of the iPhone that had just been released.

I'd always gotten my mom's hand-me-downs before, so having a brand-new, never-been-scratched-or-accidentally-dropped phone was completely new territory for me.

I opened the box, excited to see what color he'd picked for me. When I looked inside, I saw it was light pink.

He'd been listening when I'd told him my favorite color.

There was also a sticky note with his name and number stuck to the screen that said, *For when you want to text me.*

I powered it on, curious if anything was set up on it yet. But once the Apple logo disappeared, it prompted me to set up my new iPhone.

I'd have to have my mom help me get it on her plan and all set up later. Because unlike the nonsense I'd spewed on the yacht, I quite liked saving money by being on my mom's plan.

I carefully set my phone back in the box, not wanting the beautiful gift to get any scratches before I could find the perfect case for it. Then after finding a special place for it on my cleaning cart, I got back to work.

I had a big evening ahead of me. I didn't want to be late.

46

KIARA

NASH CAME up the stairs just as I was returning my cleaning cart to its closet. He looked handsome in his suit and tie, and I couldn't help but smile at him when he made it to the top of the stairs.

"Hey," he said, returning my smile when he saw me in the hall. "Just finishing up?"

"I was just heading out."

"And how was work?" he asked. "Anything exciting happen?"

"As a matter of fact," I said, picking up the phone box from where I'd stowed it on my cart, "I went on a treasure hunt and found a new phone. Apparently, someone really wants to be able to contact me."

"He must be smitten with you or something," Nash said, his eyes sparkling.

"I'm pretty smitten with him, too," I said, loving that I could say that out loud. "Thank you for the phone. I really appreciate it."

"It was a purely selfish gesture." He grinned. "I just really wanted to have a reason for you to have my phone number."

"Well, I have it now," I said, holding up the box. "And once I get this all set up, I'll make sure to text you so you can have my number, too."

"Finally!" he said with a smile. "If I'd known the only thing I needed to do to get your phone number was to buy you a new phone, I would have done that weeks ago."

I giggled. Then pulling the notes he'd given me out of the front pockets of my uniform, I said, "And thanks for all the sweet words you wrote. I think I may like these even more than the phone."

"I'm glad you liked them." He looked at me shyly, blushing a little. "I meant every word." He took my hand in his and pulled me into his arms. Then speaking into my hair, he said, "Man, I missed you today."

Footsteps sounded on the stairs behind him, and a second later, Cambrielle appeared at the end of the hall. A small smile lifted her lips when she saw me and Nash standing close together, and I wondered how much Nash may have told her about us.

She said hi, and we chatted a little about a murder mystery dinner she was helping Ava and Elyse plan in a few weeks, which she said I needed to come to.

"I've never been to one of those before," I said. "But I think it sounds fun."

"Great!" Cambrielle smiled. "We'll all have different roles and Nash already told me what a good actor you are, so I think it should be really fun."

"Nash told you I was a good actor?" I furrowed my brow, confused why he'd say that.

"Yeah, when you were on the yacht he said—"

"That you were really good at pretending to enjoy that

game of chicken," Nash said, interrupting whatever Cambrielle had been about to say. "I definitely didn't tell my sister that I thought you were acting when you *accidentally* dropped your phone over the edge of the boat." He winked.

"No, he definitely didn't say anything like that." Cambrielle grinned.

"Well, I got a brand-new phone out of my little acting gig," I said, unable to keep from smiling at their teasing. "So I guess it all worked out, didn't it?"

"I guess it did," Nash said, squeezing me closer to his side.

"That's actually a really good idea." Cambrielle gasped, her eyes lighting up. "Maybe I should try something like that next time we're on the yacht. I *have* been trying to convince Mom that I needed a new Louis Vuitton bag..."

"Well, if you decide to start dropping designer bags overboard," I said, imagining a bunch of perfectly good bags floating in the ocean, "just make sure to drop them from one of the upper decks while I'm there so I can grab them before they hit the ocean."

The siblings both chuckled at my plan, and then Cambrielle said, "Deal."

After Cambrielle went into her room and we were alone once more, I decided to employ some of those acting skills Nash was apparently impressed by and have a little fun with him now that I was even more sure he knew exactly why I couldn't give him my number on the boat.

So I asked, "Do you want to hang out tonight? I was thinking it would be fun to watch a movie or take Duke and Duchess on a walk together later."

Because really, did we even need the whole production of meeting at the falls tonight when we already knew we liked each other?

But instead of taking my offer, he said, "I wish I could. But I'm actually meeting an old friend this evening."

I should have guessed he'd say something like that since he was more theatrical than me and probably had something up his sleeve for our meeting tonight.

"But I'm free tomorrow night and would love to hang out," he added, playing his role perfectly.

Or does he actually not know?

Instead of asking him, I decided to play along and said, "Sure, I'd love to hang out tomorrow."

"Perfect," he said, his eyes smiling. "It's a date."

"Yes, it is."

He looked at the time on his watch, and as if surprised that it was already five-twenty, he said, "I better get changed. I don't want to be late for my meetup tonight."

"Have fun tonight," I said.

"Oh I will." Then with a mischievous look, he added, "I'm really looking forward to it."

I parked my mom's car in the parking area near the falls about fifteen minutes before the sun was supposed to set. There was another way to get there through the Hastings' property, but since I didn't want to be glistening with sweat when I came face to face with Nash in my pink wig and the peasant girl dress my mom had been able to find in one of the Hastings' storage closets, I drove instead.

There was a slight breeze in the air along with the scent of the forest greenery as I walked up the same path I was on almost a year ago. But instead of feeling anxious and uncertain about how this meeting would go, all I felt on the quarter mile toward the falls was a peaceful kind of excitement.

I didn't know if Nash was already waiting for me there since I hadn't seen his car in the parking area, but I was even more sure that he would be happy when he saw me.

In fact, I was pretty sure that if any other girl were to walk up to him tonight wearing a pink wig, he would politely let her down.

I hopped over a slightly muddy spot on the trail, and when I walked around the bend, my ears picked up on the sounds of the waterfalls roaring in the distance.

I only had to walk for another minute before the trees cleared and the waterfalls that were almost too beautiful to be real came into view.

I stood there in awe for a moment as I took in the sight of the water falling from two hundred feet above me. There were four different waterfalls visible in this spot, the one at the bottom probably being my favorite since I loved the way it looked as it cascaded over the different layers of rock.

The mist coming from the falls felt amazing on my skin after the short hike in the July heat. And since there was no sign of Nash in the clearing, I walked closer to the edge of the water, closed my eyes, and just breathed in the refreshing scents in the air.

I was just turning around to find a rock or log to sit on when Nash appeared in the clearing. He wore what could have been an exact replica of the button-up and dark-blue trousers he'd worn last summer—if not for the fact that I knew the pants had to be slightly longer since he'd grown a few inches taller this year.

He was looking at the falls, like he hadn't noticed me quite yet, so I quickly turned my back to him again, planning to keep my face hidden until the last moment.

I couldn't hear his approach over the sound of the water, so when he tapped me on the shoulder a moment later, I startled a little, putting a hand to my chest.

"Is that you, Wrong Number Girl?" Nash asked in a gentle voice.

After taking a deep breath, I turned around, looked up into his blue eyes, and said, "Yes, Nash, it's me."

For a split second, a burst of panic washed over me as I worried he might have actually been surprised to see my face when I turned around. But as he took in my eyes, nose, and lips, followed by the pink hair and the dress, instead of acting confused, he got a huge grin on his face.

"You look just like I remember you looking that night," he said, taking a lock of hair in his hand and twisting it around his finger.

"I do?" I asked in surprise. The last time he'd talked about remembering our meeting in the woods, he'd said everything was clear in his memory except for my face.

But he nodded and said, "As soon as I found out last weekend that it was you, I was instantly able to picture the face that had eluded me before." His hands gently cupped the sides of my face. Smoothing his thumb across my cheek, he added, "You even did your makeup the same."

"I guess I like getting into character, too," I said in a soft voice, loving the way he was looking at me right now.

"Well, you look beautiful," he whispered. "Though, I have to admit that even when you're not dressed like the fair maiden of my dreams, you're still beautiful. You're always beautiful to me, Kiara."

"Thank you," I said, touched by his sweet words.

I was just searching his blue eyes and about to tell him how handsome he looked in his suit when something else he'd said finally registered.

"Wait, how exactly did you figure out it was me last weekend?"

"Well," he said, a slow smile lifting his lips, "I must confess that things became pretty clear right around the time I got a call from a very drunk Wrong Number Girl on Saturday night and recognized your cute little giggle on the other end of the line."

"I called you?" I gasped and covered my mouth with my hand. "I thought I only texted you that night."

"Nope, you definitely called." He chuckled, seeming to enjoy my surprise at all of this. "In fact, that's when you told me you wish I'd take advantage of you."

"I still can't believe I said that," I said, wondering what else he might have to tell me now that the cat was officially out of the bag. "So I called you and unknowingly spoiled my own secret?"

"Yep."

"Well, in case you didn't know," I said, shaking my head, "keeping a secret like this was way more complicated than you'd think."

"Oh, I don't doubt that," he said. "I already know a few of the different lengths you had to go to. Dropping your phone overboard and pretending it was an accident being one of them."

"Which ended up being completely unnecessary, apparently, since you already knew you had my number." I shook my head. "Did you feel even a little guilty for driving me to doing that?"

"Not really," he said, a wicked grin on his lips. "I mean, I'm always up for some spur-of-the-moment entertainment."

"Well," I said, playfully pushing his arm, "if you hadn't already bought me a new phone, I'd probably be really annoyed at you right now."

"Which is why I made sure you got the phone *before* we met tonight and not when I got here."

Touché.

"So you're not mad it's me?" I asked, needing to hear the words for some reason. "Or disappointed?"

He took my hands in his, and with a more serious expression, he looked deeply into my eyes and said, "How could I be disappointed when the most amazing and beautiful girl in the world gave me a second chance to meet her at the falls and is standing here with me?"

"You mean that?" I asked. "You really weren't disappointed when you figured out it was me?"

"Not one bit." He squeezed my hands. "The only thing I felt bad about was not figuring it out or remembering you sooner." He leaned his forehead against mine. In a voice that was achingly sincere, he whispered, *"Sorry it took me a whole year to meet you at the falls."*

"It's okay," I said, closing my eyes and just allowing myself to really feel this moment. "You were worth the wait."

He kissed me then, and as his lips weaved their magic spell over me and warmth swirled in my belly, I knew what I said was true.

Because even though this year of pining had been hard and hopeless at times, having this moment and the knowledge that Nash really did care about me the way I cared for him made it all worth it.

He pulled away from the kiss after a while and said, "I guess there's just one more thing I need to do."

"And what's that?" I asked, curious.

"This," he said. Then before I knew what was happening, he was reaching into his pocket and lowering himself down on one knee.

"W-what are you doing?" I asked, my heart racing instantly.

But he didn't seem to hear me because he just continued to lower himself down, looking deeply into my eyes as he rested his right knee on the dirt.

"Nash?" I asked, my voice shaking as it rose an octave higher than usual. "What are you doing?"

He'd told me before that he fell fast and hard in the past... but he wasn't seriously going to propose to me right now, was he?

We were only eighteen.

But when he looked up at me with the most sincere expression in his eyes, my veins pulsed with anticipation. And for a second of insanity, I wanted this to happen.

I wanted to marry Nash Hastings.

So when he cleared his throat and stared up at me with those ocean-blue eyes of his, I held my breath and listened.

"Kiara, Wrong Number Girl, Matheson," he said, his voice wobbling only slightly with nerves. "Would you do me the honor of..." He swallowed, like he was suddenly choking back his emotions as he pulled his hand from his pocket. "Waiting for me as I tie my shoe?"

Wait, what? I released the breath I'd been holding as I watched him reach down like he was actually going to tie his shoe.

"Did you really just do that?" I asked, my jaw dropping. "Because you just about gave me a heart attack."

"I did?" He furrowed his brow like he couldn't understand why I'd be freaking out when the guy I liked suddenly reached into his pocket and went down on bended knee in front of me. He gestured at his shoe. "I just noticed that my shoe was untied, and I didn't want to trip over my laces when we walked back to our cars."

"You're sooooo funny," I said, shaking my head as he bent over again and tied his black dress shoe.

"Why am I so funny?" he asked as he stood up straight again, his expression all innocent. "Did you think I was going to do something else while I was down there?" He paused for a second. Then as if just realizing how all of that had looked, he snapped his fingers and said, "Oh wait, were you hoping I was going to propose?"

"No," I said quickly, feeling my cheeks heat. "Of course not. We just graduated from high school."

"I know." He nodded. "That's why I'm surprised you thought I was proposing. I mean, I haven't even asked you to be my girlfriend yet."

"I know," I said. "That's why I thought it was weird."

I was just starting to feel a little embarrassed when Nash took my hands in his again.

"Hey," he said, squeezing my hands.

"Hey," I said, squeezing his hands back.

"Sorry for almost giving you a heart attack. I couldn't help myself. But..." He looked down and swallowed. Then he met my gaze again and said, "Don't be too surprised if something like that does happen one day. I know it's super early and I don't want to jump ahead twenty steps or anything, but I kind of think we might just have what it takes to make it there someday."

"You do?" I asked breathlessly as my body went tingly all over.

"Yes." He ran his thumbs over mine. "And I actually do have a question for you," he said, taking a step closer. "It's not quite a marriage proposal..." He winked. "But it is something I've been dying to ask you for a few days."

"Yeah?"

He nodded. "You see, I know I've done a pretty good job of

playing your fake boyfriend here and there this summer. But I was wondering if you'd be okay with me leaving off the fake part and just being your boyfriend."

"You really mean it?" I asked, still worried he might be in jokester-Nash mode.

"Yes, I really do." He lifted my hands to his lips and kissed the knuckles on each hand in turn. "So what do you say?"

"I say yes, Nash Hastings." I smiled at him. "Yes, I'll be your *girlfriend*."

"Then there's only one thing left for me to do," he said.

"And what's that?"

He pulled his phone from his pocket. "I'm going to finally change your contact name from 'Wrong Number Girl' to 'Kiara Matheson AKA My *Girlfriend*.'"

EPILOGUE
KIARA

FOUR YEARS LATER

"NASH IS GOING to die when he sees you walking down the aisle in this," Mom said from behind me as she helped me zip my wedding dress up.

"I know," I said, feeling giddy with excitement as I looked at my reflection in the mirror in Cambrielle's old bedroom that was acting as the bride's room today. I was loving how everything I'd dreamed of for this day was actually coming true. "I told the photographers to make sure they had the camera ready to capture his reaction because I have a feeling it's going to be epic, and I'm going to want to have it documented forever."

It was July twenty-second, exactly five years from the night of the garden party where I'd had that life-altering first kiss with Nash. But after today, July twenty-second would also be known as the day I married my best friend.

Yes, Nash had proposed to me for real last fall—right there by that bench on the path in his backyard—and his shoe hadn't even been untied as he'd done it.

Mom finished zipping me in and I turned from side to side, just taking in the dress that Ava had designed specifically for me.

Yes, Ava was following closely in her famous fashion designer mother's shoes, and with all the press our wedding was getting, I had a feeling her career was about to launch into superstardom.

"You look so beautiful, Kiara," Mom said, taking my face gently in her hands, her brown eyes full of pride. "I can't believe that my darling girl is all grown up and getting married."

"To the man of my dreams, no less." I smiled.

"Yes." She smiled back. Then as if suddenly being hit with everything that this moment meant, she stepped closer and pulled me into a tight hug. "I'm so proud of you. And I know you're basically marrying American royalty today, but I want you to remember that he's the one who's lucky to be marrying my baby girl."

"I know, Mom," I said, hugging her back. "He tells me how lucky he is every day."

We were both lucky.

It had taken me a long time to feel like I was good enough for someone like Nash, but I knew my worth now.

Having Nash love me back the way I loved him was just a bonus.

"I'm going to see if they're ready to start, okay?" Mom said.

I drew in a deep breath. "Okay."

"This really is a beautiful dress," Addie said once my mom had left the room, running her fingers along the Chantilly lace on the sweetheart bodice, her eyes following the A-line tulle skirt with frosted beading and 3D petal appliqués. "It's actually pretty similar to the bridal gowns I was looking at last year."

"It is?" I asked, my eyes meeting hers in the mirror.

"Yeah." She nodded. And when she looked off to the side and her lips trembled like she was trying to fight back a swell of emotion, my heart hurt for my friend.

"I'm so sorry," I said, turning to face her. "I should've known today would be hard for you."

"No, it's okay." She shook her head, wiping at the tears in her watery eyes. "It's a happy day, really." She smiled through her tears. "My best friend is getting married. It's a good day."

"But it's also bittersweet, isn't it?" I reached out, taking her hand and pulling her into my arms for a hug. "All the wedding stuff probably just reminds you of all the plans you and Evan had."

"Yeah." She nodded and sniffled. Then going to the dressing table and pulling out a tissue to dab at her eyes, she said, "I just miss him. Not knowing what happened is just..." She stopped to let out a shaky breath. Then meeting my gaze again, she said, "I just don't know if I'll ever be able to move on until I know what happened when he went back to Miami. If he's still alive somewhere or..."

"I know," I said, grabbing her another tissue when she got all teary-eyed again. "Not knowing what happened is sometimes harder than finding out the worst."

"It is." She sniffled again. "I just hope he's okay wherever he is. Hope he's at least still alive."

My heart ached for my friend. She'd suffered so much loss in her life. Her parents. Her brother. And then her fiancé. It was so heartbreaking.

"Anyway," she said, drawing in a shaky breath, "I'm sorry to be such a downer on what should be the happiest day of your life."

"You don't ever need to be sorry for being human, Addie," I said. "I should've known how hard today would be for you. For you to be my Maid of Honor. I totally understand if you need to sit out today."

"No, I want to be here." She took a step back, looking up at me with her eyes that were brown again now that she'd stopped wearing her blue contacts. "I want to watch my best friend marry the man of her dreams. At least one of us deserves to get our happily ever after...after everything."

"But are you sure you're up to doing the rest of the Maid of Honor stuff?" I asked. "Walking down the aisle and standing up there in front of everyone?"

"Yes." She drew in another deep breath and stood up taller. "I can't just sit on the sidelines of life anymore."

"Okay," I said. "But if you need to bow out at any moment, just tell me. Alessi and Cambrielle and the rest of the bridesmaids will be able to take over if you need."

"Speaking of everyone else," Addie said, looking at the time on the clock in the corner of Cambrielle's room. "I'm sure everyone is anxious to see you downstairs."

I looked at the clock, too, and she was right. We only had ten minutes until the ceremony would begin. The bridesmaids and groomsmen were probably already lined up on the Hastings' terrace, just waiting for me.

I drew in a deep breath as a swarm of nerves came over me.

"You ready to get married?" Addie asked.

"I think so," I said at the same time that my mom opened the door and slipped into the room.

"Nash just went downstairs," my mom said, coming closer. "So they should be ready for you soon."

"Okay, perfect." I blew out a breath as another swell of nerves hit me.

It was almost time.

EPILOGUE

My dad was waiting for my mom and me on the Hastings' terrace when we stepped outside. He wore a light gray suit, with his salt-and-pepper hair combed neatly, his beard freshly trimmed.

"You look beautiful," Dad said, stepping close to embrace me, giving me a quick kiss on the cheek.

"Thank you," I said, straightening his boutonnière and feeling so happy that my dad was here today and in a much better place than he'd been a few years ago.

He handed me my bouquet of pink and white peonies. After looking me over again with his amber eyes smiling and proud, he asked, "Is my baby girl ready to get married?"

"I think so," I said, a flutter of nerves and anticipation flowing through me for what must be the twentieth time today.

He held his arm out to escort me. "Then let's do this."

I linked my arm through his, then turning back to my mom, I asked, "Are you ready to help walk me down the aisle?"

"Of course," she said. She linked her arm through mine so I could still hold the bouquet. We posed for a few photos as the wedding planner did her last-minute checks.

Was it slightly untraditional to have my mom *and* my dad walk me down the aisle?

Probably.

But I was excited to share this moment with both of them.

With my mom who had always been there for me. And my dad who had found the strength to fight his demons and come back to us.

The wedding planner gave the string quartet the signal that we were ready to start. A moment later they began playing a beautiful arrangement of "A Thousand Years"—the song Nash and I had danced to in the woods five years ago.

The bridesmaids and groomsmen began walking down the

stairs from the terrace to the Hastings' yard that had been transformed into what looked like an enchanted forest.

My parents and I were far enough back on the terrace that no one in the crowd could see us. I had yet to see Nash today, but when Addie started walking down the steps, my parents and I walked to the edge of the stone terrace and into everyone's view for the first time.

There was a sudden sense of reverence when everyone looked up. Even though all of our family and friends were looking at me, I only had eyes for Nash.

He stood under the wedding arch in a tailored blue suit that made him look like the movie star of my dreams. And even from across the lawn, I could see his blue eyes go wide with an expression that I could only describe as awe on his face.

I smiled at him. When he smiled back, a sense of peace and happiness washed over me. I'd been jittery with nerves all day but seeing the man of my dreams waiting to marry me just felt so right. For the first time today, I was suddenly calm.

Nash was my rock, and with him by my side I could do anything.

The wedding party all made it to Nash. As the audience stood, the quartet seamlessly shifted the song to a beautiful arrangement of "One Life" by Ed Sheeran.

My parents and I walked down the terrace steps and then down the flower-petal-covered wooden boardwalk.

I looked over the crowd, nodding and smiling at the family and friends that had come from near and far to be here. Even though I wanted to take everything in, my eyes just kept going back to Nash.

My parents walked me to the platform where my fiancé was waiting. After kissing me on the cheek, they handed me off to Nash, who took my hands in his as we came together.

EPILOGUE

"You look so beautiful," Nash said, leaning close so that only I could hear.

"Thank you," I smiled shyly up at him. "You look quite dashing yourself."

Okay, so he actually looked drop dead gorgeous, hot, and sexy, and a bunch of other adjectives combined. But since Hunter was standing right there, waiting to officiate the ceremony, I decided to just leave it at dashing.

"You guys ready for this?" Hunter asked as the music drifted off.

"So ready," Nash said, shooting me a flirty smile and a wink that still made me blush all these years later.

"Me too," I said.

"Good." Hunter smiled. Then leaning closer, he said, "Because I've been waiting *years* to tell everyone about the email I got from a lovestruck teenager asking how to get this unobservant doofus to finally notice her."

Nash and I both laughed. Then I said, "Little did you know that when you offered to play matchmaker all those years ago that it would mean we'd literally ask you to marry us one day."

"Life is wild, isn't it?" Hunter chuckled.

"It really is."

"Good morning, Mrs. Hastings," Nash whispered in my ear the next morning.

"Good morning," I said with a smile, loving the sound of my new last name on my husband's lips.

"Did you sleep well?" he asked, putting his arm around me and pulling me closer.

We'd stayed in the honeymoon suite at the Eden Falls Inn after the wedding and reception. Once we ate the late breakfast that the hostess said she'd bring to our room around eleven, we'd drop my wedding dress and his suit off at our new apartment above the corner bakery space that I'd just signed a lease for on Main Street, before flying first class to Iceland for our two-week honeymoon.

Yes, I was officially opening my own bakery this coming fall, and Nash said he'd even help taste-test all my new recipes. *When he isn't busy shooting the movie he's already set to film at the end of August, that is.*

That's right, Nash had recently landed a supporting role in a thriller that would start shooting in Vancouver next month—playing the half-brother of the lead that would be played by the A-list star, Justin Banks.

"I slept really well," I said, snuggling closer to his chest. "Well...you know, for the few hours you let me sleep last night."

He chuckled. "Hopefully, we'll be able to catch up on our sleep on the plane."

"Yes," I said. "And hopefully, having other people close by will keep you on your best behavior."

"Are you complaining then, Mrs. Hastings?" He arched an eyebrow as he began tracing his finger down my shoulder then my arm, causing goosebumps to rise on my skin. "Are you saying you didn't enjoy all the attention I paid you last night?"

"Oh I definitely enjoyed it," I said, unable to keep a smile from my lips as I remembered how much fun we'd had on our wedding night.

"Are you sure about that?" he asked. "Because it kind of sounds like I might need to convince you that Casanova Nash is here to stay now that we're married."

"Oh, I like Casanova Nash," I said, unable to keep a huge grin from my lips as I remembered the first time he'd told me about his alter ego in the parking lot at The Italian Amigos.

EPILOGUE

The alter ego whom I could now confirm, from experience, was indeed the most casanova-ing Casanova around.

"Good, because I think he just might have enough time for another visit before breakfast gets here."

And before I knew it, Nash was pushing me onto my back and climbing on top of me, so I was pinned beneath him on the bed.

I held my breath as I waited for him to lean down and kiss me. But as he bent closer, instead of resting his muscular chest fully against mine and kissing me like I expected, he got a devilish smirk on his lips at the last moment and suddenly started tickling me.

"No!" I squealed as I arched my back and tried to get away from the tickle torture. "I wanted Casanova Nash, not tickle-monster Nash."

"But aren't they the same thing?" he asked, purposely playing dumb. "Because I thought this was how you liked it."

"It's not—" I said, trying to catch my breath.

Why had I ever thought it was a good idea to tell him I was the most ticklish on the sides of my ribcage?

He was totally going to use that knowledge to his advantage for the rest of our lives.

"But isn't that what you whispered to me last night?" he asked, enjoying this way too much. "That tickling your ribs is the best way to turn you on?"

"I definitely—" I started to say, my words broken by my uncontrollable giggling, "—didn't say that."

"But I could have sworn—" he started to say when there was a sudden knock on the door.

We both froze and looked at each other. "Do you think we're in trouble?" I whispered, sure I'd made too much noise and we were about to get kicked out of the inn.

"Maybe it's just breakfast?" he whispered back.

He climbed off me, and after quickly pulling on some gym shorts over his boxer briefs, he went to open the door.

"Hello?" he asked, standing in front of the crack in the door so I couldn't see who was on the other side.

"I'm sorry to interrupt," an elderly woman's voice sounded on the other side of the door, "but your breakfast is ready."

"Oh," Nash said, reaching his hands out for what must be a tray of food. "Thank you. My wife is famished after the night we had."

My jaw dropped.

Did he seriously just say that?

To a seventy-five-year-old woman?

But instead of sounding like she was surprised by what Nash had just hinted at, the woman said, "Oh, I bet. I saw how pretty your bride was when you two arrived last night. That's why I made extra eggs. I figured you two probably worked up an appetite." Then in a lower voice that I could barely hear, she added, "I know me and my Harold were famished by the time morning came after our wedding night."

Oh my heck! I covered my mouth to stifle a laugh. *The little old lady is just as bad as Nash.*

I loved it.

"Well, we appreciate this," Nash said, amusement in his voice. "I'm sure this will help reenergize us."

The woman said something else that I couldn't hear. Then after pushing the door shut with his foot, Nash carried the tray over to the little table and chair setup in the corner by a window.

"Ready to refuel, my darling?" He gestured at the two plates containing French toast, bacon, and eggs.

"Definitely," I said, my mouth already watering as I took in the delicious-looking spread.

I climbed out of the bed and walked over to Nash. But

before sitting down, I stood on my tiptoes and wrapped my arms behind his neck for a hug.

"Thank you for making me the happiest wife in the whole world," I said.

He pulled me close against him. After pressing a gentle kiss to my forehead, he said, "Thank you for making me the happiest husband in the world."

I pulled back so I could look at his handsome face. "We're pretty lucky, aren't we?"

His blue eyes sparkled when he smiled. "I really think we are."

Addie and Evan's story is coming soon. Make sure to pre-order your copy here: https://authorjudycorry.com/products/hideaway-with-you

STAY CONNECTED!

I hope you enjoyed THE CONFESSION! If you haven't already, please sign up for my newsletter so you can stay up to date on my latest book news. https://subscribepage.com/judycorry

Follow me on Instagram: @judycorry

Join the Corry Crew on Facebook: https://www.facebook.com/groups/judycorrycrew/

ACKNOWLEDGMENTS

Thank you for reading The Confession. Ending a series that I've loved as much as this one was a daunting project. You'd think that after writing as many books as I have (this was #19!) that it would get easier. But I have to say that it's a roller coaster every single time.

But even if it took me longer than usual to find my groove again and get this book baby of mine in your hands, it has also been such a rewarding process. I say it all the time, but I really do have the best job in the world. Hanging out with my characters and daydreaming about new ways to torture them before I give them their happily ever after really is the best way to spend my days.

I need to thank my amazing editor, Precy Larkins, for taking this book in several chunks, since I'm *always* behind schedule. I always feel so lucky to work with her. Basically, she's the best editor and I'll keep begging her to take my books as long as she'll have them.

I also need to thank my amazing proofreader, Jordan Truex. She is the kind of reader, cheerleader and friend that every author needs and I feel so lucky to have her in my corner.

Thank you to my beta readers, Kera Butler and Sofia Simpson for fan-girling over this book. It's always nerve-wracking to put a new story out into the world and let readers into my weird brain. So hearing your thoughts and reactions to each chapter helped give me the confidence to put this out there for everyone else. You're the best!

Thank you to my assistant Lindzee Armstrong for helping me with some of the business side of things as I raced to the finish line of this book. Having someone else to help me make sure things are running smoothly has been a lifesaver.

Thank you to Wastoki for your amazing cover illustration. I have loved working with you on so many of my books.

Thank you to the readers, bookstagrammers, booktokers, bloggers and reviewers who read my books and share them everywhere. I appreciate all the care you put into your posts and reviews. It truly means so much to me and makes my day when I see another reader has connected with my book babies.

Thank you to my children, James, Janelle, Jonah and Jade for putting up with another crazy book deadline. Life is busy and chaotic at times, but I'm the luckiest mom in the world to have each of them.

Lastly, I need to thank my husband Jared for supporting me as I wrote another book. I love that he's my ultimate hype man and always open to listening to me as I talk about all of my imaginary friends. He really is the reason I can write love stories in the first place.

And if you made it this far, I just wanted to say thank you, dear reader, for taking a chance on The Confession. I seriously couldn't do what I love without your support. So thank you!

Also By Judy Corry

Eden Falls Academy Series:

The Charade (Ava and Carter)

The Facade (Cambrielle and Mack)

The Ruse (Elyse and Asher)

The Confidant (Scarlett and Hunter)

The Confession (Kiara and Nash)

Kings of Eden Falls:

Hide Away With You (Addie and Evan)

Rich and Famous Series:

Assisting My Brother's Best Friend (Kate and Drew)

Hollywood and Ivy (Ivy and Justin)

Her Football Star Ex (Emerson and Vincent)

Friend Zone to End Zone (Arianna and Cole)

Stolen Kisses from a Rock Star (Maya and Landon)

Ridgewater High Series:

When We Began (Cassie and Liam)

Meet Me There (Ashlyn and Luke)

Don't Forget Me (Eliana and Jess)

It Was Always You (Lexi and Noah)

My Second Chance (Juliette and Easton)

My Mistletoe Mix-Up (Raven and Logan)

Forever Yours (Alyssa and Jace)

Standalones:

Protect My Heart (Emma and Arie)

Kissing The Boy Next Door (Lauren and Wes)

ABOUT THE AUTHOR

Judy Corry is the Amazon Top 12 and *USA Today* Bestselling Author of Contemporary and YA Romance. She writes romance because she can't get enough of the feeling of falling in love. She's known for writing heart-pounding kisses, endearing characters, and hard-won happily ever afters.

She lives in Southern Utah with the boy who took her to Prom, their four awesome kids, and two dogs. She's addicted to love stories, dark chocolate and chai lattes.

Printed in Great Britain
by Amazon